A Crown
for
Two Islands

Planters of the Crown Book II

Patrick Highers

Independently Published

Richlands North Carolina

https://www.facebook.com/authorpatrickhighers
https://www.pinterest.com/pmhighers

Publisher's Note: This is a work of fiction. However, several names, entities, incidents, and descriptions included in this story are based on persons of historical interest. Locales and public names are sometimes used for atmospheric purposes.

Cover design by Patrick Highers
Book Layout © 2017 BookDesignTemplates.com

A Crown for Two Islands/ Patrick Highers. — 1st ed.
ISBN 978-1-7323817-4-2
Library of Congress Control Number 2018908782

Dedication

My thanks to Michelle Wilson, Deborah Horn and Angie Solum for their unending friendship and valued commentary of this novel.

Editing by Samantha Ladha

The Jesuits in 1581 endeavored to effect, in their own peculiar way, that which Pope Pius had failed to accomplish by specious promises in 1560, viz, the subjection of England to the Papal See; and if they should not succeed in this "project," at least the result of their machinations would be to sow dissentions, foment divisions and bring the Book of Common Prayer into con tempt.

– The Close, Exeter,
February 18th, 1856. No. I.
(Vol. xi. No. 291. Page 401.)

iii

They Were Who They Were

Hibernia.
Éire.
Ireland.

An island apart— severed from the body like a foot in a jagged shoe that traced a soul to Scotland. Of this soil came the people: born of full heartedness in song and script. They sang to the sun... they sang to the sky... they sang to the sea. In their nakedness, whilst riding across the plain, the people splayed out their hands as the wind took their hair: wild, wild and free.

They were who they were, and upon seeing them, the birds sang, Hosanna... Hosanna in the Highest; blessed is he who comes in the name of the Lord.

To the birds, the people replied, *Aye. Aye to the bread, and aye to the song, and most surely a yea for wine.* Then a walker walked from hill to shore and sang Hosanna for all time. He was of the Word. He was power.

Éire.
Ireland.

An island standing apart. Four kingdoms formed, united in the majesty of their heart. To each of the four came a whisper: *Where art thou? Whilst thou drift alone forever? Give out thy hand to thine sister.* The people were who they were and the birds sang in a multitude: *Holy, Holy, Holy, Lord God almighty.*

Heaven and earth are filled with Your glory- Hosanna in the Highest.

The kingdoms answered, *Aye! We hear thy song and a bridge we will build between us. Hear the Word, feel the power, know the Lord.*

Ireland.

An island. Thy kingdoms blurred; thy turbulent word imposed. High towers belied their keepers. Raised castles, flooded moat, stony walls, and the sister's unfamiliar note: *Hear not the birds any longer. Off the cliff, damned stony beach amiss, whence the ocean hath cleaved away, their music is of bones, bleached white of malady.*

The Word had changed to a song of metal, and as for the people, they found the birds as still as ice. Had all their beaks been broken? And where was the sister but in their house?

In their rage, whilst riding across the plain, the people splayed out their hands and the wind took their hair: wild... wild and free. They were who they were and remembered... they could sing without the birds.

"*Sing!*" sayeth O'Neill.

Book Map
Planters of the Crown

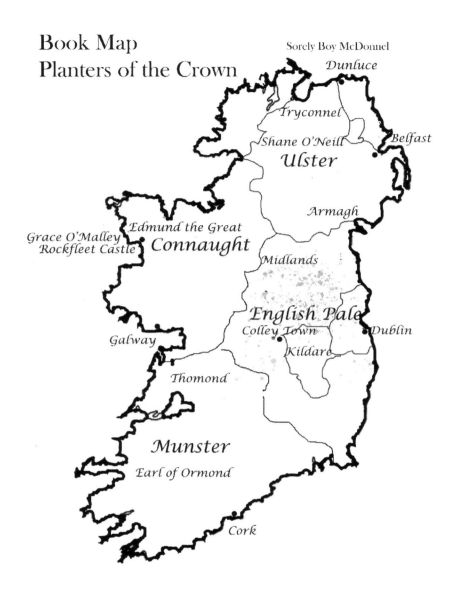

Sorely Boy McDonnel

Dunluce

Tryconnel

Shane O'Neill

Belfast

Ulster

Armagh

Grace O'Malley
Rockfleet Castle

Edmund the Great

Connaught

Midlands

English Pale

Colley Town

Dublin

Galway

Kildare

Thomond

Munster

Earl of Ormond

Cork

INTRODUCTION

In the year of our lord 1558, Queen Elizabeth claimed separation from the Holy Catholic Empire and returned the governance of religion to her monarchy. It was a proclamation to the world that all of England and the fife of Ireland would stand apart from papal rule. Seeking a foothold on the slippery slope of dissolution, Pope Pius IV scrambled to strengthen alliances with chieftains in Ulster and Connaught. From the Vatican, he ordered the collection of annals containing the births, deaths, and property of Catholic nobles. A Jesuit underground was formed and zealots were sent to report and spy on England. Thusly, Ireland became part of the holy order to counter the reformation.

Contents

CHAPTER 1

Red Sagum'

Ulster was but a few days march for the Englishmen, and the soldiers moved quickly with a spring in their step. They had been told the north was a collection of farms with disloyal bands of peasants and a few petty warlords. Strong, fearless, and certain, a throng of pikes swaggered above shoulders, from the front of the army to its rear. The largest assembly of fighting men that England had ever sent now marched into the north. Wearing long coats with red capes, called sagum', they bristled of thorniness, sang and found war good cheer.

Following the foot soldiers, a league of horsemen, adorned with two corselets each, pranced with military adornment. Chainmail, black stockings, and steel, hardened in heart, the lords of an Irish parliament sat tall. Among them were the Butlers of Ormond and Fitzgerald of Munster. At the head of this column, riding on a mountainous horse, was the Lord Deputy of Ireland himself- his cape ruffled in black and gold to strike a figure upon the battlefield. A thin man with a goat beard and eyes that glistened with the cunning of a raven. Men, boys, squires, and foot soldiers all hailed the lord deputy- the army knew him as Radcliffe.

A plume of smoke arose from Armagh. "Lord Radcliffe, a storm is coming," Thomas Butler said. How long they had been riding he could hardly fathom; it seemed an eternity. All vestige of hope waned as he wiped the sweat from his forehead with a linen kerchief. White skin, brown eyes, and cheekbones rising over a neatly trimmed mustache gave Thomas Butler a youthful appearance. He was accustomed to nobility and drilled in the art of war. In his thoughts, he would have much preferred being a lover.

Radcliffe turned briefly to acknowledge Thomas as their horses bobbed over the rocky ground. The measure of respect between them hinted that reason might yet prevail, so Thomas urged his mare forward to broach his intentions. "We have pushed too far, your Grace."

Radcliffe slowed and stared off to the endless stream of men who occupied both sides of the road. "Bloody far," his voice resonated with nostalgia. It was time, Thomas thought- but then, with a tone that vexed Thomas's desire completely, the lord deputy's voice became determined. "Lord Fitzgerald has left for England and still his men did splendidly. What say you? Shall we not advance to Dungannon?"

Thomas felt the rumble of men and wagons and thought again of his dilemma. He liked O'Neill. Hell, he even respected him. His voice paled, "What slurping do I hear from this giant slug creeping over land and hill? It is, I fear, the river, your Grace."

"It is but a river," Radcliffe replied.

Even as they spoke, the rush grew louder. Daunting in size and volume, the current raged as they clicked ominously toward Tyrone. Thomas felt it reverberate in his chest. He felt each step and stone and wanted nothing of it. "We must disperse our men and begin a camp, your Grace," he said, dreading what lay ahead.

"Do you not wish to lead us into the north?" Radcliffe asked.

"Aye, your Grace. With all my heart, I wish for that honor, and yet the rain soaks us. Perhaps it benefits our cause to look ahead whilst the men retreat before battle," Thomas advised.

"I have made a survey already, Lord Butler," Radcliffe replied sternly.

"A survey?" Thomas took the sight of his army in. He gazed back and turned up his chin. "With whom did thee survey, your Grace? Nit witted vagabonds and scoundrels?"

The lord deputy appeared to find humor with his words and it reddened Thomas's face with shame. Dismissive and yet decisive in his manner, Radcliffe replied: "Ralph Lane gave a goodly report."

Thomas raised a brow of apprehension. "Hmm, a cur. Art thou certain of his judgement? These men look wearied. Let us see the condition of the river before you commit. I know this land, and the rains that came could make the crossing untenable."

Radcliffe stroked the mane of his horse and thought of victory. "I bet on the cur- and bridges are for crossing lest ye not forget." He had heard enough of the doubting. It had taken months to prepare for this war, and now with the strength of England behind him, it was finally within his grasp. Ulster would be defeated in days and after that, Connaught would surely fall. "We have Fitzgerald of Kildare and we will have O'Neill," he replied.

The thought of delay annoyed Radcliffe. How could the queen entertain the whimsical pleas of Kildare or Ormond in the face of such treachery? O'Neill was a villain and a ruthless thug. He cast his gaze to Thomas suspiciously. The Butlers were powerful; Thomas was powerful. "We both know that a storm is coming." The thought of any delay repulsed him and he squeezed the ribs of his warhorse with both knees. The animal blew hard, sending a mist of exhilaration from frothy nostrils.

As Radcliffe dashed forward, Thomas Butler thought of his queen. Having pledged his fealty to Elizabeth, he looked forward to the reward but distained the thought of shedding blood for the want of such little gain. He would maintain his land. His people would reap the grain from their fields, and the order of life would not change regardless of any military outcome. That was the bargain. *The bargain*, he thought of all he knew of Shane O'Neill and the power of Ulster. *Unpredictable*.

To the front and on either side of Thomas, dirt trodden heaps of grass and flat bush marred the boundary of his travel. Soldiers had parted for Radcliffe leaving him in a swath of begrudging eyes which turned away like the wind that rustled through his fine black hair. They rode a bit further and Thomas caught up as the river came to sight. "There are limits to what even England can do outside the Pale, your Grace," he said as the slop of the mushed ground splattered at his boots.

Radcliffe laughed, "Are you getting squirrely on me, Thomas?"

"Nay," they slowed, and Thomas' horse showed its fine breeding with a prance, "my archers are ready, your Grace. It will not be a Butler who forsakes thee. I'll leave that to nature. "

Radcliffe turned to the embankment. *Nature? By God's breath, nature had been on their side all along. They were winning and it was good*, he thought, *Lane had been right.* "God be..." he said looking at Thomas as if to remind the Earl of Ormond that nature was indeed his redeemer. "I say we cross. It will take a day or two for the rear to catch up and we need the infantry on the other side. You can see as well as I, the bridge is still intact."

A soldier ran out to the center of the span and tamped the wood as they watched. The testing was solid and men began to push across to the other side. On the northern bank, the timber had been felled and an opening of grass extended to a separated pasture. Thomas saw the makings of a stone fence in the distance. "'Tis crossable, your Grace," he replied reluctantly.

Radcliffe smiled like a mischievous child. "I want to be eating beef in Dungannon Castle before the bullocks of this army slaps at its own ass. Can you promise me that?" he asked.

Thomas looked at the river. "Will you free O'Neill's prisoner if we succeed?"

Knowing there was a benefit to saving the Earl of Tryconnell, Radcliffe referred to the earl's wife instead: "It would give me great relief to bed a dowager of Scotland, but little happiness in the establishment of the dispossessed. The man has no resources that will benefit England," his tone was provoking.

"It would be our duty to save him," Thomas paused and then added, "O'Neill has also placed a great value on the countess. I have heard he intends to marry her when the earl is dead."

Radcliffe continued, "For that alone, I would take her," and then he waved his arm toward the bridge. "Our camp will be made at the castle. Tell your officers that progress will be made and to get out of their tent beds. That is the only way to keep our Dublin safe, Thomas. We shall take every measure to bring the queen's will into the north."

"It will be done," Thomas exclaimed pulling at the reins to turn toward his men. He did his best to project certainty, but inside he was not so sure. The prospects of the archers drew down the spirits of the men. Such a volley- such are fools- and Dungannon was a formidable tower house waiting to greet them.

In a short while, Thomas's doubt resounded across the knoll overlooking the road and river. "Prepare the archers!" he shouted to his men.

❈ ❈ ❈

To the north of Armagh, near the township of Dungannon, another force gathered. Northern men with beating chests and shields made of wood and bone. They wore open sleeved shirts of saffron and had long curling hair. The old clans had gathered, and behind them, the wilderness loomed dark, wild, and unrestrained.

Sovereignty: the people of Ulster proclaimed.

A man who dared to oppose England had risen, and he was known as O'Neill Mor. Descended of Conn, the king of the north, Shane O'Neill carried the crest of the red hand and fashioned himself the high lord of Tyrone. In the fervor before battle, O'Neill's army drank the blood of slaughtered sheep and prepared as they had never prepared before. His men believed they would cross into the south and smite the Queen of England. Their nerves were steeled with the promise that the Holy Roman Empire was with them.

On the 18th day of July, at the river where Radcliffe refused to camp, O'Neill attacked and rains caused wagon wheels to sink deep into the mud. Englishmen cursed and shouted to God for the rains to stop. The great battle had begun, and in the midst of the chaos, a sergeant of the footman guard cursed the queen who sent him.

❧ ❧ ❧

An Uisce Dubh was what he had been told the Irish called it. The words seemed harsh with a rasp catching the very back of his throat. Now the river's name mattered little. The sergeant hated everything about it. Around him was utter chaos, and he wanted nothing more to do with soldiering or the torrent that soaked him to the bone. He pulled his hands from sodden mittens and hugged the bronze cannon to keep from being swept away. The rains had caused the water to rise. First, the storm took the pilings, and then the main deck began to sheer apart the swaths and chunks of wood. One of his mates struggled with a pintle and gudgeon just before it snapped, releasing six mules in a web of leather straps and clattering buckles. How loud it was when the river broke them free. How forlorn he became as the hastily constructed bridge shattered under the weight of Radcliffe's massive cannon. Ten soldiers disappeared in the muddy waters rushing past him. Black fingernails gouged at the slippery film that coated the iron—entrenched in the sludge of the river's black bottom.

Sergeant Whitaker heard: "Hold on!" *A shout from a friend,* he hoped. The artillery unit of the English division in Armagh fought the current from both banks. "I can't..." his will began to fail, "I can't feel my hands... hurry!" His rescue was sure to fail. The sergeant knew his fate as he watched what came out of the dark woods. The O'Neill cavalry were now taking turns riding into the beleaguered men. Like death, they came... but he could not turn back. On the English side of the rolling water, high above the fighting, the lord deputy had made his orders clear. A section of archers who bore the standard of Ormond had already assembled. They stood with bows at an upward bend. If they loosed their arrows, it would not be the Irish but the sergeant's men who would be slaughtered. It would be done the lord deputy had said, *"For the Queen!"*

It was the grind. Some had crossed already, but most had not. Even as they rebuilt the bridge and watched the spectacle of war, woolen coats of Englishmen turned red from blood and gore. The Irish chief they fought mocked them. Shane O'Neill who stood against England in an open display of sovereignty- with that O'Neill... more and more now stood ready. None could surrender, not English nor Irish, and that is what marked the rise of the terrible war.

In the torment of soldiers, the sergeant heard men curse the queen herself. It seemed as though the entire army was uttering death upon her. He had refused to speak such a thing but now the river was his battle. Now, if he turned, it would be for her that the arrows would pierce his flesh.

Sergeant Whitaker cried, "Damned the queen! Damn her to hell!"

Across the river, Radcliffe's army was running away. Behind each flailing arm, a red sagum fluttered in the air. English soldiers ran and fell, scrambling to dash into the water. So many reached out as the current sent their bodies hurling past him. Soldiers who did not call out their names; he did not know who they were; but he was... Tobias Whitaker- the last upon the bridge in that blundering effort to make a crossing.

"Hurry..." Sergeant Whitaker yelled. He clung, he cried, he cursed his anchor as water jetted up to choke him and pull his body away. Once he had been optimistic. When he boarded the great warship called the *Pinnacle*, Tobias and those without names, felt as though nothing could stop them. *All of the young who died- Had they not all been trained to fight and die for glory??* His lips moved faintly, "Hurry..." he could not feel his hands; his breath was short and quick.

A group of soldiers shouted, "Whitaker, Whitaker, hold on!"

Sergeant Whitaker faintly heard the attempt to rescue. *Were the words an echo or some cruel joke?* He did not know.

The pulsating water overpowered him. He heard the thunder of horses and witnessed a sword rise on the far side of the bank. The blade came up and then swiftly fell without mercy- cleaving a friend in half. His chest ached, not from the cold, but deep, deep inside his heart. The thought of never seeing or touching another who might have loved him filled him with an overwhelming heaviness. Then he felt the sting on his face- a bloodletting bite of a knotted rope. His eyes closed and swelled shut.

"Tobias Whitaker…" he whispered.

Hands released their grip and for a moment, his stiffened body stuck to the cannon. Tobias convulsed, aware that his last breath had filled his lungs, and then like those who would be forgotten, he entered the abyss.

CHAPTER 2

The Wolf
of the
Battlefield

L ater, on a hill overlooking the town of Maghery, a
Spaniard named Miguel placed his hand upon an altar
of stone. He was tall with the blackest of hair and his
dark silk robe fluttered in the wind. Around his neck was a silver
crucifix and he held a purple biretta. Miguel kneeled as a rider
sped toward him.

"For Your glory… oh God," Miguel prayed.

There was a solemnness about him; pressed in thought, holy
war, heaviness of the heart. As he lifted his head from prayer,

Miguel noticed a saffron shirt streaking across the plain of high grass between him and Maghery. He looked closer… not truly believing what he saw. A single warrior who thrashed his stallion to flight. Even as he rode, he raised himself above a battle shield painted with the red hand of Tyrone.

Miguel turned his face toward heaven, "I praise Thee… I praise Thee!" he shouted, looking into the sky.

When the messenger arrived a glint of victory showed in his eyes. His fur cape obscured wide shoulders and the beating of an exuberant heart. A battle-axe smeared with blood and shards of bone rattled at his side. He had piercing blue eyes shining brightly below red waving hair and he was surely alive. The wolf of the battlefield.

They shared a moment of silence as the grass bent across the lonely countryside. Then the warrior shouted: "We have done!"

Miguel saw the heavy wool of leggings swirl to the ground. It was Turlough and he remembered the man's fierceness from Omagh. Turlough was breathless, brilliant and proud. "We have done!"

Miguel stood and the wind blew between them like music. He crossed his hands in front of his chest, "Thy king will be remembered and glory to God in the highest!" The thought of what he had just heard sent a surge of energy through his soul. It revived him and removed the struggle of his doubt. How long had he been in Ireland, he wondered, long enough to make amends? He was conflicted and yearned with every fiber of his soul for the Holy Father's blessing. Ireland had changed him. Surely, his father who had taken the name of Pius would see that now.

"I am Turlough Luineach, cousin to O'Neill and messenger of Tyrone," Turlough said before bending to kiss the massive stone.

Miguel nodded, "The weight of that cross was carried by the holiest of my disciples."

"Let it stand forever then," Turlough replied reverently. He took a knee, said his prayers of thanksgiving, and then crossed himself before speaking the great news of Shane O'Neill.

"I know you," Miguel replied.

"Do you, Father?" Turlough asked.

Miguel dipped his head with acknowledgement, "Yes, now tell me, how many have perished?"

"Twenty," Turlough replied sadly, referring to his brothers.

"And of England?" Miguel asked.

"Hundreds, Father," Turlough exclaimed.

Miguel looked mesmerized, "It is a sign. Our Lord will not abandon the faithful. This will be my petition to Rome. Rest assured I will travel shortly," he said as he stepped to embrace Turlough. They clasped arms and Miguel asked, "Will you give O'Neill my message?"

"You yourself would leave us? Art thou to be made a cardinal?" Turlough asked.

"Nay. I have disobeyed and must make penitence to His Holiness. But you may pray for me and hope that our Lord will guide my hand against the Anglican."

The warrior hesitated, "Why would you do such thing?"

"It is my sacrifice. My decision," Miguel offered a kind expression, "tell your King that I shall not rest until we have all of Spain behind him."

Turlough looked apprehensive, "I will do," he said before looking off toward the waters of Lough Neigh. He expected the worst of news but hoped for the best. "Have the ships arrived to Dublin?"

Miguel touched Turlough's shoulder regretfully, "I have not seen them in Dublin."

Turlough looked disheartened. Everything rested on the ships and Spain. "Perhaps the storm has delayed them. The lord chancellor of Belfast has said that Spanish ships have taken shelter in the port city. Shall I take my best men to see for myself?"

Miguel saw hope in Turlough's eyes but he had not heard from King Phillip or the Pope in months. "Be careful. If Spain has accepted, you will know the galleys sent by the green standard of the cross. They will be flown at mid-mast if the soldiers are onboard."

"For all our sake, I hope they are there," Turlough replied.

"As do I," Miguel said.

The sky was a startling blue. Turlough saw the huge body of water known as Lough Neigh and the village of Maghery smattered with the doings of work. Fisherman were fishing, plows were churning the earth. O'Neill had stopped Radcliffe's advance but for how long? "Is there anything else he should know?"

"There is more, but first tell me of Ulster," Miguel said, knowing the heartiness of this one meeting would not last.

The smell of rain had been replaced with that of lilies and wild clover. The unusual cold of the past days now turning back to warmth. It eased Turlough's senses. He imagined that things would be different in Ulster now that the English had been confronted with a loss. He also thought of Shane O'Neill's provocations and those who had not made their pledge to his cause. "Well for one thing, O'Neill has taken the Earl of Tryconnell, Calvagh and his wife Katherine a hostage. I fear that may bring the Scotts against us."

Miguel looked concerned, "The Scotts?"

Turlough replied: "He wants assurance that the Earl of Argyll who sits with a fleet of island boats does not take us at advantage. O'Neill has already sent couriers to Katherine's father Hector and also to Archibald of Clan Campbell. They must be told that O'Neill has liberated Katherine from Tryconnell and that she will not be harmed. As for me, I feel it a mistake."

"Liberated?"

"Aye. It's a bit of a stretch… but there it is," Turlough said.

"And if the Scotts rise against you to reclaim the dowager countess?" Miguel asked.

"Between you and I, I believe Katherine enjoys her captivity. She may well have played her part in the whole complicated mess."

"Risky," Miguel said.

"Ah… the old codger O'Donnell deserves everything he gets. He could have simply turned the English away but instead he welcomed their offer and opened up London Derry as if it were an English whore house. Fine way to become an earl it is," Turlough said with disgust.

Miguel frowned, "Be smart with your words Turlough. The Lord cares not for vulgarity."

Turlough laughed, "It matters little what me thinks. Katherine will be the first to die if we are attacked by Argyll. If that happens there will be nothing to stop Radcliffe from gaining the full allegiance of the isles. It's more than a gamble. It's reckless. What O'Neill truly needs is men, powder, and for the sake of Christ's blood, a commitment from Spain!"

Miguel sensed a fracture in Turlough's voice. Imperceptible at first but the sense of uncertainty was there. "It's hard to say what my countrymen will provide let alone the Holy Father." He did not like Turlough's tone but he needed him.

Turlough countered with his own recollection of duty. He had fought for freedom and also for faith. "The clans that matter have stood and made war already. Should the Pope forget his promise," Turlough replied.

"Indeed. The situation in the Pale is at O'Neill's advantage. I will tell you that the Archbishop of Armagh has over extended himself among Parliament. He is a far greater threat than Radcliffe." Miguel's eyes lit up and Turlough sensed the passion that he felt and saw the insightfulness of his expression. "The archbishop holds the true cross on display in Dublin. This boldness has caused a stir in the church and many believe him wrong. You see, Turlough, that even with the Anglican mandate, true believers understand that you cannot steal something from God."

"Loftus is a liar and deserves a traitor's death. Why does this surprise you? Does the Pope not know that with England comes the destruction of all that is holy? What else have you learned?"

"That there are still lords of parliament who wish the true cross returned to Rome and perhaps even hold some sympathy for O'Neill. But Loftus insists that all the Catholic treasure be retained for England. As for Radcliffe he imposes his will so greatly on the lesser lords that none dare to oppose either man.

But it is Loftus who has the most influence. I would urge that O'Neill summon the nobility of the northern cities to engage the clergy directly. Presently, the archbishop believes I travel to London for the benefit of one of the English plantations that brings a profit to the crown."

"Why would he believe that?" Turlough asked.

"That does not matter right now, but I assure you… he does," Miguel replied.

"It is good that you have gained this trust but I doubt that the lords of parliament will ever get off their asses. Parliament? What is a parliament of lords who hump the leg of England like impotent dogs?" Turlough asked.

"It is not the law which concerns the Pope about parliament. It is the dissention and it is the wealth that has been seized in total disregard to the faithful. I will do my part to stop this sacrilege. I plan to leave in a fortnight, so I do not have much time. What O'Neill should know is that while the lords bicker, the midlands remain unguarded. Dublin however, has been fortified and so have the garrisons in Meath."

"I cannot control what O'Neill does or where he will lead the men. He has his own vision but he will want to know who will take your place amongst the disciples?"

Miguel's expression darkened with the thought of what had already been lost. He had wondered himself who might be trusted. Of the twelve he had mentored, three were dead already. "We were betrayed from someone within and captured near Geashill. Peter and Matthew were tortured to death in front of a gathering," he said, fighting back his emotion. He knew Simon was alive and Thomas but the others had fled.

"And you escaped?" Turlough asked.

"Nay... I was rescued," Miguel replied as if it were a revelation. He looked to his feet and felt the phantom pain of a missing toe. It made him feel cold again. It made him remember, Jodia. As Turlough looked at him Miguel wondered how much he should tell or how little. "It was a Fitzgerald what saved me."

"A Fitzgerald from Kildare or Munster?" Turlough asked.

"Kildare," Miguel answered. "The Fitzgerald of Kildare were loyal to their catholic faith. It was a measure of boldness that cost the earl dearly."

"Then there is hope and mercy for Kildare. Will God avenge the disciples or shall we?" Turlough asked bitterly.

"I have handled it. You will not like what I have to say but I believe we were betrayed by Jodia," Miguel replied.

"Are you sure?"

"I'm as sure as I can be. Yes," Miguel whispered.

"Did you kill him?"

Miguel looked to the ground. He knew Jodia was of the clan and yet there was no other answer. That was the problem that seeped into every corner of conspiracy. Who could you trust and who could you not.

"I want to know how he died," Turlough insisted.

Miguel stepped back. For a moment he considered Jodia's fate as Turlough looked on expecting a reply. How could he tell him the truth? The assassins he had sent were strong and they returned to him to say that Jodia had not suffered. It had given him some relief, but was he truly dead? "I pray you never have to make such a choice but there was a perversion in him. He could not be trusted and I believe it was he who sent the Sheriff." Miguel explained.

"I asked how he died?"

Miguel answered as if he himself threw the final blow. "He was struck down with a stone." The two men stood in silence as if examining the truth of each other's souls. Miguel pondered his mission and Turlough the doubt of betrayal. Miguel spoke first, "There will be none who I trust in my stead. I will go alone and O'Neill will need to take caution in the priesthood."

The answer instilled a belief in Miguel's truth and Turlough held out a scroll. "This one is for Spain," he said, and as he handed Miguel a second parchment he took him by the hand. It was an embrace of trust and hope. "These are the names of those who will help you."

Miguel took them both, "I will protect them with my life."

"The risk you are taking may well end your life. I will pray for you Jesuit and will tell you that there is a friend to our cause at Saint Bartholomew's of London. The others I do not know," Turlough told him.

CHAPTER 3

Sailors
and
Saints

Ten days after the battle, to the south of the An Uisce Dubh, near the docks where English soldiers once felt safe, a ship known as the *Pinnacle* arrived to the city of Dublin. The first mate stood at the forecastle and hammered a copper bell. *Ding, ding, ding,* rang the bell as the ship approached the quays.

"Call to the dock master, the *Pinnacle* is arriving!" the first mate shouted. The ship prepared as it had a dozen times before.

21

Men scampered up ropes and others unfastened a long wooden ladder descending from the side hull.

"Sails down from the top crew!" the quartermaster shouted.

To the rear of the vessel the pilot spun the sternwheel whilst the captain strode to the middeck. A stoic man by nature, the captain knew the burden of Her Majesty's need. Upon the wood he stood a rigid figure of order. The ship carried soldiers, articles of powerful men, and the coin for England's war.

Hearing the first mate, the men of the upper crew worked to bring in heavy canvas sheets as the eighty-foot ship lumbered into the bay. "All sails down, was the command from the quartermaster! All sails down from the top mast!" the first mate shouted.

From high above, a grizzled voice responded: "Pull tight the outer, lads, and cinch the main sail stay!" The voice came from the sail master. Three sets of sheets stretched below him and he moved quickly on the tallest gallant and gazed from above with dirty hands gripping the top brace rail. The wind was pressing, the bay was deep and their wake would soon reach the tug boats.

In the top sails, the sail master was all to all. Bare feet, calloused and red from climbing, a shirtless back of scars, he heaved with his torso, blinked away the sweat and ogled the doings of the crew with eyes as grey and cold as the winter sea.

In the midst of things that should be done a cat scurried across the cargo hatch with a frightening yawl. The animal bounded up to the foredeck and circled the first mate's highly polished boots. This feline presence distracted the crew... oddly out of place... oddly uncontrolled. Even the captain on the mid-deck gave his glance of disapproval.

"Lieutenant Brinson!" the captain shouted into the wind.

The first mate was all the more exasperated. With things to do and orders to give the cat slinked perilously close to its own doom. In a fit, he slapped pristine white trousers with one hand and pointed with the other. "Patterson!" and he shouted again, "Pat...ter...son!"

Kenneth Patterson was not at his post on the larboard rails with the other sailors. He let loose a line and ran after his feline antagonist as the unruly rat chaser slipped away. Blackie was the bane of his existence. The cursed cat with two cunning green eyes of treachery gleamed back at him over a bristled black and shiny coat. He had failed— and the cat his brother had coddled, zigged and zagged its way through grasping hands.

The captain called out: "It's a problem, Lieutenant Brinson!"

The captain referred to the cat; the captain referred to Kenneth, and most of all he referred to the lack of discipline that should accompany an able crew. "If ye cannot contain a single feline, how will ye land this ship?"

Lieutenant Brinson flushed. With a flash, Blackie had eluded even the quickest of sailors with lightning speed but there was just one sailor on his mind.

🐾 🐾 🐾

Kenneth Patterson slumped forward and shuffled as if his feet were made of tar. He thought of his brother and walked slowly toward the forecastle in hopes that Blackie might leap down into his arms. Anything would be better than standing in front of Lieutenant Brinson. He and his brother Ryan had been warned of that.

Ye don't feed-em, the gunners had told them. *And doon-ever let the critter topside*, he remembered. The cat was important to the mates because the ship had rats. Big round flea infested rats and it was Kenneth the crew had blamed. Now, for all to see, he had no choice but to go and take his due. *Today*, he thought, *it is good ye work in the top sails, me brother; for I will surely dash your cats filthy head and throw its wretched carcasses into the sea!*

The first mate stood with both hands planted firmly on his hips. His legs swayed, the ship rolled and he looked angrier than Kenneth had feared.

"Aye sir, apprentice mate Patterson, reporting as ordered, sir!" Kenneth shouted before bringing both heels together.

Lieutenant Brinson or Mister Brinson as the captain sometimes called him was a figure of nobility imposing upon the serf. Tight white leggings, black boots and shiny brass buttons symbolized everything Kenneth was not. A pompous but capable officer and one who had the power to determine the fate of every soul on board. As Kenneth reported, the first mate poked him in the chest and eyed the shoreline. He spoke as if Kenneth was not even a man, but a thing to be directed. "Patterson will have that cat caged and brought to the lower hold before a single plank touches the pier," he said in an unusually calm clear voice.

Kenneth looked to the tugs and then to shore estimating the minutes he had before the ship butted against the mooring boards.

"The sails are nearly down. What are you waiting for?" Lieutenant Brinson seethed.

Kenneth felt his knees tremble. It was a terrible sensation because he was not afraid. He was mad. He tried to speak but felt his tongue knot up on the inside of his mouth.

Seeing Kenneth's expression, the first mate raised his voice, "Are thee mocking me?"

Kenneth heard ropes hissing and chants from above and felt the cold air tighten in his throat. "N...n...nay, sir," he said with the greatest of difficulty.

"Well get to it or you and your inept excuse of a brother will be keeled!"

❧ ❧ ❧

High above the center of the great ship, Ryan Patterson heard the sail master grunt as slackened lines became taught with the filling of an untied sheet. With all that needed to be done the situation was less than ideal.

"To the outward tackle, Patterson!" The sail master shouted.

Ryan looked back without reply and he saw an expression that was not just one of dissatisfaction but one of utter loathing. Being among experienced sailors, Ryan straddled the huge beam and lifted his body to stand. Each of the men except for Ryan pulled evenly to bring the sail down. Having tied themselves off they felt secure but Ryan was not seasoned enough to be wary of safety. With toes that gripped the foot line and a heavy canvas sheet above, the men strained and the sail master saw Ryan fumble.

"Eh—ya, boy-o! Cross the upper yard!" Ryan heard. He moved cautiously past the ropes and reached for the outer tackle. Many times he had practiced tying the knots on the deck below but at sixty feet his hands began to tremble. He was fearful... fearful and full of doubt as to the condition of the span beneath his soles.

The sail master waited impatiently, his piercing gaze a warning in itself. Other barrel chested men looked on with squinted brows and wind burnt faces, scowling whilst the slowest in his task struggled to secure the outer hoist.

"Tie the blasted thing!" the others demanded.

"God be damned or jump! Get it done!" the sail master shouted.

The sailing men of the *Pinnacle* were tense. They wanted off the vessel, but the captain, being a man on a commission, had said: "Nay... nay... none shall set foot in Dublin." They would not leave the *Pinnacle* until it made true her voyage to London. No pay for the shipmates, not a coin for the pocket and the sail master known as Grey Eyes was the angriest of them all.

"Fall down to them dirty Irish below and do us all the favor of dying!" Grey Eyes shouted like an old sea hag. His long deep slur more rotten than curdled milk.

Out on the yardarm, Ryan closed his eyes and pulled the hoist line. It was the very worst of things he could have done because the second he pulled, the tug butted against the larboard hull. The *Pinnacle* was now just feet from landing broadside against the pier. Ryan felt his hand slip and looked down to the mass of bystanders and shore-men who gathered to receive their goods.

As the great vessel traversed the myriad of obstacles and ebbed into position amongst other ships within the port, it groaned as if warning those people below. A deep hollow sound of straining timber cried out: *"Look out you fools! I am still in motion!"* but none of the onlookers understood the lumbering vessel as it wailed.

On the docks that joined the city with Dublin's bay, no one saw Ryan Patterson panic as his foot slipped off the spindled hemp. He hung for an instant with the look of desperation and tried vainly to grasp the girth of a loosely bundled sheet. Having survived six months already, the time had come for Ryan to meet his fate and his body knew this but his heart did not. Only the topsail crew saw him. A moment of queer fascination consuming their every thought. Would he die or would he not?

The ship butted against the mooring boards. A construction of pitch stained pilings and roadworks that joined the mouth of the River Liffey to Dublin proper. It was a place where people walked and worked and came to gather along the road. Behind the road, shops were built with entrances that opened to both the seaward side and interior of the city. There, the life blood of trade flowed onto cobblestone. Barrels, carts, chests and cages extended in a continual transition between the ships and city. Farther up the Liffey, larger cargo, such as horses and carriages accessed the street through a gated stone wall. The expanse jutted twenty feet high and a bridged crossed the river where the city spilled over to the other bank.

It was near the bridge on the River Liffey where Ryan Patterson fell. The event occurred as the *Pinnacle* docked, and when the captain sent sailors wearing black slops and grey woolen frocks to stand along the gunwales. The fall barely interrupted the boatswain mates who caught huge lines and wrapped them around the cleats. It happened after the bell sounded three more times and the dock master on shore blew a long loud whistle. On the ship itself, Kenneth Patterson held Blackie in his hands and shouted: "R...Ryan!"

❧ ❧ ❧

It was the 28th day of July in the morning and the port city was crawling with merchants and seaman. Fighting the crowd, a flock of Anglican priests jockeyed for position to watch the *Pinnacle* disembark. The sound of livestock split the air. A squealing pig, the cackle of hens and even the roar of a caged lion added to the moment when Ryan fell. Men took off their hats unsure of what to do and the crane began to swing.

The people on shore heard a scream, followed by a horrendous thump. It was an unmistakable sound and to the spectator's horror, a young life poured out onto the road. The sight frightened the children and so did Ryan's ghoulish moan. As they backed away the smell of Ryan's blood and splattering of horse dung wafted through the air. Incredibly, Ryan was not dead but contorted of limbs like a puppet that lay in a heap. His hand twitched and then his digits and with a wheeze his eyes rolled open. His suffering evaporated all sound: all except the sailors on the great ship became still.

Suddenly a Spaniard named Miguel broke through the circle of non-doing gazes. He wore a plain Anglican robe and a woman cried as he brushed past her. Behind Miguel some priests came to kneel in prayer. Their own gowns soaking up the blood and dampening their knees.

Miguel placed his hand on Ryan's forehead. "Sinner, hear my prayer," he said softly. Then he looked to heaven, "Lord and Father, almighty and eternal God, give your peace in this man's frailty. Lord have mercy. I pray for him to be free of all pain. Oh Mary, Mother of God, intercede in the name of Your Son, Jesus, who has taken every burden and infirmity away."

The onlookers crossed themselves and Miguel looked down and saw that the young lad recognized God's word and he paused to hear a confession. A sensation of wonder overtook Miguel. *Could it be that God would spare this man? Indeed, the lad's wounds appeared to stop bleeding and then he began to move!*

"I am Ryan ..." the sailor sputtered. And in his understanding, Ryan wept tears upon Miguel's hand.

"It is not too late..." Miguel whispered so that none could hear.

Even as those around looked on without compassion, Ryan spoke. A mixture of spittle and froth erupted from the corner of his mouth. "They are sick with evil, my Angel," Ryan sputtered.

Miguel felt Ryan's words. He wanted a healing and the euphoria of a miracle for he was sure that Ryan saw him clearly. Would the masses see the power of God? "Who... who is evil, my son?" he asked.

Ryan's eyes rolled back and then a trembling arm stretched out to point at the sailors in black slops and grey frocks standing all along the gunnels. They were there; they were dark—Miguel was warned. A dust devil picked up in a fierceness as Ryan began to slip away.

The crowd of onlookers mumbled and an angry voice called out: "Throw him into the river!" In answer to the commotion a terrible roar erupted from the caged lion and pigs squealed and rattled their pens like demon laden swine. This all came to pass in the instant of Ryan's death just as a hand grazed Miguel's neck. Hair raising awakenings prickled his arms with goosebumps.

Miguel made the sign of the cross on Ryan's forehead and a plainly suited man with buckled brown shoes and a wide brimmed hat grabbed his shoulder. "What did he tell you?" the man asked.

Miguel gently rested Ryan on the ground and stood to address the person he knew as Loftus. "Make them righteous, Adam. He said... make them righteous."

Adam Loftus was a questioner. He questioned the sanctity of the church and he questioned what it must be like to die. The church and death had always been closely linked to the eternal cycle of his Lord. Death being ever present but always out of his control and life being the promise of the hereafter. He paused with Miguel and observed the people's faces who stood briefly in awe. The thought occurred to him that death would usurp the people of Dublin. One at a time they all would cross over and yet just as quickly as death came, he saw that it was accepted.

"Is that all he said?" Adam asked.

Miguel replied: "Yes, my lord."

Adam turned his attention to the Anglican priests. Without question, they gathered and prayed over Ryan exactly how the living and the dead do mingle. Their movements were a spectacle of the eternal promise and yet he wondered if they truly believed.

Miguel carried a satchel of letters and pulled a trunk of cloths. Adam Loftus held just one book as they walked away, not inconsequential, *The Book of Common Prayer,* he cherished. It was the first of many to be printed for the Irish to read. After a moment of reflection, Adam turned his attention to his friend. "Is it tears for the lad, thee weep?" he asked.

"I weep not for his soul. I have never touched a saint before," Miguel replied.

"A saint?" Adam asked incredulously.

"I felt as though he was, my lord," Miguel answered.

Adam changed the subject. He did it to alieve his friend in thought but he also did it selfishly. "This ship will take you to London, Miguel. So indeed you might find yourself able to do what has been asked of you."

"Are you referring to the girl?" Miguel asked.

Adam scrunched his brow: "The girl? Oh no... I was referring to the sailing men of the *Pinnacle*." His expression remained stoic but Adam knew all good and well he needed the Colley's to be producing and was referring to the girl.

Miguel looked at Adam suspiciously, "If the crew have lost a brother, my lord, I will do what can be done."

"I know you will. As for the girl, I would not put all my faith in the hope that a child is our remedy for Colley Town. There are children here that can fill the void within Mistress Colley," Adam said.

"Perhaps, but to have the child of Kintyre close at hand may be advantageous. But as you have said so many times, Adam, it is not up to priests to decide these things."

"Bring her, but do not harm Thomas Smyth. The Colley's need his backing and Henry Colley is a friend of Ralph Lane... who is a friend of mine."

Miguel nodded politely, "As you wish, my lord."

"While you are away, I will pay a visit to the earl. I am not so sure I believe that a Fitzgerald should truly be trusted."

Miguel ruffled, "The earl has recanted his claim against the plantations and also Emma Colley's involvement with witchcraft. Under the circumstances he was in, I believe him. What else must he do?"

Adam looked unconvinced, "That is enough if he has told you the truth. But such a man comes from a family with very dubious ties. Does it not seem odd that he has given up his dispute so easily?"

"You know why he has given up his land and have seen in his own hand all that I have said. Remember, I came to you and asked only that his letter be delivered. In return for your help, I will not wear my pontifical robes or incite against your doctrine. I can live with this and so can the Holy Father, but can you?" Miguel replied.

"Yes, so you have told me and I will choose to believe the earl and also the assurance you have given from Rome, for now. As for the child in London, you'll have no trouble getting her aboard any ship destined for Dublin. Emma Colley has offered free passage for any girl with the name of Agnes. I hear that Henry is already in debt because of it. It seems that he indulges his wife and claims it a fitting honor for their dearest. It is a pity that his portion of the plantations yield has been secured to cover such obligations."

"Strange," Miguel said.

Adam shrugged, "Insane might be a better word for that woman. But who am I to judge? You were right, Ralph Lane has confirmed that a girl was taken by Radcliffe during his raid on Kintyre. She is the daughter of the chieftain McAlister. Apparently, the son was not of able mind and ran off into thorn bushes during the attack. The girl was unharmed and Lord

Radcliffe was smart in taking his hostage. He was also foolish for decimating one of the protestant villages in the Mull. I will not forgive him of that."

"It appears he doesn't act on faith alone," Miguel replied.

Adam nodded agreement, "Just get her aboard an English ship and let the captain know her name is Agnes and a bonus will be paid for her safe delivery to me. If you are successful, I will say that we found her traveling under false pretense. That will be enough to persuade the lord deputy that she should foster at the Colley farm. Of course there will be a harsh accounting for whoever sails with her."

"I will find someone expendable," Miguel replied.

Adam smiled, "Good... and for the earl's letter which offers peace, you may deliver them to Lord Burghley who will certainly scrutinize their value to the queen."

"He will find them worth every consideration, my lord," Miguel replied.

As they spoke, a cart arrived and with it were the death masks that the priests would wear in procession. The black feathers and hideous beaks caused a stir. Seeing this, Miguel engaged Adam's kinder affection as the priests lifted Ryan's body to be taken away. "Can he be buried in Mihans?"

The change of subject broke Adam's concentration and he looked at Miguel as if he were mad, "He should be cast into the Liffey, like the other paupers," he said in disbelief.

"I ask that he not," Miguel replied.

Adam shrugged, "I will never understand thee. We have just moments before you depart and yet you focus on a stranger. Who is that man to you?" he asked.

Miguel looked at Ryan's body without question, "God puts these things before me, Adam. I know that you believe in the Lord but I will tell you that I hear his voice directly."

Adam did believe in the Lord and yet he had never heard His voice. He looked at Miguel with a peculiar interest. Such a strange man and yet he was able to put forth true conviction. "I hear Him, Miguel." Adam motioned to the priests who prepared to take Ryan away. "To Mihans. Bury him!" he ordered. Quietly the priests pulled their cloaks over their heads and did what they thought was unthinkable. They would bury a sailor with the saints.

After they were gone and the docks returned to normal, Miguel thought about Adam's desire for power. They had spoken of it and Miguel had learned how Adam believed that sacrifice was as much a blessing as salvation. He spoke of sacrifice as if it were the means to his end and his end was deliverance from Rome. "Has the queen ever asked you to kill someone? Maybe a helpless person or someone who trusted you beyond measure?" he asked as they waited for boarding. Adam sighed without a response and so he asked again, "Have you killed for her?"

"For what purpose?" Adam asked defensively.

Miguel looked into Adam's eyes as the wind returned with a clanking of chains sounding down the pier. "For your own understanding, Adam. So that you know that your queen is the head of the Church of England and Ireland," he replied.

The call to board the *Pinnacle* was sounded as Adam answered: "The queen has asked me nothing of the sort. Her Majesty does not give a bishop the right to kill."

Miguel stepped closer, closing the distance to mere inches. His voice was but a whisper but it struck like a knife, "The Pope has ordered me to kill and I fear you may be asked to do the same."

The thought seeped into Adam's mind and tested his spirit. "Have the child put on the ship and she will be well cared for," he replied coldly.

CHAPTER 4

Remnant

It was called the mizzen and below the mizzen's furled sails, Captain Grimm stood with Lieutenant Brinson at boarding. Both officers wore dark blue cloaks fastened by a single gold button at the neck. They observed from above, looking down a wide set of stairs called the companionway at the very rear of the *Pinnacle*.

Captain Grimm spoke harshly, "That was a terrible display of seamanship, Mister Brinson."

"The crew will get better, sir. They are still green," Lieutenant Brinson replied.

The business which awaited him could not be avoided and Captain Grimm adjusted his scabbard apathetically. He would have no choice but to go ashore and leave the crew but would they be ready for a quick departure? "Perhaps if we do not kill them off before they learn the trade we might yet meet our obligations," he replied curtly.

"Aye, sir. It was a setback when Patterson the younger fell," Lieutenant Brinson gazed off toward Mihans Chapel. He could not help but consider the irony. A lowly sailor buried with the saints as church bells sounded across the water. "A group of Anglican priests have taken the body to Mihans… if you can believe it."

"Buried?" the captain asked.

"Aye, and one of the priests who anointed the body has boarded. He's a Spaniard who seems to be in the good graces with someone of influence," Lieutenant Brinson said.

Captain Grimm scratched his head with dismay and then brushed off the comment for other concerns. Below he observed the gathering of passengers who waited. Everything seemed in order but he could not shake the feeling that all was not well. "How many times did the sail master tell Patterson to tie himself off?" he asked, considering the misfortune.

"The sail master cannot be blamed for such a thing. It is dangerous work and although unfortunate, it doesn't change anything," Lieutenant Brinson replied.

Captain Grimm gritted his teeth, "We need able bodies. The sort of men who know the sea and will sail with vigor. Since our departure we have lost more than ten men. Did I not tell thee to find a higher quality of seamen? God forbid we come under attack when we cannot even make port without losing life and the confidence of our investors."

"The men are capable, sir. You also gave me strict orders to meet our schedule. Things being as they are, we have done exactly that. We are not crossing the Atlantic, we simply need to get ourselves straight away to London," Lieutenant Brinson replied.

"That is bold speak, Mister Brinson. Do you know that Admiral Hackett has been given permission from the court to exercise judgement at sea… and, as such, my intention was to seek a potential target on his behest? A Spanish frigate has been reported in the Irish sea and several warships loom on the outer banks of the Mull. Down ten men or not, I would wish to be ready for such an opportunity."

"And if we do not find such a vessel?" Lieutenant Brinson asked.

"It will be the Pinnacle that seizes that opportunity and not a privateer. So make good use of your time, sir. The queen wishes to send Spain a clear message."

"Aye, sir. We will be ready."

❧ ❧ ❧

Miguel had watched the captain depart in the hours it took to load the *Pinnacle*. He stood below the center mast with the other passengers as a smart looking boy of fair complexion appeared shortly after the captain left. The lad set his hazel eyes on each of them as he passed. Inquisitive and entertaining the boy threw out his legs and straightened his arms to swing them in a parade of march. The passengers loved him immediately and he smiled when people applauded and then took a gracious bow. Stopping near Miguel, he asked: "Have ye sailed before?"

Miguel smiled, "A time or two."

The child was dressed in baggy slops and his open shirt was cinched with a dandy piece of rope. There was adventure in his expression as his blond hair drifted feely over his eyes. "Good. Then ye will want to pay attention next cause the purser will be calling shortly." Such surety the lad possessed. His hands were stained from powder, calloused and dry and yet his spirit gave a lift to those around. He went from passenger to passenger to tell them the same and when he returned to Miguel, the little man held up his finger and pressed it against his lips. "Shhh..." he cautioned, and with a twinkle, he whispered: "you may call me Jimmy."

Miguel could see it was a tidy ship. It stretched fifteen feet in either direction of the huge mid timber. Large round chocks were neatly bound and stood ready to discharge their rope as the wooden capstan creaked to the even rhythm of two square shouldered men who worked a gigantic handle. Everything ticked along with precision whilst the passengers milled around in idle chatter. Very soon, from somewhere down below, a line of sailors trotted up and so did the man Jimmy acknowledged as the purser. A portly fellow bouncing below a pointed white bonnet: Arrogant, red eyed and cheeks puffed out with a stiff quill of whiskers the purser promptly discharged his pistol.

The thunder was followed by a puff of sulfurous smoke. It was quite the announcement and the purser rubbed his scruff unshaven face and took an ambitious swallow from a silver rum flask. He crinkled his glistening lips and took in the sight of the passengers startled condition. "Hear ye all! This be the *Pinnacle* and a ship of Her Majesty, Elizabeth, Queen of England and France. As such, every soul will come hither to sign me log.

When this be complete, and only then..." he gazed at them with bulging eyes, "shall ye leave this deck for quarters."

Immediately after his announcement, the purser motioned for his table and Jimmy went running. It was set in the center of the quarter deck. "This ill-do, Jimmy," he said. Pulling a quill from his pointed bonnet, he sat down and peered over a crooked nose. "Take heed to stay clear of the mid ship timber, the forecastle," he pointed back, "and the aft railing!"

Miguel watched quietly as a gentlemen stepped forward to announce his arrival. "Register in the name of Robert Lockhart and son, Noah," the man said as he held out his papers.

The purser's countenance suddenly became almost cheerful, "Welcome to board, Robert. Little Jimmy there will take ye aft and see to your necessaries. Until evening mess, would ye be so kind as to keep yourselves occupied in the royal galley?"

"We will and I look forward to the captain's good pudding," Robert replied.

Miguel waited patiently as similar men, dressed in suits and shiny shoes all took their lead from Lockhart. Thus the paying passengers, all except Miguel were well boarded. As for the rest who stood on deck, the purser's countenance changed. His eyes fell upon a poorer sort of fellow who held tightly to the hand of his wife. "And your papers?" he asked, knowing the man had yet to pay.

Aggrieved with his position, the man frowned. "We have not been able to secure our voyage but I can work and so can the mistress."

There was a bit of laughter from the crew as they eyed the woman. The purser however was not amused and he shot a fiery glance to the ships guard. "Why have ye not taken a ferry to Liverpool and found a way from there?" he asked the man.

The man sounded desperate, "Want for little time, sir." He turned to his wife who stood in a black gown of mourning. "Her mother is ill and this is the first ship that can arrive in London with good speed."

Miguel listened to the whispers of the men at work. *Yes, I am a Spaniard*, he thought, as they looked on with distrustful eyes.

"Do ye understand that this is a warship?" the purser asked the man.

"We do, sir, and I have sailed before. I can be of use on a vessel of this size," the man replied.

The purser now angered at the assumption. "You can be cast over or climb! As for the mistress, it looks like she can earn her pay with the gunner's whores!" he said bitterly.

"My wife is a goodly woman, sir. She will do a fitting task or I shall make twice the labor for her," the man replied.

"I don't think ye heard me. A warship does not extend credit. Will you climb down or be thrown over?" the purser said sternly.

"I am not afraid of heights and you have lost a sailor. Surely you must be in need of a worthy seaman. I am telling you that it is I whom can be of value," the man said boldly.

The purser shot a glance toward the old sail master who perked up with the man's brazen words. "Would you dare?"

"I can climb sir. I have done it before," the man replied.

The purser grunted and seemed to take note of the man's promise. It wasn't pleasant but he did make a mark in his log. "Do you know what I have written?" he asked smugly.

"No sir," the man replied.

"I have written that you and your wife will do exactly as you're told or be cast off for lack of payment. You will report to the sail master and she to the gun deck. She is pretty. I am sure they will like her down below."

The man stood there for a moment unsure of what to do and as he did Miguel stepped forward. "I have made pay for passage. Why have you not accounted for me in your log?"

"What say you?" the purser asked Miguel with agitation.

Miguel took another step forward, "I have made rightly for my travel and will pay for their passage as well. I just want to board and be left alone."

The purser smiled wickedly at Miguel's boldness, "I have been told to put you down in the stable. How would that suit you for interfering?"

Miguel's heart burned with the insult, "I will pay their way in silver," he replied coldly.

"And I asked who you are to interfere?" the purser replied.

"By the Holy Father and all that is dear to our Lord, I am a priest. I would imagine that ye should put me wherever you feel a priest should be."

"It'll be the stable then," the purser replied and the crew could not hold back their laughter.

Of the few passengers that remained, Miguel saw several cross themselves and look on with horror at his poor treatment. "Surely there is no law to keep me from boarding for I am here on the Lord's work."

"The captain has not forbidden it but he will be watching you. That he has made clear. Now perhaps you may offer their payment in advance?" the purser asked.

Miguel held out his papers from the arch bishop, "I have these," he said.

The purser looked them over, "A courier of the archbishop?"

"It is so," Miguel replied.

"A courier of the archbishop and also a priest of Rome?" the purser asked skeptically.

"It is so," Miguel replied.

"And your name?"

Miguel pulled a crucifix from around his neck. "Miguel Avaje Fernandez and I shall pay the weight of two pounds' silver from this cross. I do not wish to be of trouble and will go where the captain orders without complaint. I am who I am. If that means the stable it will rest on your conscience."

The purser examined the cross and held it in his hand. "You'll not find a warmer welcome in all of London but I'll take your silver. This will due for the man, but the mistress will need to pay in other ways. Unless you have something else," the purser said greedily.

Miguel took a gold coin out of his pocket, "You may ask her to labor but she will spend the nights with her husband," Miguel said.

The purser raised his brow, "Well now, look at that. Giving up the treasures of this earth. I am sure that your King Phillip would be overjoyed with such devotion. And the lads here," he pointed to the crew, "they will be overjoyed as well. Only a fool would bring such attention."

Miguel looked at them all. Their silence told him everything. "It is all I have. It will be yours when we arrive safely to London. So if this is stolen then you get nothing. Would it not be better to keep us all safe?" he asked.

As the loud long whistle blew and the crew snapped to get under way, the purser grunted. "Very smart, you are. The mister will report to the sail master and the mistress may find comfort in the stable. As for you, stay clear and remain on deck. You'll be provided an escort as per our captain's orders."

❧ ❧ ❧

As he waited, Miguel took a moment below the center cross tree to look through the many ropes that obscured Dublin and the hazy silhouette of Mihans Chapel. Ireland would soon be fading in the distance. He thought of his mission and took note of a barrel and saw that it was marked pork. There were a number of barrels on the upper deck just above the galley hold. People put their hands on them, sailors sat on the barrels and he could see the marks where some had already been dragged below. Barrels of dried fish packed in salt and huge bundles of apples. He also noticed the queen's yeomen. A complement of guards with such splendid looking red uniforms. His hands tingled when he saw them parade across the deck without restriction and pick at the apples whenever they liked. *They could be a problem*, he thought.

A hand touched Miguel's shoulder, "Do ye know where they took 'im?"

Miguel turned and saw an afflicted man, "Took who?" he asked.

"Me brother," Kenneth replied sorrowfully.

"Your brother?"

"Aye, and I saw you touch him. I saw…" Kenneth stopped as if catching his breath before continuing, "I saw him carted away."

The interruption was a distraction. He could see the struggle of good and evil on Kenneth's face. Kenneth appeared lost, hollow and used to the very marrow of his bones. *This man would not be a problem*, Miguel thought. "I am sorry. You know that your brother has passed don't you?"

"Where did they take him?" Kenneth asked.

"His body was taken to the ground of Saint Mihans Parrish across the Liffey Bridge. He will be buried in the old graves outside the abbey," Miguel told him.

"H… he will be buried?" Kenneth sighed.

"Your brother will be buried with the saints," Miguel said assuredly.

Kenneth opened his mouth as if yawning, "I am n…not stupid."

"It is true. You can go about your business knowing that Ryan has been cared for. What is your name?" Miguel asked.

"Kenneth."

Miguel put his hand on Kenneth's shoulder, "God always leaves a remnant, Kenneth. That is how I know that God is good."

Kenneth did not understand the strange priest's implication but he relished the attention. It was a measure of kindness. "I have been told to stay with you in the stable."

CHAPTER 5

Wildlings

In a junction where the trees met an open field near the English fort of Belturbet, night fell and the forest cast shadows on a horrific scene. A razor sharp knife slid through the skin with a crackle and made its way down the inner thigh to expose an un-scorched portion of flesh. The soldier had been slain. Fingers delved into the meat and the pattering of feet filled the air as damp leaves crumpled.

"Hagan..." one of the beastly men whispered.

Hagan was the leader. A giant to some but his emaciation had taken its toll and his ribs jutted out under tight skin. He looked up drunk from his meal with dark eyes set below a tall sloping forehead. "The others..." he replied gruffly.

With Hagan's words, a savage darted off into the night with toenails that gouged the earth and arms that parted the reeds. In a flurry of hair and covered in weathered pelts, he ran.

The tribe was far from their people and although summer was upon the forest no game had been found. Hagan stretched out his arm as he squatted and motioned with an enormous hand, "Tie de' prisoner," he commanded in a raspy voice.

The others moved quickly and subdued a survivor. A black silken robe and a silver crucifix weighing nearly two pounds pressed against his heart. He struggled and they muffled his cries with a bit of English uniform.

Tasting the blood and sweat of the musty wool, the prisoner gagged. Their sounds penetrated his soul. Then without a word the heathens dragged him off toward the brush and tied him at the hands and legs and went about their scavenging. Just as he thought he had been forgotten a woman of the tribe came to him. She appeared to be searching for something and stood over him with long uncombed hair and blood red eyes.

"Shhh…" she whispered. Her fascination was frightening and after examining him she lay down near his body. "Hagan my brother," she said. He pushed away as she reached out to remove his gag.

He coughed. These things were not the soldiers who had won the battle but they were something else. He was born of the clan and knew of the wild people who lingered in the darkness. Their speech was neither English nor Gal but something in between. A lost language perhaps and yet familiar enough for him to understand.

He did his best to keep his voice low, "Does your brother believe in God? For it is He who I serve."

She looked at him as if she did not understand and then stroked his face like a long lost love. He reminded her of someone. He could see it, even in her animalistic state, and somewhere deep inside he hoped she would have mercy and free him. "I am a disciple who heals and loves and needs affection. Do not let your brother do the things he has done here to me. I can reward you. I can give you what you need," he pleaded.

"Reee waard," she breathed.

"Yes, just let me go. Cut lose my legs and hands and you can come with me. I have people and food. You must not live like this. It is an abomination!" he said. Fearing the beasts would hear him, he stopped suddenly and held his breath. She listened also and off toward the battlefield the sounds of grumbling began. There was a metallic thump of a pot being hammered and the shouting of another who was disturbed. They were fighting with themselves now. Bickering over the spoils. The name Hagan was shouted across a field and his answer came from within the charred fort of Belturbet.

"Shhh.... no time for talk. Hagen kill you soon unless you be my man." She punched him in the chest. "My man!"

"No... you don't understand. I am a priest. We can go north to my village and the clan will pay you for my return. Even the great king O'Neill knows my name and he will not smite thee." She cocked her head as if thinking. "Or perhaps you would like to live in a priory that will feed you every day. Perhaps even your children. Or maybe there are others we can help escape this madness. We can teach them how to serve and work and be worthy of God."

"We have gone south and north and now west and still you make a war and bring many spears and swords. You burn the woods and kill the game. Even the fish swim down the river to escape your Gawd. My son killed by Britons! My husband killed by guns!"

"Keep your voice down," he whispered to her, looking back over his shoulder and not seeing where the others were off too. Would they come running? Would Hagen come running to kill him? "Not by clan O'Neill were they killed. Not by me or any priest," he pleaded.

"Yes… we kill all Britons! We kill all O'Neill!" She grabbed his hair and bit his ear as she hissed, "Gawd, not save my man! Gawd, not save my son!" Her hands probed him.

"He can save you," he said.

"No… you can save you," her voice seemed void of any feeling and her claws tore open his blouse. He remembered the knife that was in his pocket. A steel blade wrapped in rabbit fur. A gift from his brother with its honed edge and willow handle that he never truly appreciated until now. It was just a tool before. Something to eat or whittle with and now it was everything. He imagined the feel of it in his hand and wanted nothing more badly. As she touched him he did not look to God but to death and wanted only the feel of his blade as it entered her heart: for through her, he might escape. It would be her life or his. It would be her sin or his. Its sharpened point now pressed into his side.

"Shhh…" she said before straddling him and searching the hardness of his body for warmth. Her desire was fixated, immoral and writhing. Even as the others moved among the dead in the ash of the smoldering battlefield, she pressed him.

He closed his eyes. Slowly inching his fingers toward the object of his desire as she jostled him in the dirt and grime of war. He tried and failed and then stretched out his fingers again. She grunted in the night and then mercifully at the climax of her obsession the knife found its way into his hand. That is how a Jesuit came to know the sister of Hagan and the wild people who hungered in the forest.

CHAPTER 6

Topsails

O n the first day at sea Miguel climbed from his dungeon in the belly of the *Pinnacle* to join the masses. The crew were eating gruel in the open fresh air. He watched as the barrels for the next meal were hauled below and counted the number who took fresh fruit. The yeomen picked at the apples, the crew did not. He moved off and took notice of the large flight of stairs that led up to a spacious aft deck. There were fourteen steps up the companionway. Although he could not see the aft deck, he envisioned the sternwheel with its spindled circumference between the heavy cordage that draped down from the cross stays. It was a maze of dangerous ropes along a prickly construction. *That would be a problem,* he thought.

A distraction caused Miguel to turn. "We be one shy in the topsails, Dullard," Grey Eyes yelled as he held out his bowl, "do ye know the top knot?"

Kenneth took the bowl meekly, "T…t…top knot?" he asked.

Seeing that he had the crew's attention Grey Eyes laughed. "Aye," then he smiled mockingly, "t…t…top knot, Dullard. Do ye have the topknot or the bowline mastered?"

Kenneth looked down in shame because he was never good with knots. He had no idea why but one knot looked the same as the next and it befuddled him. His mind wandered off and for a moment there was silence and he thought he might be left alone. He had tried to learn seamanship when his brother was alive but his brother was not alive anymore and now his arm was going numb.

Miguel moved closer, quietly sliding between the sailors to see what was going on. In the middle of the gaggle of men, the old sail master was hurting Kenneth. Kenneth's bucket fell, sending the bowls spinning like tops across the deck.

"Fuck all, ye be worthless," Grey Eyes stammered as Kenneth pulled his arm away.

Before they could touch him again Miguel stepped into the huddle of men who teased and taunted. "I will teach him," he said.

Grey Eyes backed away. He assessed Miguel with an experienced eye and saw that he was tall and lean. Then he bent down and took the end of a length of cordage and released it from its coil. "Look here lads," he motioned to Miguel, "we have a sailing friar who can instruct as well as preach." They laughed. "Go on then," Grey Eyes said handing Miguel the rope. "Show us how the bowline is made, Friar."

Miguel replied: "I'm no friar, but a friar's life would suit me fine if it were Gods will." Without hesitation he turned to Kenneth, "You can do this." He saw the doubt in Kenneth's eyes and the shaking hands. The poor man couldn't even speak with the trauma of the situation he had been forced into. Miguel felt sorry for him, and he took Kenneth's hands and helped him twist the tail of the rope around itself three times and pass the end through the eye they created together. "This is the bowline knot," he said helping Kenneth pull it tight.

Grey Eyes inspected Miguel's work, "I am impressed, Holy Man. Maybe you should rise into the topsails instead of he. It would bring you closer to God. Do you not think so?"

Kenneth held the rope as if replaying the lesson over in his mind. Miguel replied for them both, "He can learn. But he needs to be taught to succeed and not be made to feel small."

"By God's blood he will!" Grey Eyes blasphemed.

The sail master's malice was palpable and Miguel said: "Our Lord is a forgiving God but you shall not take His name in vain." Then without waiting for Grey Eyes to respond, he reached out and touched the old sail master's cheek with his index finger. "You have a sore upon thee and must ask for His forgiveness."

Grey Eye's stepped back, unsure and caught off guard, "What say you?"

"I fear that you are truly unwell and must pray for God's healing and forgiveness." The brazen words caused a stir. The men did not know what to think or even if they should respond? A curse was a terrible thing.

"Get your bloody hand off me!" Grey Eyes shouted.

Miguel squared his shoulders and pushed Kenneth behind him. "You are afflicted! All of you are afflicted!"

In that instant Kenneth felt utterly doomed. Trouble was coming. Only trouble came from the old master. He would be beaten for this long after the priest was gone and his heart sank like an anchor to the bottom of the sea. His fear caused him to cower and bend down on all fours like a dog who had been mistreated. That is when the first mate's pristine white trousers glided past him.

"Is there a problem here?" Lieutenant Brinson asked the men.

Grey Eyes said nothing, the men found their way to leave and Miguel stood with Kenneth who appeared to be in a delirium, whispering and shaking his head. "Is there a problem?" Lieutenant Brinson asked.

"No..." Miguel replied softly.

Lieutenant Brinson didn't like it. He didn't like it at all. "To the topsails then," he said to the crew and to Miguel he said, "the purser has told me about you and I will watch your every move. Be cautious priest. It is not wise to provoke our sail master. Even the Archbishop of Armagh cannot protect a person from the perils of the deep."

Miguel nodded his understanding and looked over the first mate's shoulder to see that Grey Eyes had also listened. His piercing gaze measured Miguel intently and the essence of his grief left little doubt as to the core of evil.

As Lieutenant Brinson left him, Miguel spoke aloud what God had placed in his heart: *"Like a muddied spring or polluted fountain is the righteous man who gives way to the wicked."* Thusly the great ship known as the *Pinnacle* sped toward

London with the cursing mouths of sailing men, high up in the topsails.

Take not
from
the Vicar

Twenty miles to the west of Dublin in a place called Kings County, the midlands gave way to supplanting. There a company of Englishmen laid claim to a farm at the very edge of the English Pale. Governor White of Portsmouth and a gentleman investor named Thomas Smyth from London were the financiers, and Henry Colley was their undertaker. The acreage stretched from Geashill to the old Bermingham castle which stood atop a hill near a water catch made of stone. Surrounded by flat meadows and a great huge bog, the plantation occupied the border territory once called Ua Fáilghe. Now they called the place Colley Town, and like the towns of England, the vicar collected the tithes while the undertaker managed the estate.

Vicar Tinsdale was a sturdy round man and he took his meal alone on a freshly sanded hard oak table. He fancied himself a carpenter but lately his interest was of stone. Today the vicar enjoyed a potted lamb. As the delicious aroma infused his chapel he fondled a piece of schist. "This is the stone we shall have. It will be beautiful."

He had expanded the church and the nave was nearly complete. So much had been accomplished since Henry Colley marched off to war that he dared to wish it never end. "To the war," he said as he raised a glass alone.

Outside the church where the vicar dined, an old woman sat on a huge pile of stones. Mam thought about the old days as she waited for her next task. She had experienced hard times and hunger before but this change seemed different. The Colley's had allowed her to live in her own cottage, and they called it the brown house. *Allowed?* Mam thought. She also pondered Vicar Tinsdale and the Colley's who came to the old Bermingham castle with a guard of English soldiers. She had never seen such an undertaking, and this time the head mistress was Emma Colley. A poor grief ridden woman who slinked away alone in a musty room void of life or love. *Yes... things were different*, Mam thought.

Mam pulled a wool quilt she was making, over her knees and threaded a tin needle with a strand of horsehair. "I'll not be idle whilst a moment can be had," she said. Each square of her quilt had a special meaning and before winter came she would want this one to keep her memories warm. She had made another once… in a time of longing. Today she would add the square of white with a perfect red hand embroidered into the fabric. She was proud of who she was and felt her needlework to be as fine as ever. Mam placed her square as she watched two women down in the field. "Old biddy am I?" she whispered under her breath. Her crooked digits splayed out the material, "they'll not take everything," she stuck the needle and slid it through, "this one is for power."

Off the main road which led to the castle the wild fields of dead brown grass swayed in the wind as high as a horse's mane. The fields were like an ocean, all the way to the great bog- a swampy vast plain that touched both the old world and the new. It was a place of mysterious mist and hidden gullies filled with dark amber water. What Mam knew about the bog was that it certainly held secrets. "I wonder if the terror will be coming tonight?" she said with a sheepish grin.

The two women working in the field were Annie Beth and Mary. They were near the edge of the bog when they saw Mam waving for them to return. Annie pretended not to notice Mam but she could not deny the sound that came from the fog. "Did ye hear that, Mary?" she asked.

Mary cocked her head, "Sounded like a horn or a cow?"

They looked at each other nervously, "Thought I heard something else 'bout an hour ago," Annie said.

Mary felt it also. A feeling of lonely unsettled calm. She flinched as a large black crow took flight with a screech and flapped off into the deep overcast grey. "Best we heed the old woman and set our feet a-moving." They picked up their things quickly and looked around as if something might lurch into their midst.

Annie shivered instinctively, "I don't like it here. And I don't think Henry Colley will be returning this time, Mary." Annie's stomach rumbled as she bent over to lift the last stone into the cart. "Let us go," she said.

"Don't you believe the vicar, Annie?" Mary asked.

At twenty-nine, Annie Beth looked old beyond her years. Her gut told her something was not right in the midlands. It had been quiet since the soldiers had left— much too quiet. "Thank God for you, Mary." Annie wiped her forehead, "I don't believe the vicar and if it weren't for you, me and m' boys would be lost."

Both women wore plaid dresses and white cotton shirts that were stained from their days at work. They hadn't been given time to wash their clothes nor the cloths of their thin children. It had been that way it seemed for nearly two years. That was when they had left London on a rickety ship called the *Humbart Keel*.

"Do you believe?" Annie asked.

Mary tried to sound reassuring, "It's not just the vicar, Annie. Ela Hubert told me that her son might be gone for weeks. They say the brigade was to secure the roads north into Meath before returning. Ya shouldn't worry."

"Meath is a stone throw away, Mary," Annie stated with apprehension.

"They will be back. All the men will be back just like before," Mary said.

"All the men didn't come back before," Annie replied.

"Stop it. The captain took the men to secure the roads to Meath. That is what the vicar has said, and that is what we must trust."

Annie couldn't shake it, "Don't believe anything the vicar says."

Mary lifted a pick axe and then she grabbed the nose ring of the oxen which staggered forward in the mud behind them. The animals grunted and Annie pulled on the wooden yoke while Mary trudged forward. "Our boys will be hungry again tonight," Mary said.

"Not tonight—" Annie replied curtly.

Mary looked at Annie Beth as if she was dreaming again. She had been acting strangely and even had fits of laughter for no apparent reason as of late. She was worried about her friend. "There isn't any food, Annie. You know that... don't you?"

Annie gazed off vacantly and Mary felt the need to repeat herself. It was the work she figured. The work and the lack of food that made her Annie so clouded.

Annie's hair was disheveled and her tiny frame shuddered with a giggle. They had always told each other everything. *Hadn't they?* This time, she had kept her secret, secret even from Mary. She wanted to laugh and she wanted to cry and finally she couldn't take it any longer. She just blurted it out like a child, "I have food Mary. Been hiding some of the grain we harvested and I buried two barrels of butter."

Mary's eyes opened wide, "Where?" she whispered.

Annie pointed out into the bog. The grey mist cooled the ground even as they spoke. It was the perfect place to store such things Annie had thought. It was a place that the planters did not like to go.

"In the bog?" Mary questioned fearfully. She wondered if Annie Beth was delusional.

"In the bog," Annie confirmed, shaking her head so vehemently that her eyes threatened to fly right out of their sockets. "Took it before the vicar hauled everything off to market, I did."

Mary's heart pounded. She was afraid but even with the fear, her stomach panged with want. It was exciting. "You stole it?" There was a hush between them.

"No. We worked for it, Mary," Annie insisted.

"Do you know what they will do to ya, Annie? If they catch you?" Mary asked.

Annie knew. They all knew what the stocks did to a person. Captain Colley had built a set of the crude devices for an unruly farm hand, and that poor bugger lasted just a few hours before crying out for mercy. It was a risk, but for her children, Annie would risk anything. She wished she didn't have to. They lived and worked on a farm that produced grain, meat, and cheese, and still her children were starving. "What else can I do?"

Mary replied: "We must trust the vicar, Annie. He wouldn't let us starve to death."

Annie turned a frown at the thought of their spiritual leader. "The vicar brought no payment back from that grain. Not a groat did he get. The merchant took the entire lot and put it on wagons headed for Armagh. Then the merchant told the vicar that Captain Colley would have to reconcile the debt himself."

"How do ya know such a thing, Annie?" Mary asked. "And slow down, you're hurting my hand."

Annie released her grip on the oxen. She had not told Mary everything but she needed Mary to believe her now. "John

Goodrich was with the vicar. He heard everything. The vicar even put a lien against the next harvest so he could hire a stone mason. Can you believe that? No payment and the vicar didn't store any grain at all. He sold everything!"

"Makes no sense?" Mary questioned.

Annie continued, "He told John that we had enough wild onions and livestock to get by. He's a fool, Mary."

"I hope to God that John is wrong. But if there be no food tonight, I'll ring the bastards neck myself," Mary replied.

"Well, forget I said anything then. I really don't have any food, Mary."

Mary laughed and shook her head but Annie didn't think John wrong at all. "I have enough for two weeks if we are careful. What's mine is yours but we cannot tell a soul. I need you to hold your tongue on this."

"Done," Mary replied.

"If Henry Colley has not returned with our husbands soon, I will be taking my boys and running."

Mary looked back thinking she heard horses snorting in the bog. She gave a pull with everything she had and lengthened her stride. Annie kept pace. "Not even if our men come back shall I utter a word," she promised.

"Good," Annie said with relief.

They both walked without talking for bit as the laborious breathing of the oxen warmed their backs. It was hard work in Colley Town; muddy, blister-bursting work. Mary tried to remember better days, and Annie tried not to think what might happen to her children.

"Does it not seem strange that the vicar hasn't mentioned anything about our men?" Annie asked as they got closer to the main road.

"Aye, it is strange."

Mary saw the vicar standing with Mam as they approached. He was wiping his mouth. "Fuck the vicar!" she snapped, thinking about all that Annie had told her. Her voice startled the oxen who immediately locked their legs in protest. The sudden jolt sent her reeling into the mud.

Annie bent over, hoping no one had heard. She extended her hand and broke out into one of her unusual fits of laughter. "See, Mary, a day in the fields with me and your spirits have already lifted. I didn't know you had such feelings. Look," she pointed so Mary would see, "he is just up there and may have plainly heard that you wish to bed him."

Mary didn't know what to say. She didn't want to rise and she didn't want to haul any more stones. She was numb, just plain numb. Not even her friends senseless humor could change that.

Annie grabbed Mary's hand and kept talking. It was nonsense and she knew it, but she couldn't help herself. "I might understand if you had those feelings for a man like Dennis of the hill clan. That soldier is a good looking fella. But the vicar?" she asked with a playful grin.

Mary glared at her, "Quiet your mouth," she exclaimed.

Annie giggled, "Well... I didn't say it, Mary. You did. You want to fuck the vicar."

Mary thought about her cursing. It was so raw and vulgar and everything she did not want to be. Her anger flew out in a swing toward Annie and she missed. It shocked them both until Annie started laughing hysterically. It was the way Annie laughed, that made her realize that she was acting the fool.

"I guess Dennis wouldn't be that bad if he shaved," Mary said with a twinkle of humor inspired by her friend.

Together they tittered with their wicked thoughts. It was like a dam breaking after a long rain and Mary realized Annie meant everything to her. She would die to keep Annie's secret and knew that she would never trust the vicar again.

❧ ❧ ❧

Vicar Tinsdale stepped out onto the road as the women carted their load to the rock pile. He watched them quietly and turned to the old woman called Mam.

Mam raised her brow, "It seems to be the busiest of seasons, Vicar," she declared with her usual tenacious banter.

"Verily, I believe it is, good mother. Were there just two maidens to pull stones for the church today?" he asked.

Mam knew the others cared less about stones than she dared admit, "Aye, the other women are setting poles for the common stable." As he stood there full and happy, Mam eyed a dribble of gravy on his blouse. "Did ye enjoy a good supper?" she asked.

Vicar Tinsdale smiled and rubbed his belly, "If you must know. I had lamb with beans and a very fine ale," he confirmed shamelessly.

"Oh my, you had meat today. Very nice, yes… very nice indeed. It makes me mouth water with the thought of all the good food ye might have in that home of yours," Mam remarked.

"It is a church, Mam. A growing church," he corrected.

"Ah yes, it is growing," Mam said, thinking that any church, especially the vicar's lowly vacant church, should be for the people. A place where the common folk could worship or even eat in times of need. "We women have been working hard ye know. Me, Annie Beth, and Mary just plodding away at the stone piles. Must have added four or five feet to each I'd say."

Not catching the subtlety of Mam's expression, Vicar Tinsdale smiled with lackluster approval. "I see... and I saw... your helpers enjoying themselves."

As the vicar looked on piously, Mary and Annie Beth began to empty their cart of stones. Mary squared her shoulders and Annie took a deep breath. Then without a word, she and Annie heaved the last of them onto the pile. For a moment, the women stood awaiting their dismissal but the vicar indulged Mam with needless banter, so Mary grabbed her skirt and marched over to where they stood.

"That will be the last of it for the night, Mam. We have children to feed," Mary said hoping the vicar might offer some food.

Mam put down her quilt, "The children are working with the others near the yellow house. How ya going to feed 'em?"

Annie looked at Mary and then to Vicar Tinsdale. She could see the question in both their eyes and wanted to cry out to Mary: *Stop! Stop and don't say another word!* Instead she put her hand on Mary's shoulder. It was just enough to remind her friend, *they had a secret.*

Mary asked: "Is there nothing for us? For all our work there is not even a scrap of meat for our table?"

It was the question he had been asked again and again, and one which caused his lips to purse. This time he made the appearance of reflection as if to offer a glimmer of hope. "The mistress has said that the workers will have food tomorrow. She has said so, and so it will be. Today we will make do with the milk that can be taken at the stable and the onions of the field."

Mary's heart sank, "There are over thirty of us and not an onion has been found in days. How many cows are milking without any calves and how many sheep will give their milk now that the last of our lambs has been taken?" It was a question she should not have asked but she did. She stood firm with her hands on her hips as Annie Beth looked on in silence knowing that they would eat tonight. They also knew the vicar was a taker. He took but did not provide and above all he hated a challenge.

Mam cocked her head with an expression of admiration turning up the corners of her mouth. The old woman appeared indifferent to the suffering she endured. Immune. She was like an old battle ax or indestructible tool, but she liked a good fight, and that is what changed her opinion of Mary and Annie Beth. She was delighted with them.

Mary let out a deep sigh, "Annie and I have picked stones before and it was for the dying. We won't be picking any more. Ye 'll have to bury us first."

Vicar Tinsdale balled his fists and stepped toward them. "And if a large blessing of food arrives as planned, you will get nothing!" He paused for dramatic effect and then eased his tone to continue, "The stones are for the church… not the dead. I will tell you that the stone mason has earned his keep. He can split a rock like this with one solid strike and for that you should be grateful. Because it will lesson your work!"

Mam turned her head away as if looking for something in the bog. Annie Beth wanted to rush away. They had heard these things before.

Vicar Tinsdale pointed at Annie. "Grab that mallet and wedge!" he demanded.

Annie Beth did and Mary set her jaw as Vicar Tinsdale refused them their leave and snatched the tools angrily. As he bent down and picked up a large heavy piece of schist, which had a silvery orange thread running through it, he looked at the stone and then at Mary. He could see she doubted him. The schist was hard but he had watched the stone mason strike similar material along the grain of color to split them open. "A stone in itself is one of the hardest things. Like you, Mary. Hard. A nearly indestructible creation of God's hand and yet with the right force," he paused and looked at the women as a bead of sweat trickled off his forehead, "with the right force it can be cleaved apart as easily as butter!"

Mary puffed and turned up her nose and noticed his eyes lingering at the curve of her breasts. He did not frighten her anymore.

Vicar Tinsdale felt an excitement in diminishing Mary. She needed to be taught. Oh yes, he would teach her. "Every rock can be broken," he said.

Mary and Annie Beth stood silent, waiting and watching as they were told. They saw him grunt and sweat and bend at his fat belly. If they ran away he would only have the guards fetch them back and so they stayed. When he raised his arm, Mary wished with all her might that the hammer would crush his hand. He hesitated, and down came the weight of his blow. It took a moment for the vicar to register what he had done. His body remained perfectly still in an awkward position and then to Mary's gladness he let out a scream. Bleating and dancing like a wounded goat, they watched with glee, as he stamped his foot into the ground. Mary felt herself dare to relish his pain. It wasn't much but it was something and she felt emboldened with the sight of his blood that dripped like crimson pudding.

"Damn you ungrateful bitches! Damn you to hell!" he shouted.

It was Mam who had the courage to say what they were all thinking. "The only thing better than a good fight is when the fight is with yourself. Eh... Vicar?" she chuckled.

Vicar Tinsdale pointed to the stone he had struck. "Broken!" he shouted as he glared at the three of them. They stood united for the first time. Two mothers and an old woman named Mam. With no men around to support him the vicar bit his lip spitefully. "Maybe so old hag but I am still the vicar. Go tell the townsfolk, I..." he paused to grab his hand, "I have words. Words from me and words from Dublin," he hissed.

Mam smiled, "Oh, Vicar, ya have no idea what is coming but I'll gather the towns folk gladly."

To ensure they understood and that all the men would come, Vicar Tinsdale made an unusual promise. "There will be food tonight. One cow may be taken and be sure to bring the healer," he said pathetically.

When the women reached the only road in town, Mam turned to Annie Beth and Mary. "Go and fetch your children and make your way to the bog. I know ya have food out there. Let the others eat of the old cow tonight."

CHAPTER 8

A Coin
Before
the Serpent

As night fell aboard the *Pinnacle*, Kenneth Patterson held Blackie and sat quietly near Miguel Avaje Fernandez in the depths of the ships cold hull. A horse whinnied as the sea crashed against the bulkhead. Tonight he had a companion, and Kenneth remembered the way that Ryan would hold him so they both might stay warm. He missed his brother. The bickering and laughter which came with Ryan had left with him also. A large candle burned overhead and he focused on it dreamily as the flame batted this way and that. It didn't give him warmth, not like his brother.

"It is good that you came back," Miguel said.

"Th... the crew is angry," Kenneth replied fearfully.

Miguel leaned over in the hay and kicked off a boot. It was a long day and his feet and back were sore from the labor of cleaning pens. After a moment he offered Kenneth a lesson: "Angry men are sick men, Kenneth. They choose to be as they are."

Feeling out of sort, Kenneth said: "Cato has put his hands on me."

"Did he hurt you?" Miguel asked.

Kenneth shook his head no, realizing his pride was battered but his flesh was not. He had not been beaten very badly. They sat there in the darkness for some time and then Miguel heard someone fiddling with the handhold above.

Kenneth grabbed Miguel's leg. "It be Cato. He said he would be coming to brain me."

Both men heard the lifting as the hatch opened and sucked the stale air up and out toward the light of a lantern. The sailor landed with a thud, "Gilda, be that you?"

Kenneth sat up, "N...n...nay," he replied.

"Patterson... should have known. Put that candle out!" the sailor spat.

Kenneth quickly snuffed out the wick and the sailor continued past them. There were many people crammed into the stable and some even made their living down there. It reminded Miguel of a brothel. A filthy brothel of swine and dung. The sailor called out again for Gilda and soon after, he found her. There was some chatter, a bargain was struck and the grunting of livestock muffled their deed. Miguel pulled Kenneth closer so that he would not be heard: "I will help you when we get to London. You should not have to fear every night alone."

Miguel's kindness made Kenneth feel warm. For a moment he thought of his mother and father but then he became sad again with their memory. It seemed he could not escape his life but he also did not feel able. He was pressed to service on the *Pinnacle* and life aboard the ship was anything but easy. It was a time that would haunt him. "It is a year before I can be freed but I will bear the scars of this crew forever. Why would ye help me?"

Miguel sighed, "Because you will die here with these evil men before a year is up."

Kenneth thought for a bit, wondering to himself how a stranger could understand so much without even knowing him. He was dirty and Miguel seemed clean no matter how much work he did. This priest always appeared clean. "And ye have seen this? Ye know for certain I am to die?" Kenneth asked.

"I have been given the vision and hear the voice of God and he put you in my path," Miguel replied.

Kenneth had witnessed death on the ship first hand. Cold, hard death that came without compassion. He had seen it in the vacant eyes of an oarsman, whose lifeless head bobbed for hours until he was finally cut free of the line. That type of death made his brothers fate seem merciful.

Miguel slid closer to him, "Do you think they will treat you better when we arrive to London?" Kenneth sat there thinking, hoping, dreading. There was another long silence between them before Miguel defiantly lit the candle. "Why do you stutter when you speak to the sailors but not with me?"

"Nerves," Kenneth replied.

"Nerves?" Miguel asked.

Kenneth nodded.

"If God cures you now, this very instant, will you believe me?" he asked.

Kenneth wanted to believe, he needed to believe in something. Before Kenneth could answer, Miguel placed a hand on his head and raised the other out of the darkness and into the candle light. His words flowed unrestrained and beautiful. They were like freedom and hope, and they warmed Kenneth like a blanket. After the prayer, Miguel looked at him with such certainty that Kenneth did believe. He could feel it. His tongue would not be fouled and his hand had ceased to shake.

"You are healed," Miguel said knowingly.

A rat scurried across Miguel's foot and to Kenneth's gladness, Blackie leapt out to chase it. A few minutes later the cat returned and purred with the content of success. The rat dangled from its mouth and Miguel took the time to tell Kenneth of the Lord. They spoke for hours, and then late in the night they slept. It became day and they worked apart, but Kenneth looked forward to the cold dark stable and having companionship in the following nights.

On the third night, after the chores, Miguel gave Kenneth a carrot. It was long and orange and crooked like a dagger. Miguel took one also and they sparred in play with their meal. "Eat only of the carrots from hence forth Kenneth. They will clear your vision at night."

Kenneth took a bite. "I like carrots," he said.

"Do you know where the captain has secured the coin chests?" Miguel whispered.

Kenneth replied in a hush: "The soldiers guard the treasure in the brig cell."

Suddenly Miguel put down his carrot with gravity and he took Kenneth's hand. His voice changed from that of the teacher to one of trust, "It is that treasure and the men who guard it that can change your life. And I need you."

Kenneth bit his lip anxiously, uncertain but yearning to please. "I shouldn't speak such things. Someone will hear and turn us over for their reward. I cannot…"

Miguel put his arm around Kenneth and whispered in his ear. "Just take Blackie to the yeomen's bunk in the brig cell and see what awaits you. I need your help with this and am sure you will be unharmed."

"Are there rats in the brig cell?"

Miguel paused for a moment, "There are rats. I have heard the yeomen talking on the upper decks. They are plagued with rats, and this I know to be true."

"Now?" Kenneth asked.

"I will not sleep in a stable tonight for there is something I must do. Go and clear the rats from the brig cell and when you have finished, put a few drops of this into each of the pork barrels closest to the galley deck." Miguel held out a small vial and Kenneth took it as their eyes met. "Do you understand that when you do this, you fight the evil that binds you?" he asked.

Kenneth felt numb, "The captain has ordered me to stay with you and tell him if you sneak away."

"Do not be afraid. I have prayed that you will be protected and I give you permission to tell the captain whatever is in your heart. I trust you."

Kenneth kissed Miguel's hand, "Aye, and I know who you are, my angel," he said.

"You will leave this mark before morning. Use a knife and make sure the marks will not be missed." Miguel traced the number on the dusty floor and held his candle over it so that Kenneth could see and remember.

❧ ❧ ❧

It was a tumultuous night at sea and for most of the crew and passengers, it was a night that confined one to quarters. The *Pinnacle* rocked from side to side and Kenneth stretched out an arm to steady himself in the passageway. He held his cat nervously, expecting to be chastised by the yeomen of the brig cell. It wasn't a place he ever wanted to enter. "If ye don't kill … they will surely beat me," he whispered in Blackie's ear. The cat purred, "You have to Blackie. It is the only way," he said as he pushed at the brass handle that would certainly unlock his fate.

The cabin sat just below the bow mast where a huge timber wrapped in cord split the compartment like the pivot of a giant clock. It was a place of his past confinements. Kenneth mustered the courage to hammer his fist into the rough wooden beam. "It is the rat chaser!" he announced. He was certain the door would open or a voice would command him away. He felt even more unsettled when there was no reply. He hesitated and grabbed the brass handle a second time, knowing as he turned it, he might very well be shot. He took a breath, the hinge squeaked, and the door swung open with the heavy smell of vomit in the air.

Blackie leapt inside. Something round and heavy rolled across the floor to hit the wall with a thud and it caused him to flinch. "It is the rat chaser," he whispered.

In the dark, foul brig cell Kenneth took out his striker to light a lamp and when the flame took hold, he saw their faces. Glazed hollow eyes and stillness marked them all as if they were frozen in a fit of agony. The chief yeoman was not in his hammock but slumped against the timber unnaturally. The others swung to the rhythm of the sea and their arms dangled. Cold, white fingers curled forever in death all around him as he held his breath to step forward. They had been such beautiful men in their royal uniforms. Blackie gave a hiss as the white cotton of a yeoman's undersleeve fluttered with a hint of movement. *Could one be alive,* he wondered, moving to check for breath. He examined the man and reeled back when a rat poked out its twitchy nose and squealed off into the corner. The yeomen of the queen's guard were all dead, each and every man.

Men were cruel, cold and unkind but he had never seen anything like this. He did not feel remorse, it was just a very, very bad thing. As he stood there Kenneth began to realize that he was not alone on the ship any longer. Something greater than himself was happening here and although it was not good... it was better. His voice filled with solemn understanding, "When I am done, I will feed you, Blackie."

It was among the dead where Kenneth found himself able. He retrieved the keys to the brig cell that hung unguarded on the wall. Even as he heard footsteps above and shouts coming down the passageway, he continued. He would die in less than a year anyway and the trueness of Miguel's words were ever so real. In the dark and gloomy cabin where none were allowed to enter,

Kenneth remained calm. He opened a chest to find it full of silver crucifixes, goblets and candle stands. He saw coins in another and counted as high as he could count. Then he took a single coin for his own. Finally, after all but one thing was accomplished, he finished his task with a knife. The tip dug deep into the timber and his work left shaving on the floor. Six hundred and sixty-six was the curse he would leave behind and each of the six's where perfect. And then he stood back wondering if his work would be sufficient. The chief yeoman's head lulled invitingly. "You shall get a number also," Kenneth said as the keys to the treasure jingled in his pocket.

After going straight away to the galley, Kenneth emptied a vial into the pork barrels and made his way back to the stable. He would sleep now, not knowing that Miguel Avaje Fernandez opened the top hatch and let the cold salty torrent of sea spill down into the hull.

"Lord, if he is righteous, stay my hand from the sea," Miguel spoke into the cold of night. He needed to hear His voice as he moved silently out into the open air. Calculating, observing and noting the position of fourteen men who braved the weather above, he slipped into the shadows. Four sailors perched in the top masts, eight deckhands, and the pilot who cursed his sternwheel would never see him. He thought of Shane O'Neill, he thought of Ryan Patterson, and he thought of the girl from Kintyre. She could be the key to everything. The wind beat at his face as he moved toward a single flickering light. It guided him through the treacherous ropes and handholds along the outer gunwale. Below him the whitecaps splashed up toward his boots in waves that did all that they could to sweep him away. Miguel heard the shrill whistle to announce the changing of a watch. He hoped that they would be delayed in their duty, when the ship was found to be flooding. He must become the ghost, the angel or something not of this world.

Not far from where he clung against the torrent a fish flopped wildly before slipping over the side. The one he had come to test was near, standing on the bow spar and grasping a life line, the lone sailor stood his watch. He rose and plummeted and the lantern above him hissed through salt stained glass. Black greasy hair clung to a bright red forehead and he was unaware of who came up from behind.

Miguel grabbed a rope and stood, "Might there be another on this vessel who is righteous?" he shouted into the night.

Hearing the strange voice, the bow watch turned around. "Who... who is there?" he called out.

Miguel stepped from the shadows, "I am the priest. Whom might you be?" he said so the bow watch could hear.

The man shook his beard and gave his gruff reply, "Cato."

The two gazed at each other and then braced themselves as water washed over Miguel's feet and spilled off the forecastle. "Have you seen what I have seen, Cato?" Miguel shouted.

Cato held his lanyard tightly, the sinew of his forearm stretched across muscle and bone in tight bands that joined his wrist. His legs bent, his toes gripped and he rode the bowsprit like a stallion. "What! What have ye seen!" Cato shouted back expecting Miguel to be washed away.

"The serpent, Cato! I have seen the serpent!" Miguel replied.

Cato turned madly to scour the sea, "There is nothing!" he yelled.

Miguel knew what he had seen and searched again before raising his arm, "There!"

Cato's eyes traced Miguel's finger to the oncoming swell. He saw an unnatural swirl and tried desperately to see what broke the surface. He was unsure if it was a tail or a huge leathery back but he saw something swimming in the deep. Something huge! "I see," Cato shouted.

The wind howled and the sea crashed into the bow as Cato turned to an empty space behind him. The lamp gave another terrible hiss. It was as if the Spaniard was never there and suddenly Cato felt utterly afraid. Did he have the fever and imagine it all or had the holy man been swept away?" He returned his attention to the sea in hopes that he was dreaming and shuttered as a long neck slipped out of the wave. This time what he saw, he saw with his own eyes. A rigid back and scales that came crashing toward him.

"What in God's hell!" Cato shouted.

Miguel slipped out from under the sail mast with his robe snapping behind him. "Yes indeed, Cato. What in God's hell…" he said as the bow watch braced himself again. The next wave brought a tremendous crack of wood. Everything came at Cato in that moment. The violence of the storm, the serpent, and the priest. He fought them all. He fought them with the fanaticism of madness.

CHAPTER 9

Turbulence
of
Believers

I n Kings County, the Bermingham castle overlooked the town and Emma Colley extended her shaking hand to pull a curtain away from her window. Something outside was happening, something wrong. She let the drapery fall and nibbled on a crust of bread before brushing the crumbs off her dry plate. She paced and then poured herself a glass of wine and placed the opened bottle on her night stand. Emma picked up a horse hair paint brush and swiped it across the corner of the sill. It left a streak of red. The room was dark with high ceilings and plaster covered the stone and mortar. Emma had examined every part of it over the past few days, both in daylight and in dusk. She knew every crack and patterned flower and even the fingerprints that scarred the white lacquer of her freshly painted baseboards. She had tried to pretty it up but the rosy paint had not lifted her spirits. It did not change where she was or who she was. It did not take away her pain.

Feeling anxious, she put the paintbrush down and took a breath of the pleasant fumes that hung in the air with oily sweetness. The smell reminded her that her senses, although dulled, could still be detected. Then she walked back to the window.

"Everyone is against me!" she blurted. She knew the women of the community despised her but somewhere deep inside Emma's heart... she knew why. She had given up all that she held dear. Her pride, her sense of self-esteem, and most difficultly, the notion that her cherished daughter Agnes was somehow with her.

A chill ran up her spine. Agnes, who had died. Her child's light had slipped through her arms and there was nothing she could do. *Had it been two years?* The vivid memory seemed as though it happened just moments ago.

As night closed over the town, she picked up an empty wine bottle and moved it to the corner of her room and grabbed another. Dry, bitter wine. Her hand shook, causing her wedding band to rattle against the dark green glass as she struggled with the cork. It was bitter but so much needed. She poured. "I love you," she said as a tear streamed down her cheek. The fluid that sustained her went down easily. "I love you..." she said secretly, wishing for her daughter's soft voice to reply, and the burn hit the back of her throat.

Emma walked slowly over to the window to look outside. Another night would pass. She felt the country both beautiful and merciless. A place that needed to be tamed but Emma did not want to tame the land any longer. Now that Henry was gone, she could not find her way. He had left her to chase the thing that he thought might bring her happiness. *Henry was a fool*, she thought. He must be, because only a fool would leave an ailing wife alone among the planters.

Gazing out the window, Emma turned her attention toward the church that budded up with new walls of stone. She saw the people gathering, "Vicar…"

❧ ❧ ❧

In the center of Colley Town, Vicar Tinsdale raised his arms. The comers included John Goodrich, the blacksmith from Middlesex; two carpenters and their wives, the stone mason Percy, and twenty or so women and children. They did not run to the vicar. They did not cheer, and the oldest living soul on the plantation came not at all. Mam had stolen off alone or that is what she wanted the planters to believe.

Vicar Tinsdale raised his arms to quiet the crowd, "Brothers and Sisters, I have news from the archbishop that each of you must know," he proclaimed.

"We came for the bread, Vicar," John shouted.

With the disquiet of the gathering Vicar Tinsdale swallowed hard and stepped up onto the rock cart. Did they not know he was obliged to lead them? "You must listen!" Vicar Tinsdale screamed as he gave a telling look toward the stocks. Henry had instructed the Vicar to use his discretion with punishment and also with the four soldiers he had left behind. These men were his protection and he paid them and ensured they had good food. The soldiers stood ominously in grey and tan wool coats as Vicar Tinsdale insisted the workers quiet.

"When ye have heard, ye will have bread!" he shouted to settle them. "First, you should know that Captain Henry Colley and our men are alive. I have been told they will be back in just a few days," he lied. The people were angry but they wanted to believe him. Many had sons or husbands who had left for war and any offering of the soldier's fate always proved to be effective. Seeing he had struck a chord, he continued. "Second, you should know that a shipment of coin and common English flour has been secured in Dublin for this estate. The flour and also sixteen head of cattle are awaiting delivery at the stock pens near the quays. I will take you," he pointed at John, "and you may select four helpmates." He hoped his words would ease them into the topic of his desire.

"And of today?" someone asked.

Vicar Tinsdale held out his hand and from behind the mob, one of his loyal men led out an old cow. "As I have said, there will be meat." His words calmed them and seeing he now had control of their tongues, his hand twitched with anticipation, "The Earl of Kildare, Gerald Fitzgerald has been taken to Dublin's castle for treason. There he has recanted his claim for the land in Geashill and confessed to harboring papists. God be praised."

"God be praised for the mistress you mean!" Susan Goodrich shouted. Susan stood there remembering the earl's claim that

Emma Colley had cut out the eyes of her own child to gain the power of witchcraft. She had not believed it, but rumors abounded, and the Earl of Kildare was the one who had caused such mischief.

Vicar Tinsdale raised his voice, "I did not say that the mistress had been cleared of blame. I said that the farm in Geashill is no longer in dispute. We will soon have more land and more crops to plant. But that is not all. Adam Loftus has written a message for the faithful. For you, Sister Goodrich and for all the believers." The planters fell silent. They looked to one another and then back to him with hope. "Your archbishop, the provider of spiritual leadership and consult to Queen Elizabeth, urges peace on all the borders. He has assurance that the son of Conn, Shane O'Neill will accept the queen's favor of earldom."

"We have heard this before," John shouted.

Vicar Tinsdale did his best to look earnest and sincere, "I myself have been given this knowledge directly from the Anglican Assembly of Dublin. Lord Radcliffe has announced a victory in the north. England shall have dominion over all of Ulster and peace with Tyrone!"

John took his son's hand, "Does that mean our children might profit from a bit of grain?" he asked.

The crowd rumbled, "Or that a queen's coin will come forth for the widows?" another shouted.

Vicar Tinsdale balked, "No, no, no. You must understand that matters of state come slowly to the people. It will take time." He looked at them as if they were children. "John, you will not be getting any grain today. I have no grain... but the Lord will provide for those with faith. We must all do what He puts in our hearts to do." Vicar Tinsdale saw them ponder his words knowing they were unable to dispute the logic he conveyed. "Do not be confused by your anger. Can you not see? He spares your sons a soldier's fate and provides hope for your daughters."

"And what of Captain Henry Colley?" John asked.

Vicar Tinsdale's bald head wrinkled with his brow. His lips felt dry and he lifted a wineskin to quench the fire in his throat. "Peace John. There shall be peace in the midlands. Let us dwell on prayer and the news that our good captain is returning. Should we not give thanks?"

John Goodrich, with his six foot four frame and greying hair, pressed for more than the vicar's smile. As a tradesman he held a place of honor in Colley Town and deserved an answer. "Will Thomas Smyth of Westenhanger continue to send us aid?" he asked.

It was the moment the vicar had been waiting for and he held up a letter in triumph. "He is the source of our flour and has sent more from London as well. It is written down right here."

John knew every word the vicar said was based entirely on the fact that the planters must depend and trust in him. "None of us can read, Vicar," he said questioningly.

"Well, I shall tell you. Thomas Smyth has never been more committed to our welfare and continues as the queen's true and loyal customs officer of London. That is why he left Ireland to resume his business on our behalf. I assure you John, nothing will deter Thomas Smyth, except..." he held out his battered finger, "a plantation of unruly workers."

John looked at the vicar and then out across the fields into the bog. His stomach rumbled, his back hurt and he hoped his eyes deceived him. "Does that look like peace, Vicar?" he gasped.

From the window in her room, overlooking the town, Emma Colley watched as a cavalry of horsemen streamed into Colley Town. The riders carried torches, battle axes and swords. Two columns of warriors mottled with the orange glow of fire. The flickering light undulated as the black powder of gunfire puffed at muzzles to announce their arrival. Men with saffron shirts and black kilts with long waving hair.

"Barbarians..." Emma exclaimed in fear. She quickly twisted her fingers to turn down the lamp, evaporating the artificial light with a sooty puff of smoke. Then she ran to lock her door, realizing there was no time to escape. "Where are you Henry?" The unmistakable onslaught of horses turned to the sounds of invasion. She heard the shattering of glass and then the terrible dread of boot heels clattering up the old stone staircase.

"Go away...go away...go away," she whispered. There was a sudden jolt that broke the hinge and then her armoire fell over. Emma clutched her chest as the heat of a warrior's torch swung in to her bed chamber and she gasped when she saw him. Standing there at her bed was a fierce looking man. His hair was pulled back and braided all the way down to his shoulders and his beard dangled with beads. She heard him grunt with an approval that put a knot in her side. What a strange and terrible thing he seemed. Emma pulled back, focusing on the scar crossing his upper left temple. Surely it had been formed in battle to trace a jagged line over his whiskered cheek. He was everything she was afraid of and the menacing stories she had heard in the comfort of civility did this man justice. Wild! His arms rippled as his sword clattered to the floor.

Her words were dry. The kind of words that are barely heard but felt in the very core of a being, "I am not young... I am not beautiful," Emma whispered. He said nothing and Emma knew, as all women know, what was about to happen. She clutched the bedsheets with the dread of it.

His English was estranged by a Celtic tongue, "Nay lass, there be no need for a covering," he told her.

The words hit her with the reality of what was. An eternity of thoughts whirled through her mind and then ended abruptly. She needed a covering but not a single sheet. She needed Henry, she needed Henry, she needed Henry. Henry who had brought her from London to begin a new life. Henry whom she had trusted.

With one arching movement the warrior tossed his torch into Emma's unlit fireplace. His action caused her to flinch. She hoped with all her heart that the flame would be smothered. The fire took hold and his shadow rose on the wall in front of her with outstretched arms. She smelled his sweat. The freshly painted room never seemed so small as her eyes darted from him to a cobweb and then to a tiny spider she had examined before. She looked toward the door with one last desperate hope that Henry might come rushing in to her save.

The barbarian touched her face, "Da ya not like me?" he asked.

Emma felt the beating of her own heart and the salty taste of a tear. Before her was a bristling shoulder of scars. She heard the creak of her bedframe and her bare heels dug into the down. "I am not young. I am not..."

He covered her mouth with his and Emma heard the pop of buttons as he exposed her breasts. Then she felt the weight of him in the hardness of his body which pressed her down. She clawed at his face and finally closed her eyes to the screaming outside. The screaming of terror in Colley Town.

All Cheers
for
Noah

The captain's mess was the finest cabin on the ship and the rich wood was carved with ornate markings befitting a royal suite. It was the gathering place for the officers and gentlemen who enjoyed leisurely talks and supper. The chief cook brought them pork and biscuits and fretted about a pie he left simmering in the galley. Captain Grim sat at the head of his table and felt satisfied in the company of gentlemen. He quickly finished his meat and looked to Robert Lockhart for a word. "Mister Lockhart, can you regale us with a story?" he asked.

Robert flushed, "I would truly be delighted if it does not displease my son." The boy looked up with approval, sitting there among the men in his fine tweed and high white collar, Noah felt alive and at the age of twelve he also felt the brandy. "He's a good lad and one who will make a fine living someday. So it will be the story of Noah Lockhart that I tell ye." Robert said as he ran his hand over his son's head and nodded politely to the only lady of the table, Beth... who blushed.

As the mess fell silent, Robert began. "Two years past, when me boy was just ten years old, we had a visitor in London. The man came to our home when I was away on business, much as I am now. As I have been told, the man appeared to be a gentleman, so my house servant let him in." Robert stopped for a moment and took a sip. He looked at his son and shook his head as if knowing something the others did not. "That I am afraid was a mistake, because, within minutes of entering, he took my entire house hostage. For two days that man kept my wife and Noah a captive. It is disgraceful but true, right in the very city that I protect, if you can you believe it."

The table and those who stood close suddenly viewed Noah differently and stared on with anticipation. Certainly he did something remarkable. Robert could spin a story like no other and he could see he had their full attention as the silence embraced them. It gave him a measure of pride to be able to orate with such skill. He took the moment to let them ponder what might have been and left them wanting for more. When Beth raised her kerchief to her mouth and fixed her eyes on Noah as if to speak, he knew it was the precise moment to continue. "Yes, I tell you he was a crafty fellow this thief. A man like that should be feared." The captain perked up for he was accustomed to sea stories and high adventure, but this was something else. This was a story that came from Robert's own experience. The whole table was enchanted with the account. Noah felt his head swill and thought of how each time he heard his father's tale, how better it turned out. It was as if he was hearing it for the first time tonight and his heart raced because of it.

Robert's voice became low and serious, "Aye, it is so. For two days the thief kept me family bound as he loaded our carriage with the wealth of our home. He took both silver and paper, and even rounded up the fine musical instruments of our estate. When the thief could load no more or eat no further of our good bounty, he climbed the stairs to do an end to my dear wife and son. This I am sure he intended because he did so dreadfully dismember our servants." Robert looked down at his son with pride, "Do ye remember, Noah?" he asked.

Noah nodded with the horrid memory. Robert looked at those around the table, "Well it was a good thing for me and my dear wife that Noah escaped the bonds of his confinement during the horrific commotion taking place below. He did so by dislocating his right hand, and when he was free he undid my wife and hid her away in the attic where he knew she would be safe. If he were any other young lad of the same age, he might have hidden himself away as well but that is not in the character of my son. No... my son took out the blunderbuss that we kept under our bed and he charged it and loaded the ball. I can tell you he was a smart lad for doing so, for after the murder of my servants, the handle to my wife's chambers turned and then..." As they listened waiting to hear what Noah had done, Robert lifted his hand and slammed it forcefully onto the table, "Bam!" he shouted. Everyone reeled back in their chairs and Robert beamed with pride. "Yes, I tell ye all that that was the end of the gentleman caller. My ten years old son had done him in. He shot that bloody thief dead!"

Captain Grim stood up and applauded Robert's son. "Well done lad. Well done, by criminy, that was as good a tale as I ever heard. A toast I say."

They all raised their glasses for Noah that evening, but not long after, Lieutenant Brinson entered the captain's mess. It was hard not to notice the stoic nature of the first mate so the captain addressed him quickly to not sully the moment. "Why so solemn, Mister Brinson?" he asked with good spirit.

Lieutenant Brinson took in the pleasant aroma of cooked pork and biscuits. The cabin seemed cheerful, he did not. "I shouldn't sir," he said smartly. There was an awkward silence in the air as he refused the invitation.

Captain Grimm insisted. "Come sit and eat before the storm gets any worse. You will need to be on watch tonight."

"Not tonight, sir. I would ask for a private audience," Lieutenant Brinson replied, taking his hat in hand and setting his eyes to the floor.

Captain Grimm slapped the table. "Nonsense, we are in good company. I was just about to tell Robert and our guests about the adventure in Libya. What could be so urgent to interrupt us?" he replied.

"There's no good way to say it, sir. We have a serious problem that might well cost us our lives."

Captain Grimm became utterly sober, "Speak it then?"

"Captain, several of the crew have signs of the pox."

"The pox?" Captain Grimm replied. He considered and calmly took a clean white linen from his lap and wiped the corner of his mouth. "Are thee certain?"

"There is something wrong, sir. Of that I am certain," Lieutenant Brinson confirmed.

"Who might be infected?" Captain Grimm asked.

"Grey Eyes is covered with sores and a goodly number of the top crew are showing signs of the sickness. I am not sure how many others and so I have sent the quartermaster to take count."

Taking care not to alarm his table, Captain Grim spoke calmly, "This is solemn news you bring us, sir. We will take precautions… I want the treasury and brig cell checked first and secure the front quarters and top-deck. Where are you moving the sick?"

Lieutenant Brinson cleared his throat. He had never dealt with sickness like this but he had heard of such things and so he had acted. "The sick," he hesitated and took a breath, "the sick, have been confined to their bunks on the gun deck and elsewhere. If it is bad we may wish to put them in a lifeboat and set them adrift," he reported gravely.

"We will not!" Captain Grim replied.

"But if it is the pox, sir?" Lieutenant Brinson questioned fearfully.

"Have Patterson the older care for the sick. He is as useless as tits on a boar. As for the treasury, you make sure the crew understands that we have the means to protect it. I want armed guards posted immediately. Pass the word and then make an example," Captain Grim told him.

"I understand," Lieutenant Brinson replied.

"We'll not be casting anyone over. We don't even know if it is the pox. As for the rest of you in this galley, steer clear of the lower decks and report anything suspicious to me. I also want a report on the health of our pilot within an hour. If he is not ill, he shall be quarantined in my cabin. No one except the pilot and those we know do not have the sickness will go anywhere near the aft deck. Is that understood?"

Lieutenant Brinson nodded.

"I will confine our movement to the upper rear decks. Make sure that those who are sick are taken to the stable. We might need those gun decks, Mister Brinson!"

The surgeon, who dined each night with the officers, stood up quickly. "I will need to inspect every hand but I will not be doing it in the stable. The stable will not offer the warmth for recovery. Might we locate the afflicted on the lower gun deck?"

"No, Jacob, we cannot. You will only examine the officers and you are forbidden to go below," Captain Grimm ordered. Jacob was a man who had compassion and the captain had often been glad of it, but not on this night. "We may not have the crew to man the guns or set the sails if we don't act quickly. The sick to the stable, the well to the upper aft decks and that is the order of business."

Jacob took the news terribly. "I would advise against this, sir," he replied.

The captain grimaced, "Your advisement has been noted, now go to your cabin and return here with your kit."

Robert Lockhart stood with his son as the surgeon left, "Is there anything we can do?" he asked.

Captain Grimm's grave expression said more than his words, "Shut yourself away, Robert. I will send a report to your quarters and meals will be placed outside your cabin door at noontime each day. Do not come out."

CHAPTER 11

Cursed are the Midlands

Besieged with war between the borders of the Pale and the realm of old kingdoms, in those places that the wildlings live, neither Irish nor English were safe. The feral clan of men and women were stark figures of humanity, being remnant of those forgotten by the law. They dwelled in the margins, migrant and wild, seeking shelter in caves, or sifting through streams, the abscessed people ate the flesh of any living thing. Skin and long nailed, bony bodied, dirt trodden heels of bare feet, they lived and hunted, scavenged and stole.

101

To some they were a myth, simple legends of the wood. Others knew of the wild people at the edge of the field at night. Fleeting movements and bending limbs: the only clue to their existence. The sightings were happening more frequently now. Some near the River Shannon had even seen them in daylight.

From Belturbet, the wildlings moved through Longford where the land was low and flat to find cover near Lough Ree, east of the watery maze that formed the River Shannon. To the west was Connaught, and to the north lay Ulster. Here and there in the low country, a smattering of villages had seen them, but more often than not, the clan thrived in a tangle of thickets and flooded marshes. Somewhere, between the towns called Ballynahone and Grenard, these beasts were afoot. In a territory where farmers latched their shutters at night.

Jodia ran through Longford after cutting his hands free and his mind raced with the thought of the wildling woman. He was tall, blond haired, and young. He tried to catch his breath and feared those that chased him relentlessly. *Why?* he thought. *Why had he not killed her?*

Now the flies of Longford's drizzling summer swarmed near his face. Ringing deafened his ears; a lump began to form near his temple, and he rose from hands and knees upon hearing his pursuers who were not far behind. The land itself seemed to swallow him: a place where common law or the rule of chieftains could not hold back the evil spirits. A bird chirped, a tree branch rustled, and the darkness deucedly encroached to consume his hapless soul.

Jodia stumbled forward, falling headlong into the river. He remembered being left for dead. He remembered the terrible wild people who found him. As he entered the cold river, a ripple blurred an outstretched arm bending unnaturally toward the stone bottom. With his pain he rolled over and began to float in the current that married with his blood. He drank, gagged, and pushed away toward the distant shore. As he faded, Jodia thought of his mission, and that failure penetrated his heart. Ireland was falling fast. He felt the change in the people and tried to warn the priesthood.

They did not listen!

A rush of emotions consumed his thoughts. His obsession brought him to the point of uncaring- bitter and broken. Was he so wrong to love the man who once rallied his heart to the Jesuit order? His teacher, his prefect, and the Spaniard who was sent by Rome. Had he not been promised to fight the English by Miguel's side? To serve next to the holy man who wished to be everything to everyone.

Everyone except for him!

As the water grew deeper and blended with the great pool of Lough Ree, the thought of eternal life called to him. Hands loosened their grip on a slick moss covered rock and soon he allowed himself to drift. He wanted that peaceful sleep that came with the penetrating chill. That is what Jodia wanted, but instead he heard splashing feet. Secretly and quietly he hoped they would kill him and spare any suffering. His heart fluttered and brought a tremendous pain to his soul and then a spasm struck him as a hairy arm grazed his cheek. A gurgle escaped the back of his throat when he was lifted in a vice like grip with fingers as strong as iron. They bruised his ankles and he remembered: *These were not men! There was nothing good or human in the eyes of those that took him.* Then he heard them growl and grunt like animals, and smelled the stench of their fowl breath.

※ ※ ※

South of Longford a tent was raised in Colley Town near the stone piles of the vicar's budding church. O'Neill's army had arrived in full and Shane stood to receive the accounting of his men. His most trusted general marched toward him.

"There are none here who can fight us, your Grace" the general said upon arriving.

Shane replied: "Secure any who might resist, and leave the others unharmed." It was a moment shared in victory, and Shane's hand clapped at his cap for the general's exquisite manner. Both men stood wearing pristine white cloaks with the red hand of victory embroidered on the breast. They had shed their war bonnets and appeared civilized and resolved. It would be time for recovery.

Shane was the O'Neill Mor. The High Lord of Ulster but the warriors saw him as king. Wherever he went, the men bid him honor. It was an honor he knew would not last, and he pondered what life would be like with the blessing of England. Near him stood a tall thin man who dressed in fine stockings and an English long coat. The mayor would barely have acknowledged him a year ago, and now he seemed well pleased to wait patiently at his door. They entered the tent together.

"Thank you," the lord mayor said politely.

"Do you understand that we will camp here and await the signal fires?" Shane asked.

"I do. I will enter the city alone," the lord mayor replied.

Shane looked to his general, Barre Conn, "After we are refreshed, take the lord mayor into the castle for the night and arrange for his escort in the morrow. Then return here as soon as you can."

Barre Conn was a man who said what he thought. He was a warrior's warrior and one who Shane O'Neill's men admired. Seldom did he question his high chief but the tone of Shane's voice alarmed him. "Shall the lord mayor not evening here with you, your Grace?" Barre asked.

"I would prefer he stay in the castle lest we come under attack," Shane replied.

❧ ❧ ❧

While the nobles met inside the huge tent, Colley Town became a fort of Irish soldiers. Horses were tethered and games of dice began. A regular guard was posted at the main road and perimeter. In short order pack horses were unloaded and Shane's officers took flat bread and honey. They were not of one accord. Radcliffe had been routed and the bulk of the English army were in retreat or penned up inside their tower houses between Meath and Dublin. To the north, the county of Cavan was no longer occupied and so the midlands were fair game. Some wished to occupy and others wished to press into the city of Dublin.

After the meal, the Lord Mayor of Belfast was taken away while the others took off their sandals and drank a sweet ale. Shane took it all in, realizing they were much too eager. After some time, he found the opportunity to whisper in his general's ear, "The mayor knows too much already."

The tent was abuzz with debate, "I don't understand, your Grace," Barre replied.

"You will," Shane told him. "Turlough has returned with a message from the Jesuit. Things are not as we have been led to believe."

As Barre Conn bowed and took his drink, Shane knew he must soon address the group as a whole. The men he saw were loyal. If they had the queen's blessing rather than his each of the chieftains might be earls already. They all held land as did he. Men who wore the fur and cape of battle and bore the names of O'Neill, McMahon, and Maguire- these chieftains were the heart of Ulster and each ruled with a second at his side. Chieftain and Tánaiste, as it had been for centuries. *Would they ever change? Could they?*

He watched a minor chief named McCarty and his second whom he knew to be called Caleb. Caleb was as thick in the arms as most men were at the waist. The two warriors had the look of seriousness in their eyes but never actually spoke harsh words until now. They had angered when Caleb's drink was mistakenly given away and Shane watched McCarty put his hand on the hilt of his sword. They were hard men. Ready to fight amongst themselves as well as against another. The man who had errored had a look of surprise on his face which might have been mistaken for humor. Caleb confronted him. It was a situation they did not need and had the potential to go very badly. *It was time*, Shane thought, as he stood to put an end to the squabble. "Do thee not have a field full of men who might enjoy your company, Patrick?" he asked, hoping Patrick would find the honor to leave. Patrick puffed briefly but moved off without confrontation.

Shane now had the attention of the chieftains. "Radciffe has escaped with a small detachment." His announcement caused a stir.

Barre Conn dumped out his ale with a tightening of his fist, "The teller of lies will be caught another day," he said bitterly.

Shane laughed, trying not to seem alarmed. "I suppose Radciffe will tell the queen he has attained a complete victory over the wild Irish of Ulster. Can any of us who saw him flee imagine that?"

There was a commotion of nays among them as chieftains shrugged off the setback and moved toward the map table. The division of land was their reason, and the table a foundation on which an alliance would rest. It sat prominently in the center of the large tent so that all could see and have their say.

Barre Conn spoke first: "It may be hard for Radcliffe to make such a claim. We have enough numbers to march to Dublin as planned."

"Aye," McCarty said with zeal.

"Do thee not have enough land already?" Shane asked.

"It is not the land we want, but justice," McCarty replied.

Shane listened as they grumbled. These men did not want to be ruled. He could hardly blame them for England was damned far away. What could England truly offer but a tax on the land they already possessed? For many the proposition was pure folly. To further their grief, a ban from parliament on wool not shorn from English sheep had been enacted. This was the tipping point and a parliament led by Radcliffe was the one thing that these chieftains would not abide. Their sentiment echoed around the table with fervor. Ulster was Ulster and it did not need Radcliffe or the queen to impose upon their trade.

What made matters more difficult was that the laymen, the alderman, and the clergy of the chartered cities were attempting to impose these laws within Ulster itself. The law and the Anglican mandate! One in the same he surmised. After listening to them bicker for as long as he dared, he finally spoke out. "I fear Dublin is not the battle we should fight."

Barre Conn looked down at the map, "If not Dublin, then we should move against Thomond." It was a declaration that brought a rumble.

Shane saw the favor of Barre Conn's strategy take hold with the McMahon and Maguire chieftains who gathered at the map more anxiously than before. They looked at Barre Conn's finger as he ground his nail across Shannon Bridge and on past the hill country toward Galway. "If we attack west and put a siege to Galway, we attack with the support of Connaught and the O'Malley of Upper MacWilliam. They have ships, and perhaps with the Spanish, we will drive the fucking English away for good. I say there is no better time than now for such things."

Shane raised his voice and he raised a hand to stop such talk. "That is what the Lord Mayor of Belfast would want us to do, but that is not what we should do. The chartered cities are a part of England and if we lay siege to Dublin or Galway, England will fully commit her navy to the cause of our annihilation. Do you think the mayors of the chartered cities want to answer to chieftains or deal directly with England in their trade? Without our influence who would set the fair price of wool to the people? Who would benefit from the sequestration of our own land? It would be the mayors of those cities themselves and also the guilds within. So I ask you, do we want England's attention at sea as well as Radcliffe's army coming against us?"

"Does the lord mayor know you urge not an attack on Dublin?" Barre asked.

Shane replied: "He has an inkling, but before I left him, he said that the Mayor of Galway and his friends in Sligo would not close their ports to the English unless Dublin was well secured. I also know he has been in contact with the mayoral council of London Derry. Hell, he has even been in cohorts with Calvagh O'Donnell who I hold prisoner in my castle. We cannot trust him."

"We do not need Sligo, but Thomond cannot be allowed to continue. The O'Brien is in league with Radcliffe and so we must take either Dublin or Galway to secure a further alliance with Spain," Barre advised.

The chieftains agreed and began talking amongst themselves with the knowledge that they had of the countryside. Shane felt his heart sink and could see the burning of fields and crying of babes that would follow. It would be a disaster and he cleared his throat again to try to sway them. "I have sent many letters to the queen, most of which offer reconciliation." They looked at him gravely. They wanted war and free pasture and to hell with the bloody queen. That is what he knew his people wanted and he wanted it even more himself but not at the cost of all of Ulster. "We are at a crossroad here. It is worth considering all our facts before rushing off to fight where Radcliffe has the advantage. Dublin is walled from the priory lands to the river and Thomond has not sent an army against us. Think about it lads."

The men stirred with disagreement and like a hot bed of coals the flames were hard to extinguish. "O'Brien is aligned with

Radcliffe, what further cause do we need?" Barre exclaimed, referring to his desire to attack.

Shane countered: "Much more. O'Brien never sent an army into Ulster as did the Butlers and other lords of parliament. Why would we attack them? Remember, the Jesuit brings a message of peace to England. If our queen does not accept, there will be time for us to attack. Or… if she fails to hear us, perhaps we may attack on English soil to spare our own fields. Have thee not been deprived of the liberty to farm in your own pastures whilst our enemy grows fat from the newly planted fields in Kildare and Meath? Do ye want more of the same?"

Shane put his sword across the table and it rattled like a beat in their hearts. It was a map of Ireland and yet the hilt landed off the sheet entirely. "We are apart from England… so if a battle must be had… let us bring it to their shore and not our own. I have information that Spain has not sent the promised invasion force as the lord mayor has claimed. So if we believe we can take Thomond and Galway with the help of Spain, our hopes will be dashed. For now, we have shown that Radcliffe can be beaten. Let that sit with Elizabeth and see if her impotent council might advise a truce."

Turlough stood. He had been to Belfast and saw no flags flying the green cross. The Jesuit had not lied to him about this uncertainty. "Let me go to Dublin while you wait, your Grace. I may yet find the truth of Spain within the port itself and if that truth is treachery I will take the lord mayor's life."

Shane replied, "He has people in Dublin that will protect him and does not know that I have come upon this information. Therefore, if he tells us the truth and an army is waiting on ships in Dublin, I am sure Pope Pius IV has offered England a way out. If Elizabeth retracts the Anglican mandate, what then?"

They grumbled with their sullied taste of victory. Shane rested his faith in Turlough who continued. "It may be us at war with Spain." The implication sat with them all heavily.

Shane said, "If we hold now and find that Radcliffe has been deposed by Elizabeth, as I have requested, what harm is there in negotiation?"

Turlough replied: "At least send a small group of men to infiltrate the city. It is the rumors that will shed light on the queen's intent. The lord mayor's informants have been unreliable and the Jesuits of Meath we know have been slain. How else will we make a good judgement?"

Shane replied: "I will consider, now tell the chieftains more about what thee have seen in Belfast. Let Barre Conn hear how the lord mayor has defied us."

Turlough began to circle the table and let his voice trail low. He knew, as did Shane that his words would change the hearts of both McGuire and McMahon. These men were vital to the trade and peace in Ulster. "As we turned Radcliffe back, he headed northeast with a detachment of cavalry rather than retreat with the Ormond Brigade to Armagh. I followed him after the battle of Monaghan and I nearly caught the bastard. He had only a small force of men but he escaped into the city of Belfast."

The chieftains looked at each other apprehensively.

Shane frowned and directed his attention to McCarty who relied solely on the markets of that city to export his fleeces and horse stock. "Belfast is not our city any longer."

Michael McCarty was aghast, however, Barre Conn angered. "You should have killed the lord mayor rather than bringing him!"

Turlough replied, "It is not for me to decide. Do not believe for a moment that he works for our best interest but to kill him would not be wise. There are also a large number of Scottish mercenaries roaming his streets and these men were not the type for trading. So... I ask who exactly has the lord mayor welcomed into his city. It certainly does not appear to be Spain!"

Shane spoke tellingly to the chieftains, his voice was deep and low, "Again, I put to you all. Do we look after ourselves and Ulster or do we put our trust in just one man who would benefit from our demise?"

Barre along with the chieftain Maguire wanted to know more. "Could it have been the McAlister Clan from Kintyre that you confused with mercenaries?"

Turlough was sure. "Kintyre was sacked and Sorely Boy of Castle Dunluce has gained the trade rights for the MacRihanish. Our brothers, within the city, believe that all the McAlister have been wiped out. We have no allies across the sea anymore. Not without Kintyre."

Shane saw the sting of this betrayal hit the chieftains like a hammer. They spoke of revenge, they spoke of murder and they spoke of hate. "Lest not forget we hold the earl Tryconnell and his wife at Dunluce. Sorely Boy may dally with England but he will not raise a sword against the dowager Katherine of Argyle. Hell, her father Hector may even thank us for taking her from O'Donnell and join us against the English invaders. The marriage to O'Donnell was to strengthen his clan against

Elizabeth not join them." They quieted, and he heeded their emotion with levity, "I would put coin to wager that the entire clan Campbell will be boarding their long boats just to kiss my ass."

Barre replied, "Aye. England sits not so poorly with Sorely Boy if this is true."

Turlough offered another bleak consideration. "It is also a possibility that Radcliff has taken a portion of his forces to mass at the northern sea. He has the English ship, *Great Harry,* and he has been using it. If the Isle of Man is a staging point, Sorely Boy opens our back door to England and leaves Ulster vulnerable."

They debated for some time in that tent erected at Colley Town. It was a night of realization and disappointments. Shane understood without question that these chieftains wanted war.

❄ ❄ ❄

Emma Colley sat up in a broken room. Outside she could hear horses as more men from Ulster piled onto her husband's land. The brute who had taken her left her lying on the bed where she spent the remainder of the night alone. She thought about what had happened and felt the overwhelming weight of her life. The scarred man had not beaten her and the thought of him left her unsure. He had kissed her and in that moment where her resistance turned to surrender, she felt whole. With his touch, she became beautiful, worthy and desired. Was she so weak, to have fallen in the moment, or was she tender and frail? His eyes accepted her without knowing who or what she was and the intensity of his hunger exposed her own longing. It awakened her. The force of him shattering her conception of what was right or wrong. She felt, she listened, she smelled, and Emma Colley remembered that she was alive. She did not want her life to end. She did not want to be known as the crazy witch of Colley Town.

Emma got out of her bed and suddenly felt that the room, her empty kitchen, and the whole of the castle itself was in fact her prison. A place where she could never truly feel safe. She took the time to straighten her hair and looked at the crib and broken window. Then, she got onto her knees and bowed her head. "Lord, let a child come from this," she prayed.

As she stood, she listened and heard the sound of O'Neill's army. Henry had not returned for her. He was no longer her covering, and she struggled with her emotions. Outside, the wild Irishmen sang songs and danced around a beautiful tent. They were clearly the victors of England. Men who sounded of life and hope and sang in Celtic tongues. The words no longer seemed so harsh or evil to her soul. Henry, wherever he was, had not prevented this thing. She hated him for it!

As she listened, Emma looked out of her window and wondered if Henry was alive at all. Had he lied to her? The men she saw were not the merciless beasts of the field or eaters of human flesh. She rationalized that they were just men and she might now carry one of their children. A tiny bit of hope or a curse to the English plantation. "I choose hope, Lord," she whispered.

CHAPTER 12

Beyond the Pale and Priests

alking up Main Street, as if he were going to church, Vicar Tinsdale wore a lavish robe. He had hidden in a secret room set below the small staircase of his church. He warned of O'Neill; he had spoken against O'Neill. Realizing he could not stay hidden for longer, he dared to see O'Neill. The chieftain appeared in a white surcoat with a thick full mantle. He ate and drank near a wonderful tent with nobles by his side. Men of armor and honor, it appeared.

Vicar Tinsdale picked up his pace, *this man will listen*, he thought as he watched Shane O'Neill enter his grand tent in the middle of town. He marched past four of the finest horses he had ever seen and reached out to touch one of their blankets. The magnificence drew him. A strangely familiar crest with the marking of a red hand.

"Hold!" a guard shouted as Vicar Tinsdale passed the horses.

"I am not a threat," he paused to hold up his hands, "I am a man of God who seeks your master."

The guard wanted nothing of him and pointed away.

"Wait," Vicar Tinsdale said nervously.

❧ ❧ ❧

From inside the tent, Shane O'Neill saw a disturbance. A flash of metal and then his guard stood over a fat little man. Behind Shane, Barre Con covered his head and the others who were distraught rested. They had allowed their warriors this time of celebration, but the time had come to act and Shane lifted the flap to see what caused this foray.

Vicar Tinsdale rolled on the ground, "Have mercy, me lord," he said as the guard placed the tip of his spear at his throat.

"Let him stand," Shane commanded.

Vicar Tinsdale picked himself up. "Do not have this man kill me. I beg thee for the sake of your children," he pleaded.

"For my children?" Shane asked.

Vicar Tinsdale dusted himself off and extended his hand expecting a greeting. "Aye, me lord. We are not soldiers here in this town. To kill a man of God would surely bring the curse of seven generations."

The vicar angered Shane. "Lies!" he screamed.

The reaction stunned Vicar Tinsdale who fell backward as Shane drew his sword and prepared to strike him down.

Barre Con rushed out of the tent to stop him. "If it must be done, let the weakest of our clan bear the burden of this coward's death. We saw him flee into the church and hide before the first arrow was loosed."

Shane stared down loathingly at the Anglican who crouched before him. "Is there a woman among us who has lost a husband to the Anglican?" he asked.

"Nay, your Grace," Barre Con replied.

"Not even the old one?" Shane asked.

"She has done so much already, your Grace," Barre replied.

Shane pondered the situation as Vicar Tinsdale realized his grave mistake. "You are right. It would dishonor any warrior to kill such a coward," he admitted.

Vicar Tinsdale lifted his hands in fear, "My lord, I did not wish to offend. I am closest with the Anglican brothers of Dublin. If I am spared, how better I can tell them that you are not a brute of ill nature but indeed a gentle lord?"

"I see," Shane replied, "you have ties to the crown, and also to Dublin."

"Aye, me lord. It is true," Vicar Tinsdale replied.

"Are you ordained?" Shane asked.

"Aye, me lord. I am nearly a deacon within Queen's County," Vicar Tinsdale brushed off his robe for a second time and glanced at the golden crest embroidered on his shoulder. "I would go to Dublin in the morrow. There is a great assembly of the faithful this very week. People of influence."

"That is good to know," Shane replied.

Vicar Tinsdale let out a huge sigh of relief. "Is there anything that I should tell the brothers on your behalf, sire?" he asked as Barre Con stepped forward to take him away.

"I know what you will tell them," Shane replied.

Vicar Tinsdale knew exactly what he would say in Dublin as well. The negotiation would raise him in standing, perhaps even to chaplain. It would be good. It would be right for his appointment as such a minister after peaceful achievement. A minister to Queens County. The thought made him smile.

As Shane turned away and Barre Con escorted him in an expeditious fashion toward the castle, Vicar Tinsdale felt utterly alive. There was a high bounty on O'Neill, perhaps information might rather be the better option. They walked peacefully for a few minutes and then the general urged him more forcefully. Before he knew it, two of the Irish warriors joined Barre Con and he told those men to see him to the castle. They squeezed his arms and did not let go.

"What is the meaning of this?" Vicar Tinsdale fretted.

They did not answer but his heels dug into the ground when he saw Mistress Colley strolling toward them. "Mistress Colley!" Vicar Tinsdale shouted.

Emma whisked past the commotion quickly. *What could I do for you, Vicar?* She wondered. *Should I surrender to your talk of witchcraft and give you my power?* She turned back briefly when he began to cry like a babe. He had been careless with his words. Coaxing the town against her as if she were a devil. None of that mattered now. Soon she found herself where she wanted to be. In the midst of the warriors who stood by the tent.

Emma's voice was crisp, "Is it not an Irish custom to marry the woman whom you seed with child?" she demanded in the company of chieftains.

Their jaws dropped and Emma saw a handsome face look up at her. Shane had a black beard and glistening white teeth and he appeared much different to Emma from the warrior who raped her. The chieftains of McMahon and Maguire turned to her as well and then all of them began to laugh at her condition.

Henry had laughed at her often, rather than understand her. The women of Colley town had mocked her and now the chieftains were no different. She was done with whispers and gossip.

Shane stood up seeing that she refused to leave their company. Emma had an air about her that he recognized as redeeming, if not misguided. He moved quickly with an athletic gate, closed the gap between them and was within arms-reach before she could utter another word. For a moment, he thought Emma might be noble and had no desire to inflict harm upon a woman of birth.

"Has one of my men offended thee, my lady?" he asked.

"No!" Emma seethed, and she rolled her head and shook her hair frantically. "One of your men has put a child in me! I know it as only a woman can know!"

Hearing the English swag of her presumptuous speech, her tone removed all doubt that Emma was noble. She was strained, "A child?" he questioned, looking humorously concerned that one of his men had done such a thing.

Shane's mockery enraged her, and her voice became frantically quick. "A Celtic child will grow inside me! And that alone demands your law!" Her hands moved strangely and her fingers curled inwardly as if she invoked some great power. Heads turned with the unexpected deluge of excitement.

Shane felt her countenance chilling. "Can you tell me which of my men?" he asked with more concern.

"I can— when I smell him." A bout of laughter filled the air and Emma beamed with a wide and wild smile as she continued, "And the doer of this deed bears a scar across his face."

Shane held out his hand gracefully to Emma, "I see your distress, and will not add to it." He looked to the chieftains around him, "The law is the law," he told them with a shrug.

Emma's words cooled and she stood as if made of stone, "I have been defiled, lord. I am not beautiful or young but a lustful bastard has taken me, and for that, I will have my justice."

"Justice?" Shane asked, as those around heard the resignation of her heart. Emma was humming. Such a sound tested his conscious. He looked at her kindly, remembering the words of the old woman, called Mam. *Spare unneeded burden for the mistress*, Mam had said. Surely, the very same mistress stood before him now. He could see the sorrow in her eyes, but he also saw strength. She did not appear too old to have more children and her hips and stout frame offered a promise of sons. "We shall find your suitor when I know you are free to marry and have your name."

"I am the Mistress Emma Colley and my husband has undoubtedly been killed by your men. What am I to do without a husband?" she asked.

"Do you know with certainty that we have killed your husband?" Shane asked.

Emma felt detached from herself. The sensation of lightheadedness overcame her as if her feet hovered above the ground. "If it be not so, I will take my own life," she replied emphatically.

He had never loved the raping part of warfare and the man who disturbed this woman's mind would surely get his due. "Was your husband an English soldier?" Shane asked.

Emma's voice became a whisper, "He was a captain of the Kildare Brigade and none have returned from battle."

"The Kildare Brigade fought bravely, but I could not know of your husband. I think you should wait for your man here. I will see to it that no further harm comes to you."

Emma felt like crying. She had waited. She waited alone as the vicar used her condition of grief to turn an accusation of witchcraft against her. The vicar did not know why she had done the thing she had done. He had never known her daughter Agnes. She remembered Agnes's eyes. She had waited for Henry endlessly. She had endured the loneliness without knowing when or if his planters would come to burn her. "If Henry is not dead, he has failed to help me. I claim only the man who put his child in my womb, for if my husband returns, I will be slain because of it." Her strength ended with those words and a flood of tears came streaming down her cheeks. *A child, a child, I will have a child.* The words began to swirl around her mind and take away the pain.

"Would not your priest intervene and provide you shelter?" Shane asked.

Emma replied, "I claim not the vicar, who has spread lies about me..." Before Emma could continue, she heard the voice of her assailant, familiar and grating. The sudden interruption returned her memory and again she became afraid.

"It was Gowl!" one of the men yelled. They released Gowl and he fell on his knees in front of them all.

"I meant not to disgrace you," Gowl stammered.

Shane looked at the humbled warrior and then at Emma. He straightened his robe to stand firm before the men, "Rise for this woman whom you have claimed," he commanded.

Gowl stood up befuddled, "Your Grace, I see one who gave herself freely," he said with discomfort.

The men murmured dissentingly. Shane raised his voice, "Is it the way of women to give themselves to you?"

Gowl turned to his fellow clansmen who watched with gilded smiles and then he replied, "It is the way of war. How many maidens has this army taken and yet no others have been subject to the old law?"

Shane heard more laughter. A laughter that told him his men did not believe in the old ways as much as he would like. "No maidens have come forward to claim that right. None but this woman whom you have made your own." He paused to ensure everyone listened, "Do you remember what shall happen if you refuse her?"

Gowl's left hand dropped knowingly to his loins, "It has been years since the clan has done such a thing, your Grace."

"Years do not matter. The law is the law," Shane replied. He waited in silence and looked to his good friend Barre who had returned from the castle. "Take him, Barre," Shane ordered. The other chieftains joined Barre and together they lifted Gowl so that his toes just barely touched the ground. When Shane stepped forward, a McMahon handed him a sharp dagger.

"Wait... wait!" Gowl screamed.

Shane lifted his hand, "So you accept this lady?" he asked, knowingly.

Gowl's face burned beneath his scar. The jagged line turned white and his whiskered cheeks glowed with his fury. "Aye, your Grace," Gowl spat.

Shane wanted this done quickly so he did not hesitate. "You... Gowl of Tyrone... will take this woman as if she was your wife. You shall cherish her and protect her from those like yourself and give her the comfort of a cottage." When Shane concluded, he turned to Emma Colley and took her hand. "You are not his wife. Until you can prove you are free to marry or your true husband claims you." Then he turned to his men, "So says our Lord, and so say I."

Gowl replied, "I have not a cottage, your Grace."

Seeing that Gowl still protested, Barre Con cracked him on the forehead and stripped his kilt away. Gowl cried out in his nakedness, "I shall build her a cottage, your Grace. A fine cottage of earth and stone."

Shane surged forward with a look of murder in his eyes and ordered Gowl's legs be restrained. Emma turned her head. "The name of Gowl will be remembered this night and your story shall be told for generations! The nut-less warrior who refused a woman's right, they will sing." His tone left no doubt that he was intent on fulfilling the ancient law and Emma was certain that Gowl would bring her justice.

Gowl pleaded more urgently, "I shall give her the land of me mum and bring four sheep to her each spring!" he shouted.

Shane turned to Emma. He could see she blushed at Gowl's nakedness and he asked her, "Does Gowl still please thee, my lady?"

Emma paused, which caused Gowl much concern. Her eyes became wild and her teeth clattered as she snapped at him. "Do you promise a cottage?" she asked as she twirled a strand of hair on a finger.

"A fine cottage," he replied urgently.

"It is acceptable, my lord," Emma said as calmly as she could.

"So be it then. Gowl of Tyrone, all that I have spoken has become the law. This woman will lay with thee in thy mother's fields and later in a strong cottage. You have until the child is born to make it so," he proclaimed.

Gowl fell to the ground shamefully and when he looked up to see Emma, he believed that she would kick him. Indeed, the woman was mad. She bent over and lifted his chin by the whiskers. Then in that instant of her rage, when she saw that Gowl was meek, she pulled him to his feet and kissed him. He held out his arms afraid to make a move as Emma parted her lips and bit down hard. It caused his eyes to water and he tasted of his own blood.

Emma threw him back. "I can ride and have ten horses of my own!" she said with the intensity of a woman possessed. Her words sent a cheer through the chieftains who stood in witness. Each of them slapped the other just as Emma had done to Gowl. They were a hearty bunch of men whom she had joined. Some were warriors and some were noble, but none would forget her now.

"For the horses then!" Gowl shouted.

Therefore, it came to be, that Emma Colley became the mistress of a wild Irish warrior.

CHAPTER 13

Judas Becomes
the Beast

In Longford, close to the place where Henry Colley would soon ride, the nature of a holy man was tested. The feral landscape offered shelter for the wildlings. They avoided the horse trails and traveled south along a winding shoreline. The leader Hagan guided the group into some timber. "Build a fire and bring our people here," he ordered. Two of the clan ran off through the willows to do as he instructed, others dropped sacks of meat. There was a division among the group that was born out of suffering and hunger. Some of the clan believed they would do better to the west and believed they should cross the River Shannon. Hagan warned them of the danger of rival clans.

One of the younger and stronger youth of the wildlings spoke out. "We need naught carry alive what might flee or try to kill us. He should die," he demanded, referring to Jodia.

Hagan turned to his sister whom he loved. She had lost a husband and also a child. The blond hair of Jodia seemed to affect her. He couldn't order the death of someone that was bringing her back to her senses. And yet the man had been civilized and pampered in a life of privilege. It would be better for the man to be tested. For if he failed then he could be killed without bringing his sister's distrust or scorn. She couldn't blame him again for the loss of her man. It wouldn't take long. The man didn't appear strong enough to survive more than a month and then Etha could join with a proper warrior. Someone who could hunt and feed her. He wanted that for her, if nothing else, he wanted her to survive. "No, not him," Hagan replied.

A fire pit was cleared among the alders and leaves where taken for bedding. They clicked their teeth and split branches and Jodia understood the crudeness of their words. He remained conscious through his bashing. He was bruised and tied with rawhide lashings. After they had secured him, his eyes darted from one ghastly form to the next. What he saw was the fur of animals and the bones of wolves and foxes hanging from their necks. Their human form under the furs could barely be discerned. A cramp hit his side and he grunted as his lungs strained to find air. It caused Hagan to look his way as his body hung like a stag on a game pole.

"It be right to kill him, Hagan," the younger one insisted.

Hagan pursed his lips with disagreement. He was stronger and smarter than those who labored in sweat. "No!" he shouted.

The others hissed and moved away to help pile sod onto a strange looking mound. Their feet were bare and covered in hair and Jodia was poked when he struggled for air.

"Leave him," Hagan yelled.

The leaves rustled on the ground as a scurry of feet came running toward Hagan. Jodia watched in his upside down state as the younger wildling pulled out a knife. Full of hate and pride, and all that he thought he should be within this abscess clan, the younger one attacked.

"He belong to Etha!" Hagan bellowed.

They collided like rams as their heads glanced off each other and their shoulders sank in the rut. Hagan avoided the blade and rolled to the ground in a tangle of arms and legs. As they crashed into the trees which suspended him, a loud snap sent Jodia tumbling to the ground. He felt their bodies on him and wanted to bite and kick or run. To tear at the flesh that ground his face into the earth was all consuming and yet he could hardly move.

"No!" Hagan cried out in the brawl.

In the struggle that ensued there was a pounding that intensified in rhythm until it ebbed to a shudder and then stopped completely. Jodia heard a wheeze of asphyxiation. The weight of both men were atop him, his face pressed into the cold leaves. He felt the popping. He heard the little cracks like that of a stiff joint sounding in his ear and then there was stillness.

Hagan pushed the body off of Jodia and stood. "You not die until Hagan say!"

The others bowed their heads to Hagan as he held out his hand for each to rub. It was then that Jodia was allowed to stand. Hagan cut the bonds from his feet and Jodia knew he did not have the strength to run. He took water from a gourd that Etha brought and tasted the sweetness of the mash that she had ground. Her name now had meaning and Jodia indulged her kindness before they tied him again.

Later, a fire was built and Jodia smelled the aroma of sizzling meat. He bit his own cheeks and held his breath wishing he did not want it. The overpowering sensation left him shaking like a frightened bird. He prayed silently so that they would not hear him and as he did his mouth watered. Within an hour other people came from the forest. Stark figures who wandered into the camp with longing. They arrived with the snapping of branches as thickets obscured their number. For the dispossessed, time had no meaning, the sun breaking through the canopy provided little warmth. They were dirty with a blackness in their eyes that hinted of dark and sinister souls. People who were at the very edge of their resilience.

Soon Jodia heard women and saw thin distended bellied wildling children who jumped up in horrific play around his battered head. They poked his sides and screamed in frantic enthusiasm of his size. He was theirs now! He would sustain them! The redness of their bleeding gums, a smile of famine on their faces.

An old man came toward him. "What you called?" the elder hissed. Aged eyes glimmered through unkempt knots of hair obscuring a blue painted face.

Jodia rocked back in disbelief. *How can they even speak*, he thought? *They are animals!*

Drool formed as the beastly figure stepped away without Jodia's answer. The group knew what the elder wanted. Each of them having been given their own names now wanted to know the power of his. The breath of the old heathen's frustration creased thick lips that protruded through his scraggly grey beard. He paced around Jodia waiting for his answer. What would the man with golden hair be named? A man who his daughter had chosen.

"What you called?" the old one asked with a hiss.

Jodia's eyes rolled up to show the white of unconsciousness and the questioning ended abruptly.

❧ ❧ ❧

Hagan, Etha, and the elder moved to the fire and talked of taking Jodia into their clan. The father did not believe Jodia strong enough, but Etha pleaded. An hour or more passed and then the old one went to Jodia and began again.

"What you called?" he said as Jodia opened his eyes.

Jodia did not answer and so the children were given instruction to mark Jodia's face. They did it with crushed berries and stretched him out upon the ground. He was dizzy when they brought the blood to his lips and painted them with glistening delight. After the children were done, a hand rattled a string of bones around Jodia's head.

"What your name?" the elder hissed.

This time the question was followed with the dropping of a hot ember onto Jodia's leg. The pain was instantaneous and he shook his head and cried out: "No!"

The elder repeated his ritual until Jodia's legs were scorched and raw. He trembled and as his eyes saw the mass of the last stone being pulled from the fire, Hagan opened the robe to bare his chest. This one would surely kill him. Jodia gave his name with such power that it sent a flock of sleeping birds fleeting away.

"Judas!" he shouted. Oh how he had wished they killed him in the forest. How he wished that the priests who had once called him friend had listened. Miguel, his teacher, he felt nothing but rage. He let out his fury and cried: "Judas, Judas, Judas…" into the night.

"Ju-dous…" the oldest one said as he took the hand of his daughter.

"Yes…" Judas replied in delirium.

After the torture, Etha came to him. She walked with an arch in her back that accented the slenderness of her malnourished thighs. She dabbed his legs with oil and salt and covered the blisters in moss. When he woke some time later her face was near his.

"Take," she said giving him a smoldering piece of meat. Jodia turned his lips away and so she grabbed his face to force a bit between his clenched teeth. "Eat…" she hissed in his ear.

"I am a priest…" he panted as she stopped his sound with the flesh.

Etha ran a greasy finger over his chest. She touched his head and Jodia could see they were inside the strange earthy mound that the wildings had built. The others were outside dancing by the fire.

"Never!" Judas cried.

She reached between his legs and grabbed him and felt him rise in her hand as Judas opened his mouth without control. She tore at his tattered cloths like an animal while he listened to the others chanting. Their souls were beyond any hope of redemption. As her treatment of him continued, the crackling embers of the fire began to snap with an overpowering smell of roasting flesh and this woman took his battered soul.

"Lord God, be merciful," was now just a whisper upon his lips.

"Ya, Ya, Ya, Yah!" A symphony of voices sounded out and many hands cast their stones into the fire.

"I am Judas," he yelled as the sweat of her dripped across his chest. The intensity of his shudder made her cry out, and like those who had subdued him, Judas became the beast.

A Lesson
well Learned

The *Pinnacle* sailed toward London with a crack along the bow sprit. On the fifth day at sea Lieutenant Brinson walked onto the aft deck in the company of Captain Grimm.

"If the sickness was not bad enough, something struck the vessel at dusk, sir," Lieutenant Brinson reported.

The captain searched the water. In contrast to the desperation of a sickened crew, he found the sea to be uncommonly peaceful. It was of little comfort to the terrible reality of their condition, but it was something. His men had suffered and the fever was spreading very quickly from one mate to the next.

From his experience, those that were confined would inevitably start clustering with accusations. He could tell his first mate was showing signs of the sickness, and even now he imagined his crew assembling in the dark places to embellish his reputation for disaster, and bring down what little morale remained. He cleared his throat and took a deep breath to put forth his best face. He was Captain Grimm after all, the captain of eighty feet of English sail. He opened his arms to feel the sun and bathed in it. *Yes, the light will keep us safe*, he thought.

"Captain Grimm, did you hear me sir?" Lieutenant Brinson asked.

"I felt nothing in the night," Captain Grimm answered defensively.

Lieutenant Brinson felt a stirring in his gut, "Perhaps the Captain was preoccupied in the officer's galley, but it happened, sir," he replied curtly.

"What is the damage?" Captain Grimm asked, regretting that the sun did not abate his first mate's condition as it had his own.

"The hull is intact but the bow sprit will not hold a sail. She's cracked at the stem and a portion of the front timber is showing fatigue," Lieutenant Brinson replied.

The captain pulled out his looking glass to verify rather than walking past the crew. The bow was cluttered and shards of wood littered the deck. "Why do you not wrap it and be full on our way? We will need to be sailing not sitting at anchor."

"Aye, sir, sailing," Lieutenant Brinson said, feeling sicker by the moment.

"Is there anything else you should tell me?" Captain Grimm asked.

"We must begin to bury the dead, sir. Little Jimmy came running to me pleading for it to be so. He said it would be our curse if we did not send their souls off in prayer."

"The boy is right. Why haven't the preparations been made?" Captain Grimm asked.

"I understand, sir, but the bodies are covered in sores. And then there is the matter of the queen's yeomen. None of the crew will go near them," he gasped.

"The yeomen?" Captain Grimm asked.

"Two dozen or more," Lieutenant Brinson responded dryly. "That is how many are dead and among them are all the yeomen. We found them just this morning and the marks of the devil himself were etched all about the brig cell."

"That's nonsense," Captain Grimm responded.

"Six, six, six, sir. It was cut right into the chief yeoman's forehead. I've never seen anything like it." The captain looked up with a newness in his expression that baffled his first mate. He almost seemed pleased. It was a bizarre response.

"Bring them to the decks to finish preparing the bodies and we will complete the burial quickly. It must be done soon and the men must see we honor our sailors regardless of the risk," his voice gave tell to his improved spirit as he continued, "the markings you describe might just be the salvation of our crew, Mister Brinson! Do not fret about it further."

"I don't understand you, sir. Not one bit" Lieutenant Brinson replied.

Captain Grimm thought of all that he remembered from Africa. He had known two hundred men under his command when the last outbreak of pox hit his crew. Of those men only twenty survived such a plague. If this was the pox he doubted

Lieutenant Brinson would last another week but the markings of the devil were not of the plague. "Have ye posted a guard on the silver?" he asked, ignoring Brinson's doubt.

"Bradford. He and five of our soldiers have secured the brig cell but refuse to go inside," Lieutenant Brinson said.

The captain scowled uncomfortably. "Afraid. Always comes the fear before the calamity. Remember that, Mister Brinson, if ye make it through the day."

"The crew will not touch the bodies. I don't know what else to tell you sir," Lieutenant Brinson said.

"Foolishness and treachery!" the captain declared. "Make sure the crew understands that foolishness and treachery will be punished severely. I have lived with curses, Lieutenant," he spat before continuing, "and I can also be one!"

After giving his direction, Captain Grimm's gaze fell upon Miguel Avaje Fernandez who stood on the forecastle. "I don't like that man," he said, noticing that the priest was basking in the sunlight.

"None do. He is a peculiar," Lieutenant Brinson sighed.

"Let us make use of his talents with the preparation of the dead. And in the future, Lieutenant, keep that bastard off my foredeck. He and the dullard will get the bodies where they need to be. Any of the crew who refuse to assist will be cast over immediately!"

※ ※ ※

Miguel Avaje Fernandez observed much from the forecastle and he took a moment to share his faith with two who remained untouched by sickness. "How long have you been at sea, Jimmy?" he asked.

Jimmy held up two fingers. "I was ten when me mum gave me up. She got twenty shillings." The boy raised his chin proudly, "She loves me."

Miguel smiled, "I know she does, Jimmy," he said.

Jimmy sat down near Kenneth and crossed his legs as Miguel took note of the purser and quartermaster below. The men were talking. He saw them look toward the captain and then turn suspiciously away. He turned back to Jimmy wondering what the vile crew were up to. "Do you want to hear the story of how the world was made?"

Jimmy's thoughts were as distracted as the crew. He had never seen sickness overtake so many with such speed. "Are we all going to die?" he asked.

Miguel spoke calmly to reassure the frightened boy, "No one can know the exact day or time of his own death and so when we have the opportunity we must learn as much as we can. I want to teach you, Jimmy. Will you listen?"

"Aye," Jimmy replied nervously.

Miguel spoke as though he was reading from the scriptures directly and his surety was a comfort to the boy. "And after the fourth day, God said, *'Let the water teem with living creatures, and let birds fly above the earth across the vault of the sky. So God created the great creatures of the sea and every living thing with which the water teems and that moves about in it, according to their kinds, and every winged bird according to its kind. And God saw that it was good. God blessed them and said, 'Be fruitful and increase in number, and fill the water in the seas, and let the birds increase on the earth.' And there was evening, and there was morning—the fifth day."*

Kenneth let out a deep sigh, "Did God create the monsters of the deep?" he asked.

Miguel replied: "They are only monsters if you do not know their purpose. God has made everything for a reason."

Kenneth looked at Jimmy, "Don't listen to the crew of the topsails, Jimmy. Even if they did see a serpent last night, it was not made by God to kill us."

"How do ye know," Jimmy asked.

Miguel hushed them and looked toward a sickly first mate who pulled himself up the ladder to where they sat in peace.

Lieutenant Brinson's head beaded with sweat and his trousers were dingy. He'd yet to shave and his voice was hoarse. "This will not do, Holy Man," the first mate said sourly.

Miguel, Jimmy, and Kenneth all looked at the first mate as if he were already dead. He looked terrible and Miguel replied: "They are listening. Surely there is no harm in the hearing of God's written word?"

Lieutenant Brinson steadied himself, "The work for seamen is never done. If you wish to issue prayers, do so over the dead that will soon be buried."

Jimmy stood. At twelve he understood his purpose. He would clean and make ready the powder and then scrub the decks below. That is what he did and that is why he had been called a powder monkey, with kind affection. Today he would do his duty with thoughts of death all around him and as he passed Lieutenant Brinson, he hoped he would be alive to hear about the sixth day.

Lieutenant Brinson gave Jimmy a nod of approval. "The boy knows his place. How 'bout you, Patterson?" he asked Kenneth.

"Aye, sir," Kenneth replied meekly.

"Crack on then," Lieutenant Brinson told him.

Kenneth turned to Miguel. "Thank you, teacher," he said clearly.

"Thank him, do ye?" Lieutenant Brinson quipped. "Did this Spaniard give thee back your faculties?"

"I have done nothing wrong, sir," Kenneth replied.

"Thou speaks clearly. How curious. Let us see if your mind remains clear as you drag the corpses from the brig cell. That's where I want you to go. Get below and drag those honorable men topside and do it with care," Lieutenant Brinson commanded.

Kenneth knew what he was being told to do. He had seen the dead be buried before and when it came to sickness, those that touched the dead were often doomed. He looked at Miguel who nodded for him to obey and then made the sign of the cross for his understanding.

"Go," Lieutenant Brinson demanded, looking at Kenneth with distain.

Miguel clasped his hands together as Kenneth left and faced Lieutenant Brinson head on. *It was good that the crew were afraid to touch the bodies,* he thought. "Have thee heard of the serpent, Lieutenant?"

"What serpent, Holy Man?"

"The serpent seen last night and the creatures of the deep," Miguel replied oddly.

"I am not interested in serpents or sermons. I am only interested in your assistance with the dead..." he raised a brow of warning, "as is our captain."

"It is a lesson well learned, Lieutenant. But I can see that for a man such as you, the lesson might be better learned through experience."

"Perhaps, but in the present, our captain will have thee at mid-ship in an hour. Do be there and ensure you have the right words for the deceased. Take note also, that this be the foredeck, and ye are neither sailor nor officer to set thy feet upon it," Lieutenant Brinson replied.

CHAPTER 15

Prodigal

Far to the north of Colley Town, a detachment of horsemen came upon the English fort of Belturbet. The soldiers wore ragged uniforms of blue wool and sat heavy in the saddle. What they found caused stomachs to lurch as Captain Henry Colley took the sight in and began to investigate. Mutilation.

A scout assessed a cluster of bare footed tracks leading away from the smolder of human flesh.

"How many?" Henry asked.

The scout placed his hand inside a single footprint and splayed out his fingers. "There are a dozen or more but some of the tracks are gigantic."

Warrant Officer Blanch grabbed at his arm with a grim understanding. He had believed in Henry. He had even ordered an attack against the farmers who had chosen to leave their land behind and flee to Connaught, but he had never seen the type of barbarity which befell the English fort. "Where are they heading?" Blanch asked gravely.

The scout replied with certainty: "South, the same as we."

Blanch leaned uncomfortably forward and nosed his mare toward Henry. "We cannot engage again, Captain," he coughed with a rattle of infection and then finished his thought, "turn west toward Meath and avoid this thing."

Henry adjusted himself to sit higher in the saddle. He made the same gesture that Blanch recognized each time a vital decision was upon him. "We may have no choice. Best the men make a camp here and I will head out to see what lies ahead," Henry replied.

Blanch steadied himself, "No, sir. We must keep moving and we should take the eastern boarder around the bog."

Henry spoke quietly, as if he was thinking rather than telling: "There will be fish in the river. Have Dougherty and Kevin take half the men out to find food and the others shall set a watch."

Blanch didn't respond. It would take hours to collect fish and berries. He knew that it was far more likely that the men would become injured and exhausted of what little strength they still had. The edibles of the field had been so scarce in this area that the idea seemed preposterous. Blanch considered himself a professional soldier but even so it was hard not to imagine taking Henry out of the equation all together. His angst was palpable. He could feel it rising in his gut.

"Blanch!" Henry shouted.

"Captain, we cannot engage again," Blanch said with a menacing tone.

"Have Dougherty and Kevin take half the men to the river for fish and then set a watch!" Henry ordered.

Warrant Officer Blanch rubbed his ailing wound discontentedly, "Aye sir, we shall set the watch." Looking down at his mangled appendage he did not feel like setting the watch or hearing another word from Captain Henry Colley but he was unsure of the others. What would they do if he struck out and killed the man? His arm began to throb. It seemed as though every insect that could find a nesting place took their relish in his wound. It was all he could think about and everything he wished would go away. He looked at Henry distrustfully. "Did ye not see what was done to the fine soldiers here?"

Henry answered: "We are in charge of the midlands until relieved by a living English commander. We will send a rider to Armagh to inform our lord deputy of what happened here. In the meantime, and before we go another yard toward home, set us in a secure position."

"Home, Captain..." Blanch said as if dazed.

Henry turned to the scout who looked up over a sweaty brow with his curling brown locks falling over his shoulders. Dennis of the hill clan they had called him and he wore the uniform well. Although mal tempered he appeared less worn than the others, more athletic and alert. "We will continue south along the river, toward Colley Town... when the men are rested," Henry told Dennis.

Dennis gave a nod of approval. He wanted to get home like the rest but he was used to fighting and the trail was nothing compared to the prison he had left behind. He was a free man now, a soldier.

Warrant Officer Blanch continued to press Henry, "We should never have come this far north, Captain. It was a mistake," he said.

"No Blanch, we should have come more quickly," Henry replied.

The words sat in his craw. Blanch knew Henry was a good businessman and he had the potential to lead but he was not a good soldier. They had pushed the Irish out of Geashill by force, but when the Kildare Brigade entered Cavan, things changed drastically. No longer were they chasing the helpless farmers of the midlands. In Cavan and also Longford, the resistance was fierce. "If we pursue, let us hope we find only women and children and not the giants which made those tracks. I doubt we could handle an adversary like that."

Henry took off his hat. "We have miles to go, Blanch. Miles until we reach Colley Town and if between us and our home we must fight… then fight we will surely do. Nothing will stop me from returning to my wife. I am not the only one who feels that way. Look around!"

He may not be the greatest of captains but Henry had not yet lost the men, and that is what Blanch hated most. He would be alone if he moved on Henry. "I will wager that once ye have seen what made those footprints, ye'll know that England is very far from taming the north. I will do as you wish, Captain, but we need to act quickly."

Henry didn't waiver, and seeing that Blanch was aggrieved, he knew he would have to keep him close. "We will, Blanch.

Take some hard tack and tend to your arm, then be ready to ride in one hour."

"I have already lost the arm," Blanch replied bitterly.

Henry watched as men rushed off to the river and others cut limbs for shelter. His voice was calculating, "We are well South of Cavan now, there may be a physician loyal to the crown ahead. Perhaps I should take Dennis?"

Blanch riled, "It will not matter. No, it will not matter at all, and I'll not have the men's fate left to the judgement of a felon from Tipperary. I'll be ready in an hour."

Not long after their quarrel, Henry and Blanch rode into the darkness and somewhere past the region east of Lough Ree, they came upon a crackling fire. They did their best not to be seen and crept toward the strange sounds that filled the cool air. There was yelling, there was fire, there was hell!

What are they?" Henry whispered.

CHAPTER 16

Long Neck
of a
Monster

Calm waters marked the passage into the English
Channel as a burial was made ready at sea. On the
quarterdeck, Kenneth Patterson kneeled among the
tarps near the tall sided gunnels and stripped the leggings from
one of the dead yeoman. "I am Kenneth the rat chaser," he
whispered. He had taken nearly all of the yeoman's clothing,
having been told to fold the uniforms neatly, to be aired for later
use. The dead where now all around him and so were the living
feet of those who watched. Lieutenant Brinson was closest.

147

"Another has perished," a sailor told Lieutenant Brinson grimly.

Kenneth finished bundling the yeoman and slid over to the next. He worked slowly, listening to every word, and his heart nearly leapt from his chest as he unbuttoned the grey frock and then the black slops of the old sail master known as Grey Eyes.

"Another one?" Lieutenant Brinson asked drably.

A hush came over the man as he looked at the line of bodies which littered the deck. It made him question his own fate and he scratched nervously at his beard.

"Who was it?" Lieutenant Brinson asked impatiently.

"The last of the top crew," the sailor replied with horror.

The first mate looked up toward the gallant. The crows-nest was empty. Not a single sailor from above could be seen. "We will make do, even if I have to climb the sail mast alone. You know how to rig a line as well, don't you?" Lieutenant Brinson asked, avoiding the appearance of doubt.

"Aye," the sailor replied with uncertainty.

Lieutenant Brinson glared down at Kenneth: "Do ye still retain the quality of speech, Dullard?" he asked distastefully.

"I have not realized a change," Kenneth replied steadily.

Lieutenant Brinson had noticed a change. It unsettled him, "Wait to cover the sail master and keep quiet. We do not need the ramblings of an idiot at this hour."

Kenneth sewed and he left a margin of air in the canvas ensuring the bodies were not tied too tightly. He thought of Grey Eyes and left his face uncovered as he was told. Just then, a whistle blew, calling the first mate away to leave Kenneth alone with the menacing sailors who still survived. Many of them worshiped Grey Eyes and they appeared mournful.

"The first mate has the sickness," one of them said.

"Aye, and it would be good to have him gone," another mumbled looking back as if he was afraid he had just revealed their plan. They were dirty men, even for sailors, and the nearest of them turned away.

What Kenneth heard, he did not want to believe. It was the talk of mutiny! "There be silver below. Silver enough for us all, and we'll be see-in' land on the English side in less than a day." More talk which Kenneth could not hear and then: "It might be that the prick dies sooner than later." A mischievous laugh hushed their talking.

Kenneth pretended not to hear their careless words. They were not pulling together to survive this thing. The sailors were fractured. Earlier he heard the master gunner plotting the same thing, except the master gunner was taking the silver in the long boats. "Broken," he said, as his thoughts consumed him.

The sailors stopped and looked at him briefly and one of them held his finger up to his lips. They... like the gunners... had no inclination that his mind was whole. "Shhh..." they warned him. Then he heard something else. "The priest must be killed, and also the passengers." Their whispers continued to drift across the dead as he worked.

※ ※ ※

As the sun shined down on the aft deck of the *Pinnacle*, the first mate approached the captain. "Where is the priest?" the captain asked.

"I asked for him and he has not since been found. It is as if he vanished, sir," Lieutenant Brinson replied.

"Don't be a fool! Find him, Mister Brinson. You find him and bring him to the middeck." The captain looked ill, disconcerted, and began to show the signs he had been infected.

"Are thee well, sir?" Lieutenant Brinson asked.

"I will be well enough to stand with our crew. This has to be done now... not tonight... not tomorrow... but now! We have lost two more passengers since dining and the cook has reported the pork to be fouled." The captain pulled a white handkerchief out of his breast pocket and patted his forehead. "Do not look disturbed, Brinson," the captain said.

"It is most disturbing, sir," Lieutenant Brinson replied.

"It is better than the plague. Do we know how many have eaten the rancid meat?" the captain asked.

Lieutenant Brinson shook his head, "I have no idea, sir."

The captain felt his gut churning, "Get the damned priest on deck. The meat may kill us all but I fear not roaming about. Make sure you tell the crew what has happened. Bad pork is much less terrifying than the pox."

"I will do, Captain. I will," Lieutenant Brinson replied with haste.

❧ ❧ ❧

At sea the *Pinnacle* dawdled, and down in the lower hold a woman named Claudette clung to her ailing husband. His breath was fading and the tears washed over her face. "What will I do without you?" she whispered.

He smiled weakly and gazed up at her as if saying goodbye. He had been good to her and sacrificed his own labor to maintain her honor but he too had become ill. It seemed an irony and a cold terrible truth that their journey to see her ailing mother would cause the loss of her own true love. She prayed that it wouldn't and huddled down in the stable trying to warm him under the straw. As they languished, two sailors clattered to the floor. It angered Claudette that they would be so thoughtless in such a time. Then her anger turned to fear as one of the brutes swung a club and killed a passenger who was not more than ten feet from where they lay. She looked to her man and covered his mouth and then she peered down the stable hall to see the other passengers falling over themselves in an attempt to flee. The men were swinging and swinging toward anyone that moved! The thrashing frightened the animals and they too screamed and kicked at their pens, and before she knew it, they were coming toward her. Claudette kicked at the assaulter as another man lifted his arm to deliver a devastating blow. Then just as the two were about to dispatch them, a porthole blew open and she saw the flash of a dagger.

Claudette felt a rush of movement breeze past her like the beating wings of a dragon, and the dust flew up to cloud her vision. She tried to stand. She was trembling and then it became still and quiet.

He stood like a vision before her. "I have made a place for you to hide," Miguel whispered. She watched him gather his robe and then bend down as the few survivors cowered in the shadows. He lifted her husband and she followed him out of the stable without uttering another word. They stopped near a cabin door toward the very front of the ship and Claudette noticed a stairwell spiraling up to the middeck above. Once again, she thought, the priest had interceded for her care.

"Are they dead?" Claudette asked looking at six of the ships guards who lay face down and pushed against the bulkhead.

"This is the brig cell. It is important to us both that the crew fear it cursed," Miguel told her. He quickly handed her the keys, "You will go into that cabin and cover yourself with the blankets of the dead yeomen. They will keep you warm and hide you both."

"My husband is going to die," she whispered affrightedly.

"That is not certain. If I can save you, it will be done," he told her.

❧ ❧ ❧

Topside, the ship sat lazily at anchor and Kenneth ran his knife through the last piece of rotten canvas. It was time for him to cover the face of Grey Eyes, and the purser stood above him to see the task done right. The purser spoke as if the old sail master was still alive and it made Kenneth wonder if he was. "Ye got no pay living but ye will get your coins for the gate keeper," the purser said as he bent down and placed two pennies in the sail master's eyes. After the purser recorded the death of Grey Eyes, Kenneth began to sew, still wondering if his greatest fear might come true. "Do the last stitch right, Patterson," the purser demanded.

Kenneth's hands began shaking so badly that he had trouble holding the needle. He was being watched by everyone and over his shoulder he saw Miguel appear and wave his hand across those who had already been sewn into their canvas sheets.

"Hurry— God be damned," the purser complained.

Kenneth cringed as he pierced the sail master's nose and saw a trickle of blood. Fearing the old man would arise, he quickly pulled the sheet closed to finish the covering stitch. As he sewed he heard a little puff of air under the sail master's sheet. Not a cry or movement but something.

"Is he dead?" someone asked.

"Dead," Kenneth replied not knowing.

Suddenly two sailors pushed him away and took their sail master to the gunnels. A few moments later as the captain and crew looked on, the first mate and cook arrived to the mid deck and a quiet fell across the deck.

Captain Grimm cleared his throat and began. "For Her Majesty, Queen of England and France, this day will be recorded as a terrible loss." His words ignited some emotion. Some took off their bonnets and held them to their chests. Others stared out to the ocean and did nothing at all. The latter seeming to have little time or patience for delay. "Here lies the complement of yeomen who did suffer a miserable fate, and so too an honored member of my crew." As the captain stepped back, the ships drum master began a rumble on his snare and in good fashion, the rudiment ended with a loud thump. It was time for the names of those who died to be announced. The crew listened intently, for not all of them knew who had perished.

The purser held out his log. "Yeomen Bentley of the queen's royal guard," he called out. After a customary lag, a further twenty-five names were announced by the purser as the living silently looked on. There was relief amongst some and sadness in the face of others. The names of the additional sixty bodies of impressed sailors and low class passengers were never mentioned. That is what Kenneth noticed as he remembered the crew throwing the poor over as soon as they had died. For Kenneth, the calling of names was his reminder. He was not of this ship in spirit but only a member of the body.

After announcing the solemn dead, each of the men were prepared for the board. Then with ceremonial precision, the sailors lifted the corpses four at a time to let them slide away. Four splashes were heard… and four more… and so on, until just one remained.

"Bid them a prayer, Holy Man," Captain Grimm said as the cook pushed Miguel forward.

Kenneth saw a resistance in his friend. A defiant and solid stiffening of Miguel's back warned him that something bad was about to happen. He moved silently away and watched as Miguel lifted his hands to the sky just as Grey Eyes was hoisted to the side railing. "My God!" Miguel shouted into the sky. The bearers held Grey Eyes uncomfortably as Miguel hesitated and turned to the crew who stood with salt stained beards and sweaty frocks to give their intention away. A horrid lot of men by any standard. Near them the captain expected the priest's words to be prophetic, inspiring or comforting in some way. His words were not. "My God, you have given to these men, that which they deserve. Smite the wicked as they relish in the sins of their desire!"

The outburst shocked them all, and Grey Eyes slipped into the sea. Hearing these utterings, a calamity arose that hinted of confusion and Miguel shuffled to the side nimbly, continuing as the crew pursued, "Feed the creatures of the sea with their earthly flesh and let the demons of hell consume their souls!" he shouted as they closed him off from escape. It was madness, and madness consumed the deck of the *Pinnacle* like a flame.

Not understanding the true nature of what was happening Captain Grimm screamed out not to kill Miguel. His mind immediately went to the fouled pork and the mysterious and undoubtedly intentional killing of the queen's guard. Having this traitor alive might allow a trial. It would certainly save his career. The crew moved at Miguel with knives and his voice was feverish, "Do not kill him!" he commanded.

The crew looked to each other with uncertainty and obliged their captain. They did not kill Miguel but they held him and Miguel watched helplessly as the malcontent turned on the first mate and then the captain himself. Lieutenant Brinson had never suspected. The captain was caught unawares as well. Miguel felt the weight of two men who pulled his arms and kicked at the back of his knees. He was at their mercy. Men who despised and cursed his Lord. Men who had risen against their own. "Keep him down and cast the captain over!" the leader of the mutiny shouted.

As they held Miguel, four of the sickly crew struggled with the first mate, and Captain Grimm blocked a jab which sliced open his hand.

"The bodies float!" little Jimmy exclaimed with horror.

The words penetrated the fray. A curse was a terrible thing and the child's terror stifled the killing blows. Everyone's eyes went to the sea. Everyone except the captain who stood and curiously studied Miguel Avaje Fernandez. The momentary distraction had given them both a chance. A single opportunity to fight. The oddity of this circumstance was that Miguel saw an expression of allegiance wash over Captain Grimm, but there was no time to be sure. He hesitated and together the captain and he were soon being prodded to the rear of the ship at knifepoint. They were not dead but they had lost control.

"Ye have passed your curse to the dead!" A man named Ebbs declared.

It was apparent he was the leader of the revolt and Captain Grimm spat at the cur with venom. "And it shall pass to the living as well, Ebbs," Captain Grimm hissed defiantly. Most notably the captain regretted not scuttling the ship when he had the chance and leaving the mutinous crew to a cold death at the bottom of the sea. He was pulled, he was bullied, and he was beaten all the way up the companionway. Around him, was the chaos of mutiny and the men forced his resistant body to the aft rail. He hit the wood bloodied as the mutineers gawked at the white canvas clinging tight to those hapless forms below.

Ebbs was a slender man with a thick red beard and rotten brown teeth. He immediately turned the attention of the crew to Patterson. The blame for such a thing would fall to Kenneth. Although not yet restrained, Kenneth instinctively followed in trace of the commotion and it was he who bungled the burial at sea.

Kenneth, who was now also on the aft deck, stepped backward under the pressure of responsibility. It was a moment, to Captain Grimm's sheer relief, of opportunity. The mutineers became distracted.

"He cursed our brothers!" Ebbs shouted accusingly.

Kenneth replied: "No, I am a dullard and was not told."

Lieutenant Brinson who was also kept alive and forced to the rear of the ship struggled to break free. The first mate was angrier at Kenneth than the mutineers it seemed. He glared at Kenneth and shouted: "Fool! I will kill you myself!"

The men holding both the captain and Miguel loosened their grip to get a better look at what transpired in the water. They saw all of the dead trailing behind the ship. Some floated on their side and others bobbed like sacks of wheat.

"What in God's hell have thee done?" Lieutenant Brinson screamed at Kenneth. Ebbs saw the first mate's anger and he motioned for the men to release Brinson and they did. These sort of men relished a good fight and were glad that Lieutenant Brinson had lost his mind with fury. Lieutenant Brinson shot a glance to Captain Grimm who in turn looked to Miguel and then he attacked Kenneth with all the fierceness he could muster.

Seeing Kenneth fall, the crew chanted, "Kill him!" They circled the fight, enthralled with the first mate's delirious and vicious assault.

Kenneth fell beneath Brinson and saw a black streak of fur out of the corner of his eye. The cat his brother had loved screeched across the deck. It seemed out of place, uncontrolled. He also saw the captain slide free of his restraint and then everything became a blur.

Captain Grimm saw the feline as well and he shouted: "It's a problem, Mister Brinson!" The captain referred to the cat and he referred to Kenneth Patterson and the lack of discipline of the mutinous crew. In the moments that followed, Kenneth realized he should already be dead but he was not. Brinson's hands were light upon his throat. He let his eyes close and his arms lay flat upon the deck and in his mind he felt able.

"See what you have done!" the first mate shouted as Kenneth's moving ceased.

Blackie raised its back in an arch and let out a hiss between stomping feet. "Get it!" Brinson yelled as the cat darted between them. In the confusion the first mate turned away from Kenneth and grabbed a knife.

"Leave the cat be!" Jimmy shouted.

Miguel spun on his heels when his captors reached out for the black streak that whizzed past them. His momentum broke one of the men's arms and he shoved another over the aft rail. The captain fought also and the first mate found his footing. The tide of mutiny was turning in a fray of flailing arms and legs just as Jimmy shouted: "Grey Eyes is alive!"

For a second time, Jimmy's words struck the crew with horror. In the moments that followed, the first mate pressed Ebbs against the aft rail and from the companion way up came a son and his father. It was Robert Lockhart and Noah who leveled their muskets on the mutineers. The remaining crew dared not fight. Instead they moved away from the muskets and the struggle for control was finally over.

What happened next struck them all. Both the sick and the dying now feared for the old sail master as they peered over the aft rail. Miguel took the opportunity to grab Jimmy's hand, and he and Kenneth sped the child away. Miguel spoke out to heaven as he gathered his foundlings, "I am here my God. And I will obey thee," he said as Kenneth and Jimmy listened to him faithfully. As they made their way down to the brig cell, they heard the first mate's words echo off the bulkhead.

"Serpent!" Lieutenant Brinson shouted.

There, at the very back of the ship, all those present witnessed the thing that was until now just a fable. An unbelievable exaggeration that had come to life. Scales and fiery eyes with fins and teeth and a body that dwarfed the imaginings of legend.

"It's the serpent! The terrible serpent!" Lieutenant Brinson shouted. They all watched it dip into the water and their eyes followed the shadow. The animal undulated just below the surface. The long neck touching the floating corpses one by one until finally choosing the last. It was Grey Eyes the serpent fancied. The canvas sheet that showed movement of the squirming soul struggling inside. It drew the beast as the sail master's face appeared for a confirmation of life.

"All bloody hell!" Grey Eyes gasped as his face hit the open air.

"Swim!" the crew shouted.

There was nothing more terrifying for those who witnessed the sinful life of Grey Eyes coming to its end. It was a reminder that any of them might die most horribly. None of the evil doers could remove their gaze from the scene. They were drawn by fear, as if their heads were fixed with iron. They watched, immobile, with heat flashing and hearts racing as Grey Eyes tried to escape. Out came one arm before the splashing began. Then came his cries from out of the water when the serpent shook its head violently. The beast shredded the old sail master, and there was nothing they could— the long neck of a monster.

CHAPTER 17

Where goes
the Mistress

West of Meath and east of the River Shannon the gnats swarmed around two shivering soldiers of the Kildare Brigade. Private Hubert was a proper trooper and Dennis Hill was not. Both men now found themselves on lookout below a full moon after the rains had duly soaked them. Dennis Hill of the hill clan near Tipperary was an oddity among Henry's men. He was neither planter nor soldier but claimed upon his indoctrination to be the finest fighting man to have ever set foot on the Kings County plantation. Indeed, that may have been true for he managed to bludgeon a tinkerer near Fleming. Thusly, Dennis's punishment for marauding was an assignment to the Kildare Brigade. He was now official, paid four farthings a month whether he needed it or not and he looked forward to the luxury of what Hubert called the dreary tents of Colley Town.

Hubert reached up quickly to swat at the flies which clouded his vision and then felt the unpleasantness of Dennis's meaty hand tighten around the back of his neck.

"Don't move!" Dennis said through clenched teeth.

The two of them had crawled through a thicket of briers and thorn bushes upon hearing the thundering horses to their front. "Why are we on our bellies when we should be running toward the men of Radcliffe's army?" Hubert whispered.

"They are not English, you fool," Dennis advised.

Hubert felt a lump form in his throat as he looked more closely at the men on horseback. They carried swords and wore the saffron color of the enemy. "How can it be?" he asked.

"Quiet," Dennis told him.

Hubert did his best to assess the long column of riders and his eyes caught the glimpse of something familiar. Something very, very strange. His first instinct was to yell out and rush the heathens who had taken the mistress. Dennis continued to hold him back and Hubert realized that Emma Colley did not appear distressed.

Dennis saw his partner's arms tense and he pulled at Hubert's back. "Don't... move... you... fool," he hissed in his patently English twang.

Hubert hated being called a fool. He was no fool. The insult compelled him to slap Dennis in the mouth but the compulsion ended quickly. They both pressed into the ground and flattened their bodies against the thorns and thistles as the column of Irish warrior thundered by.

"When I say so, fool, get up and run," Dennis whispered as the last of O'Neill's horsemen passed.

After the rumbling ceased, Hubert and Dennis leapt up from their position. Dennis grabbed his musket. Hubert adjusted his crotch and dusted himself off only to realize he was now alone. "Wait!" he shouted as he picked up his lance and dashed off into the woods. A branch slapped him in the face and he fumbled with his gear. Then upon hearing nothing, not even a bird, Hubert ran.

Dennis arrived to the camp breathless and found the Kildare Brigade scrambling to pack the horses. Something was wrong, or perhaps the cavalry of O'Neill had been spotted by the other outpost. In either case, he found the aura of the men to be daunting. Warrant Officer Blanch in particular, who sat numbly by the fire, appeared utterly desperate. Perhaps they had seen a ghost or maybe the banshee of the forest, Dennis thought. His speech was more a slur than an intelligible formation of thoughts. "D' come!" he shouted.

Henry leapt to his feet upon Dennis's arrival and he too was out of sorts. "Have thee seen them?" he asked frantically.

Dennis could not know that his captain referred to the hideous men of the forest. The memory of a large hairy beast breaking a human leg bone had sunk deep into Henry's mind. Surely, he thought, the O'Neill cavalry were what Henry referred to and so he gave his reply apprehensively and answered," Yes!" The thought of such an overwhelming force coming against the small group of soldiers was all that Dennis could think of. "We must flee, sir!" Dennis added.

The words sent Henry into a tirade. "I told you! I bloody told you!" he shouted to the group.

Instinctively the remnant Kildare Brigade gathered around Dennis and Henry as Hubert found his way to the camp. Henry spoke grimly, "Have I not told you that we saw men who eat the dead?"

Hubert broke the silence that followed the outburst. "Mistress Colley was with them! Mistress Colley was on a horse and laughing! They have taken your wife, sir!" he exclaimed.

Henry's eyes became as wide and white as porcelain saucers. "What?" he asked in confusion of the things he heard.

Dennis was vexed. "There is a whole troop of horsemen, sir. They are O'Neill's men and they are heading north. That is what we saw."

"And Mistress Colley," Hubert added.

The soldiers who listened believed Dennis much more so than they did their captain. Henry's story seemed outlandish and Blanch had said nothing at all since returning. Everyone understood the terror of Ulster. Their comprehension preempted the gut wrenching vision of their families at home. A troop of Irish horsemen should never have been riding freely across the open country of the midlands. It was a fear that overshadowed any delusion.

Hubert continued to Henry's dismay, "She rode beside a fearsome man. A terrible rough looking Irish warrior with a scar across his face."

"Shut your fucking mouth, Hubert!" Dennis yelled.

Henry turned in shock and the soldiers began moving toward their horses. The surviving men of the Kildare Brigade were rattled into action. Men jumped in the saddle ready to die. Men like Annie Beth's husband who had taken on with the soldiers after the crops had been sewn. Thirty of them in all, staring at Private Hubert, and expecting Henry Colley to act.

Suddenly Hubert remembered the whip and lash received by an undisciplined friend who had been beaten for stealing an onion. He also remembered the stocks that crushed the poor resistant farm hand that dared speak ill of the plantation. Henry Colley and Warrant Officer Blanch had done those things. The recollection made him feel small. Stealing an onion was nothing compared to the defamation of the head mistress. "She was taken, sir. Mistress Colley must have been taken by force. That is what I meant," he said apologetically.

Kicking dirt over the fire as he stood, Warrant Officer Blanch asked: "Do we the men of Kildare, go to fight in Meath and give our glory... or do we live?"

Dennis Hill, not yet appointed any rank, gave a further report: "We never made it to see what happened beyond our outpost, but there was a trail of smoke beyond the riders. The savages roam freely with axe and spear and they number several hundred. We have no idea if they even came from Colley Town or if the woman was the head mistress, sir."

Henry's thoughts overwhelmed him. Could it be... Emma? Had the O'Neill army beaten the entire division in Armagh, only to vanquish an isolated plantation with little advantage of land?"

Warrant Officer Blanch spoke out again. "There is no certainty that Hubert is right. It may not be Mistress Colley but we know for sure what is to the south near Shannon Bridge. They are animals!"

Henry turned to Hubert, "Are you mistaken?" he asked.

"I, I no longer believe it was," Hubert replied desperately.

"No, it was not Emma," Henry conceded. "We are too far from home. We go south and will take the heathens on the trail to Colley Town."

❧ ❧ ❧

Colley Town, oh so dear, and yet they were in the bog. Annie Beth held her son Jacob and the child was covered in mud. She stroked his hair; she shed a tear and then Jacob kissed her. "It's ok, mum," he said. The white of his eyes seemed to glow; round and beautiful.

"Aye, my child," she couldn't help but touch him. "It'll be a' right," Annie told him.

Mary was not far away and she too had her sons, and they had eaten from Annie's stash of grain. That was before the horses came. Before the fire and before Annie Beth or Mary understood what was going on. They felt guilty in the bog. It was such a vast place; so easy for them to hide away when the screaming began.

Mary poked her head up as Annie Beth listened. It was silent now.

"They are gone," Annie Beth whispered.

Mary's children were fast asleep with only grass for a blanket.

"It looks terrible," Annie Beth whispered back.

"It sounded terrible," Mary replied with a whimper. The women looked at a black stream of smoke that stretched from the castle to the sky.

"We must go back," Annie Beth said.

"For what? To be put in stocks for stealing?" Mary replied, looking at her children.

"Stay here, Mary. I am going... I have to," Annie said, as she stood to leave.

"And of your son?" Mary asked fearfully.

"If I do not come back you take him and leave," Annie whispered.

❧ ❧ ❧

People did survive in Colley Town and that is what Annie Beth saw after the walk back to main street. John Goodrich was alive. He was digging near a stone pile and the rubble of the ruined church. John stooped and sifted through mounds of ash as she approached. Annie put her hand on John's shoulder and without thinking, her words just came out: "What happened, John?" she asked.

John took a deep breath as if smelling the air. He was shaken and hollow and his silence frightened her.

"Is it Susan?" Annie asked with the certainty that John had endured an unimaginable loss. The crease in his forehead pinched his brow. John wore his leather smock and canvas breaches. Quiet by nature, hardworking and tall, his expression made Annie uncertain. Today he looked older than she had ever remembered.

"John, what happened?" Annie Beth asked vehemently.

John stared off without a reply. He looked toward the shallow hill that inched its way toward the castle. The old stone tower house and water catch that they knew so well. Annie felt relief to see Susan rushing toward them. Susan was kind but as she grew closer there was no kindness in her eyes.

"They burned Vicar Tinsdale in front of the old Bermingham castle!" Susan shouted as she came within earshot.

John grabbed Annie Beth by her arm, "How could thee not know?" he said accusingly.

Annie turned to see Susan already behind her, "Where were you?" Susan demanded.

Annie Beth felt her heart sink with the dreadful things they were asking. She thought of her son and Mary. She wished her husband was here to protect her. The thought of her husband and the sounds she heard over the past two nights was almost too much to bear. First there was screaming and gunfire and then strange singing. Suddenly it struck her. She realized what John was smelling as he covered his nose and stood repulsed. Sweet tainted smoke that reminded her of scorched hair.

Susan's voice was strained, "Where were you, Annie?"

"I was in the fields when they came," Annie said cautiously.

Susan's questioning eyes told Annie she did not believe her.

"I was... I was with Mary and our children," Annie Beth admitted.

Susan frowned, "Everyone was made to watch, Annie. We had to account for everyone and came up five short. You, Mary and the three of your boys. I wanted so badly for John to tell them your family had run off. They would have searched for you. They would have found you. Instead he lied and said that all were present."

"I did not know..." Annie cried, raising her hands to cover her eyes.

"Put your hands down! You wouldn't know that they moved us all to the front of the castle and then beat the men to ensure we told the truth." Susan glanced at her husband with sadness before turning him around and lifting his shirt for Annie Beth to see.

Annie's knees crumpled. John was always a good man and deserved nothing but admiration. It was true that she had not suffered and also that her actions had caused John's torment.

"You should have stood with us," Susan cried. Her voice left no doubt that she no longer trusted Annie Beth. "Where is your son?" Susan's brow raised, "and Mary... where is Mary, your dearest friend?"

Annie Beth fell silent as some of the other women began to walk toward them. She couldn't risk telling. The planters looked possessed.

John reached down into the pile of ash and picked up a single unburned book. It was the *Book of Common Prayer*. "This is all that's left," he said as Annie stood there crying.

Susan grabbed Annie Beth by the arm. "You need to see something and then tell us exactly where Mary and the children are." Annie said no, and Susan yanked her into a trot toward the castle. She resisted and Susan pulled harder, stomping in the mud and crushing the grass. As they approached Annie wondered if Emma Colley could see her. Emma would surely order her into the stocks if she had any knowledge of theft. That fear only added to her dilemma and she quietly wished for Mary to sneak her child away.

As they arrived, Annie turned her eyes away from the huge wooden stake that held the vicar's body. She wanted to look toward the pear trees, instead the smell of him slapped her in the face. It was horrible as Susan pushed her forward, causing her to fall just below the vicars remains. Her gown was now soaked in dew and it began to absorb the ashes floating down like snow. Little bits that gave her dirty garment a purple hue.

"Look," Susan said as she pointed. Annie Beth whimpered. Her whole body shook with the sobs. "Look at his face!" Susan yelled.

"I cannot," Annie cried out before bending over to vomit.

Susan grabbed Annie's hair, "We know... but I did not believe at first. I could not believe that after all that we've been through— you would steal!"

"I am... I am sorry," Annie Beth sobbed.

Susan's countenance changed as she forced Annie to stare at the grizzly sight. The utter repulsiveness of it overtook her. "Do you see?" she said as her voice cracked.

Annie tried to turn away as Susan held her face to the vicar, it was grotesque and she wailed with horror just as all the others had done in the face of such barbarity. Then as Annie accepted her fate, an unadulterated hatred of the wild Irish consumed her to the very core of her soul.

It was Annie's loathing that reminded Susan of everything she did not want to be, and as Annie trembled Susan released her. "Go and get your son."

Annie spoke softly, "I am afraid for him."

Susan's voice softened, "We have work to do here," she paused and reached over to touch her husband, "John will go to get food today and your son will not be harmed."

Annie stood up, her voice still trembled, "I will cut down the vicar and bury him proper," she promised.

"We cannot. The Irish left someone to ensure the vicar remained in place until a message could be delivered to the archbishop. Only Adam Loftus may cut down Vicar Tinsdale. That is what the King of Ulster, Shane O'Neill demanded," Susan warned.

"Why?" Annie asked, noting that Susan called Shane O'Neill a king.

John's voice sounded haunting, "The vicar must hang there, and I have been ordered to go to Dublin. There is nothing else to say," he said dryly.

Susan grabbed Annie's hand and squeezed it, "We cannot cut him down. He will know," she said as she pointed toward the castle. Annie looked and indeed a stranger was approaching. He was not a soldier at all. The man was certainly born of privilege and walked directly toward them. Clean and finely shaven with hair cut neatly and hands that had never seen a plow. He had the powder of a wig.

"Do you have one?" the stranger asked, as if a dead vicar burning on a pole was nothing to be concerned with.

Annie Beth looked down. The man's accent struck her as beautiful and his graceful countenance did not inspire the fear that John had shown.

John answered, "I have found one book and am prepared to take thee to Dublin."

CHAPTER 18

The Bringer

I t was the fourteenth day on the water and a week since the incident. Miguel Avaje Fernandez stood as the rain washed over him and thanked a silent crew. He heard the clanking of oars and watched Jimmy's face as Kenneth rowed the survivors toward shore. They would start anew, and for that, he was thankful. The skiff sat low in the water and Miguel touched his silver cross with thoughts of his own father. He had always wanted a family but never had the opportunity to achieve it. His father had been strictly intent upon business, never one to discuss or teach a young man about the intimacies of a human relationship. For a moment he allowed himself to dally with the thoughts of what might have been, if only his father had allowed him to love. The thought left him empty.

As the Pinnacle tracked toward the heart of London with a rudder fixed in place, Miguel considered what still needed to be done. The treasure which belonged to the Holy Catholic Church was secured in a long boat, and most of his belongings were in that boat as well. Everything he needed was ready. His letters from O'Neill and the Earl of Kildare had been hard to preserve but within his satchel the seals remained unbroken. He also had another vile of poison and understood its toxicity and time of effect. He would need clothes, so he scavenged the captain's cabin for a suitable arrangement and as he brought the last of his necessities topside, the cat darted between his legs. "Blackie," Miguel whispered.

A horn blew from shore, where a lighthouse was visible on the horizon. The amber light penetrated a heavy bank of clouds and then faded with the moonlight. *Dawn will come soon,* he thought as the rain came down divinely to wash away his sin. "Yes, Lord," he said, looking forward to the city of London that loomed ahead with the glow of many fires. "I hear You."

Miguel's eyes caught a flash of lightning as it streaked across the water. He did not feel alone, even without the presence of the living. He thought of Ryan and the innocent. He thought of the girl who was held against her will, as the weight of God's intent rested on his shoulders. As the finals hours of his approach came to an end, the clouds gave way to a purplish red sky and the moon hung like an orb behind him. He picked up his trunk and leather bag and climbed the companionway to stand beneath the aft sail. The waves crashed into the bow, the wind increase the ships speed, and Miguel raised his hands to let the Anglican robe he wore flutter behind him.

"I am here my God! I am here as you have commanded!" His answer came with the shouts of fishermen who called for the great vessel to bring down its sails. Their voices were frantic; the wind began to howl; his heart raced. "Yes, Lord," he cried, "I am the bringer!"

CHAPTER 19

Uncertain Liaisons

The O'Neill's army was heading north. They spoke of the Hill of Tara, and Shane heard the nostalgia of men who failed to understand the season. "We cannot dally in Meath, Barre," he told his general.

"The men want your honor at Tara, your Grace," Barre replied.

"Kildalkey will offer us shelter with those we trust. Shelter and water, Barre. We must not turn east now. Send our lead forward to ensure we will be welcomed and block the road to Armagh.

"Would thee begrudge it?" Barr asked smartly, referring to the ancient rite to declare a king.

Shane mused the notion, "Aye. In the present I would. We don't have time to wait on a mythical stone to sing, while our enemies become emboldened. The old law will stand regardless of where our feet are."

Barr replied, "We should give the men something, don't you think? If not a battle, then they should feel the worth of their sacrifice in custom. You owe it, your Grace."

"Tis what Radcliffe would expect us. He paused and took in the air. "Kildalkey, Barre. That place of small things where no map does betray our purpose."

※ ※ ※

Further down the column of warriors, Emma Colley pulled on her reins and looked at the brute beside her. Throughout the day she had heard the men talking of Tara and tradition. The stories had helped pass their time in the saddle. They were interesting tales and Emma wondered if the warriors truly believed their colorful take on history. If so, giants had built a place called Tara and Saint Patrick climbed Eagle Mountain to cast away demons with a sacred bell.

She wanted to know more. "What is Tara?" she asked Gowl as they rode through the low country of Meath.

Gowl's expression was sour. "What does it matter?" he replied flatly.

"It matters because I hear the men talk," Emma said.

He bit at his mustache and spat out the trimmings. *It matters because I hear you talk*, he thought to himself. She had a look of trouble about her and that was a surety. *This Emma will be like an anchor and I, a ship refused the sea*, he mused as she persisted with her questions. His predicament had been eating at him for most of the day. *How worse could it get,* he wondered.

Emma closed the distance between their horses. "Are thee not talking?" she asked as he tried his best to avoid her gaze. "Come on then, give us some words," she coaxed.

The horses whinnied and the nose of Emma's mare brushed against his leg. "Get thee off," he said gruffly.

"From what I have been told, Tara is where the heathens shed blood instead of honoring God," she prickled, waiting for his reply.

The tension mounted when his horse threw back on him. She was goading. Inquisitively digging into the depth of superstition to meddle with the unknown. He felt the sting of it on his lips as the horses settled into their stride. Glancing over his shoulder, he gave her his answer. "It is the ancient place of inaugural stone. Older than time forgot. Now don't bother me further."

Emma liked that he angered. She had found his weakness and Gowl didn't even realize. She took the sight of him in and saw how raw he was. Failing to heed his warning, Emma moved her horse closer. It seemed to her that everyone talked except for Gowl. She wanted to hear of Tara and also of the wizardly sage who lived in the woods near Dunnamore. A conjurer so powerful that he saw everything between the two worlds. Perhaps such a man could see her future. "Is the wizard a real person?" she asked.

"He is real," Gowl replied.

They rode a bit longer in silence and arrived near the River Boyne and Emma nudged her mare close again. "I will cut your hair when we get to Omagh. I don't like the braids," she told him.

Gowl reached up and pulled his strands across his shoulder and gave her a glance of disapproval. "Cut my hair?" he asked.

"And that filthy beard. Do you not think it could use some soap and a good brushing?" she asked.

He frowned, "There's nothing wrong with it," and then he turned his face from her so she would be denied further examination. She made him feel like a bull being assessed for market. *What did she know?*

"Says you," Emma replied as Gowl kicked out his foot to urge her mare away. She laughed. "Ye'll not be getting close to me until you learn how to bathe. That's a must, Gowl of Tyrone; who smells of the pasture," she told him plainly.

"You should not look at me or speak to me," Gowl said.

"You should not have laid with me then, you shit!"

The thought sank into him. He did not need the old law to tell him his actions were wrong. He had lost his honor and in the deepest part of him, which he did not show, he was shamed and sorry. Had his hatred of the English made him do such things or was he an animal? He was sick with himself and knew, deep inside that he would never be able to make amends. "I am…" he couldn't finish.

She sniffled and sat back high in the saddle to gain her position. "Are thee?" Emma asked him. "Are thee sorry?" she repeated in a voice loud enough to cause his discomfort.

He looked at her, but she couldn't tell.

"I am…"

Emma could not help but think of Henry as she measured him. Henry had spent a lifetime to become a gentlemen undertaker and captain of other lord's men. It was a life of calculated appointments and graces offered that they could ill afford. All done so that their family might rise in station. Gowl, on the other hand, had been humbled for his actions and carried on as if nothing had occurred at all. His crime was altogether going unpunished in her eyes. He had no need for station. He was simple but she did not know if he was truly sorry.

"That village over there," she pointed, "that is English?"

"The pasture is the land of O'Farrell but there be a few English cottages as well, for sure."

His answer pleased her and took away the bitter sting that she felt. Every word he spoke gave her a reassurance. She was committed. She had no choice and he had many. She softened her tone, his countenance began to change. *Yes*, she thought, *that is how I should speak to him*. "Why are they not coming to fight?" She really didn't care about any English farms anymore but she needed his words.

"We are still in Meath but even here the farmers know of O'Neill. They have no flag and their fields are bare. Their sons have been taken away. Did you not see that they have no livestock or stores of grain, lass?"

He called me lass, she thought. "I assumed the farmers fared poorly. Colley Town had an abundance of grain this year. It was sold by the vicar. Perhaps those people need to learn how to care for their crops," Emma replied.

"Are you so blinded? They had grain and cattle until the English army came. The army of the great deceiver whom we call Sussex. That is who took it all." He saw Emma withdraw with his contemptuous words. Women were such fickle creatures.

❧ ❧ ❧

After hours of riding, O'Neill made camp because he had to. Between he and Ulster, an English regiment was moving to the west. The northern army retreated into the hills. A hundred men and horses put on their cloaks of dispersion and blended into the high mustard and weld. The pollen floated up into the air and doused their tunics.

Gowl took a position in the open fields and brought Emma with him. "You bring war so strangely," Emma said, wondering if Henry had spent his days away from her in such freedom. War did not seem so terrible.

He motioned for her to move down into the grass. "Away now, it is time to rest and keep yourself below the hilltop." He was glad she had decided to speak again and Emma was relieved that Gowl began to smile. The hours of silence had not inspired confidence in her decision to leave Colley Town. Her only indication that he would try to please her came when he stopped and begged a bar of soap to wash his beard. He did it in a stream as the other warriors rode past with questioning eyes.

The reality struck Emma that she was beyond any chance of return and her thoughts returned to Henry and also the vicar. Henry was not a bad man, nor had he been a poor husband. Her hands began to tremble and the haunting thoughts of fire and brutality washed over her like hot tar. She could never go back. Not now that the planters had witnessed her setting the vicar ablaze!

"Does this place disturb you?" Gowl asked, seeing that she was deep in that place she feared.

Emma turned to him, "I am a murderer," she whispered.

"Aye, as are we all," Gowl replied.

Her mind drifted back to the Bermingham castle where they had tied the vicar just a few nights before. She could see in her mind's eye all those people she had lived with. The familiar face of Susan Goodrich and the planters of Colley Town all standing silent and afraid. "Would that man have beaten John to death?" Emma asked.

"Aye... he would have. His name is Turlough," Gowl replied without question.

"And did the O'Neill provide the gold he promised for the sacrifice?" she asked.

"Aye," Gowl replied.

"It is so strange and cruel," Emma cried.

Gowl took Emma's hand. She fell into him, allowing her arms to hang on his shoulders like he was a prince that had delivered her away. She knew it was not the truth. Her life was a record of shattered truths. "I will make camp with you," Emma whispered.

"And I shall tell thee another story," Gowl replied in a way that eased her heart. He made her feel young and beautiful. He made her forget. She watched him as he cut down the grass and laid out a position to defend. He held up a pistol, charged it with powder and showed her exactly where it lay.

"Are you not afraid, Gowl?" Emma asked.

"Of what?"

"That Radciffe's army will come and kill us all before I truly get to know you?" she asked.

"Aye, lass," he said before she kissed him.

CHAPTER 20

Poor John

John Goodrich had made the trip to Dublin many times before and today he traveled with a stranger. The man called himself the lord mayor and as far as John was concerned he was both dangerous and cryptic. Supposing the worst, John considered how he might kill the lord mayor. Quietly, when they were well beyond the outskirts of Colley Town would offer his best chance. The thought was all consuming. As they rode without words he then supposed it might be he that was killed, and yet that made no logical sense— John also thought of the gold. It was not a large sum. It was just enough. He envisioned buying a meal with some of that gold. He closed to the lord mayor and looked for a ditch or clump of trees to conceal the body. A dog barked, and to his disliking, the road from Kings County lit up with activity several hundred yards ahead. It was a family from Carbury he had seen before and as they passed, the father and his eldest son struggled to right a turned cart. They looked up expectantly as John continued without offering a hand. The lord mayor kicked his Arabian into a canter. The sudden increase in speed and the questioning eyes from Carbury, broke his delusion. He rode with the enemy. He had been seen, and with dread, O'Neill's warning came rushing back. The dark lord of Ulster might return again, or perhaps he had sent someone to watch John, secretly. That notion was hard to dismiss, so he was trapped in this thing: the taking of the lord mayor to Dublin.

They entered through Ormond Gate. "These people are little different than those of Belfast," the lord mayor told John as they passed market square.

The words put a place and face to him. He was from an English city. "I would not know," John replied. The revelation of such a circumstance caused John's hands to tingle. A traitor who conspired with the wild chieftains of the north.

The lord mayor's voice became pompous, "Would you know if you were hanging from a noose?"

The words struck John with a sense of foreboding. Without reply he followed, thankful that the conversation did not continue. He was a blacksmith by trade and lived in the state of now. A job that might need doing or a family concern he could understand. The lord mayor was something else. He was aloof, meticulous and cunningly articulate.

"Why have you come?" John asked.

"Justice," the lord mayor said piously.

John thought differently as they passed the market and turned on Worbers Street toward the center of the city. Entitlement exuded from this stranger and the consequence of dealing with anyone who was entitled prevailed heavily.

They drifted through Worbers Street without notice and John saw Skinners Row. Several of the planters from Colley Town had worked in the tannery of skinners. They were glad to be free of that place and he understood why. The stench of hides permeated the crowded street with the smell of decay.

"Are you with me, John?" the stranger asked, covering his nose with a kerchief.

John nodded and they passed carts forming an intricate maze of vendors. The noise of horses clicking, people talking and the bustle of trade made it hard for him to put the pieces of the lord mayor's story together. "How much further must we go? Do we have a purpose?" John asked.

The lord mayor replied, "Have you any recollection of what has occurred in Armagh, Galway, or Derry?"

"I have never been to those places," John replied.

"There have been hangings!" the lord mayor answered accusingly. John remained silent as a merchant's cart halted their progress. "They are hanging Catholics and old clan chieftains wherever the name of Her Majesty is exalted. Of course, you are Anglican, so it matters little, I imagine."

"It matters," John said, realizing he had stumbled into a conversation he did not wish to have.

The lord mayor frowned, "Yes… you are right. It matters. It is the northern cities what pay the price of this dispute between Lord Radciffe and the O'Neill Mor. We have not, however, fabricated crimes to kill the Anglicans that meander through our gates."

That hypocrisy struck John as wrong. "No, you just burn them," he replied defensively. This man may be a lord and he may be a mayor but he was neither for John. John's anger caused him to stray. He knew that when a thing like this was begun it would not end with a single death. He had a vision of many people burning. Could be that the archbishop would incinerate the Catholic citizens of Dublin. Dublin was the heart of London and also an Anglican city. "Me thinks the vicar has paid a higher price than required in Ulster," John said bitterly.

"It wouldn't be smart to joust with me, John. Now off with you and find a good hitching place."

John dismounted, tied the horses and returned. They carried on through old town on foot and passed St. Worbers Church to arrive near a place called Center Pub without further discussion. John considered it an odd end to the journey.

"We will sit here and wait," the lord mayor said patiently.

Center Pub was located on Worbers Street, near the Holy Trinity Church of Dublin. It was in essence the communal source of good spirits, where one might partake with the brethren in the sampling of Irish brew. On Sunday, John knew, business was always good. It was a relief for him that that the lord mayor took a table on the patio and paid for two large portions of ale. He took a sip, the lord mayor did not, and from what John could determine, the lord mayor waited impatiently for mass to discharge for some particular reason.

"There are some treasures over there. I have been told that your archbishop has sequestered a specific cross inside." The lord mayor pointed toward Trinity's chapel, "Right over there..."

"Is that why you are here?" John asked. "To see a cross?"

"You'll find out soon enough why I am here," the lord mayor replied curtly.

John held out his hand. "And rightly I should do. Have ya not dragged me into this tangle for the promise of reward?"

The lord mayor smiled teasingly. "Ah yes. You think of the gold. What if you were someone who was entrusted with a very special gift and another who was also trusted stole that thing and later reported to your master that it was you who was the thief. What would you do?" the lord mayor asked.

The taunting frustrated John who thought to turn and walk away. He could enter the church and speak with the archbishop. Perhaps he could even deliver O'Neill's message for himself and then ask a loan of the merchants for grain and provisions. The futility of those thoughts, however, held his feet in place.

"You don't have to answer, John?"

"No, my lord?" John replied.

"And since you cannot answer, I will tell you what you should do. You should take your large body and overburdened mind into that church and smother the life from the liar who took from me. I can see you are a man of action, even if you do not say so."

"I would not, my lord," John replied.

The lord mayor's expression changed to disbelief. "Perhaps. Or perhaps you should concern yourself with a matter much larger than yourself."

"I will not kill anyone," John insisted.

The lord mayor paid little attention to John's reluctance. "The Earl, Conner O'Brien of Thomond took this cross which I seek. It was in route from Galway as an honor to my good city. He paused to receive John's full attention, "The Pope himself was to come to Belfast when it arrived. I have been told it now resides in Christ's Church of the Holy Trinity."

John looked underwhelmed. "How will that benefit the condition of Colley Town? We will surely be doomed regardless of any cross," he replied defiantly.

"Everything, John. You have seen the power of Ulster first hand and I retain the gold that will feed your people. So I see little choice for you. Enter that church and confirm what I know to be true. It could very well mean the end of this terrible war. Or, it could cause O'Neill to continue his advance into Dublin and Spain will surely follow. Do you want a war, John?" the lord mayor asked.

"That does not sound like a bargain to me. To openly run in and give you or O'Neill the right to attack another city. Even if what you say is true, it would take months for Spain to arrive. What I do now has nothing to do with war," John replied.

The lord mayor smiled, "There are ten Spanish ships already docked along the Liffey. Ten! And Radcliffe is reeling to regain any cohesion of his so called coalition of faithful earls."

John wanted to run. They were in a public street. People were everywhere and the lord mayor would most assuredly not want to draw attention if such a thing were so. Even the gold was no longer enough to keep him.

The lord mayor reached out and grabbed his arm. It was the first time he had seemed uncertain. "Wait! I am not playing here. There does not have to be war, John. I despise O'Neill and the other mayors of the chartered cities have made a choice also. A choice beyond Shane O'Neill or Radcliffe. A choice we need you to help us convey to Adam Loftus. If you do not, I will ensure that O'Neill will continue to Dublin and Spain will enter into the trade of our cities. It is a war you can prevent!"

John felt sick and confused, "Why not go yourself? I will never be permitted to speak to the archbishop," he replied.

"No. I cannot enter that place. But I will offer the same choice to the Lord Mayor of Dublin while Radcliffe is without the control of his army. After speaking with the Loftus, we shall visit parliament together. There are others who are ready to take control of this city. But not Loftus. Up until now, he has refused to meet with me for he is truly an Anglican. You, however, he will see. You will be allowed to speak with the archbishop for what you hold."

"I understand nothing," John replied.

The lord mayor held out the charred *Book of Common Prayer.* "It has always been for you, John. Take this through the foyer and then make your way to the altar. You will see the *True Cross* there and then you will hold Adams book above your head."

John felt the sweat trickle down his back, "There are crucifixes in every church and so I am not versed in the difference," he said.

"You will not mistake it," the mayor replied.

"And if it is not there?" John asked.

"It is there, John. So hold your book up high. I wish to see the archbishop here at Center Pub and he must come alone. You make sure that is exactly what happens."

On the great stone staircase leading into Christ Church of the Holy Trinity, John removed his straw hat, wiped the sweat from his brow and dusted off his jacket. In front of him two huge black doors hung open. He could see a number of priests and heard a soft murmur of voices inside. He entered the foyer where an expansive arch rose with intricate stone and walked through the sanctuary below a vaulted ceiling. Once inside, he made his way toward the altar.

"Can we help thee, brother?" a priest asked as John continued reverently with his head held low. The priests had joined for their morning devotions and on either side of the missal, the floor of a wooden choir was being swept by two young lads.

John held the book closely and he also had a knife hidden in his belt. His tone was nervous, "I have come to see the cross." His words hushed the testimony of a plainly suited man standing in front of the pews on the left side of the sanctuary. He realized after speaking that he should have said something else. There could be any number of reasons that a common man would approach the altar. But it was too late, the priest who addressed him gave him an odd expression. Even more disturbing was that the tall man wearing plain cloths turned and walked to the center aisle exactly where John had just been.

It was clear he had errored and the other members of the hall fell silent as they examined him intently. John looked over his shoulder and then back to the suited fellow not realizing that he was in the presence of the archbishop already. Suddenly he wondered what he should do. Should he fall to his knees and feign a deep and meaningful prayer? The suited man said nothing further so John loosened his robe slightly so that the knife's handle might be more easily reached. He took another step toward the missal and began to kneel. There, he could clearly see a sacramental cloth draped over a cross but he could not discern if was the one true cross. As he held the book and prepared to stand he received his answer.

"Take him," the plainly suited man commanded. Then as the sanctuary doors were closed, three of the clergy came so quickly that he did not know whether to run or fight. He did neither and they easily restrained him.

A thunderous voice called out, "He wishes to see, so let him see."

Obediently, two priests removed the sacramental cloth from the stand, and there it was, the silver crucifix displayed under the light of stained glass and candles. It was exactly as he was told and below the cross was an ancient book.

"Who sent thee?" Adam asked, seeming to know already that John intended ill.

"The Lord Mayor of Belfast," John replied meekly. Seeing he was not believed, John said it again. "The Lord Mayor of Belfast... please believe me. I will show you!"

As they pulled at his arms, the book he held went tumbling to the floor.

Adam looked down and his voice became scornful, "There have been lifetimes spent translating that text and you dare burn a sacred copy?"

"I did not burn it. We were attacked by Shane O'Neill, the King of Ulster." His words caused a stir. "He burned our church and vicar! After which I was forced to travel with this terrible man and it was he who threatened and made me do such a thing. Open it, please… I beg you," John pleaded.

Adam picked up his cherished word and gently lifted the brittle cover. The inscription read: *This man's entire family will die if you do not come across the street to the Center Pub.* He raised his eyes slowly to the others, "They are here, brothers," Adam told his clergy.

"It cannot be," an alderman said, knowing that the rumors of Radcliffe's defeat seemed all but impossible. The gossip in the streets was one reason they were meeting. The clergy was to act on England's behalf and counter the prevailing mood of instability within Dublin. People were saying that Lord Radcliffe had deserted the city and O'Neill was coming to take control. It was a subversive movement but one that had good effect in the poorer corners and now it seemed it was true.

Adam closed the book gently and placed it on a pew. "We have not seen Lord Radcliffe return as expected and this book comes from within the Pale. Our council spies have warned us that the chartered cities could side with Spain should a northern army be successful in securing the midlands." Adam replied.

The alderman appeared confused and then waved his hand toward John. "Are they here in the city without our knowledge?"

John, realizing that he had only this one opportunity, spoke out: "Shane O'Neill has an army outside these gates and has already captured Colley Town. This book came from our chapel. Our vicar, God rest his soul, hangs on a stake!"

Adam considered his words and ordered John released. "If the army of Ulster is upon us, we have little choice. One of you must go to Dublin castle and inform the chancellor. He will know what to do about closing our gates and securing this city. I will go see this Lord Mayor of Belfast who dances with our enemy.

"Will you parley?" the alderman asked.

"I am the archbishop, he is the Lord Mayor of Belfast, who apparently has the O'Neill's force and favor. I am sure we will come to an agreement if our Lord Deputy has not been keen enough to secure our great city.

CHAPTER 21

Pinnacle

aving just pissed off the bridge, Thomas Smyth of Westenhanger buttoned his fly and resumed wading through the crowd. Sunshine warmed him and the River Thames cast its iridescent glow of purple and red. It was his second crossing this week, and he was glad to be done with the buggery of Southwark. Atop the bridge, structures heaped in crooked defiance of gravity seven stories high. Above the crawling masses, tenants and tinkerers of the filthy bridge scurried to open windows. Thomas grunted with distaste. It was a fiasco really- the bridge and people who tempted their fate above the water. Business— the business of life had drawn him to cross and it left a queasy sense of unpredictability to the day.

"Is there a pike for another head here?" Horatio asked looking at a vacant impalement that jutted up hungrily from the guard-wall.

Thomas gave a telling glance, "Rumors are that O'Neill will be arriving soon."

"I thought so," Horatio concluded, seeing that someone had taken the liberty to scribble, *Shane O'Neill*, on a wooden board that hung near the bake tower.

They walked a little further and passed the archway of the fishwife and Horatio ducked into a narrow door. "A crumpet, Thomas?" he asked.

Thomas waved his hand, "Off with ye," he said curtly.

"Best this side of Southwark, Thomas," Horatio replied.

Thomas wondered how anyone would dare take food from such a filthy place and declined. "Go, I'll keep William here company," he replied. Horatio nodded appreciatively toward the skull of William Wallace and then departed. *William Wallace traitor to the crown*, the plaque read; and old William's mouth was fixed open as if he shouted for a meal. Still had some teeth though, Thomas thought. "Ye haven't had a crumpet for over two hundred and fifty years, have ye, old boy?" Thomas held his hand to his ear and smiled with his own imaginings, "What?" he asked.

William said nothing.

"Why certainly," Thomas replied. Then he reached out and grabbed the shaft and turned it counterclockwise so that William's skull faced away from the sun. "Is that better old fella?" he asked.

William still said nothing.

It was as it should be, Thomas thought. The bridge was both industrious and medieval. A mantle for the heads of traitors; boiled, tarred and stuck for all to see. *I suppose England has a lot of traitors,* he concluded. There were nearly three hundred skulls upon that bridge. They were his reminder as he looked down on the oil of London spilling out like a rainbow of filth to mottle the water below.

A few moments later and Horatio grabbed his shoulder. "I'm back. Shall we go?"

Upriver from the bridge was London Tower. Downriver, along a four-feet tall seawall, apartments rose up between the docks of Broken Wharf and Black Friars pier. It was his city, not perfect, but within the realm of his reality and Thomas surveyed the barges making their way out to sea with the thought of collecting the appropriate customs. Then as the shimmer of the sunrise struck his eyes, he had to stop and make sure of what he saw.

Thomas pointed as Horatio shielded his face from the sun. "Is that what I think it is?" he asked.

"It is the *Pinnacle*, Thomas," Horatio confirmed.

Their alarm was simultaneous. The ship was at sail and bearing down with speed. It was battered and torn and set true upon a course for Blackfriars! "Look at it, Horatio! Can it be?"

"Not bloody good," Horatio replied with disbelief.

"We'll never make it in time," Thomas said with a fright. The men turned together, pushing their way through the mass of people like salmon struggling against a tide. It was Friday, the market was open to trade, and the noon bell of Westminster had already begun to chime. "Send for Gilford the moment we get there!" Thomas shouted.

Someone slapped Horatio's face. He shoved out an arm, "Aye, Thomas," he replied as he felt the dread that came from Ireland.

❧ ❧ ❧

Ireland in the Midlands

Henry Colley thought of Thomas Smyth, he worried over his wife and saw the structures of Colley Town. His soldiers had fought the beasts near Shannon Bridge. It was an engagement of desperation and yet here he was. They had made it home and the Kildare Brigade limped toward the cottages and castle. It was Percy, the stone mason, who first met them near the bog.

"O'Neill came with his army!" Percy yelled to the beleaguered men.

Henry stopped briefly, his horse reeling, "Where is Emma?" he appeared affright, "did they kill her?"

Each of the soldiers who had survived the encounter at Shannon Bridge bore the wounds of a heated engagement. Warrant Officer Blanch, Private Hubert, and Dennis Hill of Tipperary were among them. Also with them was an emaciated form of skeletal repugnance. The blond specter rode without cloths or shame. Percy had never seen such a thing... his feet trod backward... their horses encroached.

"Did they kill my wife!" Henry shouted.

"Nay sir! Nay sir! Nay sir!" Percy cried. He screamed it out remembering the terrible thing Henry's wife had done. "The Vicar was right! The Mistress is a witch, sir! A bloody evil witch!"

Henry trampled Percy as his horse surged forward under his boot heels. The tradesman fell injured to the side as Henry's soldiers followed. Only the naked man held his charger from bolting and the abomination of his condition was manifested in a fanatical grin. Like a banshee he passed with crisply dried blood and hair fanned out from head to shoulders. He was young. He was hollow. He was hungry.

Annie Beth saw the riders also and took Mary's hand with the sight of them. There were so few who rode back to town. The women searched the soldiers faces in hope to see their husbands, and Annie Beth breathed a sigh of relief. Mary did not. Mary's heart sank to the very depths of her own existence for her husband could not be seen. They gathered up their gowns to run behind the soldiers who headed straight for the stone piles and ashes of the church.

Mary's voice trembled, "He's dead! My man is dead, Annie!"

It was a good day they had thought, before Henry Colley returned. Mary and Annie Beth both said a prayer in the sunshine just moments before. They had found a new hope in Colley Town as the planters welcomed them back and they learned that Emma Colley had gone with the Irish. The women and all of the children had been on their own now for the past two days. They had found food and shared their grain and butter and John was surely to return with meat and flour soon. What they did not expect to see was Henry Colley or any of the men from the Kildare Brigade. For Annie Beth and Mary, the arrival was both a blessing and a curse.

Annie tried vainly to quell her friends fear. Her voice was an indication that she barely believed it herself. "We don't know if he is dead, Mary." As the women approached the riders, they could see the men were not right. They were weak and Captain Henry Colley kept turning in his saddle with confusion. All of the townsfolk came running. The children from the fields, the women from the common stable and Susan Goodrich who longed for her husband John. Their concentration fell to Henry and his men and not to the naked man who cantered behind the mob like an apparition.

Judas watched the women take flight and remembered the wild one who had taken him in the forest. It stirred him and enticed his imaginings as Annie Beth and Mary ran ahead with wide and rolling hips. Were they civilized?

Annie Beth covered her face as silt showered her from the horses. A tan and blue shoulder emerged from the dust. There were several men who had made it back alive but Mary turned with the realization that her husband was truly missing.

"Where is the Mistress!" Henry shouted. He could see they looked at him with broken hearts. They all stared and their arms hung loosely at their sides without the courage to speak. He hated them for it. As he circled and his horse panted, his vision blurred. Sweat and blue sky, the cusp of his trousers and a tree all began to swirl around him. He saw their faces. All of their faces except for Emma's! He did not see his wife! Henry began to topple.

"Grab him," Susan yelled.

Warrant Officer Blanch fell to the ground with a thud, and Hubert slumped in the saddle as his family came rushing toward him. "We need help!" Hubert shouted.

Annie Beth let go of Mary's hand. She dashed forward and caught her husband just as her son came running to her side.

Mary fell to her knees and Judas became excited behind them. The children gawked as he passed through the town toward Bermingham castle. He did not speak, but fondled his hair and smiled wildly as he skirted the commotion of the scene. It was the smell that drew Judas. So unique and powerful that it caused his mouth to water. Naked and alone he rode up the hill as the shouting faded behind him. His thighs chaffed with the bristle of horse hair and he picked up the pace. *The smell*, he thought, *the wonderful smell*.

The image of the wild woman of Longford consumed him. She and her brother Hagan had escaped the battle that liberated his soul, and it made him glad. His horse snorted and tapped the ground as he circled the smoldering corpse of Vicar Tinsdale. Leaning ever closer, stretching, poking with his finger until he could no longer resist, Judas grabbed hold. A piece of the vicar tore off and he shoved it in his mouth and took another. Then he turned with the blackened grizzle on his face and rode back to the men who saved him.

London

Aboard the *Pinnacle*, a sudden jolt threw Miguel's head forward and he felt the impact of the landing, and rushed to free himself. Below the wreckage, a skiff awaited. Would they see him shimmer down a ladder made of rope? He moved quietly, as quickly as he could.

Boats and barges, rowing men and porters all focused on the *Pinnacle*. It was the chaos that cloaked Miguel as he drifted away. He steered himself toward the stony wall where an apartment met the river. The sun was full. The air became filled with commotion and Miguel pulled himself up to enter the city of London. "For Thy Glory, Oh God," Miguel said.

CHAPTER 22

Cheapside

O f all the places in London that a girl might want to be, Cheapside was not one of them. Cheapside was a place of beggars and scurvy looking sailors slinking off into darkened alleys at night. The street bristled with those that wanted, and takers wandered from Church Hill to Black Friars, then back again. It was the ward by the river, not far from the bridge, two crooked blocks above Tame Street.

Miguel had been instructed well on the doings of Cheapside and he blended into the surroundings without any problem at all. He had come to pay a visit to one of Thomas Smyth's establishments. He pounded on the pub door and then pounded some more until finally he broke it down. Inside there was a vile man and he struck him to the ground. He also found the girl from Kintyre. She was unmistakable with her tight locks and pouty face that hinted of the highlands. Her name was Jade McAlister and she was being hunted by some very powerful men. Jade wrapped her arms around his shoulders. "You will be called, Agnes," he whispered in her ear.

Jade thought of her mother and sister named Miah. She remembered how her brother had fled the soldiers and then cowered in thickets before she was taken. Why she had been separated from the others and taken away she still did not know, but the stranger who killed her cruel master seemed to recognize her immediately. Had her family sent him to save her? She wanted for nothing else.

Her months of fosterage had been cruel. She had been taught her place and now she felt a hesitation. If the mistress found her she would surely be punished. Mistress Talles had left no doubt in her mind about running. She would be killed or worse. For Jade, life had gone from being a chieftain's daughter to one of chores throughout every hellish day. At nine years old she had no idea how to make it back home. Not until now. Not until this angel had come to save her. She felt the ripple of his arm and her heart fluttered as he moved toward the door. She hoped in the way a child hopes.

"We must go," he told her. They left quickly and Joshua the sheep man tilted his head their way. Joshua had always watched Jade. He could have helped her, but did not know how.

Miguel held her as they blended into the masses. They traveled through the back alleys so quickly that she knew it was her escape. A blurry rush for life that she added to her memories. *Why was her name to be Agnes? Why had he whispered in her ear?*

They worked their way past Bread Street and on to Hog Street, littered with the slop of the morning swine being driven to meet the butcher. After that she didn't recognize where he was taking her. Dogs alerted the men and women clattered with wooden soles all up and down the cobblestone streets. Faces turned, a finger pointed, and Miguel kept on as if nothing mattered. He slowed only when they approached the wall near the Tower of London. The great moat and stony barrier closed them off from escaping any farther into the city. It was then that the stranger put her down. She hadn't really thought until then. She hadn't noticed how intense his brow was or the look of desperation that revealed his uncertain expression. When he took her within the pub, he had seemed sure. He must have known that she needed to be rescued. Now the cold look in his eyes gave Jade pause and she began to cry.

His voice was heavily accented, "You will walk next to me now," his face was sweaty, "hold my hand and don't let go. Don't talk to anyone. If you do... the bad people will take you," Miguel told her.

Jade looked confused and hurt. She felt the devastating disappointment that he had not come to return her home. At least she did not think so for she had never seen such a man in her town of MacRihanish.

"Be quiet and don't answer any questions," Miguel cautioned.

Jade wiped her eyes and took a deep breath and wondered if she could escape. *I could run and get away, I should try!*

She felt his hand tighten, "Where would you go?" he asked as if reading her every thought.

"Where are you taking me?" she whimpered as the pace of her captors steps lengthened.

"You don't need to be afraid, Agnes."

She had heard that before, the very words of doing as she was told gave her youthful anger a reason to resent this man. She pulled against his hand and then he yanked her to his side and they were off. He was training her. Every bit of independent thought or tug against his grasp quickened their pace until Jade's legs burned and her breath was short.

He pulled her quickly into an alley and stopped. He was looking for something, she could see him searching and then they went off in a different direction until he finally slowed after what seemed like an eternity. They had circled the entire inner city of London. Shops had given way to market fields and cobbled streets turned to earth and back again. Her feet felt as though they were on fire.

"No," he told her, as she pulled at his arm.

As he struggled to hold her, they inadvertently struck a beggar woman carrying a heavy basket of coal. Her grey cloths were tattered and her hands looked dry and cracked. At first, the stranger and the beggar held each other's gaze. Both were surprised and ashamed that they had collided. Then the woman bent down to pick up the bits and Jade saw a crucifix dangle from the woman's smock and her captor's face went pale when he saw it. The woman looked up as his gaze shifted from her to the token of her faith, which now hung openly in the air.

"So sorry," the woman said quickly. Her eyes were like emeralds sparkling from a sooty rock. She smiled briefly to reveal clean white teeth and her dry cracked hand brushed a strand of brown hair away from her face.

"Are you lost, Sister?" Miguel asked.

Jade kept quiet… just as she had been told. The man had called the beggar sister and the woman looked up at him in awe.

"Do not call me that," the woman said.

Miguel bent down and urged Jade to help as they gathered each and every piece of coal that spilled out into the street. "I am lost myself it seems," he said awkwardly. A carriage rambled by and Jade heard the driver crack his whip. The loud noise frightened her.

The woman stood with her basket to straighten her back. "You shan't call me sister. My name is Mary Margaret. Please, call me Mary."

Miguel hesitated and then took Jade's hand. He looked utterly dumbstruck. "We could use your help, Mary," he finally said. Jade heard a hint of softness in his voice. Again he appeared to be the kind one who whispered in her ear.

"What are you looking for?" Mary asked.

Miguel looked down at Jade, considering what to say. "I am looking for St. Bartholomew's and a man named Rodrigo Lopez," he said truthfully after another awkward moment.

"Have you been watching me?" Mary asked cautiously.

Her tone befuddled him, "I only need to know where. You do not have to take us," Miguel replied.

Mary's back hit the brick wall behind her and she nearly dropped the basket a second time, so great was her angst. "Who are you?" she asked fearfully.

"It is very important, Mary. I have just arrived here in London," Miguel said.

"Are you hunting me?" Mary asked.

"You're not hearing me, girl. I am a Catholic priest and have come with urgency. I need to find Rodrigo Lopez," he told her.

Mary saw a desperation in his eyes. She cast a glance toward the child who was now beginning to shiver. The poor thing, she thought. The girl was exhausted. She set her coal basket down and touched Jade's damp cheek and hugged her. Then she stood and threw up her hand to hush his mouth. "Don't ever say that here. Don't ever, ever say you are Catholic—again."

Blackfriars Pier on the River Thames

Thomas Smyth walked the docks of Black Friars pier holding a ledger. "It is a debacle, this is," he told Horatio.

The ships were stacking up all along the river and the *Pinnacle* was lodged in the pilings like a beached whale. "Aye and couldn't have happened at a worst time," Horatio replied.

Thomas cursed and slammed his boot heel into the deck. "She's impaled. How long will it take to get her free?"

Horatio was at a loss. The ship was wasted, full of sickness, death and disease. A black cat had survived the voyage but it darted off and escaped upon the docks. He held a kerchief up to his nose. "She'll be lighter after the offload. How in hell did it find its way back to Blackfriars with a diseased crew? It's a ghost ship I tell ye," he replied dismally.

"Cursed," Thomas mumbled. London was crowding him once again and he had the most overwhelming feeling of remorse. "Ireland," he continued with the memory, "it has brought yet more trouble."

Thomas watched another raft go out. It's black smoke rising as the flames consumed more of the bodies. *There would be a quarantine at Blackfriars and possibly even the upper wards*, he thought. It might be days before things returned to normal.

Horatio turned to him. "Thomas, we have the lord mayor. Don't ye remember?"

Thomas cringed. He wanted to be free of this particular obligation. What would it be like to wield the power of the Lord Mayor of London, he wondered. He had never liked John Lodge, yet felt himself ever more entwined with the man during each of their encounters. Lodge was devout and his sense of piety exuded into all of his transactions. He even called himself a purist. Upon his appointment to mayor, Lodge had insisted that Thomas join the guild of skinners and then expected unreasonable detail in the accounting of furs from Russia. *It would be another one of those meetings*, he thought as his desire for private enterprise evaporated with Horatio's words and the hulk blocking access to his trade.

Horatio followed Thomas out onto the docks like a puppy lapping at his heels. "Thomas," Horatio said as he breezed along the boardwalk, "Lodge has received the charter for two ships. He now has the Prymrose and Mynyon, and seeks a goodly portion of coin from the *Pinnacle*. How will we manage that if you must close Cheap Ward and a quarantine is enforced by the watchmen?"

Thomas replied: "No."

Horatio raised a brow, "No? No, we shall not be transferring the coin or, no we shall not send the lord mayor a warning to close Cheap Ward?"

Thomas did not slow for deliberation. He had other things on his mind. "Even the lord mayor must await the mints accounting. I shall issue him a voucher for the captains of the

Mynyon and Primrose and he can sort the details out with the gold smiths," Thomas replied.

"Thomas, the captain of the Prymrose is fully prepared for sea. He has sat tied in anticipation of this coinage for far too long and the Mynyon departs from Broken Wharf as we speak. To delay the lord mayor's venture would not be wise," Horatio informed him.

Thomas threw a bit of candied paper he had been holding into the water. The sweet fruit was bad and he spit it out. A gull swooped down and grabbed it up and then flew off into the distance. It was gone. He watched the bird until it was nothing but a spec. *Yes, the candy and fruit were gone as if they never were. The only thing left now was the residue on his fingers.* "Have you made an accounting of the chests?" Thomas asked, ignoring his aide's concern.

"There are some discrepancies with the captain's log and the actual number of chests. It appears that there are actually more chests of silver than the captain reported in his inventory," Horatio replied.

Thomas heard a hunger in Horatio's tone. He tried to hide his thoughts, for this was not the first captain whom he knew to under account the queen's inventory. It was an arrangement that served him well until his catastrophic mistake of trusting Captain Grimm. "No, you shall not concern yourself Horatio. The captain and all the crew are dead so we will never know if a mistake was made or who made it. Let us be glad that the treasure remains intact and be grateful for the increase. As for Lodge, at dinner tonight, I will convey our greatest regret that he must wait until this can be sorted."

"Do you think that wise?" Horatio asked.

Thomas sounded tired, "The lord mayor has many resources. If he wants the *Primrose* put out, he may borrow from his Russian friend George Gubko. They seem to have quite a bit in common."

Horatio saw an opportunity he simply could not resist, and as far as he was concerned, it was within his rights to question. "No, Thomas. I think I must involve myself," he said stubbornly.

Thomas stepped back, wondering at what point Horatio had found his courage. "Have thee grown a pair?" he asked sarcastically.

"Aye, two big hairy balls in fact, but the matter remains unchanged. We should investigate." Horatio watched Thomas's expression hoping to see him flinch. Thomas remained cool, calculating, and stoic. It immediately put Horatio off and left him wondering if Thomas had finally made a mistake.

Thomas turned toward the offices, "Come with me inside. I don't wish to talk about this in the open." They walked to the customs office overlooking bank side market before another word was spoken. The silence was unnerving and when they arrived, Horatio finally saw Thomas break. "Get out. All of you," he told his workers. Thomas's crew left quickly and Horatio suddenly felt it was he who had been mistaken. The customs office was a place of order. A place where everything depended upon trust. Would Thomas trust him? He looked around to see a drawer left open, a lantern spilling off some oil and papers everywhere. Suddenly he was not so sure. The two men walked over and peered out the window through a yellowed glass infused with lead. The *Pinnacle* appeared as heavy and worn as Horatio's burdens and the efforts on the ship were not going well.

As Horatio stood there, Thomas removed the lord mayor's records from the drawer and made a quick note before handing him the inventory. "See that the chests get delivered to the carriage guard and then be back here tomorrow. You may divert the appropriate coinage to the captain of the Prymrose."

Horatio looked puzzled, "So we will pay him now?"

Thomas slammed his hand on the desk. "Pay the damned mayor or pay the captain! I care not!"

"Aye, sir," Horatio replied skeptically.

"And before you do, put a guard on that ship and shoot any porters who try to come off. In fact, put guards on the tugs as well and keep the torches lit at night," Thomas said bitterly.

Horatio suddenly knew he had struck the wrong chord with Thomas. It wasn't the reaction he had hoped for. "Our porters, sir? Some of those men have wives and children."

"Are thee daft?" Thomas asked, looking at Horatio with discernment.

Horatio's face went pale, his voice betraying his apprehension, "They are our men, sir."

"They have been exposed! Would you have the pox fester in summer? Have the porters finish burning the bodies and spend the next ten days in quarantine. Their families should be thanking me!"

The thought of what Thomas Smyth had just told him turned Horatio Philpot's stomach. "I will do this thing, sir. So help me God, I will… but it will cost."

"You get a stipend of twenty pound per annum. Were thee not just paid?" Thomas asked resentfully.

"Twenty pounds is a meager sum. I have been watching you and your ledger is thorough but the chests from other ships appear to have required fewer porters at the mint than they did during offload. Can you explain that?" Horatio asked.

Thomas reeled back as if the room was closing in on him. He never expected this challenge from Horatio. Horatio had been nothing before he had given him employment: nothing at all. "If you have an accusation to make, I would rather you make it directly. You see and count the same coin as I."

"I don't know how or why the treasury chests are off. Certainly none of the records appear out of order, but the silver smiths have been complaining of a poor quality as of late. I find these circumstances dubious. I get paid to investigate the dubious. Do I not?"

"Are thee now an alchemist, Mister Philpot?" Thomas asked defensively.

"No. I am a man of little knowledge of fine metal, so you need not worry on my account. I make no accusation; albeit, if there is business to record, that business should benefit us both."

Thomas was flabbergasted. It appeared that he had underestimated the brittle little man and his payroll would become very costly. He had those that served him and a wife of position and yet London's air was stale and the bread was now sullied with grease. Everyone wanted into his pocket. After a moment of dire consideration, he gave his answer halfheartedly. "Your discretion will be rewarded, Mister Philpot."

Later, as Thomas left his office, in the crowded bankside market, his man named Gilford waited for him on Tames Street. *Yet another of my thugs, and the chief administrator of Cheap*

Ward has his tentacles in everything from my market shares to the merchandise, he thought as Gilford approached.

Gilford was a tall slender person with eccentric taste. He fancied hats. All kinds of hats, and today, Thomas saw Gilford wore a black round top with an upturned brim.

"We have a problem at the pub on New Gate Street, Thomas," Gilford claimed.

"You look ridiculous in that garb. Must you dress yourself like the fool?" Thomas said dryly.

Gilford snugged his finger around the felt in good fashion, "I have no idea what you mean. Will ye hear me or will ye wank off in that fancy carriage of yours?" he asked pretentiously.

Thomas was not amused. "I am bound for Westenhanger and have an engagement with the lord mayor. You do understand the lord mayor is quite concerned at the moment? Can you not handle the rent for a single pub?" he asked.

"It is not the rent that's the problem, Thomas. Your tenant has been murdered and his wife and two daughters are refusing to leave. The woman is a demanding bitch. I'll tell ye plainly that she has already stabbed one of my lads who tried to evict her."

"I have no time for this, Gilford. Take the rent or remove the tenant. That is a simple thing and within the law," Thomas replied.

"She is holding a hostage and says she will burn your pub to the ground before another person steps foot through her door," Gilford waited for a response but seeing Thomas delay, he continued, "unless it is you, sir. I should have said."

Thomas clenched his fists, "Is that a gold tooth in your face?" he asked incredulously.

"Do you like it?" Gilford asked, revealing its shine with a broad and vexing smile.

"I hate it. I have told you not to make a spectacle of yourself but you don't listen."

Gilford went silent. A single gold tooth was nothing to be concerned with.

"What in bloody hell is wrong with this city today!" Thomas exclaimed as he motioned for his coachman who polished his cherry wood cab. The man was taking too much time with Thomas's fine new carriage. After some thought, he asked: "What is the harpy's name?"

"Mistress Talles," Gilford replied.

"It was Osbert Talles that was killed?" Thomas asked, finally understanding which pub Gilford had meant.

"Aye sir. I have had our men ask around and the sheep man, Joshua Tinkle said a stranger was poking about the pub and asking questions. A Spaniard with strange looking markings on his wrists and he asked about the girl."

Thomas suddenly cared very much about this news. It could not be a coincidence. "The girl has gone missing?" he asked praying the answer would be no.

"She has," Gilford replied.

"A Spaniard?"

"Aye," Gilford confirmed.

A few moments later they were off together and Thomas's mind drifted back to his other worries as they rattled down the crowded street. He had been told of a Spaniard when assessing his plantation in the midlands. Henry Colley's family was attacked by a Spanish sailor who they had rescued from sea and later the same man had been seen by Henry on a road near

Geashill. *The sailor with the strange tattoos who was also the priest...* Henry had said. *Was he mad to think it could be?*

Elizabeth

Hampton Palace sat in the ward of Richmond surrounded by hardwood forests, dappled with pine trees and ferns. It was tall and beautiful, fragrant of lilies. An integral part of London sitting a good distance from the inner city, Hampton nestled near the River Thames. It was the queen's favorite place.

Elizabeth could not sleep and sat in her privy chambers holding the weight of her burden in a single letter. Thought's haunted her as she pondered the nature of man. The hungry animals that might run or jump in the fight against the coming of her light. Tomorrow she wished to see a stag while riding horses and forget that the wild of Ireland had risen against her. The wild of men, she supposed could not be avoided. Men who wanted to kill her. The rain beat at her windows with a wind that could easily obscure her enemies hiding outside the walls.

Elizabeth sluffed off a blanket and then walked over to take a porcelain cup of tea. She lit candles and rubbed her hands meekly. Wanting more, always needing more, she looked down at the fireplace. She took a sip... hesitated... thought. The tea was cold. She slid off her chair and onto her knees to blow. The ash released a puff of smoke that caused her to blink and cover her face. She felt helpless. She felt alone. Outside, the storm gusted and brought the smoke. It was if the wind itself sought to smite out her life with toxic fumes.

A guard alerted. The yeomen had been posted by her gentleman usher. Robert Dudley, the Lord of Leinster and her friend insisted that only capable and loyal guards protect her. They had selected both her huntsmen and her personal guards together, so why did she fear?

With an anxious mood, Elizabeth stoked the log and hoped for privacy as the smoke seeped into the interior brick and began to warm the slew. *Tis too much for want of warmth?* She struggled to lift a log so that the air might achieve a flame. For thirty minutes the queen dirtied herself to get what she needed. She did it privately as was her way when she did something she should not.

Ah, there it tis. She dusted herself off, picked up the letter and sat in front of a growing fire. She had succeeded in a small thing. A brief moment of satisfaction overcame her and then the wind crashed her window open. Cold wet wind and the tea splattered on the floor. "Be gone!" she screamed out into the night.

Hearing Her Majesty's cry the guard broke from custom and came running to her side. "Tis nothing," she said as he closed her window.

"It is secure, my Queen." he replied reverently.

She did not answer. He could not know what lay outside her walls or the magnitude of those who plotted against her. *Never safe! I will never be safe*, she thought.

Outside her room and down the hall of the privy bedchamber six trusted maids slept in the night. *Where are my ladies?* She wondered. Now that her thoughts had been interrupted she wanted someone to come to her, but like many things in the life of a queen, what one wanted and what one received were not always the same. She watched as the fire grew and began to feel hot. *I have a flame, and now I am ablaze, but how could it matter?* Alone in the room once again, Elizabeth took the broom and poker and put her bed chamber back in order.

She sat down to read in a plush royal chair that dwarfed her slender body. "My dearest Queen and cousin," she read out loud. From the hand of her Lord Deputy of Ireland, Thomas Radciffe, came a clear message. "Sussex, thy crafty bastard, what shall we do now?" His words gave her hope but also a solemn understanding that a larger conflict was inevitable. The Lord Deputy painted a bleak picture and to help convey his concerns, he had sent the Earl of Ormond, Thomas Butler to her court.

Thomas was a handsome man. She remembered him fondly from childhood. Soft spoken, elegant and noble: a better man she could not imagine. What this war would do to England she did not know. What it might cost the Earl of Ormond she could scarcely imagine. Her handsome earl with his black hair and armor would benefit her more upon the field of battle, but his presence meant everything to her. Her mind wandered briefly, *what a scandal would he bestow upon England, if she dared to entertain him? What would her maids do if they found him sleeping in her bed?* She tried with all her power to envision him clearly. Anything to dislodge her untenable feeling of loneliness in a house filled to capacity. She thought of his smile, his hand, his touch. That is most likely what troubled her most, but yet she was unsure.

As the fire died down, the storm outside picked up and sucked her breath away just like the northern chieftain who fought against her. It was a betrayal! She threw the letter into the fire and stood dizzying with the fear that her enemies were somehow already waiting in the woods. Having crossed the expanse of an Irish sea to fester and nest in her forest. Thomas Butler was not enough to sway that fear. She heard the windows rattle and saw the candles shake with thunder. Like invisible hands that closed all around her body, she felt the demons coming.

"God's Wounds!" Elizabeth shouted in her rage of Lord Radcliffe's report. She ran to the window before the guard could come and threw it open to shout out into the night: "Come then O'Neill to England! Come and deal with me!"

Dungannon Castle, Ulster

In the Castle of Dungannon, Emma closed her eyes and focused on the sound of harps and fiddles. So much and so little was familiar. They had arrived to Dungannon and then joined the festivities within the stone walls of a fortress. They were greeted as victorious and the castle had been set for a king. A diversity of people in assorted dress came bristling in and it reminded Emma of the Kilkenny Castle and the Earl of Kildare. She had feasted once in Kildare and that time where she once thought herself entitled came closing down around her like a terrible dream. It was at that very feast that Earl Fitzgerald had accused her of witchcraft. Henry had argued against the charge with anyone who would listen but she was ordered to remain a hostage in her own home. That was then, she thought, and this was now. These people were different and did not know what she had done. She took a breath and then opened her eyes as in hopes that her past would go away. Gowl was with her. He was loud and strong and puffed out his chest with the sport of showing his courage. Emma cringed as men lined up to take Gowl's challenge.

"Ye be the man of a fishwife!" someone shouted. A cheer arose and then a bout of laughter followed as Gowl squared his shoulders and prepared to be punished with another gut wrenching whack from a hard oak staff.

"Bugger off you whore mongering fool!" Gowl shouted back.

A second later Emma heard the swoosh and her man set his feet to take the force with a determination that Emma found remarkable. "Thank you, my lord. May I have another!" Gowl shouted.

The mood was intoxicating and Emma bit her lip as Gowl gently pushed her behind him. He tensed, raised his hand to signify he was ready and then Shane O'Neill stepped forward.

"I will bust your gut like a plucked goose, ya bloated cur!" Shane shouted before Emma heard the undeniable snap of O'Neill's effort.

Gowl took the brunt of O'Neill's force without flinching and smiled at his lord for doubting his strength. "There be no O'Neill, O'Hagen or McCarty that will ever bend my knee or cause me to quake," he shouted triumphantly.

There was admiration in the warriors' eyes who surrounded them and also humor. "That was not what ye whimpered with your cock stripped bare in the midlands," another chimed, to incite more laughter and drinking. Emma was appalled at the rough language and mocking. In England such a thing would be seen as undignified. Gowl made no issue of the offense but rather seemed to like it. She calmed, thought to keep her composure and pushed the indignity aside. She would not be lead here in this castle by a man. She had made that promise to herself the moment her feet left the soil of Colley Town. Never again would she allow the failings of others to bring out the worst in her.

"Enough! Shane exclaimed with pride. "Gowl has redeemed himself. Far be it for his withered member to ever be seen by our kinsmen again. It is time for feasting."

Gowl turned to Emma triumphantly and she offered only her disapproval. His words gave her pause: "There are green hills where my mother's house is and I will wager that once you lay with me in that grass, you will forget all about that cottage I promised."

Emma turned up her nose pretentiously, to feign her dislike. On the outside she appeared of stone but within, she could not deny that there were things about Gowl that impressed her. She allowed him to take her hand as the men of Dungannon sloshed their pewter tankards soaking them both with a clank of Irish brew. Her mind swilled with the aroma of malted barley, intoxicating smoke and the dusk and musk of men. A moment later she found her feet being swept off the floor as Gowl hugged her and placed her safely near a table. She stayed there at that table for a bit and watched as others entered the festivities. Her attention fell to the old one who dragged his cane pole creaking across the floor. She wondered, no, she wanted the old man to be a wizard. Since being accused of witchcraft she had wondered if magic truly existed, even if she did not possess it.

The ceiling of the hall was vaulted and all the torches of Dungannon Castle flickered when Farleigh made his entrance. Here it seemed that magic was embraced and Shane was quick to recognize the old man. "Farleigh... old sage. Fare tell that Brehon shall live forever."

Farleigh's crooked hands gripped his staff and he planted both feet squarely. Emma could hear but could not understand all that was said as the room became quiet. After Shane's greeting, Farleigh scanned the faces of the gathering with clear blue eyes. He had ribbons of white hair and smiled with the gape of his blackness. With a nod of approval his aged voice rattled off a snippet of praise: "Be it Brehon and the law of the fathers, which liv-eth forever!"

A cheer arose from the men and then a young boy whom Emma believed to be as fine a looking lad as she had ever seen, confidently entered the hall behind Farleigh and stopped to turn to the old wizard for acceptance. He was dressed in nickers and an English doublet. "And will the Barron of Dungannon be well received in the old law?" the lad asked.

Farleigh looked down on the little man without speaking. It seemed to him he had little choice in the matter. England had recognized the child and not his pupil, Shane, when Con had died. With Irish hands, England had planted a seed. It was not the child's fault, and Farleigh knew that, so rather than reply, he took his cap off and made a feeble bow.

Shane turned happily to his nephew, "Lord Brian, the Barron of Dungannon and perhaps a chieftain of legend. You are the blood of your people. It is for you that I come directly to Dungannon to share this victory."

The lad beamed with Shane's words and he took his uncle's hand to walk to the head of the table. It seemed odd to Emma that the child did not understand that Shane had attacked the very country which titled him a Barron. He sat there in the center of things alone and without company. Emma felt a loneliness in the child's heart. She could see that he so dearly wished to be loved but did not see that he was truly the Barron of Dungannon.

Farleigh looked at Shane skeptically, when the latter returned to him to offer the old sage a hand. "Get ya filthy mitts off me auld bones, ya fool!"

Emma understood Shane's reply and it intrigued her. "Have thee not dwelt stooped down under the tree for a century? How well will my hands serve you for another."

So there was magic in this land, Emma thought. So many questions she had that even her questions had questions of their own. Platters of meat lined the long oak table and soon women came out to serve. One of the women, who later sat near Shane O'Neill at the head table, was beautiful. Gowl said her name was Katherine.

Those present by clan or by association, paid homage to O'Neill as well as the beautiful Katherine. It was a custom to honor the king, Emma presumed. There were so many people present to honor Shane that they took breaks to eat and make merry. After one of the bouts of toasting and food, it was Gowl O' Hagan's turn. He struggled to stand.

"Gowl O'Hagen and this woman," he pointed, "I pledge one tenth of the cows that survive till winter!"

Emma felt utterly slighted and plucked awkwardly at a platter of robin eggs. He could have at least said her name.

"Bring her here, Gowl," Katherine said.

Katherine's response was something Emma had not considered and to her nervousness, Gowl took her hand and delivered her. More disturbing than her nervousness was that Gowl waited for a quick nod of Katherine's head and left her there! He left her standing alone. She bowed her head low. At the same instant of her deference, the boasting and toasting began again. Katherine joined in and so she remained bowed for an uncomfortable period and noticed a chain attached to Katherine's right leg. It didn't look heavy. Apparently the chain was made of tin thread which was clearly visible over her elegant shoe. It was a chain none the less. Emma's eyes traced the tether up to the velour of a bonny green dress and from there it disappeared from sight.

She felt a hand on her shoulder and looked up. "Stand, woman. I am not the queen but Katherine, daughter of Hector the Great and a prisoner to the O'Neill."

"To the prisoner!" Shane shouted for all to hear, raising his glass with apparent and open affection. The entire hall let out a bellow and Katherine smiled cautiously as Shane stood to mingle and feast. Emma remained perfectly still. Unknowing, unbelieving.

"Am I a prisoner?" she asked quietly.

Katherine let out a wild laugh and fanned her face. "I believe you are. And you are called?" she asked.

The question struck Emma sadly, "Emma... Emma Colley," she said as the room began to swirl.

"I do not know of Colley. Is it an English house?" Katherine asked.

It did not seem real or civilized to talk openly of her husband or his house. He was not a bad man... but he had not returned. One of the very men in this room might have killed him for all Emma knew. "It is a common name," Emma replied meekly. The words set hard upon her heart for she saw that Katherine was more than an Irish lass of the field. Emma knew that she would never be her equal.

"I have been told you had a husband," Katherine said.

Emma felt a sinking in her heart. She truly had no idea if Henry was dead or alive and had thought that all these pressures would have been left behind. *How could it matter? How could any of it matter?* "I was taken by the man named Gowl in my own castle. If my husband is alive, he would surely despise me."

"Do ye know that he would?" Katherine asked.

The hall seemed so loud around her. She wanted to leave her life regardless of the war, or God, or even the memory of Agnes. She wanted to be free and yet she told Katherine the truth, "I do not know for certain."

Katherine let out another laugh. She pursed her lips and throttled her hips and Emma stood back aghast. "Aye, it matters not. Do it," Katherine said provocatively.

"Am I being mocked?" Emma whispered.

Katherine settled herself, "Not at all. It be finer to be an auld Irish whore than an English bride on any day." Katherine sat up whimsically and put an elbow to the table with a devilish grin. "I should know, my fair lady, for I am one myself." Her voice trailed off with a twang that led her gaze to Shane O'Neill. When she turned, Katherine motioned to the women who had put down their platters of food and now found themselves falling into the laps of very friendly men. "They do not treat us badly but I pray your husband does not suffer as does mine," she said.

"I do not understand?" Emma replied, not knowing whether to laugh or cry.

"Come now…" Katherine said seeing the ale take effect of her guest.

Emma heard felt the floor begin to rumble as the men drummed the tables. The men began shouting as a maid's tit flopped out, and Shane O'Neill bent down to kiss it. It was more than she could handle. She did not want to be a prisoner.

"Sit over there and please him," Katherine said, pointing to the chair next to Gowl.

"You don't understand. I am a proper lady and Gowl has been pledged to my virtue," Emma replied.

Katherine shook her head and lifted her voice so that Emma and all could hear, "Until your husband has been proven to be adulterous or dead, Gowl will not be allowed to marry you. If you have a child with him, he will be required to care for you but when that child no longer needs your breast, he may cast you out. You should please him, Emma of Colley."

Emma flushed in the realization that Katherine knew everything that could be known about her. She felt her old feelings coming back, the feelings she could not control. "What did they do to your husband?" Emma asked as loudly as she dared.

Katherine looked around the room. Suddenly she felt less festive and her legs tightened as she sat and crossed her knee. "My husband is caged at the front gate, and like you, I cannot be wed." She smiled at Emma's courage and saw that she would be genuinely met. "Good for you, Emma," Katherine replied. And then she asked: "Do you want your husband caged?"

"No," Emma replied.

"You will see mine at the front gate and when you do, you may give him your body. It might do the auld geezer some good."

Hampton Court, England

Hampton court was flooded with the aroma of hot spiced cider and bacon. The bakers of Henry's kitchen had been cooking since dawn. The wonders of the castle ingratiated the elite as a string of servants hustled the meals from kitchen to court. Their work would be an all-day affair and the ambassadors of Spain ate first with delegates of Portugal who befogged the condition of France. Outside, carriages arrived in a procession from Molesey to bring together the royal household. In the upper privy room, along a polished cherry wood table, Elizabeth's council met to discuss the condition of state. William Cecil, Thomas Gresham, and Robert Dudley were among her most trusted few. As they waited, they spoke of Spain's embargo of Antrim, the affairs of Calais, and the tension that brewed in Ulster.

The privy council stood as a courtier announced Queen Elizabeth, who promptly strolled in with magnificence beneath a wide carriage and buxom blue gown.

"My lords, may God find thee well," she said formally. Her favorite, the Earl of Leinster, Robert Dudley, took the place of her gentleman usher and gently, reverently, pushed her seat to table. The hardwood floor caught the iron clapped feet of her chair and made a scuffing sound that interrupted her cumbersome silence. There was a seriousness in her posture, straight and firm. They waited for her dutifully, in the stillness of Her Majesty's grace.

"Rumors..." Elizabeth began as if everyone in her presence understood what she meant. William Cecil, prepared mentally to give his report as she continued with a glance of utter dissatisfaction, "I hear the war with Shane O'Neill does not progress for the benefit of our people."

The council turned one to another with wide eyes and humble awe. They had bad news but had yet to give it to her and wondered who exactly had informed their queen. Lord Burghley, also known by his God given name as William Cecil, cleared his throat. The other members said nothing.

"Lord Burghley, pray tell?" Elizabeth asked expectantly.

William softened his face, and refocused his voice to suit her, "My Queen, it is true we have unsubstantiated reports that the army has been stalled at the River Boyne. We do not however have accurate and timely communications with Sussex to know why."

"Balls!" Elizabeth interrupted with a slap of her wrist.

The room of men stiffened, William continued artfully as if her outburst was a pleasure. He was clear voiced and even keeled, "It seems there has been little success with correspondence received from Armagh..." he paused, made a regretful sigh and continued with notable concentration, "correspondence which can be depended upon... at the very least."

"And that is somehow a reason to make your judgement?" Elizabeth asked.

Judgement, William thought, *I haven't even finished speaking.* He looked at his fellows and then to her. "The council has met daily on this matter while you have been ill. We seek to put an end to the Lord Deputy's..." he cast a glance about and continued, "unending and unpredictable campaign. And..."

Elizabeth interrupted: "You will refer to him as Sussex! Lord Deputy is merely a position and not the title I afford him!"

William balked, "Of course, Majesty," he replied. Seeing that she had finished the drama of her intent, he continued: "A legion of post riders being lodged at Liverpool will be ferried between the Isle of Man and the city of Belfast. We will use these riders to deal with the mayors of the other cities directly. The mayor's will then close the gates of trade to both Sussex and O'Neill until a peace can be achieved."

"You do not find sufficient enough communications to provide us a victory, Lord Burghley, but instead seek to undermine the commander on the field?" Elizabeth asked.

William looked to Francis Bacon and then to the others to ensure they did not recant, "No. Not undermine... but protect. A victory cannot be had."

Elizabeth countered: "No? No is not the answer, Lord Burghley.

"My Queen, Sussex has garnered the support of Antrim and has made a pact with a notorious traitor: Sorely Boy of the Scott's. He has also asked for additional troops and has neither informed nor succeeded in delivering any positive results. Our concern is with the trade and the tax which we must now ensure comes swiftly due to Sussex's folly."

Elizabeth did not endear the resistance of her council. "Tell us then, Lord Burghley. How does my cousin, who is encumbered with battle, find the opportunity to get on a ship to retreat to Dublin without sending you more detail? I have faith in Sussex and have sent him an aide to assist in your understanding of what is going on in Ulster and Connaught. Have you attempted to communicate with Ralph Lane?"

William replied: "Ralph Lane has sent somewhat conflicting reports. In one, he has stated his firm convictions that the army will secure Ulster before winter. In another letter he reports that the Ormond Brigade sent a fury of arrows into our own men, thus allowing O'Neill to advance into Meath and Kings County."

Elizabeth slammed her fist into the cherry wood table. "O'Neill in Kings County! O'Neill sixty miles into the heart of the Pale!"

The room festered with unrest. "We do not know if O'Neill has remained in the Pale. Further investigation needs to occur. Perhaps our best bet is to query Lord Butler. He was at the battle and arrived to court only yesterday. Your cousin, my Queen, has not been forthright."

Elizabeth felt trapped. If they were correct, she could lose Ireland and then Spain would tighten the noose around her. "I would have Admiral Hackett's opinion on the shipping and security of this correspondence," Elizabeth said with resignation.

"We have sought his advice. Lord Hackett has effectively provided a blockade of Belfast, and he has endorsed a privateer to secure the royal correspondence and articles of war."

Elizabeth looked utterly frustrated, so much so that the powder on her cheeks turned red with her fury, "A privateer? The wealth of conquest secured through a privateer?"

"My Queen, it is a matter of speed that is of the most import. Admiral Hackett has trust in this privateer. He has used the captain to ferry war materials before and the ship known as the *Abigail II* has proved to be the fastest vessel at our disposal. You will know the sail captain as Benjamin Roderick. He is the one whom your own charter was issued six months past to patrol west of Connaught against the pirates of the Upper MacWilliam. Since receiving his charter, Captain Roderick has sunk several vessels off of the western Ire'. His service has brought a goodly portion of gold to the crown and so every confidence has been given him."

She took a moment to ponder what her council had already thought through. "What say you, Thomas," Elizabeth asked gravely.

Thomas Gresham found his own words troubling, "This war is more about timing and finance, my Queen. At present, we cannot sustain a prolonged encounter if the army you have sent is not sufficient for the Lord Deputy."

"Sussex," Elizabeth corrected.

"Yes, M' Queen, Sussex," Thomas said with a bow of his head.

"Will O'Neill have control of all of Ireland before this agreement with the lord mayors has comes to pass?" Elizabeth asked.

Thomas looked doubtful, "It is possible, if Connaught unites and Spain provides assistance against us."

Elizabeth sat a moment and closed her eyes, took a breath in reflection and opened them with purpose. "I want you to use every resource you have to explore loans from the banks of Antwerp. We may have no choice but to send more men and more men will require gold bullion that I do not have." The queen then turned to William Cecil, "If my recollection is accurate, I signed the charter for the *Abigail II* so that Connaught could be pacified and placed in the hands of Connor O'Brien, Earl of Thomond. Has that not been achieved?"

William replied, "Connaught has been decimated, but O'Brien did not defeat MacWilliam and a fleet of Irish ships remains protected in the wild north of Galway."

"Right. Another failure. We have dumped our resources into Connaught and the MacWilliam Lochtar, an old and senile man I will remind you, sheds our war effort like water off a tight tarp. The same goes for O'Neill in Ulster! How has Shane O'Neill managed so successfully to thwart your efforts?"

Lord Bacon answered: "We believe that O'Neill has anticipated both your victory and defeat. Thusly he crafts his strategy concerning England in advance of either outcome. In doing so, he can quickly provide this court and his allies, with information to best serve his purposes. He is also actively engaging in both combat and the turmoil that the Roman Catholics have incited."

"And have we not done the same?" Elizabeth asked.

William replied: "Our communication to Sussex must be precise and timely. That is the disadvantage of having the burden of discernment. Sussex understands this and should have made the appropriate liaisons."

"From what you tell me now, we have been outdone. How will that sit with the memory of my father or our Anglican base? It appears... through my own council... that I would rather have O'Neill with me, than against me!"

CHAPTER 24

Enterprise of Misfortune

Thomas Smyth rapped on the door of Smyth Pub with an unsettling feeling crawling in his gut. He had spoken to the sheep man, and now he needed to speak with the trifling widow of one of his more profitable businesses. "Open up, it is your landlord, Thomas Smyth!" he shouted.

He heard mumbling above him and stepped back to show his face to a fat woman poking her head out of the second floor window. "Is that you, Thomas?" the feverish pitch of her voice told him she was hysterical.

"You will need to let me in, if you wish to speak, Mistress Talles. I'll not be having our business shouted across the street."

"Oh, thank God it is you. Thank God, thank God," Mistress Talles repeated before she disappeared from sight.

Gilford sat across the way with two of his helpers. The three men gave Thomas a look of confirmation but he doubted they were capable of giving him aid. They were his men, but they were anything but loyal. Moments later the door latch lifted and Mistress Talles let him in.

"I have something for you, Thomas Smyth. Something that will set your mind straight on why only you could see it," she told him.

Thomas looked at the poor sod that had been tied face down and strapped to a knotty barstool. The woman had been rough with him. Seeing her for himself, he doubted the man had a chance. Dodd was one of Gilford's men, dressed in black leather pants, heavily worn boots and a canvas jerkin. Gilford had told him previously, with his flashing smile, that such clothes made his fellows appear tough.

"You will have to let my man loose before we discuss anything. That is the first order of business," Thomas told her.

"I didn't hurt him bad, Thomas. Hell, the lad nearly fell down and tied himself to the stool," Mistress Talles replied, before she cut Dodd free. "Away with ya then… get your sorry ass out of my pub!" she scolded.

Dodd stood and dusted himself off. He looked pathetically toward Thomas just before Mistress Talles gave him a swift kick in the ass. "Go, you bloody fool!" she shouted.

Thomas rolled his eyes toward the door, "You may go, Dodd." Dodd sucked in his lower lip and exited quickly.

"That is one sorry, cross eyed son of a sod sucking louse," Mistress Talles quipped.

Thomas was not amused. Mistress Talles was the typical bar wench of Cheapside. She had greasy hair that may have been blond, tied up in a bun over a sweaty looking thick neck. A full bodied woman but not in a pleasing way. "You will have one week to gather your belongings and be out of this establishment. That is the arrangement your husband made with Gilford and that is the arrangement I intend to keep."

Mistress Talles leveled her gaze, "Ya might think different when ya see why I refused to leave. Ya might think to owe me a bit of favor, Thomas Smyth."

"I cannot conceive you have anything I want unless you have the girl. I was told she was taken," Thomas said dryly. Mistress Talles squared herself to him. He had to admit, the woman had gall.

Her mouth puckered and her cheeks became rosy, unlike her curt tone, "It is true and my husband was murdered, God rest his soul, but that is not why I called for ya."

"Why have you called for me then? You seem to be the only one who has any idea of what the hell is going on here," Thomas replied impatiently.

Seeing he meant to have her thrown out, Mistress Talles became more demanding. "Not until I have your word as a gentleman, that I and me poor little girls will continue on here with our business. At least until I can arrange for Osbert's brother to make good on our keep."

"You'll be lucky to keep your hands, let alone be trusted with this pub," Thomas threatened.

Mistress Talles shook her head and then waved her finger. "Oh... Thomas, what I have, ties ya to something far more important than me hands. What I have might even put ya in the darkest part of the tower."

Thomas saw a certainty in her that made her more than a cackling hen. She knew something was much more serious than he imagined. He could deal with a Spaniard in his own city. He could even recover from losing a ransom, but Mistress Talles, suddenly frightened him. He gave her a begrudging nod for her to continue.

"If you don't believe me, I will leave with Alana and Triny right now. We got a place to go. We want not for debtors' row." Mistress Talles raised her flabby arm and shouted: "Triny! Ya bring that paper down here!"

Her voice made him jump back as two stocking covered legs climbed down the ladder. Then in an instant he was handed a sheet of very fine parchment. Mistress Talles smiled for the first time since he had entered. He wished she hadn't as the yellowed expression of satisfaction made Thomas ponder her condition of oral hygiene. "Go on then," he said.

"I read it, I did. I'm the only one on this street who can read. It seems you have angered someone, Thomas. Someone with very high birth." She began laughing so hard that her jiggling breasts threatened to split out of her ill fitted girdle. The factious humor was disenchanting as Thomas read:

Catherine Bourke has sent her regards to Thomas Smyth, He glazed over the introduction and found his concentration waning with the recollection of that woman. He thought of the farm in Geashill that he had encouraged Henry Colley to confiscate by force. He thought of the war that was coming to Ireland and he thought of his lust. Catherine's words had been dear to him once, but that was another lifetime. He certainly didn't want to remember his feelings. He unfolded the paper carefully, looking for a smudge or blot of ink that may have hinted of a tear but found only her writing to be neat and clear.

May your days in London be filled with the horrid memory of what you have done. Please know, dear Thomas, that your wife and children shall revile your name. You cannot stop what is coming. You will not be able to hide. Your association with piracy is not confined to the theft of my land and I have the proof of it all. The queen will be hearing from the MacWilliam Lochtar. She will be hearing from Connaught!

Mistress Talles saw his eye's drift to the floor, "It is not a long letter is it? Albeit, it is one that might bring suspicion to one's wife or maybe the constable of the high court. I surely wouldn't want that, would you?" she asked.

Thomas folded the letter and put it in his breast pocket. "You will have all time in your matters of grief and recovery." Mistress Talles crossed her arms. "I will reduce your rent by a quarter for as long as this letter remains a secret between us. Was there anything else that I should know?" he asked calmly.

Mistress Talles perked up. It was as if her mouth watered with the next request. "Yes. I want the Scottish girl back. The one you took from the Portuguese slaver, down at Blackfriars. Oh yes, Osbert told me you was keeping her for someone's ransom."

"That is my concern, and not yours!"

"No? Well it is my concern now, as well it should. I also want the head of the man who did this. His severed head to be displayed right here in a pickle jar." The mistress slapped the bar stand so hard Thomas felt her weight through the soles of his shoes. "All shall see what happens to those that attack the Talles family."

It was a calamity of circumstances that he had not anticipated. All of it a price for his lustful and adulterous feelings toward an Irish lady. He felt himself slipping away with the dread of it all; slipping farther and farther into the devil's trap. "All that I can do, I say," Thomas replied.

Mistress Talles answered his inner thoughts as if they came directly from Satan himself, and Thomas listened: "I can make you a great deal of money, Thomas Smyth."

He looked at her quietly.

"A great deal," she repeated softly as his thoughts overwhelmed him. "I have been saving that girl for more than you could ever get in ransom."

Cheapside never seemed so small and the walls of London were closing him in. Such was the state of Thomas Smyth, that he made his bargain and made it well. All so that Mistress Talles would never tell.

CHAPTER 25

Alleluia

An iron point dug into the ground splitting the earth open to begin its furl. Below the castle and within sight of Henry, the broken solace of tilling a new pasture sent a flock of black birds beating their wings in desperate flight. He could see it all in Colley Town.

Annie Beth held her son's hand and walked toward a well with a bucket. Mary opened a window and put a meat pie on the sill and John Goodrich went directly to work a bed of coals near the stable, glad that he had returned with Adam Loftus and grateful that the mysterious lord mayor had made good on Shane O'Neill's promise of gold. The plantation would be safe for now; war had been avoided. John pumped the bellows twice and sent a current of air over the red hot coals before daring to look toward the scene where Henry Colley and the soldiers stood.

"Take him down!" Adam said after the long ride from Dublin. He was tired. Ralph Lane, the lord deputy's aide, was also tired. The six cavalry riders who pulled out their swords and hacked away at the charred ropes holding up the vicar were exhausted and so was Henry Colley.

The men held kerchiefs to their noses and Henry felt his stomach wretch. "And you say, it was your wife who lit the flame?" Adam asked.

"They say," Henry said drearily, as he hung his head low and listened to the crackling skin and wood peeling away in a char of sinew and ash. He thought of Emma, he hated the soldiers.

Adam's tone was decisive and clear, "Do not fret. We shall not record this, nor shall we speak her name. I will find a suitable wife that your father will agree upon. A wife more befitting of a captain in the queen's army," he told him.

Henry's nose ran. It was a trickle he couldn't stop, barely noticeable to the others. To him it was persistently and openly an aggravation. He wiped it with a tremor in his voice, "And if I loved her?" he asked.

Adam turned to Ralph Lane, "She will be hunted down and hanged for murder. If it was within my power, I would do the same to Shane O'Neill." Adam could see that Henry listened but he did not comprehend. Maybe the cold truth of his words would sink in. *The witch, the murderer, those thoughts to sway him? No*, he reconsidered. Henry was bereaved.

Henry grabbed the inner portion of his sleeves with white knuckles and stood rigidly in his uniform. He could hear the children playing off in the distance. The moment was unforgettable, unimaginable. A fly landed on his nose and he tried not to reach up and flick it away. It tickled, then irritated, then buzzed around his ear. And there it was again, the drain from his sinuses and his eyes felt puffy. "Have you any idea when Sussex will move again from Armagh?" he asked hoarsely as his friend Ralph Lane stood with condolence, considering his task.

Ralph nodded his head as the soldiers covered the body. "Next summer perhaps and that is only if the queen does not accept the O'Neill's offer.

"The offer?" Henry replied unknowingly.

Suddenly the sound of the returning black birds filled the air. A whole flock it seemed, ravenous and quick. Like thieves sounding their own alarm out of the brazen confidence to escape. They landed and just as quickly sped off. Ralph turned to Adam Loftus, realizing he had said too much, "Henry... how could you not know?"

Adam's brow wrinkled, "This is not the time," he advised coldly.

Henry's face was already pale, his whiskers jetting out in an uneven frill. He needed to understand how his queen would accept any offer from the vile chieftain who did this. His voice betrayed his anger, "What... pray tell, could prevent the issuance of judgement!"

Ralph cleared his throat, "I will forgive your outburst because of your grief, but you shall not forget whom you address, Henry," he said sternly.

Henry struggled to say it more clearly. The only thing he considered was his own need of violence. At least a hope of a retaliatory strike would give him the strength and purpose to steel himself against the loss. Was it too much to ask for an accounting? Everything had changed now. He was no longer an undertaker of other men's ambition. He was a killer. A soldier who needed to be fed with the raw, flowing, fucking blood of the Irish. "What things, my lord?" he seethed, wishing for an answer that would make sense of the senseless.

Adam took his time, "It's alright, Ralph. I understand Henry, and he will settle." His words were finite in Henry's ear. The man had apparently been through an ordeal and he clasped his paw on the tan and brown uniform just above the gold braid of Henry's epaulette. "The O'Neill wishes to be made a peer and England's consult."

Henry shifted back as the words struck him. "O'Neill?"

Adam replied: "It is preposterous to believe such things, but he has a legitimate claim which guarantees an audience with Her Majesty."

"Legitimate?" Henry mumbled. "Has the council lost their senses?"

Adam knew of nothing else to say. Ralph Lane had exposed it and there it was right in the middle of this debacle. *Of course Henry Colley wouldn't understand. How could he?* "There will be provisions made. You will not lose your land, Henry."

"What the fuck are we talking about!" Henry shouted.

❈ ❈ ❈

John Goodrich dropped a glowing iron horseshoe into the cold water. The steam washed over his hand with a hiss and over that he heard the shouting. He saw a dagger flash and a soldier grabbed Henry, so he picked up a pitch fork and went running. Annie and her husband went running also, and so did Mary.

The soldiers restrained Henry as Ralph Lane held up his hands.

Adam turned to see John Goodrich charging up the hill with murder in his eyes. He surveyed the pasture and the plow was standing alone and a throng of people were churning their feet to reach them. It happened so quickly. The soldier and the musket which discharged like thunder echoing across the countryside. *Hallowed... hallowed be His name*, Adam thought, as a man fell and silence drifted with the smoke over the hillside.

"Cease fire! Cease fire!" Ralph shouted.

Henry stood there shaking with rage. Susan Goodrich ran out of the stable and Dennis grabbed a sword and marched directly toward the castle where the shot was sounded.

"Order! There will be order here!" Ralph shouted. He turned to Henry, "Is this what you wanted! Is it!"

Henry fell slack against the hands that stayed him. Not ten feet away, the canvas tarp that covered the rotting vicar had already turned black with flies and his feet felt like lead in a river. There was nowhere for him to go. He had nothing left. He could say nothing at all.

Lane, being a military aide and witness to subversion, ruffled. Henry had been his friend? Was he? "You have taken a great liberty beyond your station and look what has come of it," he said bitterly.

Susan wailed: "You have killed him! You have killed the stone mason Percy!" and her husband John threw down his pitch fork in anger.

Henry's mind was spinning. The gut check he did not anticipate left him festooned with the loss of his pride and dignity. "Retreat, my lord," he sobbed.

Adam turned to face the planters, "Go back to work and you will be spared..."

Henry, fearing that more of his planters might be shot urged them to do the same. With the outburst quelled, the soldier released Henry who watched helplessly as Percy was carted away. The whole incident lasted little more than five minutes but for Henry it would continue for a lifetime. Again, he was the undertaker. A man who worked for other men's dreams.

Ralph Lane saw the utter revulsion in Henry's eyes. "Do you understand, now?" he asked in finality.

Henry did understand. He doubted that Emma could have ever committed such atrocity and knew the vicar had not shown her the slightest bit of kindness. Now he understood. Percy understood as well, because he was dead. "I am to remain a hostage or do nothing at all, as my wife is hunted down and hanged," he replied.

Adam Loftus said: "You are a military officer, and will do as you are told."

Henry cooled with an expression that left Adam uncertain of his mind. "Aye."

"You will have plenty to do here. The woman is no longer your wife but a fugitive of justice, just like that man laying over there."

Two days later and Henry had been relieved. The dreary day was grey as far as the eye could see. Bloody far. Even past the alders the sky was smitten and well into the bog where fog rose in perceptible gloom. He stood in the meadow near the old Bermingham Castle, where the planters buried the dead. The small cemetery was growing below a sloping hill of whine bushes. The fertile clearing had become sacred. The gathering commenced in front of the archbishop who had stayed with the planters to ensure their fortitude. Now, Adam's wide brimmed hat was canted downward, the droplets beaded on the supple felt and spilled over to the ground as the last shovel of earth landed in a, pat, pat, pat... of tamping. The new graves were perfectly round.

Adam felt clean, refreshed; he could see that the planters did not. They, with the mud still clinging to their bosoms. Their mottle of wool hanging damp and smeared, both men and women downtrodden. "There will be peace in the midlands," Adam said, looking down at the stone which marked the vicar's grave. After his words, he waved off the townsfolk in their dingy white tunics and brown canvas breeches. Such a plain people. Some had shoes, some did not. He also reflected on the occurrence of the vicar's death as Henry Colley shook the hand of Ralph Lane.

Henry appealed to Ralph, who looked now to be more of the man he remembered than the tyrant who invaded his home. "You have made me a promise," Henry said.

"Aye," Ralph replied.

Henry dipped his head and together the gentlemen walked toward the castle. They would enjoy eggs, ham, and biscuits. It was the meal that Adam had requested. Henry hoped it would be the last. "Will you be staying on longer?"

"We leave straight away, Henry; but before I go, I believe I have an answer to your situation here." Adam's eyes fell on Judas who appeared from the castle and walked toward them.

"Situation?" Henry asked.

"Of course. I have spent hours with your guest. Did you know that Judas heard me preach in the chapel on the hill of Dungannon just last year?"

Henry looked astonished. He had never considered such a thing as he observed Judas emerging from the front of his castle. Judas had been given a clean robe. The white cotton was unusually soft and boded loosely about his waist as he lengthened his stride in a free and happy gate. There was a glibness in his countenance as he extended his hand. Henry chose not to receive it.

Judas pulled back before his gesture became awkward. Adam spoke for him: "It was over a year past that I visited and held those people dear."

"Aye, Lord Bishop, it was a year," Judas replied fondly.

Henry appeared cautious, having heard Judas's nightmares and spasms of gibberish each night. Strange was an understatement for his guest, whom he rescued from certain death. Touched maybe. Touched within his mind and deep into the spirit. "I found him in a most terrible condition near the country of Longford, my lord, you cannot believe..."

"What—" Adam said curtly, "I cannot believe, what— Henry."

Judas stood quietly expecting to join the men for lunch and Adam turned to him. "He has a knowledge of scripture. He has a repentant heart and is learned in Latin. This is what I have come to know of the man you relieved of savages. He adores you, Henry, and has wished for nothing more than to be confirmed as a true disciple," Adam said.

"I am sure he does, my lord," Henry replied.

Without further detail, Adam turned to Judas, "You are away from Dungannon, Judas. But you are not away from the Lord" he said.

Judas rubbed his hands and thought of Brehon. The old law and the betrayal of his heart by Miguel had never caused such a change in his spirit. He could never go back to his people. "I was troubled but now I am well. All thanks to the Captain," he replied.

Adam looked kindly at Judas's face, "You may never speak against our Queen or take a papist vow again. Do you agree in front of Henry, the headmaster, to honor me in this?" he asked plainly.

"I am without obligation, Lord Bishop. I have converted with my whole heart. I cry each night with the thought of my transformation and pray on my knees that God will feed my soul. There is no lie in that," Judas proclaimed.

Henry assessed Judas with bewilderment. The shaking hand, his wandering eyes and the teeth grinding intensity of a man on the verge of insanity could hardly have abated so quickly. If he had been transformed, the transformation itself would have to be miraculous.

Adam made his intention clear so Henry would understand: "Judas, it seems these people need a new vicar as well as a meal. Would you be willing to learn from me and stay amongst them?"

Judas pursed his lips to form the perfect letter 'O' as he exhaled and then clasped his hands together in joy. It was theatrical and he stood as a figure of prayer with euphoric eyes of wonder. "Yes, my lord," he said, bending to kiss the hand of the archbishop, directly.

Adam could not have been more pleased. "It is done then, my son," he said smartly as they entered Bermingham Castle.

Henry paled. Within the castle, the lacquer of fresh paint and the rose color pattern did nothing to lift his spirit.

CHAPTER 26

Secret Sisters

Of London, Saint Bartholomew's had once been a church for the people, and for the widows, it still was. They would walk the three miles from Coleman Ward, near Moorgate and pass the skinners gild each day on their way to the hospital. For them life had changed over the past four years. They lived sparsely, but they did not beg or steal. It was a strange thing to have once been cherished in a community of believers and now be so poorly received. They were veritable outcasts, not allowed to marry or take a paying job. Such was the treatment of nuns that the Earl of Leinster had furtively advised the queen to make the dispensation of their faith unlawful and, so through Robert Dudley and the House of Lords, it was.

Occasionally, Mary would carry baskets of coal or cart scraps from Skinners Street down to the old mothers by the Thames. Such work made Mary feel fortunate; as it was with other capable ladies of the Lord who lived in a shared apartment near the former priory ground of St. Boltolph. They could all walk easily from St. Boltolph up Aldgate Street to pass Cornhill Ward to follow their calling. The widows served the sick.

Caring for the destitute was God's honor, Mary was told. It gave her and the others a purpose. St. Bartholomew's was therefore the natural hub for their purpose. The parish was neglected but not the place of healing. Within the hospital a house physician would allow them bread from Bakers Street and medicines were tested on the poor. It was not ideal but Mary knew their benefactor as a kind man and his name was Rodrigo Lopez. His only flaw in her opinion was that he mixed dutifully with the upper crust and showed no inclination of faith at all. His appointment was that of Tudor, Master of Humors for St. Bartholomew's Hospital. He kept his offices at the larger buildings, St. Bartholomew's the Greater, and also saw to the leasing of grounds to laymen.

"For God we come," the sisters told Rodrigo each morning.

"For God you may stay," he had always replied.

Rodrigo instructed them and on occasion he even rewarded them so that together the former nuns were able to accomplish truly wondrous things. It wasn't until recently that he insisted on calling them all widows. Mary did not feel like a widow, she did not look like a widow, and she knew that she would never be a widow. Rodrigo had begged her to consider it a kinder affection than being called a nun. Once, he even told them that he himself understood how it was to be dispossessed and that God would find their work most pleasing regardless of how they were called.

"Mary," Julianne called out.

"Sorry, Mother," she replied.

Mary picked up her bucket and slowly walked down the infirmary. Her mind was adrift and she could not help peeking up at Rodrigo as he spoke to Miguel. She almost felt guilty for bringing the Spaniard into their midst. He had been so insistent, so convincing to purpose. The thought nagged at her. They whispered and she wanted so much to know what they said. Why did that little girl sitting near him appear so sad?

"Mary, the cider," Julianne said with a tone that moved her.

"Coming, Mother," Mary replied.

"It will only be for a short while, Mary," Julianne said before handing her a bundle of foul smelling clothes. "You must call me Julianne, as our benefactor deems fit."

Mary smiled and in her eyes there was a little twinge of resistance. She liked living on the edge. Life as a nun had become full of danger as of late. It added to the thrill of her existence in the mundane. She kept working, taking every opportunity she could to move closer to Miguel as her mind drifted in the work. *Who am I?* she thought. The sisters had cleaned her, taken hours and hours to pick off the lice and provide her a pair of shoes. They had taught her well and asked only that she learn about the Lord. She understood now who God was. *Through Him...* she knew she would be saved. They had even written her name in the book of life. Of course it was symbolic but that too came with a wonderful ceremony and sense of belonging. But she really didn't know who... she was. Somewhere, although she didn't speak it, deep down in her heart, she needed something more. Her arms prickled when Miguel looked her way and again she felt guilty.

Miguel sat there patiently as the good physician told him all of their names. Widow Julianne Barrilich had come from the Church of Saint Mary of the Assumption at Clerkenwell. Widow Linda Bryant, and the tiny Jeanne Sweeney, had saved the sacred scrolls and scriptures and hid them away in barrels where even Rodrigo did not go. Their devotion and unity of purpose were remarkable, Miguel thought. As he stood to take his leave, Rodrigo pointed him toward the back hall and Miguel's eyes naturally fell to Mary. It may have been because she was the first he had met in London. It may have been that it was her who stood with warning in the street; or it may have been her magical eyes. She was a beautiful creature and he could see through her rags a radiant glow.

Mary Margaret dipped the ladle into an old wooden pail and lifted the cider to nurse the sick. Her eyes were as green as emeralds and her skin as white as milk. "Soy un hombre de Dios," he said quietly.

Jade squeezed Miguel's hand wondering why his attention drifted off. For some reason she did not quite comprehend, Jade resented Miguel's inattention. It caused her first utterance since leaving Smyth pub. "We should go," she said, thinking to herself again about the name he had given her.

Leaving the lessor of the buildings, Miguel and Jade marched across the street and up a half block. Jade McAlister had never seen a building so large but Miguel told her, that Agnes would have. Agnes, he had said, would have been accustomed to entering the Church of St. Bartholomew's the greater. She wondered who the girl was that he spoke of.

Where they entered a second compound, Jade marveled at the painted vault, so beautiful that it overshadowed the crumbling brick walls all around them. It was the ruins of a larger facility that Rodrigo had called St. Bartholomew's the Great. Having been left in decay, Rodrigo had said it would be the perfect place for them to hide. He himself had an office and apartment there because of its seclusion. They walked out through the cloister and on to the quadrangle to pass through a courtyard filled with rustling brown leaves. Farther down, was the old bell tower and there is where she had heard they would stay. Jade felt cold as the pigeon's cooed above her.

"We will stay only a short while," Miguel said, seeming to know her thoughts before she asked. Jade wanted to leave. He took her back into the old tower and they climbed a flight of bricked stairs. The wall was dusty and she ran her fingers up the rough mortar as they ascended. It turned her palm red. More stairs, gritty, like a sand house washing away on the beach, and each step she took caused it to cascade off the bottom of her soles, falling off to nowhere. When they reached the old attic, Miguel let her stand alone. It was as dark and black as the old castle dungeon she had once stumbled across in her father's stone house. A house of pain her Da had told her. So dark that she wished he hadn't.

Miguel pulled out a key that Rodrigo had given him as Jade wiped the dust out of her eyes. He turned to her before opening the door, not thinking of her feelings. Until this moment, Miguel had no idea of how to treat a child. He only thought of his mission and how she was part of a greater plan. He would bring her back to Ireland, but first they must survive. "It will be safe here," he told her.

Jade did not answer. She wanted to be strong. She was a McAlister.

Miguel saw the dusty dark staircase with its crumbling mortar and cob webs and he saw Jade's face. He had never wanted to parent or hold babies but her sobbing touched him. Each quake of her shoulders made him want to reach out and hug her. That too was strange. A thing he was not taught but a feeling that he tried to suppress. He attempted to carry her before, but she held back and all he could tell her was that for the moment, *it would be safe.* The lock turned but the door was jammed so he kicked at the slats and a pile of dust covered them both. He heard her cough.

"Must we stay here?" she asked.

"Until a way has been made ready," Miguel said, speaking more to himself than to her.

They entered the attic of St. Bartholomew's the Greater and he offered her the dusty floor. Miguel rolled up his sleeves and found a straw broom. He swept and slid things around and she watched him and dreamed of Kintyre and the stone house of her father. When he finished and the dust began to settle, Jade reached out and touched his arm. Her inquisitive mind made him pause and so he took her to the window. They stood there together for a moment looking at the streets below. A vast network of houses where oil lanterns began to light as evening covered the city.

"Why do you have the markings on your arms?" she asked him.

Miguel looked cautiously over her head, "I did not ask for those marks, child but a great man has taught me how to use them," he told her, referring to his tattoos.

Jade traced her index finger over a star. A tiny black speck of ink that connected to another through a line. She wondered if it hurt when they pierced his skin to deliver the ink. There were so many of them, almost as many as the stars in the sky.

"Do not concern yourself with symbols," Miguel said softly, pulling his hand away.

"They are pretty," she told him.

Miguel looked out and saw they were not far from the butcher's hall and then suddenly he pulled her back as if to prevent Jade from falling.

"Don't stand at the window or let anyone see you looking out. Do you understand?" he asked.

She nodded and he shifted her away from the glass. "Who is it?" she asked.

"The looker," Miguel told her warningly.

Her face seemed gaunt. She had learned to mask her feelings; fear, happiness, and even pain. This time it was impossible. She did not want to reveal who she was or what she felt but at this very instant, the looker seemed to be everything she needed to escape.

"Are you hungry? I can get some bread, maybe some cheese?" he asked her.

Jade had no idea who he was or why he had taken her. "Why did you call me Agnes?" she whispered.

He felt a twinge of regret, "To protect you."

She thought about what he said as she raised her hands and moved them in circles. She parted her fingers and remembered the cold dark hull of that ship and the English soldiers who took her. She had tried to capture the light seeping through in that darkness: deep, deep down in the belly of the *Great Harry*. Oh how she wished her sister, Amiah, was with her. And her brother? What had become of him?

Miguel noticed her dreaming as she moved her hand in a most peculiar way, spreading her fingers and closing them and then doing it again and again as if trying to catch a ray of moonlight. "I will do all that I can to protect you, child. I will do all that I can," he told her.

She sat there in uncomfortable silence and he knew she did not believe him, nor did she trust him. Miguel was a man.

CHAPTER 27

The Household

In the castle at Hampton, past Richmond and into East Molesey, fifteen miles from where Miguel had found the widows, Queen Elizabeth prepared to meet the lords of Ireland. Had she a victory in Ulster the earls of Leinster and Ormond would adore her and know that Spain and the threat from Rome were contained. Victory however, seemed ever more unlikely to her now. There would be no celebration to have if things did not change very quickly. The assembly awaited her in the presence chamber and she was not even dressed. *What can I offer them today?* She wondered. Lady Lettice Knollys, a childhood friend and cousin was with her.

"Do you not think it odd that Sussex sent his wife to my court rather than coming to me himself?" Elizabeth asked Lettice as they prepared for the night to come.

Lettice turned up her eyes as her comely red hair fell over an outer gown and nestled on her shoulders. Her voice was light with anticipation, "There are many ladies in court. I thought nothing of it," she replied.

"Sussex should have come himself to explain this debacle. Tonight is the night that I promised to divide the lands of our victory. Instead, I must face the earls of Leinster and Desmond and know that our own Duke of Northumberland has lost an heir to the midlands."

"Northumberland?" Lettice asked.

Elizabeth tightened her lips. "Did thee not hear me earlier? The Duke's nephew was butchered like a filthy pig and left to rot in Belturbet. That does not bode of victory."

"It is a burden I cannot imagine," Lettice replied.

Elizabeth frowned with displeasure, "Tonight will tell us what Sussex's wife intends. She has no business in the apartments or in my court without her husband. I do not want her involved in any stately affairs," she seethed.

"I was told Lady Radcliffe departed for Penshurst in order to see her father," Lettice answered. She then picked up some lace and turned to fasten the queen's carriage.

Elizabeth obliged her, "Mark my words, Lettice. She will come tonight and she should not be left alone in the presence chamber without her husband. By God's bones... I should have that bitch restrained!"

"I will keep an eye on her," Lettice said. She then turned and lifted a beautiful crimson false front and helped Elizabeth attach it to the laced under gown.

Elizabeth's tone changed with a mind that was constantly awhirl, "She does fancy herself to be a lady and a matchmaker. Do you not agree?"

Lettice listened intently and then politely nodded. It was a jolt to her sensibility when Elizabeth reached up and took her hand harshly.

"You look too much like me."

"Beth?" Lettice asked apologetically.

"These Irish have noticed you and sometimes bow in your presence. Don't think that I will not be watching you as closely as you will be watching Francis Radcliffe."

Lettice tried to dismiss the remark and then placed Elizabeth's sleeves out and smoothed her gown to the waist. "A mistake only, my Queen. I am blessed to have a measure of your beauty," she replied nervously.

Elizabeth held up her hands to have her sleeves attached, "Well, you shall make no attempt to embellish your position. Nor shall you prostitute yourself as a figure of state. Is that understood?"

Lettice pulled away and lowered her eyes, "I would never. I would never do or think such a thing," she replied. Then she picked up the red robe. Its weave so fine that her fingers could scarcely feel the thread and worked Elizabeth's torso and shoulders through to pull the black stitch of her linen through to the wrist. "It presents your form splendidly."

"Good," Elizabeth replied, as she let the material fall at the waist. She looked at herself in her mirror and continued, "I will be watching you both. Sussex's wife has my attention and you should know, Francis is a plotter, and a plotter is ill suited to advise a queen's council."

Lettice felt the affront and began to wish she had never returned to court. In the past she would have never thought her cousin to be of high temper. No longer though. Monarchy did not seem to agree with the old Beth. She no longer knew her friend or the giddy little girl who ran with her through the palace to spy with devilish eyes on the doings of those in court. She answered without freedom. "I understand, Majesty. I am but your servant and will always behave with the greatest love and affection toward you."

Elizabeth lifted her arms and then stroked the fur of her mantle as it fluffed over her shoulders. "When we are greeted by the lords this night, you shall do well to remember."

❧ ❧ ❧

Down the grand hall of Hampton, William Cecil orchestrated a house worthy of jubilation. The stonework echoed with the sound of music and his heart gladdened that Thomas had come. "Back from Calais, Lord Gresham?"

Thomas Gresham, raised a brow of apprehension, "Things did not go well. Northumberland has quite a bit of influence in Antwerp but he was hesitant to weigh in with the banks to secure our loan. It was the same in Calais." Thomas was a crisp sight, but he felt defeated.

"Nothing?" William asked.

"It would be easier for me to borrow from Spain with the promise we would use the bullion against them. It is that surety that we have, that Antwerp will provide us nothing." William grunted and Thomas accompanied him toward the ballroom.

"I am glad you came, none the less. We need the whole of our council here tonight," William said.

"Do they not know that Radcliffe is missing?" Thomas asked referring to the Irish lords who had pledged themselves to Radcliffe's support and undoubted victory.

"Nay, it must be kept between us, and us alone, Thomas. If the Earl of Ormond does not speak of Radcliffe, I feel the Irish lordship will be well entertained. I have Walsingham trying to ascertain the whereabouts of Sussex as we speak. We must put on our good humor tonight," William insisted.

"Indeed, Lord Burghley. I have heard that Sussex's wife has come even if he has not. Do you believe that will be a problem for us?" Thomas asked.

"Let us hope not," William replied.

❧ ❧ ❧

Francis Radciffe was raised to know that one never drifted far from the crown by one's own choosing. The upper crust of an inner circle of women who dabbled in Elizabeth's court. When she arrived to Hampton, Francis wanted to be perfect and rode in a carriage from her father's estate of Penshurst. She felt powerful to be back in England with his horses pulling hard and a gentleman usher at her side. Such a visit was more than satisfying, it was necessary.

"You must remain at court," her father had said. His pervasive insistence put her off and she left wishing he had shown her kinder affection. Still, to see him well, was refreshing and so was the thrill of entering court. The carriage stopped at the west gate and Francis leaned forward with gold thread around her neckline, an elegant blue gown and pearls fashioned into her hair.

"You look regal," her usher said.

"Powder my face, would you please," Francis told him.

Theobald reached out with his right hand and dappled her forehead with powder. Then, with a finger already stained of rouge, he delicately touched her pouty lips and put a dot upon her left cheek. "Beautiful," he told her.

They entered a bit late and made their own way into the grand hall which smelled deliciously of roasted meat. Her waist was cinched tight to a baleen carriage and Francis had pinned her brown hair to expose her slender neck.

As they mingled, Francis thought of her husband who was entwined in war. He was a brute to some and a hero to others but for her he was simply, Sussex. Always preoccupied with his fixation of Shane O'Neill and never having the propensity to touch her. It was a convenient union for them both, she told herself. Most likely he would be dining tonight in Dublin's castle with his own puppets. For Francis, Sussex was a man who increased her influence and her other needs could be met by someone else. Tonight she would be dutiful and belong to him, ingratiating those that the queen would acknowledge for Ireland. It was her place to do so... to be perfect: waiting, watching and serving where she could, below the queen's own ladies. After the courtesy of curtsey and bow, Francis found her place near a long tapestry where her and Theobald could observe the ornately decorated presence room and everyone who entered.

Seated to the left of where the queen would soon take a position was Lord Burghley and to his left was Robert Dudley and she noted that every seat was filled except for one. She smiled as they talked among themselves and fiddles resounded in her ear.

"Look," Francis said as Theobald took her shawl.

"I see, now hurry, they await you," Theobald told her.

Silence befell the orchestra as Francis made her move to the table. She felt as though every eye was upon her and kept hers on the vacant chair. Keeping her back straight and her steps short, she glided across the floor and felt like she was floating. It was beautiful she imagined, to see a swan that men desire. Francis understood the Irish lords would know the honor of Sussex.

Before she had reached her seat, Lord Burghley stood. "There will be stillness in this house!" he exclaimed to Francis's horror. His voice made her freeze in her tracks. Suddenly everything she had been taught came back to bring her hauntingly to her knee. As she bowed, knowing that the queen had entered, her hair toppled over to hit the floor. She could not continue, she could not sit and she had never felt so small.

Queen Elizabeth let her heels fall on the marble beneath her short train and her ornamental rough shrouded her neck like an elaborate honeycombed wheel to cast a shadow on Francis as she passed. Behind the queen, two courtiers marched in tune to the trumpet that sounded her arrival. The men rose and then everyone bowed together as Elizabeth's red gown brushed Francis's cheek as she paused just above her. It seemed like an eternity.

"You may follow my lead to the table," the queen whispered. When she heard the footsteps begin again, she felt the wave of a hand over her back and then she meekly found her way as she was told.

Elizabeth stood in front of her chair and cast her eyes to court. "I am well and the evening sup should be graced with music," she said, to Francis's relief.

William Cecil raised his hand to the orchestra as sumptuous platters of roasted lamb were paraded out ceremoniously. For Francis the meal time promised to be a solitary time as the servers poured wine and portioned out lamb, pheasant and venison.

After the meal had been tasted, Queen Elizabeth addressed Francis with acumen, "May God, guide your husband, Lady Radciffe," she said.

Francis raised her glass to the custom, "My husband is goodly. I am sure he toasts to England's prosperity in the halls of your Majesty's great castle of Dublin," she replied. Her words brought a round of approving nods and glasses raised in tribute.

Elizabeth assessed her closely and then reluctantly took a sip. A moment between rivals that did not go unnoticed. "Be it so. For that is all of my desire," Elizabeth said before biting crisply into a polished apple. She chewed it thoroughly and smacked her lips in a most unladylike fashion and then said: "Eat Francis—everyone must eat."

For the remainder of the evening the queen ignored her as Francis watched Lord Thomas Butler take the place of her husband. She may have failed to gain the queen's favor but the earl of Ormond had not. Thomas's elegant words were making their mark. She watched him kiss the Queen's hand and move closer after the sup had ended. Thomas Butler intrigued her. The Earl of Desmond, Lord Gerald Fitzgerald who moved toward the queen as well did not. She could almost feel the tension of Fitzgerald's determined expression. It was a bitterness that Francis knew well. *how will the haughty bitch handle this,* she wondered?

Fitzgerald did not wait for permission to speak. "The war sits poorly in Munster, my Queen," he said boldly.

Thomas Butler stood ruffled. "And you speak poorly for Desmond," his voice betrayed a long bitterness.

To Elizabeth's distaste, Lord Fitzgerald made his claim more vigorously, ignoring Thomas Butler and any practical form of cordiality. "The war does not prosper and shall be the ruin of all of Ireland and my people!"

The court fell silent, aghast at the earl's temper. As the music stopped and every eye turned with expectation, Francis dabbed her mouth with a roll and picked up her kerchief to cover a smile. *What will she do now?* she thought with faux disapproval.

Elizabeth took but a moment to gain her understanding. The division between her lords flushed ever to closely and now it seemed to have spilled onto her. She flashed a glance toward Lord Burghley, expecting him to rise and put an end to it. He did not. She sensed that some in the room admired the bold earl of Desmond, but she could not. His expression of self-righteousness left little to doubt that he felt empowered.

"Lord Burghley, you shall have Lord Fitzgerald taken to the tower," Elizabeth commanded.

Fitzgerald's Irish temper splayed out like red hot coals for all to see. "Ye'll not keep me in confinement for long!" he warned, kicking over a chair in his outrage as the queen remained perfectly still. Only the ambassador of Spain rose to offer his respect of Desmond. Bishop Quadra's gesture was met with a gentle hand to his shoulder. The ambassador sat down, near his predecessor Count de Feria and the two had the look of discontentment. For them, the Earl of Desmond offered the hope of a Catholic state and return to the court of Mary. To Cecil and the others however, the earl was a true threat. The ordeal was therefore put down quickly, when the unruly Earl of Desmond was forcefully removed. Elizabeth then sat and raised her golden chalice. The words left no doubt in Francis Radcliffe's mind that her queen was both resourceful and cunning.

"Now then, my friends, let us all be friendly."

Smyth Pub, Cheap Ward

The reverberating cries cascaded down the walls and up the streets of the lower city. "There are dead bodies on the bank," people shouted. Less than a mile from Tames Street and into the lower ward, Mistress Talles also heard the distressful calls at New Gate.

"Triny, ya get the fire started and don't go outside!" Mistress Talles shouted to her daughter.

"What's about Mum?" Triny asked. The child pulled a sweet roll off the bar stand and then plucked some goo from the bread.

"It's the pox!" Mistress Talles stammered. "The pox has come to the quays, child. God's speed to Thomas Smyth but no other can enter these doors!"

Just as Mistress Talles had shuttered the windows a loud knock came. "Don't answer it. Don't you touch that door,"

Mistress Talles said, as Alana, her youngest daughter smiled mischievously and lifted the brace to let it fall on the floor.

Mistress Talles pushed Alana aside just as a foot poked in. She tried to force the door shut and it was kicked open to her horror. Her ghost was in the doorway. People knew him as Joshua Tinkle, the sheep man. He had been a nice man once. A man who thought to help those in need when no one else might care. His cloths were tattered. He had worn the same gloves and filthy pants for nearly two years; refusing to take them off out of guilt. Something had happened to him people had said, but in the Talles house, it was a thing not spoken.

Joshua's teeth were as black as soot and his face was shaved to avoid being taxed. It was the constant shaving that had left him scarred. He had repeatedly cut his face out of spite in protest of London's most recent levy on the personal grooming choices of men. Joshua was not stupid but she knew without any reservation that he was dangerous... and insane. The most frightening thing for Mistress Talles was that tonight he had a remembrance in his eyes. A seething maleficent itch that terrified her. "Ye'll be dying soon," he threatened.

For all of her stature in the pub and the roughness she was used to enduring, Mistress Talles was ill prepared to greet the sheep man. He had been waiting for her. Always watching the pub and smiling from across the way. His countenance was as if he loved and hated her simultaneously. She had told the constable of his whispers and yet the watchman did nothing!

"I will choke ya," Joshua said so often that she was forced to remember. He never said it loud enough for anyone else to hear. But she heard. And she knew.

"Ya get out now," Mistress Talles said nervously as her foot slipped on the thresh of the floor. He didn't move. This time Joshua didn't back away and stood there wet from the rain with a haunting look in his eyes. She pushed her daughter aside, clutching for an iron poker, "Get out now, I said."

"Ye'll be dying very, very soon," he hissed. After the ominous warning, Joshua turned as if he had forgotten what he had said and wandered off into the night leaving her in his wake to tremble.

Alana came up from behind her, "Are ya cold, Mum?"

Mistress Talles slammed the door and spun about: "Don't ever— ever, open that door again! Do ya hear me, lass!" Her child nodded, and then darted off toward the counter.

Outside, just across the street, Joshua found a bail of wool. In the rain, as the sheep man pulled up his cloak and drifted back in time, he remembered. *So beautiful she had been.* The recollection was like medicine.

Hampton Court

In contrast to the dread overcoming Cheap Ward, Elizabeth's court remained unaware of pending danger. Certainly a curse of plague did not prevail as Lettice Knolls danced for the Irish in front of her queen. Francis stood against the tapestry once again, beside her gentlemen usher. When her dance was concluded, Lettice blushed as the Spanish ambassador announced that she was certainly the fairest lady in all of England. The Irish lords seemed to agree for they, unlike the queen's own privy council, rose up a great cheer to Lettice and began whirling her around the ballroom from one to another. Francis relished in the moment and noted Thomas Butler who condoled the queen with his good graces.

"Do you see how Butler fawns over her? And how she endears the Irish Lords to their own devices?" Francis asked as Lettice swirled over the floor like a dancing parrot.

Theobald stood crisply in a long black coat with a neat white collar pressed tightly to his neck. His long legs bent slightly as he dipped and then straightened in an odd expression of acknowledgement. His trousers came to the knees, tight white stockings covered the rest of his lank to the ankles. He was a slender man, with a long nose and receding hairline and his heron like appendages moved with precise calculation.

Francis pursed her lips as Elizabeth gave a fleeting glance of disapproval and then fell into the embrace of Thomas Butler, the 10th Earl of Ormond. "She has much to learn about the Irish, I am afraid. Even if they are her lords, they will not all bow to England."

"Act the Lady Sussex, if you will," Theobald told her.

Francis felt as though her duties as the lady might consume her soul. "I trust you Theo. You have been with me since we left Penshurst. How long has it been now?"

"Too long my lady. It is as if our time there was of another life," he answered.

She thought of it often. Penshurst, that magnificent greenery of her former self. She missed her garden and the song birds which nested each spring. Her tone was nostalgic, "Ireland changes a woman. I know how it has changed me." He looked down at her with quiet expression as she continued, "There is still a wildness— a twinge of uncertainty that sets a fear into my soul. Do you not believe it duplicitous to think that our queen is truly ruling these lords?"

"She is the queen here and wherever she is, Francis. She has power," Theobald replied.

"Yes. The queen has power, but also great weakness. There will be a lord in Ireland that will try to find her underbelly. A lord or possibly even a lady, Theo."

"That is a matter best left to others. If you wish to keep your head," my lady.

Francis relished Elizabeth's interest in Thomas Butler and she didn't mind thinking it at all. "The queen will call the night soon. I will have to depart from you, my dear Theo, I am afraid to say," she said as if he did not already know.

Theobald thought she was all the drama without the act when he replied: "I will assemble the grooms, my lady, and the maids will escort you back to the apartments." He was dutiful and also eager to retire himself.

"Do you know that my husband has increased my purse for this visit?" Francis asked.

"No, my Lady, that is beyond my position," Theobald replied.

"Well he has. And he has given me discretion on an additional eight hundred pounds to ensure the queen is well tended. Would thee not be pleased to benefit from the Queen's pleasure?"

Theobald said: "I do not think I should answer, my lady. If I dare say yea, you shall have my honor at your disposal. If I dare say nay, it would put question to your judgment."

Frances cooed, "Do as I ask and stop pretending you have never questioned my judgment. I have always taken care to reward you."

Theobald straightened his back as he looked cautiously about the grand hall. "Yes you have, my lady."

"Good, now I can go. I will put a seed in the queen's ear and you shall inform the Earl of Ormond that I wish to speak to him privately."

"I presume your husband would not approve of this private talk?" Theo asked.

"My husband is too busy fighting a war to worry about a wife. You will inform Lord Butler that I will await him in the garden when the court has cleared for evening."

"Use caution, Francis, Thomas Butler is a man with many mistresses. If what I believe you are conceiving actually comes to pass, you may well displease Elizabeth. Her wrath could be the end of you and your husband."

Francis hated when he addressed her by her first name. Theobald had done it since she was a child, whenever he disapproved. Her father had allowed that indulgence and she had been unable to break it. "Remember you are the usher, old friend. Here you are and will always be in my family's debt."

"I have not survived this many years because I have ever forgotten. I keep your most personal affairs and also my tongue. Profit me not... I say, for some of the things which I see you conspire and do, I am glad for my heart that you are not my daughter."

Francis touched Theo's hand before she left him. She always touched his hand, when he called her by her God given name.

CHAPTER 28

Vested

Thomas Smyth listened as Horatio read back his dictation: "Lord Mayor, as you have directed, the aldermen from each ward have been summoned. We shall meet in Westminster to set up the infirmaries and pyre sites. The royal house should not come to the Tower or entertain any persons already within the city. Having already been exposed, I will personally deliver the treasury to the mint and tend to the notification of St. Bartholomew's Hospital. The Lord Mayor can be assured, all measure of precaution, will be afforded London."

"That is fine," Thomas Smyth replied.

"Has the queen's house not been informed?" Horatio asked, as he dusted the parchment.

"Of course it has, the letter is a formality," Thomas said, haughtily.

Horatio looked confused, "Do you not believe the lord mayor wishes to be readily available to the crown himself in this crisis?"

Thomas grew impatient. "Take the letter to New Gate near the prison and deliver it to the box. He does not wish to have you in contact with his persons."

"So it is true then. You alone have control of all the alderman without the lord mayor's ear?" He looked at Thomas approvingly, "You are a very clever man, Thomas," Horatio said.

Thomas thought about the Spaniard and the threat. *Clever? No he was not clever he was resourceful.* "It must be known that none of the porters survived the *Pinnacle* after boarding. I have set up the burn pile on the south side of Tames Street, near the gutters. The fires are burning close to the swamp and Gilford is in charge. As for you, your carriage is being prepared to take you to New Gate and then St. Bartholomew's the lesser."

Horatio folded the letter, sealed it and put it away. "What are you speaking? Not a single porter has perished. They wait for your release?"

Thomas looked uncommonly satisfied, "You are not going to the hospital alone. Dodd will accompany you. As far as the porter's health... I feel you are mistaken, they have been loyal and their families will be compensated, but I fear their lives have all been lost."

Horatio shook his head, "They are well. Did ye not hear me?"

I heard you. You insolent piece of shit, Thomas thought. "I have already instructed Gilford on how to handle this tragedy.

None shall enter the quays, not even you, until Gilford and his men have given the all clear. Additionally, no sailors or sail captains will take flight from Broken Wharf. Now that the *Prymrose* has departed there are none here in London who will question that decision. Do you understand?"

Horatio thought of the families and those poor unfortunate men. He had seen them healthy just hours ago. His voice was but a whisper of shock and despair, "I'll not profit of murder," he replied warily.

"Aye. It appears you already have. Did thee not accept my offering of silver?" Thomas said. Horatio felt choked. As if a noose had cinched his throat. Thomas didn't wait for an answer, "Let it be known, Mister Philpot, that we believe the bringer of this plague to be a Spaniard who travels with a little girl. You will ensure the people know that such a man brings a curse to the city and should not be loose on the streets."

Horatio swallowed hard, "Do you mean, if I don't die of the pox myself before all your worldly plans come to fruition?"

"Indeed, Horatio. When a disaster is at hand, the thrifty will benefit from every opportunity." Thomas smiled, "I thought you were a man of ambition as you so eagerly informed me earlier. You disappoint me. It was my understanding you understood that prospering was important. It mattered not the circumstance, I believe you said." Thomas turned to look out the window as if reconsidering his plan and then made his tone final. "When it is done you will offer ten pounds to the families. None will question that kind of pay…" he saw Horatio's hand begin to shake, and added, "wealth does not come without sacrifice. You wanted to partner with me and now you are all in."

The bath day being the Sabbath day happened to fall after the evening ball, and Elizabeth took one bath a week whether she needed it or not. She left her royal chair by the fireplace and walked toward her private basin. Lettice folded a shawl and turned quietly to retrieve a night gown. The soft texture was so enticing that she hesitated and let the material slip between her fingers.

Elizabeth looked to her maids and then to Lettice, "Nearly all of the lords found you to be most charming, Lettice. You do seem quite adept at your impersonations of me."

Lettice looked up as she held the silk, "I am here for your pleasure and security," she said defensively.

The maids averted their gaze, down toward the basin, afraid to interrupt. Their long white cotton dresses had already become wet so they pulled at their drapery with soapy clean hands rather than face the certain scorn which came with the queen's poor temper.

"You shall remove all of my clothing for this bath, Lettice. Every stitch shall be taken and not one of you will gaze upon me or speak," Elizabeth ordered, as she lifted her arms.

Lettice gave a curtsey and tilted her head in submission, "My queen, should not the maid servants disrobe you?" she asked.

Elizabeth slapped Lettice in the face with a stinging bit of rage, "Not one of you shall speak!"

Lettice began to cry. Having no choice, she obliged her queen in silence. The lady of Oxforshire who once delighted in the company of the girl named Beth was no longer. Her fingers trembled with the release of each button. Cold hands untied the girdle and her heart ached. Elizabeth lowered her arms after minutes of perfect stillness to speak again with harshness. "Unwrap my breasts and take the linen."

Lettice felt her throat close as Elizabeth bared her true self. She stood with square shoulders and the bits and bumps of any woman, and she stood expecting. Lettice could not stare but she saw the little raised blemishes and raw impression of the tight gown visible on the skin. Her eyes narrowed, *do not forget you are human*, she thought.

"I like it cold. The water, that is, and the lavender oil should be warmed gently. Only you may put the oil on my skin, Lettice. I don't want the maids to touch me this night."

"Of course," Lettice replied.

Elizabeth slapped her face again. It was the insult that hurt more than the pain and Lettice seethed with the rejection. Four women in the room and not a sound escaped them. Only the slow trickle of water and rustle of Lettice's bodice betrayed her movement. A whisper of the activity that consumed the maids every concentration.

"You may retrieve the powder," she spoke to them all but to no one. When her bath was complete, Lettice dried her, and to ensure Lettice understood her place, Elizabeth bent over, offering her buttocks to the towel. "Do you think I am desirable? Do you not think, in my own court, I should be the most… desirable?" Elizabeth asked.

Lettice took the chance to speak again, knowing she might be punished, "You are being made to be so, and have the royal form of one who would take a king and bear many children."

Elizabeth sighed profoundly, "That is not what I asked. You cannot give a clever answer to me for I am not a man who desires your lustful cunning replies."

"You are beautiful, my Queen," Lettice said meekly.

"Do you think so? You who are wet for all the lords of Ireland?"

"I shall never, never again offend thee, my Queen," Lettice whispered.

"No... shall you not? Have I not already told thee that you have? Yet to my dismay, this night upon the ballroom floor, you found pleasure in dance and took the attention of any who would give it!"

"I shall never offend thee—I said."

Elizabeth hissed, "Back away from me and let me bow to you then. That is what you desire. Is it not? Show me your talents and do not disappoint because I truly wish to know of the proper method to give myself to a man."

Lettice held her breath as her old friend turned and faced her. "Come to me now that you have been accepted and return that kiss as you would upon my ballroom floor. Let me feel the depth of your passion with parted lips!" Elizabeth grabbed Lettice's hand and pulled her into a firm embrace. She stroked Lettice's hair and spoke with her breath upon Lettice's neck, "It is a natural thing, to desire. I feel these things as fervently as any. I feel them and must suppress them for a greater love," Elizabeth said maliciously. Lettice stiffened her shoulders as she felt the plying fingers of her queen. "But you don't feel what I feel. The magnitude of your fire cannot be quenched by will alone. Can it, Lettice?"

"No, my Queen," Lettice replied as she thought of just how badly she intended to hurt her monarch. It was more than the touch that brought the bile to the back of her throat. It was the shame.

Elizabeth held onto Lettice so tightly that she could hardly breathe and thought of all that Francis Radciffe had told her. She thought of her Earl of Ormond, Thomas Butler, and pressed with an uncomfortable moan. "You will never understand the power of a queen and what a queen must sacrifice," she was too angry to stop herself. "You will never understand!"

The Curse
of the
Sheep Man

The widows worked and then they prayed in the comfort of Lady Chapel. "Hail Mary, full of Grace, the Lord is with thee. Blessed art thou among women, blessed is the fruit of your womb, Jesus. Holy Mary, mother of God, pray for us sinners now and in the hour of our death." This prayer was their prayer and their combined voices echoed off the wall and up into the vaulted ceiling. In the hour of their plea, they knew that one of the fold was wavering with conviction. Widow

Mary had not come to the Lady Chapel this night and the mother supreme had noticed.

Julianne departed swiftly as the others prepared to sing. She walked out of Lady Chapel and into the courtyard of St. Bartholomew's the Greater, where she stood under the Oriel Window. A breeze ruffled some leaves. A glimmer of a candle struck her eye as it was dampened to hide the light. She turned quickly and marched toward the courtyard's interior door to the offices where Rodrigo should be. When she entered the narrow hallway and climbed a single dark set of stairs, Julianne heard a footstep from above. It was suspicious.

"Mary," she called. "Mary Margaret," Julianne whispered into the darkness. The hallway stunk of mildew and old veneer. A place where she ventured only upon invitation and only if Rodrigo was with her. She took off her clogs to hold them, knowing she walked in the physicians educational wing and close to her benefactor's private suite. "Where are you?" Julianne asked quietly. She suspected there were things about the physician that had drawn Mary. Things a nun must never consider. Rodrigo was a vigorous man after all. Trust, she had learned, was as fleeting as the breeze that ruffled the leaves outside. The floor creaked as she moved forward. She hoped Mary was not in this place but where else would she be? Who else but Rodrigo, had given her any attention? Her stockings eased over the smooth wood floor, "Mary..." Julianne whispered. There was no answer. Feeling foolish and convicted of her own intuition, Julianne set down her clogs and prepared to leave.

The sound of feet shuffling on the floor is what alerted the intruder. She never heard him or had the chance to cry out for help before he grabbed her.

☙ ☙ ☙

In the loft below the bell tower, Agnes sipped a cold soup that Miguel had brought her earlier in the day. She gazed out the window and down to Bakers Street and dreamt of Kintyre. Down there, way down on the street below, the legs of some poor creature being throttled into a carriage caught her attention. London was such a cruel place, she thought. Then she looked at the heavy bag that Miguel had left. The thing had landed on the floor with a tremendous thump when he had taken it off his shoulder. Agnes put down her soup and walked over to touch it. The hard brown leather and two heavy buckles were the only things that kept her from knowing what was inside. She opened both, flipped back the fold and sat back with amazement. Her fingers dug into more coins than she had ever seen. Silver coins with unfamiliar faces, dirty coins with worn off noses, smooth soft coins having lost their strike completely. Their size was as varied as their form. She stacked the round ones and put the flatter ones on their edge. She flicked one with her finger sending it hurtling across the floor like a spinning top. And, she turned to see him standing there behind her.

"Do you want to know why I called you Agnes?" he asked as she quickly picked up the coins and put them back in the leather bag. Jade felt as she had felt so many times before when her father caught her doing something she knew was wrong. She saw in that expression a disappointment. It was not of anger. It was just serious.

"Aye," she said before closing the buckles.

He lifted her gently by the arm. "Come by the window, and let me tell you a story," Miguel said softly. As she sat, he cleared his throat and reached for a bottle that the widows had given him earlier. He dusted off the top and with a twist Agnes heard a crisp sharp pop. "Take some and then give it back here," he instructed.

She did. It was a sweet wine and one she had never tasted before. She swished the grapy fluid around in her mouth and took another swallow. "Good," she said, flashing a purple grin and holding the dark glass bottle up to inspect it as her father might have done.

"Not too much," Miguel told her.

"It is much better than the ale," she replied.

"Si," Miguel said in agreement. He let her finish and then his voice became soft, like music to her ears. "Once, many years ago, there was a girl like yourself. She worked even at the same pub that you know." Agnes tingled with anticipation. She had not been told a story in such a very long time.

Miguel brushed a strand of her hair out of her eyes. Her face was pretty. The starlight was shining on it through the tainted glass window and he noticed her contentment. "The girl from the pub had a name and she was called Cora. Cora saved all of her pennies and did everything that she was told to do but still the master of the pub treated her badly. You see, Cora was pretty like you, and the pub master had a longing for her, but it was an unnatural thing. Cora did not like him and she tried and tried to always push him away."

As Jade listened, Miguel saw that she became utterly still. Seeing her in discomfort he gave her a look of reassurance. "Do not fear," he said.

"I fear not," she replied. "I loathe that man."

"Good." He continued, "The years passed and Cora turned nine and then more years past until she was sixteen. She had delicate hands but the mistress of the pub had turned against Cora out of jealousy and made her work until her hands were black and calloused. Cora's beauty was her curse, you see, so she was made to do the most terrible of things. Still, Cora endured, saving her pennies until finally she had enough to escape."

Jade's eyes were so wide that he knew she had felt every bit of Cora's pain, but she touched his arm for more.

"When she thought she had enough money, Cora asked a very kind man to help her. Do you know what his name was?"

"Nay," Jade replied softly, wantonly.

His name was Joshua," Miguel told her.

"You mean the sheep man?" Jade asked with surprise.

"Si. But you should know his name is truly Joshua," Miguel replied.

"What did Joshua do?" Jade asked in a whisper as she clutched Miguel's robe.

"Joshua actually loved Cora. He was much older than she but he loved her just the same. He loved her more than anything in the world and when Cora came to ask for his help... he became afraid."

"Why?" Jade asked, as she looked out the window sadly. "Why if he loved her did he fear?"

Miguel reached out and held Jade's hand, "Because he knew that he could never go with her. His master, Thomas Smyth, owned his debt and would never let him leave."

"What did he do?" she asked.

"Joshua thought and thought for many days of how he could help Cora and also tell her that he loved her. Finally, Joshua told his sister, whom he thought might help. He pleaded with his sister to allow Cora to buy her freedom so that she could stay in Cheap Ward as his wife."

Jade smiled, "So he married Cora?" she asked, but then she frowned, knowing that Joshua did not have a wife.

"No... Joshua's sister was Mistress Talles. It was her that despised Cora for her beauty. Instead of allowing Cora her freedom, Mistress Talles took the pennies that she knew Cora had saved."

"I hate Mistress Talles," Jade said.

"Hate is a strong word but it is not unjust to wish for a person to change. Do you think the Mistress could do good?" Miguel heard Jade sigh and then she squeezed his hand and shook her head no. It touched his heart. "Cora was sold as a slave to the very man whom Joshua was indebted to. That man's name was Thomas Smyth and he sent her away to Ireland. But she did not forget Joshua or the bad thing that Mistress Talles had done. She did not forget at all but she also made a friend along the way. Do you want to know what Cora's only friend was named?" he asked her.

"Agnes?" she asked, knowing that all he told her was true. She had heard the name of Cora on the lips of sailors and those who entered Smyth Pub. They didn't talk kindly of her. *Poor Cora,* she had thought.

"Agnes," Miguel confirmed.

"Is Cora alive?" Jade asked.

"Yes," Miguel told her.

"Do you know who I am?" Jade asked.

"You are a great chieftain's daughter and through Thomas Smyth's own greed we have come to know of you. You will be called Agnes so that we might get you on a ship and deliver you away from here. For not only was Agnes Cora's friend, but she was the daughter of someone who has promised your safe passage. But that, my dear Jade, is another story."

"Will I ever go home," she asked.

"I don't know, but until we get you to Ireland, you must answer to the name of Agnes. There are people who will be looking for Jade McAlister and so Agnes you shall be," Miguel replied as he touched her cheek softly.

Jade felt her heart fill with love and sadness all at once and she could not help herself from asking just one more question. "Will I see my Da again?"

Her voice caused his heart to ache, "In heaven," Miguel whispered.

CHAPTER 30

Prelude of Tyburn

In the upper loft of Thomas Smyth's office on the Black
Friars, the scuffle cascaded down a finished staircase with
the bully protest of a mother supreme.

"Get your filthy mitts off of me!" Julianne shouted.

They pulled off her blind and threw the sack onto the floor.
Her eyes adjusted and she saw a flash of gold in the mouth of
her abductor. Julianne tripped and the man's pedicured hand
caught her arm. "Easy, Mother," Gilford said.

She reeled away, apprehensively. Her mind was still set on
Mary. This invasion of her person was the worst possible
outcome of her fear. More disturbing was that she knew the man
in front of her. Gilford picked at a fingernail as she was sat

down in a wooden chair by a rough looking fellow Gilford had called Dodd.

Gilford's eyes reminded Julianne of a weasel's- black, small, glistening orbs that held some incalculable thought. He slid his feet across the dust covered floor and she heard Dodd breathing heavily behind her.

"We do not want to hurt you, Mother," Gilford said apologetically.

Julianne leveled her gaze and set her jaw. "How many years has it been? Fifteen, me thinks," she said.

"Fourteen," Gilford replied.

Julianne's expression soured. "Fourteen years since I saw that boy who was good with the numbers. What have you turned into?"

Gilford mocked her disappointment.

His pretense did not convince her. For a moment she saw the same lad she remembered. A confused hurt child who needed love. "Let me see your head, my son. Has it healed completely? Is there any pain?" she asked.

Her words were his memory. They penetrated him just like the hot oil that had covered him. A master's cruelty and then the beating that he endured came rushing back. Gilford brushed his feelings aside. That was then…when she coddled him in his suffering and put manure and bandage to his scalp. This was now. "A Spaniard and little girl were last seen entering your hospital. A dangerous man. You must know…" he said coldly.

"I can hardly believe it is you," Julianne said bitterly.

"Do not make me shout, Mother. Do ye not remember how loud I can be?" he asked.

Julianne did remember. The sound of his little voice crying out as she tore away his bandage each night and redressed the wound. They were screams that still haunted her. The tone of his voice left no doubt in her mind that whatever caused his change, she could never heal.

"Aye, it was my scream," he said, knowing that she reflected. He could see that he frightened her and she pushed back into her chair. "Where is the Spaniard and girl?" Gilford yelled.

"I do not know!" Julianne cried.

He persisted and took her arm in his hand and squeezed. "It will only get worse for you if you do not speak." She resisted. It made him angry and he took off his top hat and threw it on the floor. "Is this what ye want to see?" She gasped with pity as he took her finger and rubbed it on his scar. "Yes, my wound has been healed and it reminds me every day what it means to be weak. Do ye thinks me weak now?" The gold crowns on his incisors flashed menacingly and wet.

"Have you fallen so far that you seek to harm the only one who showed you kindness?" Julianne asked him.

"You must know of whom I speak," he replied.

Dodd stepped out from behind her as she answered. "I cannot say for sure, who may or may not have entered the hospital. My concern is with the sick. Was this Spaniard suffering as you did?" Julianne asked.

"Not yet, but he will suffer, and so will you," Dodd threatened.

"Be still, Dodd," Gilford said. "There will be no harm to the sisters if you answer. For you, I fear it is already too late. Speak now and know that for giving up the Spaniard you will save your flock."

Julianne thought of Linda and Jeanne Sweeney and lowered her head. There was no rhyme or reason to the madness of London's obsession with Catholics. No sense in it at all. For any answer she would give would only doom them.

"Do ye know what will happen to you?" Gilford asked as she refused. He waited for her to reconsider and wanted to hear it from Julianne's lips. "If you help us there will be no room for you at New Gate," he finally said.

"I have had so many memories and experienced such joy," her voice was nostalgic, "that it has been more than enough payment for any suffering that I might endure. Do what you must, Gilford. You cannot take my soul."

❧ ❧ ❧

St. Bartholomew's the Greater was a bricked compound in disrepair that served well the Worshipful Company of Butchers. Rodrigo entered his study just above the blacksmith hall. He had a platter with tea and scones set down on a table and gave his view through the Oriel Window. Below, in the courtyard of the former priory, Mary was playing with Agnes. He turned briskly to hand Miguel a letter. "It is from the Ambassador of Spain," he said.

Miguel opened it, "Alvaro de la Quadra…" his pause was followed by his question, "how is he?"

Rodrigo took a sip. "The Count is well. He's not pleased with Elizabeth's court, or the Anglican mandate, but he is well. Read…" he said quietly.

After some silence between them Miguel asked with uncertainty: "He has received the O'Neill's request?"

Rodrigo sat down and folded his hands across his lap, "I must say that there was a concern in his expression as soon as he understood that it was you who brought O'Neill's offer. Did you know that the Pope was searching for you?"

Miguel's posture tightened, "I suspected."

"Show me your arms so that I can see you are the same man who can read the Father's intent," Rodrigo replied.

Miguel pulled the cuff of his right sleeve up and revealed the markings. "I am the same," he said surely.

"If you are found out, those marks will bear you great pain," Rodrigo whispered.

Miguel covered himself, thinking that he had already endured enough pain to last a lifetime. It made little difference if it was here or in Ireland. He would be hunted. "I will endeavor to keep my freedom. That you can be sure of."

Rodrigo had seen men like Miguel before. The thought of martyrdom digging in to their sense and sensibility. He doubted that Miguel truly believed that he would not take unnecessary risk. His tone was not reassuring, "The ambassador told me that you have been away so long that King Phillip presumed you dead and the Pope has not condoned your actions. You are here unexpectedly."

"I am here on a mission," Miguel replied.

"The count will see you only after he has relayed your whereabouts to Pius himself. King Phillip is also not happy with the circumstances which have come about at your behest. Did you think that word would not reach back to him?"

"I had hoped it would. Spain has made a promise to those who are oppressed."

"Urging O'Neill to war has cast doubt to the Pope's intent for Ireland. The King is also your King and Phillip is closest with the Earl of Desmond. He holds little affection for O'Neill." Miguel shifted uncomfortably as Rodrigo continued. "It appears you have come to do a thing which has not yet been asked of you."

Miguel felt a swelling in his throat, "To wait is not easily done, when God Himself has spoken to me."

"Sacrilege! You are not God's messenger on earth!"

"O'Neill is prepared now and so Ireland is still within the Pope's ability to save. That is what has been placed in my heart."

"We are talking about England, not Ireland, and when we talk about Ireland, the Pope will most certainly embrace the Earl of Desmond. As will King Phillip of Spain," Rodrigo replied.

"Does Quadra know that the Earl of Desmond refused me?"

"The Earl of Desmond did not refuse the Pope. It was you who took it upon yourself to incite the O'Neill. You were to have gained allegiances in Ulster, not encouraged open attack. You were also instructed to handle the Fitzgerald of Kildare and yet the earl is still alive. That is what I was told and the ambassador assures me when the Pope hears of this he will likely excommunicate you. Did you know that?"

Miguel tore the letter up and threw it on the floor. "My own King is blind and the Pope has been deceived to believe such things. O'Neill did not attack… he defended as this unholy queen sent her demons into Ulster! You must go back to Quadra and tell him of that. It is the queen whom should be cast out and not I."

There was a silence between them until a sparrow landed on the window sill with rushing feathery flight. Then another tapped at the glass having landed on the frame to pick at the moss. Rodrigo spoke first, "If you are to be heard, you will be heard at Bear Garden. It will take weeks for this communication to occur. In the meantime, you can no longer stay here. Your very presence has brought unwanted attention to me. There is also the matter of the nuns. One has gone missing because of you."

Rodrigo stood again and walked back to the window. He scratched a fingernail along the glass and the sparrow flew away. His tone was filled with empathy and inflection, "I want to help... but you must understand my very livelihood here depends on the success of St. Bartholomew's. Should I appear to have the sympathies of the wrong people..." he pulled at his tunic and then continued with discomfort, "this hospital would be shut down and all of my work would be for naught."

"You have placed yourself in the way of harm, and I understand."

"Thomas Smyth has placed a bounty on your head and he offers reward for information about the girl. The fact that she is a Scott only complicates things. Why are you involved with such distractions?" Rodrigo asked.

Miguel replied: "Smyth has as many enemies in Ireland as he has friends. That is why I am involved. The girl is the key to trade between the free chieftains of Ireland and the Scotts of Kintyre. She will be fostered until she comes of age and can claim her right as a countess."

Rodrigo said: "That is your business, but it suits the cause ill. You have strayed far from the knowledge of Rome. Let us hope it is not too late for you."

"I appreciate the warning. I will take the girl and be gone by morning.

"Mary will bring you cloths for her and you will also take away the nuns." Rodrigo said.

"I cannot," Miguel replied.

"Take them with you. You created their condition and you will help them. I do not care where you go as long as it is not here. We lost Julianne last night and I will not risk being questioned myself."

Miguel felt the weight of what he was being asked, "I have no way to get them out of London."

"You can put them on donkeys for all it matters, but they cannot stay any longer. It endangers my mission much more than it endangers yours. If you don't believe me look what I found last night," Rodrigo said, walking over to his desk to lift a tattered scroll. "It reads: '*We have found the record of the guilty and will be coming.*' I can only assume the archives have been raided. It is one of many problems we have here in London. Names and births and confirmations that were all written down for posterity. Thankfully, I am not one of those who are in the records. On the other hand, whoever it is that took Julianne has everything they need to prosecute the widows and those that aide them for heresy. I will have no choice but to report this letter to Elizabeth's court if I am to be seen as a loyal physician."

"Even though the widows tend the sick they would harm them?" Miguel asked.

"They will. Other wards have already been subjugated to this sordid treatment and I can tell you it all ends with a tight rope at Tyburn," Rodrigo replied.

"Do you know who might have taken her?" Miguel asked.

Rodrigo answered: "As far as Catholics are concerned, there's been nothing good and nothing gained from the questions of Thomas Smyth."

London Port Authority, Blackfriars

Thomas Smyth of Westenhanger opened the door on the second floor of his office. "Has she told you?" he asked Gilford.

"Nay, Thomas. Not a word about the Spaniard. She knows nothing but feeble stories and so it would be well for her to go free," Gilford said.

Dodd held up a rope and smiled. "I can get her talking, Thomas."

Thomas looked at Julianne who sat sternly with a straight back and a defiant look in her eye. "She cannot be returned to St. Bartholomew's so she will go straight to New Gate Prison. I have already notified the Sheriff and testified in the House of Commons. All the heretics shall be collected."

Thomas paused, and then looked up at Julianne, "Do ye know what time the feme' prisoners are allowed a toilet?" he asked her.

Julianne had seen the prison at New Gate on more than one occasion. In her younger years a most notable priest had given her alms for the poor ladies there. Toilet was a necessity much better suited to the gutter than down the leg and at New Gate those things didn't matter. The feme' tunnels reeked of the sewer and the guards profited from the inmate's anguish. New Gate was the worst place to be. Worse even than the field before Tyburn of Traitors.

"I am familiar with New Gate Prison," she said, and the memory was the thing that made her cry.

"Good. These men will deliver you today for there is no need to ask you anything further. Either you know of the girl and Spaniard or you do not. It matters little to me now. I have obtained all the proof I need to ensure that you will not be alone in that prison." Thomas looked at Gilford and Dodd and then returned his emotionless gaze to her, "It must be a frightening thing to know that none shall pay the jailer for your better keep?"

"I know nothing," Julianne said with a whimper.

CHAPTER 31

O' Donnell Boy

mma Colley sat at the base of a cage which hung two feet above the ground. It was a huge iron thing, rusted and creaking in the northern wind as it rocked its captive from his sleep. The man looked almost regal in his fur. His crisp blue eyes beamed over rosy cheeks, weathered by the sun and cold. After looking closer, Emma saw he was much older than she imagined. She held out a biscuit and cup of malted barley.

He nodded with appreciation as if expecting her, "That is a fine way to start a day," Calvagh said.

"It is from your loving wife, my lord," Emma replied.

He ate the biscuit in two mouthfuls and quenched his thirst so quickly that it spilled down his grey beard and dripped from his belly to the bars below. She watched him. She pitied him and she heard him swallow. His gaze darted to hers briefly in his own realization that he had forgotten his manners. "Katherine has fared goodly?" he asked as the crumbs fell off his chin.

Emma did not think so, but she nodded politely and sat down on a stool. "She is a prisoner as well, my lord," she said, knowing that Katherine was much better off than he.

The earl smiled. "Who are you?" he asked provocatively.

"Emma Colley…" thinking that she was mistaken, she corrected herself, "Emma, the Mistress to Gowl."

"You do not seem so happy, Emma of Gowl," he replied.

"No," she said with a sigh.

"Why not?" he asked.

"I am unsure of who I am," Emma told him.

The Earl of Tryconnell laughed like he knew exactly how she felt and was kindred in her spirit. He seemed to be kindly affectionate and overly filled with zeal for being held in such a condition. "I know who I am but none seem to understand," he chuckled.

"I know also. Your wife insisted that I know how important you are. She wants you to be free and happy," Emma said.

"Do you think so?" he replied.

"You are Calvagh O'Donnell and loved by Queen Elizabeth as Lord of Tryconnell," Emma told him, longing to feel the safety of England once again. She had wished now that she had never left her room. She would have finished painting and if the vicar had been killed it would not have been by her hand.

"Is that what my dutiful wife has told thee?" Calvagh asked.

"Yes," Emma replied knowing he did not believe her. As she spoke she watched a butterfly flutter through the rusted cage and land on Calvagh's beard. His blue eyes turned down his nose inquisitively and focused on the yellow and black wings. He moved his hand slowly and it gently lifted its legs to take a finger. The butterfly moved and he smiled. "See it flutter its beautiful wings as if saying hello?" he asked her.

"It is lovely," Emma acknowledged. As he examined the bright color and blew on the softness of the delicate insect she asked: "Why does O'Neill treat you this way?"

Calvagh stretched out his arm and reached through the cage releasing the butterfly to open air. "I am not treated badly. I get a bath once a week and have walks everyday if I want them. Katherine even sends me a woman now and then," he said with a bit of glimmering satisfaction. The gesture made him appear feeble.

"Are you not faithful to her?" she asked.

He avoided the question, and laughed. "What have thee heard of Tryconnell and England?" he answered instead.

Emma shook her head as if to say she was sorry, "I have heard nothing good, my lord."

"Yes, exactly... and that is what I feared when I accepted an earldom. We are well north and west of the Pale. London Derry is not the epitome of the Queen's concern I am afraid." He clenched a fist, "I should have known." He reflected and scrunched his bottom lip over his mustache and continued, "Tryconnell is a lovely place you know. Lovely... but we did not stand a chance amongst the wolves."

"You or your own army?" Emma questioned.

"O'Neill has defeated my knights but he will never defeat me. Even when the queen does not exactly care that I sit in this cage," he replied.

"Were you taken in battle?" Emma asked.

Calvagh grabbed the iron bars with both hands to have a stretch. He flexed his arms, squatted to his bottom and then looked at the sky. "We were taken hostage by O'Neill while praying in church. Is that not what my dear wife told thee?"

"I fear you do not wish to know what she told me," Emma replied.

"Well it wasn't battle that was my doom. No...no lass... it was the pig ass and scandalous traitor O'Neill who would do such a cowardly thing as to take a hostage whilst he was praying!" His banter raised his dander and she could see his rage. "Why are you here?" he asked abruptly.

"I do not know," she said.

Seeing him isolated and locked in his cage made the earl look harmless. He was more human and even intriguing than she ever thought an earl could be. For a moment, a very brief moment, Emma pondered what it would be like to lay with such a man. And then he reached through the bar and touched her.

"Tell me, why are you here?" he asked her again.

"I am ashamed to tell thee," Emma whispered.

"Shamed?" Calvagh put his face through the bars nearest Emma as she sat on her stool. He seemed hungry to know her. Hungry for her attention. "Shamed is nothing. Talk to me truly for none have been shamed more than I. There is no fear of shame with a man who lives in an iron cage."

"None here must ever know," Emma whispered.

"Alright then. Tell me truly about my wife. Does she sleep with the O'Neill?" Calvagh asked.

Emma felt a flash of heat run across her face, "I could never speak of such things."

Calvagh saw her discomfort and sat back down smiling and rubbing his beard. "Try..." he said desperately as he began to lick his lips. "Does she like it?"

"I would not know," Emma said.

"Did she tell you to bed me?" Calvagh asked.

Emma stood, turning nervously to see if Katherine was coming and found herself alone with only the wind, green grass and castle wall to hear her. "If I told thee that I was a witch would you believe me?" she whispered.

Calvagh slapped his knee playfully, "I don't believe in witches."

"The people of my town believed it. My own husband thought I was mad," she whispered.

"Are you insane?" he asked.

"I do not know," Emma whispered.

"Nor do I," Calvagh admitted.

"I burned a vicar before I came here," Emma blurted out tersely, expecting he would reel back with loathing.

Calvagh sighed his resignation, seeing that she would not delight him. "That is a heavy burden," he confessed.

"I have done more terrible things," Emma said.

Calvagh began to disrobe, "Did I not say that O'Neill indulges me with women?"

Emma did not respond but neither did she turn away. *Maybe this time*, he thought, *maybe he would really do it.* "Oh yes. I have maidens sent to me on occasion. It is never at night, though." He raised an eyebrow in jest, "It is always during the day so that everyone will see my lust. Are you to come into my cage today?" he asked.

He distracted her, "Absolutely not," Emma exclaimed.

"Then why are you here," he asked, feigning disappointment.

"O'Neill took my town. He took it and there was nothing I could do. If I stayed I would risk being burned alive. Only my husband Henry could have prevented such a thing but he came not to save me. So I went with Gowl. Gowl of Tyrone who has given me the promise of a child," Emma said.

"Well then, Emma. Now... I know why you are here and that we are not so different." Calvagh buttoned his shirt and covered his shoulders in fur once again. "I have never been unfaithful to my wife. She sends maidens to me in hopes that I will succumb and I know she even watches now. She wants to be the wife of the O'Neill Mor, but he will not marry her unless she is divorced. So...I disrobe each time she tempts me but only to taunt her," he said with a smile.

Emma saw that Gowl returned up the path to the castle. It was strange that she felt as though she had just cheated on him. She was so naive to men, she thought. "It is time for me to go."

Calvagh reached through the bars again and held out his hand, "Will you come talk with me more?" he asked.

"I do not know. In the morrow if we have not yet left for Omagh," she replied.

CHAPTER 32

On the Inside

I t was duty day in the mint and Thomas Smyth crossed the moat below Byward Tower, and stopped for a moment to view the bridge over Thames. The shoreline bristled with a forest of static masts waiting on him to give the order. *Sail or stay to trade another day*, he thought. He knew that across the bridge in Southwark, the aldermen had assembled and the city would remain in quarantine. People didn't care really, he surmised. A groat or penny was worth taking a risk for. Within the walls of the old quarter, things carried on in a semi normal state.

"The gate is open, sir," one of the watchmen told him as he looked toward the tower.

Thomas walked with the many inside and heard the praising of the queen from the daily orator, giving the courts dictate. The man was dressed in black with a fluffy burgundy bonnet. Further on, in a tiny square enclosed by the dark wood façade of inner shops, a scribe scribbled down a figure. Thomas's inclination was to remain calm. He must appear as if nothing was out of the ordinary. That might be hard with the old fellow who always seemed to have a way of discernment. His next thought was that he had been back from Ireland for less than a month and again he was tempting his fate with the crown. The orator's announcing of England's prolific glory did little to satiate his mind and the scribe would surely take an accurate accounting. It was troubling.

"Come, come," he told his porters who carried the chests behind him. They grunted under the load and a rattle of commodities within hinted of their cargo. A few moments later he found himself standing at the entrance to the royal mint and the guards who guarded the door with puffy shoulders swayed as their arms swung forward and their boots came together with a snap. "I come with the queen's duties," he announced. There was the usual acknowledgment and then the courteous and disciplined side step as they allowed him to pass.

Overseeing the endeavors of purchasing bullion and converting the metal to a spendable form, was the chief coin maker. He in turn was scrutinized by the warden. Thomas had heard the latter would not be in the mint today. It would certainly be to his advantage if it was true.

"Over here. Put the chest over here if you please," a scribe instructed.

The porters did and Thomas stood near the fresco of Christ's Crucifixion as the porters exited the mint to wait outside. Such a sight, he thought as he assessed the art on either side of the bricked fireplace. It was an impressive mural and he understood the meaning of it now more than ever. A depiction of scales with the angel Gabriel on one side and the great evil doer tipping the odds to his favor on the other. And all the souls fell off the devil's end to a fiery death below. It was the fate for those who dared to steal from England. Thomas thought about that. He thought about the fire as he stared at the face of Satan.

"Shall we take the accounting now, Thomas?" the coin master asked, coming from a room that extended out from under White Tower. He hesitated in front of the mural. "Shall you hand me the ledger, sir?" the chief coin master asked.

Thomas held out his accounting, "Set 'em there," the older man said pointing to a table as he moved toward the chests to give his inspection. Turning back to Thomas he continued as he always did, "We shan't be striking the pennies anymore. Tis a shame really."

Thomas politely showed bemusement, "No?"

The older man kept talking and took out a key that he used to unlock the chests that Thomas brought. Thomas was the only one to have the other. He examined the contents, took the ledger and opened it. "No... not going to strike the smaller coins at all from what I have been told. Lord Gresham believes that the pennies should be pressed with a fancy machine."

"Sounds more efficient," Thomas said, not caring either way.

"The lads and I say the machine will degrade the sterling with its ability to press the harder metals. There is no need to change something if something is not broken, says we." The chief coin maker shook his head regretfully. "But... alas... who am I, except an old man in the service?"

"Well, I am sure Her Majesty has good faith in Lord Gresham and although it may appear fruitless, one cannot fight change," Thomas replied.

"I think the whole idea is rather threatening. There will be a lesser accounting of true silver and the ability to create mass quantities of pennies will certainly make them worth next to nothing," the coin master complained.

Thomas wanted out of the mint. Everyone here was so calculating. They spent days drooling over the minutia. "They are only pennies, coin maker. I suppose the true wealth will not actually ever leave England. Pennies are a trifling thing."

"No— they are one of many denominations— but they are not trifling!"

Thomas did not wish to dally, he did not wish to offend, he simply wanted out of the furnace. *Nothing ventured, nothing gained, was that not the saying? Not in the mint it seemed.* He gave no reply.

"Will you not help me to the scales, Thomas?" the coin maker asked.

"I have counted, weighed and tallied the sum and noted its value in that ledger. It can be made into bullion or refined with Elizabeth's pretty face. Do you really need to weight it?" he asked, referring to the Irish coinage taken from the *Pinnacle.*

The sound of the coins as they cascaded through the old man's fingers pleased him. They were heavy. "It is good to have you back from Ireland, Thomas Smyth. How did you enjoy the time away from this great city?" he asked.

"I would have stayed longer if possible," Thomas replied.

"I would do also," the coin maker said suddenly seeming more cheerful, "there are good reports from the Pale. I have heard that civility is common and the fields are ripe. My son has considered going. Did you make a tidy profit with your lady friend?" he asked.

The comment took Thomas off guard. "I... I don't know what lady friend you refer of?"

"Oh, what was her name? That lovely Irish woman. Oh yes, it was Catherine whom you toured in this very mint a few years back. Did she not travel with you to Ireland?"

Thomas's face reddened with the man's recollection of a single tour he had made with Catherine Bourke over three years past. "She and I have not seen each other for ages. My business in Ireland was strictly one to establish a plantation in Kings County. Thank you for asking though. I am astonished you remember."

The old man smiled, "Even one as old as I can notice a fine woman when I see her. There was much talk of Lady Bourke within these walls. She was no stranger to the tower you know. Although I believe your attentions upon her would be no different than any whom she accompanied."

Thomas looked out the door as the line of merchants began to grow. This old buzzard was drooling and that troubled him. "I have some business with Lord Gresham presently, in Windsor, and so I do not have much time," Thomas said, trying to avoid any further inquiry.

"Very good, sir, but I believe Lord Gresham is in Hampton, unless I am mistaken."

Thomas puzzled. *How in the bloody hell would he know that? The folly of a foolish heart?* Then he corrected himself, "I believe he is, it was my mistake," he replied and *bastard*, was what he thought.

"The court has not yet moved to Windsor and still resides in Hampton," the coin maker said as if he were instructing. Thomas nodded politely. "I'll make the notation of fifty pounds' silver as you have written, Thomas Smyth."

"Very good then," Thomas replied.

"You'll ensure my pennies are as good tomorrow as they are today in Cheap Ward, won't you Thomas?" the coin master asked.

"Of course," Thomas said politely.

The Prison

Of all the gates that opened to the city of London, New Gate was by far the most notable. Not far from Thomas Smyth's business and across the city from St. Bartholomew's, the widow Julianne found herself removed.

"It didn't have to go this way, you know," Dodd told her.

Julianne looked up at the six stories of New Gate and dreaded the sounds of the prison below. It was a stone wall of madness. It had windows, halls, and two arched doorways and she had walked through it pitying those who were held inside many times before.

Dodd pushed Julianne forward until they reached a drab looking yeoman of the ward. He was the type of parasite that made his living off the hapless. "This woman has been recorded by the lords and Thomas Smyth of Westenhanger for the crime of heresy," Dodd announced.

Julianne heard a racket coming up from the basement. Shouting echoed off the stone work as the guard assessed her with bulging round eyes. "Do ye have a paying husband?" he asked her.

"I am a widow," Julianne replied.

The guard spoke to Dodd expectantly, "It is a farthing per week, per bed," he stated.

Dodd cleared his throat as a child ran up from the sewer and slipped out with his shaggy hair and dirty bare feet into the street behind them. The guard didn't even bother to chase the lad. "Will you be paying for her internment?" he asked.

"No need, the biddy won't be here that long," Dodd said.

The yeomen grunted with contempt. He could make good money off some but rarely did he earn for widows. Seemingly uninterested in taking charge of her care, he questioned Dodd again, just to be sure. "What heresy?"

"She has been named for confirming Catholics, and there will be others coming soon," Dodd replied.

"She can't work and the basement is full already. Thomas Smyth will need to settle with the Sheriff and pay for a bed before I take her," he informed Dodd.

"There will be others coming whom you can earn from but this woman will do fine in a crowded basement," Dodd insisted.

The guard clarified, "One half pence each time I have to unlock her. Every day, twice a day, and one additional halfpence for her walks to the latrine. He will also be billed for the bridge toll to Southwark when she goes to meet the executioner."

Dodd reluctantly offered a two-day advance. The guard hefted it, mulled it over with his thumb and then put it directly in his pocket. "Will thee purchase her a torch?"

Dodd replied: "A bloody torch?"

An arm bending moment later, Julianne was roughed through the iron bars that led to the lower basement. She was thusly inducted into the New Gate Prison, a place where she had never thought she would be.

CHAPTER 33

Apples

A t St. Bartholomew's the Greater, preparations were being made. Miguel watched Agnes as the child slept soundly on the floor. Her hair was cut, her gown had been replaced with dirty brown trousers and she had eaten. She had not questioned him since he had told her the story.

"Miguel," Mary said, opening the door to the attic.

Miguel pulled a robe over Agnes and then turned to see Mary behind him.

"Is this what you wanted?" she asked.

"Si," he said as she handed him a bundle of carrots and then brought some of the wine that he loved so dearly.

"I do not want to wake her," Mary said quietly.

"Did you have enough money?" he asked.

Mary looked grateful, "More than enough."

Her return caught him off guard and indeed Miguel wondered if she would not be better off to find her way alone. He had given her enough coin to start over, hoping she might run away. Mary placed all but what was needed for his meager request back in his hands. "We will wake her in an hour. Are the others ready?" Miguel asked.

"Not happy... but ready. I have gone down Bakers Street and asked about Julianne..." she did not finish but her expression told Miguel everything.

"So people have seen her?" Miguel asked.

"I have an idea who took her," Mary replied.

"It is in the Lord's hands now; we cannot wait any longer." Miguel whispered.

"I know," Mary sighed looking at the window, "it is just that Julianne saved me," her voice trembled, "she saved me from the streets and now she is gone. Is there nothing that can be done?"

His words were a comfort, "It is because of me, not you."

"I was told that some of Thomas Smyth's men have come out at Broken Wharf and Blackfriars and have already detained a goodly number of people. They have been locking up the known Catholics."

Miguel saw that Mary was having doubts and asked: "Do you remember what I told you?"

"Aye, but there are checkpoints all over the city. If Julianne was taken, it is Smyth who is behind it. They look for the girl and have very detailed accounts of you." Mary looked to the floor, "Did you harm her?" she asked.

"Does she look harmed?" Miguel asked.

"No... but they have said you are a murderer," Mary replied.

"That is not a lie." He watched as Mary's hand pulled away from him. He wanted to reach out and touch it. He wanted her to know that everything he had ever done was to please his earthly father, but that had changed. His heart was changing. *My voice must remain sure, strong, not leaving her any doubt*, he thought before speaking. "At six o'clock I want you and the other widows to put on your cloaks and walk quickly up Wood Street. Do not stop for anyone until passing through Cripple Gate. Do you know a place called Draper's Alms House?"

"Linda and Jeanne have spoken of it," Mary said.

"Good. After passing through Cripple Gate, go directly there. I want you to take Agnes," Miguel told her.

"Will you not protect us?" Mary asked.

"I cannot be seen with you. When you get to the alms house, send Jeanne or Linda to ask the inn keeper for Ginger. Do not all go, and do not take Agnes inside. You need to find a place to hide until you know the house is safe," Miguel said.

"What if she doesn't return?" Mary asked.

He took her shoulder and spoke quickly, "You must find your way alone. Run as far and as fast as you can and do not turn back. If it is meant to be I will find you." Mary looked horrified as she gazed down at Agnes. "Her father was a very important man and now he is dead. Keep her safe and I will come for you all."

"And if it goes poorly?" Mary asked.

"Survive," he said.

New Gate Prison

In the dungeon of New Gate Prison, a superior voice called out and echoed down the dank tunnel of slippery brown stone.

"Deborah... Deborah Horn, is that you?" Julianne called under the flicker of a noxious torch. Julianne shuffled forward, taking care where she placed her feet. She could scarcely believe her eyes. Deborah had gone missing from West Smithfield weeks ago, and yet there she was laying in the muck. The disappearance had been the reason that Rodrigo insisted on calling the nuns of St. Bartholomew's widows. Julianne's foot slid into the sludge of human decay and she bent down to touch the nun she recognized, with pity.

Deborah grabbed Julianne's wrist defiantly, "What do you want!" she hissed.

"Deborah... it is I." Julianne answered

"I cannot see you," Deborah said, as she squinted toward the light of Julianne's torch.

"Julianne of the sisterhood, Deborah. You know me well," Julianne said, hoping that her dear and trusted friend would recognize her voice.

"They found you?" Deborah asked sadly, realizing she was not in a dream.

"No— they took me. I was abiding by the law— but they took me," Julianne said more as a matter of fact than an admission.

Deborah pointed to nineteen crooked marks carved into the sludge that coated the brick walls of the sewer. Her fingers were blackened and raw. "I have been counting, Julianne, that is how many days I think, since I have missed a toilet. I don't want another and pray they will soon hang me."

"Have none brought you alms, Sister? Have you eaten?" Julianne asked.

Deborah struggled to focus, she brushed a strand of hair away from her eyes and something inside her gave her trembling hand a bit of strength. It was her anger, "Our contracts have all been forgotten, Julianne! There have not been alms for the feme' since Smyth ordered me here," she replied.

"No, Deborah, our contracts have not all been forgotten. Even some who have sank into the depths of evil still remember." Julianne told her friend.

A cackle came from the darkness, "Lots of good that did ya! Now shut the hell up!"

Deborah rattled out a laughed, "And thieves too, Julianne," she whispered and then she tried to stand, "there are thieves down here. Any help has never made it back this far," she said.

"You just get yourself up and help me unbutton," Julianne said, turning her back to her shaky friend.

Seeing Julianne gave Deborah hope and strength and light. She found her feet and tried to release Juliann's neckline. "How did ya get so fat, Julianne?" she asked with ridiculously awkward humor.

It made Julianne smile, "I am not fat you louse ridden twit. I am stuffed. Now bite the damned button if you have to," she replied.

Deborah did and the next button popped open easily to allow Julianne's oversized gown to drop on the wretched floor. "Now help me unwrap and keep your belligerent tongue quiet."

It took them several minutes to unravel the cloth around Julianne's body. "Keep them wrapped tight and close, we may not be getting more for a while," Julianne said as she reached into her last layer of robes and pulled an apple from her bosom. "Eat," she said quietly.

"How many do thee have?" Deborah asked.

"Enough…" Julianne whispered as her torch went out.

Spontaneous Combustion

Elizabeth walked leisurely and thought of Thomas Butler as the larks sang and flirted across the pond. What a court she had; sculpted with ornamental dragons, high pillars and expansive courtyards bounded by painted red bricks. She relished the magnificence of her father's estate. The head of her stately affairs walked with her.

"Your mind seems to be elsewhere, Majesty. Maybe a walk with an old man does not please thee?" William Cecil asked.

"Your company is ever wanted," Elizabeth replied.

"Has your Majesty considered the shipping?" William asked.

The fondness between them was comforting, "We need a stronger fleet of ships, Lord Burghley. I fear that all the hawks are circling and England relies too much on privateers."

"Perhaps we need to leverage every asset that can be sourced, rather than trying to build. Ships included. Spain requires that we must look to private enterprise. We simply do not have the money for a separate state fleet."

"We must find the resources," Elizabeth answered.

"In time, but to encourage private sail captains and trading companies is the quickest way to achieve those resources. In particular, I believe we might complement Admiral Hawkins with the *Good Ship Jesus* for expeditions into the Indies. He can raise his own men at arms and sail under an English flag if we put a charter to his cause."

"That will not solve our problems in Ireland or with Spain," Elizabeth replied.

"It is a start. We must not be overextended. Look around and see a thousand souls inside your court who have heard your vision and want nothing more than to unravel it. Your credit is that those persons have proved unsuccessful. You have turned away an internal war, and unlike King Louis of France, the people love you. The whole world is watching."

"Not so well in the Ire' I fear."

William balked, "We have only to deal with O'Neill in Ireland and Connaught cannot oppose us alone. Mayhap we should consider a reformation of strategy with Ireland whilst we gain the shipping needed to secure our interests apart from papacy? Every measure in that direction will be taken for the better of England and eventually the world, if you ask me."

"That is not what my father would have done. He would have invaded outright, rather than accept the outlandish proposals of chieftains," Elizabeth replied.

"Your father was older than you, and he never had such a court," William assured her. "He also did not send an army to Ireland but had the common sense to let them quarrel among themselves and remain divided."

Elizabeth took a long deep breath of fresh air, "Enough of Ireland, does the admiral have his own investors?"

"He does and he has a competent first mate in his nephew, Francis Drake."

The Queen thought and walked with William beside her and then asked: "Spain does not rely on privateers so heavily. They have a new world of gold. Does Alvaro de la Quadra believe our resources of state to be deficient?" Elizabeth asked.

"It would be good that he did, for although Spain has found such riches, a fleet of privateers could acquire some of that gold and Spain would be none the wiser. Bishop Quadra believes there is still hope for your marriage to a Catholic. Our other Spanish friend, Count de Feria, believes us weak and his ego is as bloated as the Spanish armada," William replied.

Elizabeth pondered the condition as three white geese landed in her pond. They were free, so very free of thought or politics. What it would be like to fly away and never look back. She sighed, "Very well, Lord Burghley. You have my endorsement for Admiral Hawkins. We will invest and he must have his own crew and return a profit. Pick a trade that even Spain cannot deny. A commodity that can be sold at high margins."

At long last William felt a triumph, "Consider it done. Now you must know that Bishop Quadra wishes to have a gesture of good will extended before he meets with you today."

Elizabeth brought her hand to her mouth playfully, "What pray tell?"

"I wish it was just play my Queen, but it is not. He has asked for the release of Earl Fitzgerald."

Elizabeth grunted, "Lord Fitzgerald of Desmond?" she asked.

"And also Fitzgerald of Kildare," William replied.

"I did not want to keep Desmond a prisoner for long anyway. He is a handsome man but he is hot headed. You may tell the ambassadors that I agree to Lord Fitzgerald's release but I do not hold the Earl of Kildare a hostage."

"The Earl of Kildare is in Dublin's Castle, Majesty. He has been detained by Lord Radcliffe for months. If their presence eases the tension between us and Spain, it may also embolden O'Neill to accept your invitation. It would be good to get the three of them together right here in London where we can deal with them all at once," William told her.

"You are a crafty old man," she replied. Nothing displeased her more than the ambassador of Spain except perhaps the outlandish claims from Ulster. She needed to put an end to O'Neill and the Fitzgerald dynasty that continued to waiver in their devotion. Presently however, she had another lord of Ireland in mind. A lord who loved her. "I will consider it as I tennis with Lord Butler."

William stopped immediately when she revealed her daily plan. He stood in the gravel so she was forced to stop herself and pay attention. "It is not fitting for you to sport against your gentlemen lords. I will speak with Lord Butler and inform him that you will be engaged," William said.

"You are no fun, Lord Burghley. No fun at all. As I have said, I cannot meet with him today. You may tell the ambassador that our congress has been delayed until the move to Windsor. It would be good for him to know we are leaving. You will also ensure he understands he will need to arrange for his own apartments outside of my walls."

William looked at her like a father, "Do not play with Spain, your Majesty. We need to ease King Phillips encroachments not provoke him," he told her.

"It will ease both Bishop Quadra and Count de Feria to know they have given up their stately quarters so that the earls Fitzgerald of Desmond and Kildare are well tended by me. They cannot have everything they want. For the pressure attempted to be inflicted on me, I will not have those Spanish bastards spend another evening in a royal palace."

"Yes, my queen," William said softly seeing that he had disappointed her.

Cheap Ward

Miguel entered Smyth field where the sheep man stayed and darkness loomed over the city. The widows had made it out of St. Bartholomew's just hours before. A ram alerted. "Have thee come for me?" Joshua asked, believing the light of God stood before him.

"I have," Miguel replied as he squatted near Joshua's fire.

"Do you have the girl?" Joshua asked.

Miguel heard a nervousness in Joshua's voice, "You look afraid. Is there someone watching you?" he asked.

Joshua turned his back to the street, "Aye," he whispered.

"Have thee betrayed me?" Miguel asked.

"Aye," Joshua said again and twitched his head mechanically toward the pub. The streets were quiet, much too quiet as Miguel eased away from the fire. "Is the Mistress Talles in the house?" he asked.

"She is with a man named Gilford. I told them that you would come for me. I told her she would die. Gilford beat me for saying such things. They beat me to find out what I knew."

"You should not have told them anything," Miguel said.

"I am a weak man. It has as always been that way but I don't want to be weak," Joshua said sadly.

"I know of your weakness and say to you that to take the easy road will always make your life hard but when you have the courage to take the hard road, your life will be made easy. Be thankful I do not kill you instead of your sister."

As Miguel turned away, Joshua grabbed him by the arm, "Wait, wait, don't leave me here. I am tired but I will not betray you again." he pleaded. "They will kill you!"

"Do you not know that whoever awaits me could never harm an angel?" Miguel told him without fear.

Joshua fell to the ground and put his face into the ashes and Miguel raised him up so that he might not be burned. And then he left the sheep man without another word. The fire crackled behind him as the old ram bleated. A moment later as he steeled himself for what lay inside, Miguel pushed open the pub door.

The fire was burning. "You will not be harmed," Gilford said immediately.

"I assure you, I won't," Miguel replied, surveying his surroundings and expecting to be attacked, "where is the mistress?"

Gilford replied coldly, "She is tied in the hog yard. We have been waiting for you, my friend," he said.

Miguel moved forward and opened his hands and heart for battle. "She is a trader of young girls. I cannot imagine how either of you could anticipate the arrival of a man such as I."

Gilford picked at his tooth with a shard of wood. He knew what he was up to, Miguel did not, and he watched the strange priest move quietly toward the back window. The Spaniard was large, stealthy, and unafraid. "I have heard you are a man who can be in two places at once. That is what my master has said."

Miguel said nothing.

"If it is not her who trades in flesh, it will be another," Gilford continued as he sat on a barstool and took a sip of ale.

"It is only the mistress whom I am concerned with. She has wrongly done a woman of Connaught. I shall kill her first and then your master, Thomas Smyth. You know who I am. I can see in your eyes your knowledge of me," Miguel warned.

Gilford smiled coldly. "I do not want to die. What if I told thee, that I knew of where the sister Julianne was and could help you provide her safety?"

"Why? Why would I risk everything just to save one physical body? The sister will soon be better off with her Father," Miguel replied.

"I work for Thomas Smyth it is true, but he is not my master. There are things Smyth must do before he dies." The fireplace below the cookpot caught a flame. It could have been a morsel of fat that ignited the coals or a coincidence but Miguel did not feel it so. Gilford's hand slid to the stool next to him and he began to grind the leg into the thresh of the floor. It was as if he was playing. "Besides... I do not like the man or some of the things he has had me do. You see, when I was young, there was only one person who gave me love. It was the nun whom Thomas has arrested. I would not take her to prison so Thomas gave the task to Dodd. Dodd is a fool." Gilford hesitated and then he stood up and walked to the cookpot and bent over. Miguel watched him as he placed his hand into the flame, "I am immune to the effects of the fire. Been that way since the scalding, I have..." he said before pulling his hand away.

Miguel felt a coldness in the room as Gilford spoke, "And what has that to do with me or the mistress of this house?" he asked.

"I know who you are and so does the other I work for. I have known since you took shelter in St. Bartholomew's, and I care nothing of it. You want a holy war. It is your business and you have done me a favor by killing that Osbert bastard. His time, like the slut ridden clot of a whore outside, is long past, but Thomas Smyth is another matter. Work with me and the nun Julianne will not rot at New Gate or swing from the Tyburn Tree."

"I cannot work with evil," Miguel said sternly.

"And I do not believe you will kill me. I believe you will listen," Gilford said.

"There are others who depend upon me. Others whom Julianne would not wish to risk," Miguel said.

Gilford stroked the wide brim of his newest hat, which was nearly a foot long. "I am deformed so I cover my head with these beautiful hats. Do you like this one?" he asked, with a glint of gold in his smile.

Colley Town

In the midlands, on the English plantation of Colley Town, Mary looked up to see the young vicar smiling with gleaming white teeth. He had shaven. His face was so perfectly formed that he looked like a sculpture. For the first time, since the terrible day of Henry Colley's return, Mary smiled.

"You have done well, Mary," Judas said happily.

"Thank you, Vicar," Mary replied. It had been a time of grief but having Judas so close to her made Mary dream of a future. He had taken kindly to her in the past few days and she couldn't help but adore his affection. Judas had suffered and yet he showed a true concern for others and a keen interest in her boys.

Mary called to her children who played near the rock piles, "Time to eat!"

John the blacksmith and his wife Susan, a few soldiers, and Henry Colley all came toward the chapel at once. It was as if they had never left or been forced to start over. Mary handed a loaf of her freshly baked bread to Annie Beth and she in turn gave to her husband. They would eat near the yellow house today and for Mary, the yellow house had never seemed more like home. The sun was beaming, the sky was blue, and the children laughed.

Vicar Judas held out his left hand and caressed the blond hair of Mary's son as he sped to the table. "Cooked over a fire and never has it smelled so good," Judas said. He waited until all had arrived from the fields and stood ready to receive their blessing. Holding the bread high over his head, he gave a gleeful thanks, "Lord, we thank you for this bounty. It is through Thine hands that we shall sustain and grow together. Bless this food and bless our headmaster, Henry… for all that he does in Your holy name. Amen."

"Amen," the people said.

Judas broke the bread and handed Henry half. Then he took a goblet made of wood and poured in the wine. One man to his left and one to his right, each did the same.

"And the Lord said: *take this bread and eat it. It is my body, broken for you*," Judas said as he took a piece of Mary's bread to his mouth. As the finely ground flour dissolved on his pallet, Judas cried tears. The water came to his eyes as if the Holy Spirit had embraced him. He took a breath, picked up the goblet and lifted. "And the Lord said: *This is my blood, shed for your sins. Take it and drink, for whoever believeth in Me, will have eternal life.*" He took a sip and set the goblet down in front of him and covered it with a sacramental cloth. The communion began with the men, and each took a piece of God's body and drank of God's blood. Thanksgiving.

Heaps of lentils and round boiled turnips graced the table. The sight pleased Adam Loftus who walked out of the stonework of a newly rebuilt church and then made his way to the people. Everyone noticed Adam as he cast a smile toward Judas. "I am well pleased, Judas. Let the people eat and know that God is good," he said.

Judas gleamed with satisfaction, "I wish to make disciples."

"You will, Judas," Adam said fondly. It appeared to Adam that Judas revered those at his table and even the soldiers who sat on blankets in the grass, "We shall have wine every day when the work is done. Thanks to Thomas Smyth," Adam said, cheerfully.

Judas replied: "God's thanks to Smyth, and may the husbands join their wives each night. England needs more children." There was some laughter and a glass was raised and then another and Adam took to the notion with great confirmation.

Henry thought of Emma, *the husbands should join their wives as they wish?* It made his skin crawl.

Annie Beth smiled happily… for however odd the vicar seemed… he was changing the plantation for the better. She grabbed her husband's hand and dared to speak. "Do you hear, Ethan?" she whispered.

"I hear," he replied as he squeezed her fingers.

❧ ❧ ❧

There were many thanks given the day that Adam Loftus left Colley Town. The entire lot of planters turned out and Henry looked back at the window of his bedroom. He thought of his conversation with Ralph Lane, who departed the day prior: *The soldier is much like the horse with bearing reins,* Ralph had said. *Both must hold their head up high and prance. It will never be easy, but a direction can be found in a most elegant fashion, if both the soldier and the horse learn not to resist. In the end, the bearing rein will always achieve a precise movement.* The thought lingered. Was he still a soldier? Ralph had told him he was. He watched as the trail of dust left off from Colley Town with Adam Loftus.

Judas stood in the center of the road, looking as if he had just lost a father. Henry went to his side, thinking he would walk with the new vicar for a while. The departed had left his impression on the young vicar. An impression that would be difficult to sway. As he joined the vicar in the road, Henry shielded his eyes from the sun and saw the last sign of Adam's carriage disappear from sight as the dust settled. They would be together now; they had been paired. "I have to admit, I thought the archbishop to be in error when he made you the Vicar of Colley Town," Henry said, to gain Judas's attention.

Judas looked at the empty road meandering through the fields that bordered it in the direction of Dublin. He then faced about and viewed the distance of the road in the direction of Geashill as it adjoined the great bog. On either side in that direction, there was a great deal of underbrush. There was also a forested patch very close to the western most fields. The nearness of the woods concerned him.

Judas was meticulous; clean and free of guilt. He turned from the thoughts of the wildlings to soak in the sight of pear blossoms and waving grass near the stone tower house. He heard Henry; he felt Henry's hand on his shoulder. Along the hill were the fresh graves and near them the whin bushes cast a beautiful yellow hue toward the road itself. He liked this place and he answered with simplicity: "I do not blame you. It must have been a sight of horror to see me the way I was."

"You have proven me wrong. You are very skilled and have already found a devotion among the common. For that, I am grateful," Henry said.

"Are we not all common?" Judas replied. The townsfolk began to go about their business. Judas thought he should do the same.

"I need these people to work. I need them to be happy, and as a matter of security, I need to know that when I am gone, they continue. I can see that you are not common, Judas."

Judas smiled, "You are unnecessarily burdened, Henry. I will do my best here when you leave."

Realizing he knew so little about his knew vicar, Henry asked: "Where did you come from Judas? I mean, before we found you. You seem to have miraculously gained the full trust and confidence of the most powerful clergyman in all of Ireland. That is no easy feat, and yet here you are."

"Truthfully, before you saved me, I came from Omagh. I, like my brothers, would have made war against you. I also tried very, very hard to be a Catholic priest. I was, and I suppose I will always be, of Clan O'Hagen." Seeing that Henry listened without reply, he confessed, "I was also a lover of men, Henry."

"That is not a bad thing. It is our Godly duty to love our fellow man."

Judas replied earnestly, "It is. Oh yes, Henry, it is our duty, and I was shown so many ways to love. And then I was betrayed and beaten and left to the animals of the field. Is it any wonder to you that I now devote myself to those who have shown me I was expendable?"

It was a strange reply but Henry could see the honesty in Judas that made him accept his answer without further discussion. He had known many priests to convert and many of them were peculiar in one way or another. "Well... Judas, it is a very small island we live on. I have word from the lords that soon we will march into Omagh. Does that disturb you?" he asked.

"Will you kill the innocent?" Judas asked with remarkable composure.

"Not the innocent, Judas," Henry replied.

"Then I will leave the war in God's hands and not fear or worry."

"And that is the answer I needed for you to have my trust with Colley Town," Henry replied.

Judas looked longingly to the people. He pursed his lips, "Oh... oh yes... it is what God has planned for us. I can see that now. Colley Town shall be rebirthed."

Henry took Judas's hand and they began to walk toward the church, "Can I confide in you, Judas?"

"I wish for it," Judas replied, feeling the warmth that Henry was trying to convey.

"There is one who I loved that may be in Omagh," he paused and looked Judas in the eye so that he might see his pain, "I loved her... and now I wish her dead."

Mary walked past them and smiled as Judas replied: "I have given my lover over to the darkest of enemies for the same hurt." Judas saw Mary enter the yellow house and then her boys followed. "They will need to be protected," he said.

"These people do, but I speak of my wife," Henry replied.

"To wish someone dead troubled me, and yet somewhere in my heart it also gave me satisfaction. When you lose someone whom you loved so deeply, sometimes satisfaction is all that can be had. We must pray together Henry. We must pray to be forgiven."

New Gate prison

Julianne lay in the filth with Deborah who was ailing from a swollen ankle. Someone coughed and then a series of cackles gave tell to the insanity of their situation. "Lord have mercy, Lord have mercy on these poor souls," she prayed. Deborah shivered next to her and she could hear the squeaking of mice. She sniffed a runny nose and felt the bulge of her sour apples against her ribs. *They had only four left*, she thought and then something touched her...

From out of nowhere a torch burst into flame and the heat came close to her face. "Come, poor mother," she heard as the chain was lifted off her leg. The light blinded her, just as it had blinded Deborah the day before. She raised her hand and saw him. It was he. It was the boy she knew behind that hideous mask. Gilford freed her, and Julianne turned to Deborah to do the same.

"Get your filthy mitts off me, Deborah complained, as Julianne woke her friend from sleep.

CHAPTER 35

Gone Missing

William Cecil left the dim light of his quarters to slip down a candle lit staircase of the Hampton royal apartments. He found his way to the lower compound where he hoped to go unnoticed passing under the high white window panes of the exterior facade. Hampton was a condition of work as well as home to a variety of subjects, and William knew them all. He looked down a narrow corridor to see the dark wooded doorframe of the apprentice quarters. Cobblers, cooks, and carpenters he thought. It appeared that the house vice steward had things in order. Of course, he longed for his own estate, but the time here in court was necessary. The care of the foundations of state, much like that care of the palace, were vital.

He heard his knees crackle as he walked. The little pops and prickles of age. His joints were stiff, much too stiff for his liking and he needed this spell of fresh air. His walk took him past the wine fountain where he heard voices of laughter and a vision of drunkenness repelled him. He continued discontentedly, wondering if he should scold the ill doers or ignore their mischief all together. He decided to ignore. While approaching the compound of the fountain, the baker's wife trotted by with two full pails of red wine. The woman pretended not to see him and darted down a narrow stair toward the servant dorms. It was enough to turn his stomach.

Before he could gather his thoughts of discouragement, another dilemma crossed him and it came in the form of a carpenter. "Lord Burghley," the master carpenter called out. William recoiled that the tradesman felt compelled to track him down. Did he not see he was cloaked?

"Oh…your Grace, good evening. Might I have a moment?" the carpenter asked.

William set his tone with a note of discouragement, "Is it to discuss the laxity of our maids and butlers?" he asked sternly, gazing at the mayhem over the master carpenter's shoulder. The man had a gift to gab and he was in no mood to indulge the old tinkerer's whims on an evening when the court was disposed to leisure.

The master carpenter straightened himself with puzzlement. He seemed to have lost his inhibition and appeared to consider his next words but unfortunately the wine got the best of him. "I wish to show thee what I have been concerned with, my lord."

William stood there regretting he had allowed himself to be seen. If he dismissed the carpenter and there was a real need, he would surely regret not hearing the old man out. More likely, he thought, his eyes would slam shut from the utter boredom of some useless remedy.

The carpenter took William's silence for concern. "The cobble near the palace front has chipped away and there are portions of the brickwork in fish court that are in danger of collapse. The worst of it, sire, is near the ambassador's quarters."

William replied curtly: "Have you not taken up the matter with the vice steward?"

The master carpenter puffed. "Aye, your Grace, I have. It seems there are other priorities for the stewardship at present and that is why I bring the matter to you. Can thee imagine the displeasure of the queen if one of the dignitaries becomes injured by a hunk of falling stone?"

The thought did not escape William and even in his angst, he smiled. *Yes*, he thought, *I can only imagine*. "There is nothing I can do about it this eve. Can it not wait for the vice steward in the morrow? Perhaps you might even direct your attention to your man over there who has an arm, elbow deep, in the queen's wine fountain?"

The carpenter turned with a frown, oblivious to the red wine stains on his own gray tunic.

"Or perhaps..." William paused for effect, "tell me when the south court will be ready for plaster and paint? Should not that be discussed with the vice steward since I am sure the queen herself will expect such reports?"

The carpenter staggered back and braced himself. "Indeed, your Grace. I will get right on those things. By the by, the Irish brutes have been sticking their heads in that fountain."

"Pardon?" William replied.

"Umm…" the carpenter fidgeted, "To waste not the wine. To waste not the want… the wine, sire."

The thought soured him and the carpenter was drunk. He could have him beaten for such word. He could… but then a new carpenter would be required. "Purge the fountain as thee see fit," he raised a finger of caution, "Master Carpenter, if the fountain is not polished and replenished with a good port by morning, I won't be asking the vice steward a bloody thing about the broken cobble. Do you understand?"

"I understand, your Grace. I surely do," the carpenter replied gratefully.

Before William could think on other things and make his retreat back to the solitude of his own duties, Thomas Gresham called out to him. "I've been looking for you," Thomas said.

William was grateful that this interruption was at least from his peer. Why Thomas would seek him out though was a mystery. Thomas did not typically venture out of the castle. "And you have found me. As has the master carpenter and a drunk maid. Have you also been drinking of the fountain, Thomas?"

Thomas looked more concerned than William had seen him in ages. His voice was high with tension, "The Queen missed her appointment and she is not with her gentleman usher. I had business with her tonight. Business concerning a possible solution to her war chest and it is not a matter she should have neglected."

"What do you mean?"

"She missed her appointment with me. I have spent days working on a proposal and set our time aside for her schedule.

When I announced myself, she did not come. Tis that simple. There's no one in chambers at all."

The report gave William a chill and as Thomas's words warned him of mischief, a queen's horseman made that warning real. It was the huntsman that galloped through the gate and his pace was one of urgency. The horse bucked, a servant darted to the side, and huntsman saw what he came looking for.

The huntsman turned immediately to William and Thomas. "My lords, the queen has gone missing!" he shouted. The animal spun as he leapt from his mount to reach them. The man was breathless.

William couldn't believe the misfortunate night. It seemed that bad things came to court in threes: each far worse than the next. "Missing or..."

Thomas's brow furrowed with dread, "How?"

The huntsman was uneasy. "Her Majesty rode off, my lords! Before the sun set. We looked everywhere and cannot find her. Is she returned here?"

In fountain court, there was certainly drunkenness and an ample supply of wine. In fish court, there was loose mortar, and in the woods, the queen had gone missing. This moment took the dawdlers away with sobriety. The court cleared out completely and the huntsman's red wool jacket was stained as though he had been crawling through the swamp. What, pray tell, William thought, would the queen be doing in a place like that? There was no doubt that he had ridden briskly and was now rightfully petrified.

"Is that all ye have to say? The queen rode off?" William quipped excitedly.

"Nay, sire. I came back while the others continue in search. Her Majesty insisted for a ride and took company with Lord Butler this afternoon. It was to be a game Her Majesty had said. We were to seek them in the woods but the Queen and Lord Butler stayed there not."

William grabbed at his black gown and answered harshly, "And none were wise enough to accompany the Queen or have the skill to follow?"

The man shook his head vehemently, "There were too many tracks. It was as if the Queen wished not to be found at all," he stated in a panic.

"Fools!" William shouted. His voice was heard throughout the compound and through the gated wall where a great number of people hushed. To infuriate him more, the man's horse snorted and deposited a pile of manure near the fountain. "Clean that shit up and get your chief back here!"

When the chaos had settled, Thomas Gresham turned to William quietly, "She is with Lord Butler," he said.

"Lord Butler," William replied distastefully.

"Aye. It is not just a courting that I fear. Elizabeth has been fawning on him and the tongues are beginning to wag. She is not missing, she has left!" Thomas said.

"Let us hope it is just her youthful folly and not something more. There are dangers about the countryside. She has been warned."

🌿 🌿 🌿

Hours within Hampton Palace passed with no word from the Queen or the Earl of Ormond. With the privy council now assembled and rumors beginning to abound, the pressing matter on William Cecil's mind was order. As far as Hampton Palace was concerned, the details of moving the wardrobe and closing down the offices now rested solely with him. He would have no choice but to relocate the council at daybreak. The thought occurred to him that he should send riders directly to Windsor, but for want of additional men, he did not. Something else was afoot- there was no immediate ransom note or evidence of struggle. The impromptu investigation yielded no antagonist; there was only Lord Butler. What he did know, now more certainly than ever before, was that Elizabeth Tudor, the sole heir to the throne of England, had no line of succession. She was dangerous.

With the festivities doused, just as surely as the wine that now spilled out to blanket the cobblestone near the fountain, William was reminded that a missing queen could lead to allegations. Surely, Northumberland would make a claim for the throne or perhaps even King Louis of France, should she be ill suited in the eyes of her peers. If that day ever came, he would not have the popular support to stop it. Banishment or death without the prosperity of the queen was a certainty for both he and Thomas Gresham. That would be the fate of all who were not sympathetic to Rome.

Inside, Robert Dudley grilled the staff with high threats of treason. They knew nothing- not the mother governess, nor any of the ladies. In the out of doors, under a blanket of stars, William Cecil and Thomas Gresham swiftly rounded up each of the royal yeomen. His heart was heavy, his orders were clear and the castle came to the high order of battle. Not long after the guard was set, the remainder of the queen's party returned.

After entering the palace, the captain of her horsemen offered little consolation. The man was as crisp and ornate as a Swedish nut cracker. A thick black belt, the polished brass handle of his saber, and a high fur hat did nothing to return a sense of normal. He gave no explanation but stood in rigidity, his chin tight against the strap.

The tone of William's voice brooded with frustration, "You men will go nowhere. Take the horses to the livery and return with the greatest of haste. Do you understand?"

The officer stepped back with his knowledge of discipline. William wished he had seen only the abrupt face about but the guard's expression was sobering. The cold snap of two heels hitting the stone hinted of his ineptitude. The captain's dutiful resignation of failure creased his lips and echoed in each movement. It was a weakness, William thought.

A short time later, after William dispatched Thomas Gresham to notify the council that they must be prepared to adjourn by morning, he turned to the queen's hunting escort resolutely. Behind him were the trumpeters who held their long instruments at the ready. His hand raised, they sounded three times, and then he waited. There was no reply from the forest. He pointed to the battlements where a flag had been raised in signal and torches were lit along the entire periphery. Silence was the answer they received from the queen and with the silence, the yeomen of the wall paraded out of the barracks like ants exiting a mound. A veritable army who could fortify the gates or battle from within the walls. William had instructed them clearly. He knew exactly what must happen next and so his ants lifted up their claws and surrounded the queen's huntsmen. Their long harqubus' prickling toward the men who failed her. It was the thing which ensured the captain did not hesitate.

"The one who last saw her," William commanded.

"Baxter!" the Captain replied. The words left a bitter taste in his mouth.

The youngest of the lot felt the weight of the world upon his shoulders and lost his bearing. This thing, this terrible thing was not folly and he feared they intended to kill him. "My lord... my lords have mercy for I am of the greatest sorrow!" Baxter pleaded as the guards leveled the tips of their spears. He was unsure as to why it was he who they had blamed. His heart quickened and in his youth he kicked out and struggled to break free.

William hesitated as the young Baxter was restrained. The royal guard's skin was without wrinkle or blemish. He was noble, he was pure, and the queen had chosen him for herself. *A suitable offering*, he thought. "Take his head and put it in a box," William Cecil ordered resolutely in the silence of Hampton Palace.

CHAPTER 36

Black Husband

The branches snapped back as two of the finest horses of the queen's stable crashed into the open green pasture near Windsor Castle. Elizabeth let out a whelp of utter excitement. She bolted past a hay wagon; streaked with clods of earth flying through the air and passed the stone houses of Maidenhead. *He is in chase*, she thought. Thomas had stopped at a stream trickling into the Thames and he touched her near the cool clean water. They had built a fire and she napped in the warmth of his arms. The exhilaration was mesmerizing and so was the chase.

"Hold, my love!" Thomas shouted as Elizabeth gave flight toward the gate house of Windsor.

"Do not be without valor!" she yelled over her shoulder.

The wall was open and a flag rose like a white sail with a bright red cross. Triumphant fashion, a ruffle and then a furl billowed out with a puff of wind. Then as they raced onward, the heavy cloth sank with a sputter, and like Thomas, the material hung breathless. Daunting. The slope of the hill rose in obscurity before him and beyond the hill was the imposing castle. Dwarfed in the landscape he felt himself a speck of a man who had lost control and failed to catch his damsel crossing the infinite plain. He was soaked with sweat from ass to saddle.

Elizabeth darted through a narrow passage and she saw him follow. Grey stone walls on every side and carriages being ushered along an interior that looked more like a city, than a home. "Over here… you fool," she called.

Thomas Butler slowed on his entry and nosed his mare toward the alley as candles and lamps began illuminating the fortress's arrow loops. *Where did she go?*

"My lord," a child's voice echoed from behind.

Thomas looked down to dirty feet which shuffled across the straw. Toes black from the mire of cobble and crusted with dung.

"I will take her, my lord," the stable boy said plainly.

Thomas heard a baby crying and then a rooster crowed as he dismounted with a quiet. "Very good," he said. The lad beamed at the sight of him and the child's wooden sword clicked on something hard when he jumped up with youthful joy. Thomas smiled, "That's a fine arm ye have boy. Whilst thou defend your lady's honor?" he asked playfully.

"Aye," the lad replied.

The child took the lead and Thomas's horse puffed and raised a foreleg. "Better ye take her first. This mare is ill content to wait on her oats."

"Aye, me lord," the child said.

"Where is your queen?" Thomas asked with a bow.

The lad turned as he led the horse away. "Gone through the kitchens, me lord."

The giant clock tower chimed to announce the morning. He had no idea where the kitchens were, but they could not be far. His feet drifted forward. He peered about as the town of Windsor came to life and through the gate he saw the masses as they entered. Women, children, servants, and administrators hustling up the ramparts. He knew the kitchens would be first to come to life and he followed the keg line knowing the cooks would soon enjoy their mead. Seeing the white bonnets and aprons, he entered the stone house where the wood was being stacked for the fire.

"Where is the queen?" he asked.

"Gone," a fellow replied hastily. Thomas cleared his throat as a blister scarred servant took his meaning. "This way, me lord," the cook said, showing Thomas the way. They exited the kitchen together and walked through the service door and into an arched hall. It was a tunnel of sorts where inside the lamps burned brightly and continually marbled the red clay with patterns of smoke. It smelled of oil, perfume and curing cheese. He stopped briefly to take off his cape as a formation of women walked dutifully past him with fully laden arms. "Here, my lord," the cook told him.

Thomas followed without reply as the interior door opened and there, where the maids and servants had passed, he entered into the expanse of Windsor Castle. Dim and yet intriguing. "This is where the lords should stay," the cook said.

"And the queen?" Thomas asked.

"The queen? I have no idea where the queen is. Have you not been to Hampton?"

"Never thee mind, I'll find her myself," Thomas replied. The man nodded and turned to his business, leaving him alone. He felt intimidated and unsure. *I know her not so well*, he thought. Elizabeth paled to the beauty of the other ladies he had known, but she was the queen. He droned forward like an insect drawn to the pheromone of power.

The staircase was grand and so he took its steps and wandered. Unable to resist the stirrings he felt rise with the danger of the encounter that might come. It was intoxicating and he dared to imagine how she waited for him somewhere in this gigantic palace. Two maids descended as he climbed to his fate. They giggled and one gave him an impish glance and then nodded her head to the right. They too, he thought, may have listened to the tantalizing encouragements of Francis Radcliffe. The remainder of his journey to the privy hall was unimpeded and the carpet hushed his steps. Tight woven Indian thread that patterned the privy floor with plush pile. His sweat made him shiver as his hand reached out to take the handle of her door.

Inside the room, Elizabeth lit candles and threw off the sheets of her furniture. This was her moment and she could hear the slow creaking of a squeaky hinge. *That'll need some oil*, she thought. She laughed out loud. Her race had bought her time, just enough time to make herself ready. Thomas would come and she would not look upon his face. She wore nothing except a silk gown. The texture teased her as she sat in her padded chair in front of the fireplace. They might enjoy hours together before the household arrived. She hoped it would be hours and struck the match to ignite the kindling. The contrast of the heat on her hand and the cool feeling of soft material intensified her desire. She did not want to hear a man's voice. She wanted to feel. She wanted to feel him and accept his passionate embrace and if he pleased her, she would reward Ormond greatly.

Thomas entered without a word and his armor fell to the floor. He did not know his cousin well but he knew of women. He reached out and touched her shoulder, "What will you tell the council?" he asked, lowering his head to kiss her neck.

His lips sent a tingle shimmering down her arms, "I will tell them the truth, my love," Elizabeth whispered.

"Will you?" he asked.

"I will tell them…" she licked her lips, "you are my black husband."

He ran his hands down her silken gown and felt the erectness of her nipples and Elizabeth let out a long deep sigh. Her head rolled back and her thighs quaked at his touch.

"I am your servant," he said softly.

She kissed him openly on the mouth and her breath quickened and then as tormented as she was, she put her hand on his chest to stay him. "We shall not go further, Lord Butler."

Thomas stepped back with his eyes fixed on what she had denied. His full black beard still damp from her mouth and his heart racing. "Are you playing with me?"

"You may sleep at the foot of my bed."

His face reddened. He felt such fool, doubting she knew anything of men. This was the behavior of a child who licked at the flame. "I will not disgrace thee with unwanted talk. If your heart and body are not in this, it is sufficient that I have ensured your safe travel." It was a relief and disappointment.

"Shall you sleep in the apartments that have not been heated?" she asked him.

"That would be fitting," he said. Thomas thought of Francis Radciffe who had urged this encounter for her own gain. "What is in your mind for Ormond?"

"Always favor," Elizabeth replied.

"And for Ulster?"

Something in her eyes told him whatever she said would be a lie. "I would welcome a negotiation with an open and peaceful heart," Elizabeth said, regretting the passion had turned to talk of state.

Thomas retrieved his armor, "I shall build a castle for you, my Queen. If you ever wish to ride like we rode today, a stallion will be yours to command, and then when the day is done, you may become a woman. Only then will I be... your black husband."

🐝 🐝 🐝

At midday, Thomas Butler stood near the Windsor docks on the River Thames and prepared to greet Lord Burghley. The ferry arrived with a rhythmic sound of wood and water droplets cascaded off the oars to wet the outer gunnel. The birds were chirping and it would have been a pleasant day if it were not for the expression of Lord Burghley. He stood in the boat with his seal skin coat and plied his leather gloves together. The rail of Windsor's dock made contact. He was certainly vexed and well in a hurry.

Thomas extended his hand, "The queen is safe, and I have waited here these hours for you to arrive."

"You error in that assessment," William replied.

"If I do, I do it for the devotion of our queen. Even now, she rests unmolested in her chambers," Thomas said.

William appeared relieved. He straightened his gown and turned to the boatman. "For the queen's virtue, you shall be rewarded, Lord Butler." The boatman and two guards then came up to the dock and handed William a box. "The queen adores her huntsmen and even allows them to enjoy sport on occasion. Did you enjoy your sport with her?"

"I did, Lord Burghley. The men were most gracious and devoted in their conduct."

William handed the box to Thomas. "The huntsmen are the guard and must accompany her everywhere. She has relied on their skill for both leisure and protection. Did you get to know any of those fine men?" Lord Burghley asked.

Thomas felt sweat form in his hands and replied cautiously, "I found the queen's men to be most pleasing, my lord. I spoke to each of them throughout the day."

"Good, then this gift to you will be most fitting. I hope you share this pleasantness with Her Majesty as you shared the day and evening," William replied.

Thomas stood in William Cecil's shadow. The man was calculating and calm and for all his imaginings he never thought a statesman could look so imposing. "Have I overstepped, and offended thee, your Grace?" *He knew he had. He knew it even before he departed.*

"You are ambitious, Lord Butler. I cannot find fault in that. As a lord, your apartment will be guarded here in the country. I do not want to alarm you, but two guards will be posted at your door. Please treat them with the knowledge that if they fail, they will fail to honor England."

"I understand, Lord Burghley," Thomas replied.

"I know you will, Lord Butler. I truly do," William replied as he departed for Windsor Castle.

The Courage of Insanity

E
mma looked up to see the hill and a chapel. A field of hay between her and the future. She stood on the road with Gowl, which wasn't truly a road but a swaddling footpath cut between the whine bushes and ferns. There were a few places in the road with stone abutments supporting a haphazard array of boards that spanned irregular ditches. Oddly, the lack of good construction bothered her.

Others made the trek also and the church bell rang across the lowlands as she took sight of the large gathering already massing at the church. It was talk, she hoped, only talk and so she kept walking with Gowl on the precarious path.

Gowl and his mates were not alone in wanting to impress their chieftain on this particular morning. They all wanted to be chosen. Every farmer, chieftain, and wandering shepherd had heard of the rumor. Word was that the O'Neill Mor had finally received his reply from London. *The word*, Emma thought. It gave her a sickening nostalgia.

A few boys ran by, waving their arms and cackling like banshees. Gowl hesitated and looked back toward Dungannon. "Do they distract you?" she asked.

He caught her by the arm when her foot snagged a loose board. "Look at all who come." His voice indicated he was unsure himself. Could it be that the queen would allow their security? The banners of the McCarty, McMahon, and O'Hagen septs flew in the wind along the hillside. "It is the day that the O'Neill has waited on. Is it not beautiful?" he asked her.

"I see a rush of clansman and wool leggings. Where is the beauty in that?" Emma replied.

Gowl shrugged off her displeasure, "Come... let us get to it. It'll be a long day if nothing else." He took her hand, "They will pledge themselves one sept after another and then Da O'Hagen will declare in Brehon Law that O'Neill should make his case."

"True enough," Emma said.

"Hard to believe," Gowl replied. They seemed to be of one mind and that was a mind of distrust. It was a quality that Emma admired in her man.

"Then why would you even come?" She asked.

They continued walking, "We shall hear soon enough. It takes a pledge for such a thing to happen and O'Neill has always been pledged to the law. If he does go, I would want to go with him. He will choose the greatest of the warriors to take this victory to England. When that happens, he will need men like me to protect him from the certain attempt on his life."

"His victory?" Emma asked.

Gowl laughed at her words, "Aye lass. Victory or death be the only way a chieftain of Ulster would leave the land, and O'Neill is still breathing. Would ye not have your man ride to protect such a thing?"

"Do not believe it, Gowl. I know London and the ways of England better than any here. It will not be a welcome you get. I am certain. Least ways the O'Neill will find a queen's guard to restrain him since he holds an earl his hostage. Those that go with, will find only a noose," Emma said.

Gowl looked at her questioningly, "I don't like you talking to O'Donnell. He puts these things in your head but fails to tell you why he is caged. Stay away from him and look not to his wife for advice either. Those two are as foxes circling the hen house."

Emma didn't think so. "And will you now tell me that God has blessed O'Neill?" she asked.

Gowl picked up his pace, "Aye, I will do. We go to hear God's word and if it weren't so, then O'Hagen would not strike the bell as he has done. You hear as well as I." Gowl replied.

They made their way to high ground with some effort and Emma felt flushed and out of breath. She could see Lough Neigh off in the distance. "I feel not like attending church," she said apathetically. "It is a war that brews, and not the O'Neill's victory. And no, Gowl, I do not here the call to London."

At the church she saw a priest and the old sage, who leaned on a willow shaft. It was contrary. Men who had taken off their armor and a priest who ushered them in. She watched with apprehension as Gowl knelt down and tied the leather strap of his sandal. "I will never feel the same about a church again," she said.

"What?" Gowl asked.

"Nothing," Emma whispered. She knew he was leaving. The same sensation of dread came over her just as it did when Henry had ridden away.

"Go find the women folk. You should get to know some of them for it is the women who manage and bond together in the absence of their men," he told her. As he took his place in the line to enter and the others found a reason to talk, Emma found only the need for silence.

❧ ❧ ❧

It wasn't a large church but it was large enough for the chieftains. Gowl stood behind Con O'Hagen of the O'Hagen sept who covered down in the right row of pews. The Deacon of Dungannon, Calvin O'Neill was present as was the episcopate and presbyter of the Franciscan Order who stood like ornaments along the wall. Oddly among these catholic priests, the old sage known as Farleigh also stood with a thin willow rod in his hand. It was the old man and faithful that made Dungannon unique in its own magisterium. To the left pews were the McCarty and McMahon and Shane O'Neill stood behind the missal, dressed in the tweed of his clan.

Shane raised his right hand, and displayed the ring of Con. "Settle ye chieftains and hear the judgement," he announced when the least of them were finally seated. Shoulder to shoulder, crammed into the wooden pews with elbows to ribs and a few punches to boot, the clans waited to hear of their sovereignty.

This was the day within the walls. The day that the chieftains would choose a future.

"And what shall we hear that is different on this day than any other?" McMahon began as he stood at the head of his sept. They were fierce looking men, the type that guarded their border with impunity. A commotion arose, which boded of a continuance of war.

Shane stepped forward, "Ye know as well as I, what we have been promised. And ye know after Turlough's report of Belfast, that much is different on this day than it was before. The Pope himself was pledged to defend our shores and send an army. That has not happened!" His words were sobering. The quell began to abate.

"Aye, Shane," McMahon said sourly, turning and raising his hands, "but it taketh not Spain nor the blessings of the Pope to hold our land. Have we not rousted England on more than one occasion?"

The church became like a hall of laughter as a cheer arose. Michael McCarty of sept McCarty sounded out as well: "We can hear her Majesty even now... 'Listen...' sayeth she, 'Me lord, me lord... can ye reach in and pull dis Irish boot out me arse?" and the chapel erupted in laughter once again.

Shane smiled dutifully. "I would not take the victory or such humor from glad and noble men but for how long can we continue?" He looked at McCarty and his second in the sept who all knew as Caleb. "You are burly fighters and of good spirit. Hell, if it were only of my choosing, I would pledge all of Tyrone to your arms. But alas, it is not. How many times must we fight? A month, a year... a generation? God only knows." He paused and began to walk among them as he spoke, down the center isle; prideful and confident as his sandals smacked on the stone case floor. "None of us alone can sire enough children to oppose the whole of Britain without end."

"But we can surely try, can't we?" Someone chided. It was enough to distract Shane with more laughter even as the old sage Farleigh reached down and grabbed his junk. Such a cackle of men and the mood was daunting as their jest covered the trueness of their situation.

"Aye," Shane replied resting his humor with Gowl. "Some indeed fare better with trying to sire a nation than others. I myself have pledged to put a few children in the bellies of Scotland but it will take more than our humping to win this war." Shane nodded politely to the deacon who feigned to cover his ears. "No offense, father."

Father Calvin rolled his eyes, "The Lord covers your multitude of sins, Shane."

Gowl took his opportunity to speak: "Does He cover my sin as well, Father Calvin?" Gowl asked.

Father Calvin's expression turned to revulsion, "Nay Gowl. He do not. You will always be a filthy bugger." Shane nodded agreement and a few began to laugh as Gowl shifted uncomfortably with the realization that Father Calvin was not joking.

In the very loud and small place of worship, Da O'Hagen was next to have his say. He was the leader of the O'Hagen and the first to sway for a vote. "Ye'll be casting your yeas for the O'Neill I suppose," he said, looking at the McCarty and McMahon, "but for the O'Hagen clan, me says it is a nay. Nay for Gowl, nay for sept O'Hagen, we shan't be going to England."

With the first of the tribes against him, Shane O'Neill smiled at his old sage Farleigh who had told him of his right long ago. Then he turned to Barre Con, who stood silently by his side. "What say you, Barre?" he asked.

Barre Con said his peace softly. "If I am a yea, whilst thou take a vengeance on the Jesuit who killed me brother, Jodia?"

❧ ❧ ❧

Emma found her way to the women who sat on blankets and spoke Gaelic. She reached out and brushed the hair of a little girl who breezed past her in a surge of youthful energy. The child couldn't be but four and four years past, she thought, the girl could have been her Agnes. A pang fluttered in her heart.

"God be," Emma said meekly as she came to kneel beside the women who sat on a blanket. They immediately became silent in their white puffy blouses and none moved to make space for her. They were rude, and being ignored was something that Emma would not endure. "Do none of you hear me?" she asked.

A red haired lass answered Emma, "We hear you."

It was Ingrid of the O'Hagen sept. Emma had met her at the castle where she was cold and despondent in their every encounter. "What do the men do in the church that we cannot join them?" Emma asked.

"We'll be joining them shortly but first the O'Neill Mor must get blessings and advisement. That is how it is done here. That is the way of Brehon," Ingrid answered curtly.

"It seems the decision has been made already by the queen," Emma said.

Ingrid, shook her head as did those who sat around her. "If O'Neill goes, we hear he will be made the queen's deputy of all the island. She has even sent word to Ulster that Shane will be accepted at the Maundy Ceremony of Westminster. So I presume the decision for who goes with him and who stays has not been decided," Ingrid told her. The women giggled with speculation as Ingrid incited their imaginings. Then with a waft of her hand she said: "You should know better than we of England and the Maundy. If you go, you may even be chosen to wash the queen's feet for a bottle of rancid wine," she said with a hint of sarcasm.

"I didn't know," Emma replied bitterly.

"Oh yes. Radcliffe has been returned to London and when our O'Neill Mor comes home, he will send a member of every clan that have entered the church today out into the counties and English shires. They will remove the Sherriff's and return our land to the people. We have no need of English laws here. So it will be for each of the earls of those counties as it has been for Calvagh O'Donnell. And we all know how much you love yourself some Calvagh."

Emma flushed with Ingrid's implication. "I know the man little," she replied not wanting the rumors of her talks with Calvagh to be mistaken for whoredom.

"That's not what we hear. Even his own tortured wife has said that you visit him in his cage," Ingrid replied rudely. Seeing her effect on Emma, Ingrid continued while the others looked on, "I have heard that Gowl will make his homestead in the midlands, and will leave you there because of your unfaithfulness," she said smartly.

Emma stepped back with a placid smile refusing to be taunted. She would never go to the midlands again and Gowl had told her nothing of the matter. She fought to kept her composure, thought of the strange Calvagh and prepared herself mentally for any other surprise that the women might offer. "I pray Gowl is offered Geashill," Emma said as Ingrid scowled up at her.

"I know of no town named Geashill," Ingrid replied.

"Oh yes. Geashill is a stout farm and I have been there already. Often I fancied the town and also the people. I would love to live in Geashill," Emma replied.

Ingrid found herself with no reply as Emma gloated in the silence of the dumbfounded hens. "Tell Gowl, I have returned to Dungannon castle to bid farewell to my lover, Calvagh. I must feel his cock once more before we depart. Believe me, Gowl knows all that I do and he has conceded to share my affections while we linger at the castle. But now that we must depart, what a blessing it will be to return to the midlands before our child is born. I should not dally here any longer lest I be not ready," Emma told them all.

Ingrid reached up suddenly seeing that Emma was committed to the insanity of what she had just confessed and tried to pull at Emma's gown. Gowl would brain her and her husband if she ever uttered such things to him. "I was teasing. Mind you, Emma, they must go to London first," she said with haste.

Emma shook her head, "No. Gowl would never go to London and as you have said, I visit Calvagh in the flesh. I am no man's wife so if I am to leave with Gowl I should at least explain this to the caged earl. Gowl will understand and we all know it is his duty to take care of me until this child is born. At least I will be back in the midlands when he leaves me," Emma replied sternly.

Ingrid said nothing else to Emma as she watched the strange woman in English clothes untether a dapple pony. She knew it wasn't Emma's horse, but she dared not say another word. In her frustration, Ingrid knew it would be best to avoid Gowl and never again tempt the woman known as: Burning Emma of Colley Town. Not long after Emma left and the hillside became quiet, Ingrid turned to her flock, "Come girls, it looks like rain," she said pointing to the common house very close to the chapel of Dungannon.

❦ ❦ ❦

Emma trotted at a canter and pulled at her pinned up hair as the rain began. She felt the cold droplets hit her face. Small specks that hinted of the shower to come and the air smelled of it. Her heart began to beat wildly as she dared release the emotions that she so cleverly hid on the hill of the chapel. She felt heavier as each droplet struck her. She was like the storm. Struggling to stay upright and moving. A few drops she could manage but eventually the rain was too much to bear and her life was the downpour. When she reached the castle her dress clung to her legs and chest and her hands were red from gripping the mane. It was he that saw her. The Earl of Tryconnell.

"Calvagh... Calvagh... they hate me," Emma cried.

"Why are you out in this foul weather?" Calvagh asked as he lifted his skins to show his face.

"I...I am being cursed!" Emma shouted.

Calvagh adjusted the leather tarp that protected him. He pushed it up with a stick and a pool of cold water came down with a splash. It finished the soaking of her hair. "Stop..." Emma shouted.

Calvagh laughed, "I am so sorry, dear. Here, take this," he said reaching his hand out and handing Emma a knot of twine. She looked at him with disbelief: "Pull it tight, lass," said he. "I do not wish to be wetted and you are able," he urged pleasantly.

"You have soaked me!" Emma screamed. He looked down on her kindly and she took the twine and began to tighten his awning to keep his tiny space dry. The work took Emma's mind away from her own troubles. She pulled and tightened, bent and circled and pulled again until his tent was secure.

Calvagh motioned with his head, "Take that rock there and hammer down the stakes lass," he instructed.

Emma did. Her hands were full of mud and her dress became stained as her knees hit the ground. She struck the first stake hard. It felt good. She lifted the rock over her head and struck again and again, stopping only to drink the rain. She cried out with her energy and desperate life.

"Enough!" Calvagh shouted.

Emma turned to him in her own terrible nightmare with eyes smeared and black, "I wish to come into your cage," she said pitifully.

Calvagh smiled through his whiskers, "Come in then. It is not locked," he told her.

Dublin Castle

The Earl of Kildare missed his wife and longed to ride in the green fields with his knights once again. Instead he listened to the young and boisterous banter of a delusional Kevin O'Hagen; the eldest son of Bair O'Hagen; the keeper of Tullyhogue of clan O'Hagen. The people all called Bair, Da. As if he was everyone's father but truly Kevin was the son he loved most. He was also the lord deputy's only trophy from the bloody campaign in Ulster.

"My cousin will come for us and raise this retched city!" Kevin exclaimed.

"If he does, if by some far reaching miracle, Shane O'Neill can breach these walls and take the castle, you would be wise to kill yourself," Gerald replied.

"He would not harm me. I am of clan O'Hagen the keepers of his ancestral ground. It is you that should be a-feared, traitor!" Kevin hissed.

"If I am a traitor and not a noble earl, howbeit we sit together?" Gerald asked.

"I do not know," Kevin said looking down at his feet, "they do not torture you," he said angrily.

"When I can help you, I will," Gerald said.

"Will you pay for me to eat?" Kevin asked.

Gerald looked up as he heard the old timber door open with a click of iron on the stonework. It was cold in his cell, and as he exhaled, his breath condensed and reminded him that he was now in the lowest part of the castle and probably his life. He sat down on the floor and ran his hand across the hay that served as a bed. "I have been robbed of any riches and cannot even pay for my own food," he said.

Kevin bit at his fingers hungrily, "Some glory you are of Kildare. At least I have fought to keep what is mine. Yours you gave to the English freely."

Gerald heard the unmistakable shuffle of feet down the drafty stairs and then the lighting of a torch.

Kevin heard it also and crouched in the corner, "They come to torture me," he said and then he backed against the wall. "They come to torture the son of a chieftain and warlord!"

Gerald slid his back against the wall, pressing himself with his feet to steady his shaking legs. It would be hard for Kevin this time. Very hard. No matter how he tried he could never dampen his ears. Lord Radcliffe had been unmerciful to the son of Bair O'Hagen.

As the stealthy figure walked by Kevin's cell, Kevin lunged at the bars of his prison and shook them as violently as his youthful energy would allow. "I dare thee to touch me, you filthy English swine!" he shouted. It was a pitiful effort. A display of uncontrolled rage that left both Kevin and the man outside of his confining world expended.

Gerald wanted it to end. He closed his eyes and swallowed in preparation, all the while thinking of his own family. He had not seen them for months. The figure passed Kevin and stopped at his cell instead. *This was it*, he thought, *now Kevin will have to dampen his ears*.

"Do you know who I am, my lord?" The man asked.

Gerald let out his breath fearfully, "No..." The man removed his cloak and Gerald saw that it was Adam. The archbishop whom he despised. Such a man who took out his anger without revealing any emotion and reveled temporarily in the taking of his former land. He had seen this unwelcomed tenant before and he considered him the lowest of ministers. A protestant.

"I am the Archbishop of Armagh," Adam said.

Gerald recoiled, "If I am to die, might I speak with a Catholic priest?"

"I am not here to take your admissions. You have been summoned by Shane O'Neill, and the lord deputy has been commanded to release you," Adam said.

Kevin cocked his head as he listened and licked his lips with the delicious sound of his King's name. His heart pattered and he scraped his beard with long fingernails and wailed. "Aye! Aye my cousin will come and burn it all. He will burn it all down and shit on the queen!"

"Silence idiot!" Gerald shouted.

Adam ignored the banter that came from the cell and calmly looked at the Earl of Kildare. "I came to tell you that the holy relics of St. Patrick's and all of the papal wealth will been returned."

Gerald asked, "And the congress of mayors of the chartered cities?"

Adam replied, "All of the northern cities have given their support to the House of Fitzgerald and O'Neill."

It was utter relief to his ears and he could scarcely believe. *How many letters had he written to Spain? How many times had he dared to oppose the lord deputy in secret? Too many and look where it had gotten him. Was it worth it?* "Why have you, the archbishop, come to tell me such things? I am a lord of England and a sworn knight of Her Majesty, the Queen. Is it not for she that I have been suffered?" Gerald asked.

"Her Majesty will entreat thee and you shall go to England with O'Neill Mor," Adam said as he looked menacingly to Kevin O'Hagen. "He will not be so fortunate. Sussex is bitter and has already departed for London and his supporters will take their flesh none the same. If Shane O'Neill becomes as powerful as I believe he may there will be no trace of O'Hagen to be found here at this castle."

Gerald Fitzgerald spat: "That is not justice!"

Adam raised his hand. "You'll hold your tongue or all of Kildare will be lost to flame. That is all you need know in your travel. The queen needs not the details."

Gerald turned and kicked his bare and bruised toe into the hay. He wailed and then took Kevin's hand through the cold iron between them. An expression of compassion washed over them both. "Don't be the fool," Kevin whispered.

Adam continued, "I shall not wait all day. Will the House of Kildare once again be righted in the Pale?"

Gerald released Kevin's hand, "Aye," he whispered with the heaviest of hearts.

"In your earldom, I need an assurance that my churches will not be destroyed and the vicars turned to ash," Adam insisted.

"There will be no such endeavors within Kildare," Gerald promised.

Kevin shouted in his insanity: "Traitor! I told thee! I told thee!" and he grabbed through the bars vainly.

Adam looked at the guard who had followed him into the dungeon, "Let him wail for another day and then we shall set him in the courtyard." Then he returned his conversation to Gerald Fitzgerald, "It would be best for all if you gave wise influence to Shane O'Neill."

"Only if Kevin be spared," Gerald said.

"The writ for O'Hagen's execution has already been signed. I do not dabble in the taking of life, and so I will not interfere." Adam replied coldly.

Dungannon

Emma sat in the cage and the rocking reminded her of the sea. It moved with the wind and she felt a spray of the afternoon shower blow onto her face. Calvagh lit a fire in a large clay pot and both of them warmed their hands together. He was remarkably dry and his hands were neat and clean as he pulled a fur robe over her shoulders.

"You came back to me..." Calvagh said.

"I don't know who I am, Calvagh. Will I become my husband's tormentor?" Emma asked.

"I told you. We are not so different, you and I," Calvagh said.

"Does the O'Neill truly go to England to become the lord of all Ireland?" Emma asked.

Calvagh hugged her, squeezing her shoulder as she sat up on his bed. "Who can say what a queen will do. My wife has told me that when that bastard departs, he goes to seek her release from our marriage. She said that so that I will know she does not require me to be unfaithful in order for our union to be dissolved. I wonder what her father, Hector of the Isles, would say if he knew of her clandestine plans. She has also told me that she is with O'Neill's child so you might understand how I doubt the truth of anything Katherine confides to me," Calvagh said.

"Why do you not just leave?" Emma asked.

"Here, in this cage, I am still the Earl of Tryconnell. I am married to the dowager princess of Argyll. In that, I have hope that her father Hector and the Earl of Argyll will turn their gallowglass warriors against O'Neill. If I divorce Katherine, Tryconnell will become independent of Argyll and Shane will be free to both marry Katherine and take his war back to my people." He sighed and then rubbed his hands some more, as if plotting. "Should I just leave? Such a thing would bring Katherine to her gladness for O'Neill can justly order my death. He would do it by the old law, if it suited him, for I am surrendered to be his hostage by honor."

"That is a terrible place to be," Emma replied.

"It will not last forever," Calvagh said.

"Would you really lay with me during the day, so that all may see?" Emma asked.

"What do you think?" Calvagh replied.

"I think not," Emma said as she began to warm.

"I think you worry too much over what a queen might do. Gowl is a warrior, not a governor. If O'Neill is anything at all, he is not stupid. He will never rule all of Ireland and you shall never be burdened with life in the midlands," Calvagh said.

"Maybe the queen will execute O'Neill. That will return your wife and land to you, my lord," Emma said.

"You called me lord?" Calvagh questioned.

"I see thee truly now as a lord," Emma replied.

"You are very sharp for an English woman," Calvagh said as he hugged her.

CHAPTER 38

Consequences

Miguel Avaje Fernandez pulled the drapery away from the small window on the first floor of Smyth Pub. Pacing and then checking the rear of the establishment he noted a line of sheds that might support escape from rooftop. If needed, he would climb to get away, and with little else to do, he thought of his father. There was paper here, mostly scraps of parchment but he found what he needed and sat down to write. His hand trembled as he reached out to take the ink well. The tattoos on his wrist called to him. It was his bond. The secret language that only his father knew. He laid out his parchment and quill and removed his robe that revealed a scarred back from his own mortification. *Was he his father's sin?* Everything seemed small in the pub except his guilt as he stooped over the makeshift desk by the fireplace. "I am sorry…" he whispered. His hand moved; a streak across the yellowed paper that made his writing blurred.

It has been long since I have written thee, but I am alive and in your service. The O'Neill gave me your letter in Omagh and I must confess to beg a forgiveness. I find the Ire' to be full of idolatry and vigorous enchantments against the true faith of your teachings. There are also many here in England that are being martyred. It is a despicable onslaught. I fear England will never return to the fold and caution of your belief that such a place can be redeemed. As for I, your Holiness, who have failed to complete your will, there is only regret. The lands of Kildare and Connaught do truly support the House of Fitzgerald who have risen against tyranny. So do the chieftains of both provinces in Ulster. This I tell thee sadly for if there was a measure of solidarity within the Ire' it had come without your aide. Where were you? It does pain my heart that I have believed wrongly.

Truly your great admonition of sin at the council has reached my ear, even here in England. By this revelation, I know also that my brother and I are your natural sons. I beg that Your Holiness has mercy on him and do not trouble in your thought of me. As we are your beacon of sin and understand implicitly the true nature of your love. Even though what was promised to me and my brother and also to Ulster has not been received, I will still send to you and the Holy Church every blessing. I am now, and forever will be, a Jesuit. Your trusting and loving son who resigns himself to God and your infallible judgement. I wish thee, my Father, the Head of Rome, and all the world through Christ Jesus, unity.

Miguel folded his letter and tied it with twine. He put his words away and steadied his mind on the present. Should he have trusted the golden toothed man with his fancy hat? Trust was a hard thing to give an Englishman but in the hours after noon, he received an answer.

Joshua pounded on the door with the two girls standing near him and the door opened. "Where are they?" Miguel asked as the three entered.

Joshua looked at Triny and Alana. The girls resembled their mother and ate without running away. "They'll be here soon. May I take them to the loft?" he asked.

"And of Gilford and Dodd?" Miguel asked.

"Dodd will never bother us again, and I have visited the silver smith just as you have told me. Master Smyth will be given a year's payment for this pub and believe the money came from my brother in Chilworth," he said.

Miguel put his hand on Joshua's shoulder, "Verily, it is good that you may care for them and have found your courage. Go and tend to your nieces," he said.

"Thank you. Thank you for giving this to me," he said. Then with a bit of swag, he motioned to Triny and Alana, "Girls, we must go upstairs. I fear your mother has been very, very sick. Did you know that she was my sister?" he asked.

"No...," Triny replied as she took Alana's hand.

A moment later a carriage arrived at Smyth Pub and Gilford emerged with the nuns. Not a soul on the streets turned a questioning eye to him. He was part of the burrow. An indistinct feature of oddity and ambition.

Dungannon Castle

Gowl had come for her, and it cost him dearly. "Ye shouldn't a leaved me," he told Emma. His countenance was like a great ox which yarned against an enormous load. They "had" ten horses, now they had only seven. Because of Emma, Da O'Hagen passed a very steep and swift judgement. "Ye don' steel a wee pony nor borrow without consent!" It was a most egregious thing and now he rode indignantly away from the castle with the shame of being chastised.

"You fuss like an old hen. Cannot you see I am here," Emma said as she turned toward the castle and gave a wave of her hand.

Gowl wore his leather. Of the seven horses they now had, two they rode and five were packed while the last of their train pulled a bundle of tarps for ill the cost of a wagon. Emma giggled; he jostled his sword begrudgingly and set his jaw like a stubborn old mule. Such a sight they were: the warrior and the witch, bound by an old out dated law. Emma found it to be both humorous and fitting.

"Gowl, what will we do in Omagh?" she asked.

For all his agitation he answered: "We shall build a cottage and tend a herd of cattle."

"Cattle? Are we that rich to have such a herd?" she asked.

"They belong to the O'Neill and to the O'Hagen and McCarty. They will be delivered to pasture and we may take only if needed. That is the arrangement, and that is what we shall do. This herd will feed a northern army."

"Is that an honorable thing that the O'Neill has placed on our family?" Emma asked.

Gowl fumed. *Honor? Well... not actually.* The old sage Farleigh had laughed profusely when the O'Hagen had passed his judgement, saying: "Ye should a taken the nutting, Gowl... it wouldn't have been as painful as the trouble that English woman's going to bring thee for the rest of ye auld days." The old squeaking voice rang in his ear like the strike on an anvil.

Gowl ran a hand over his head which was now trimmed and bushy. *Fuck*, he thought. He had let her cut off his locks so that he might find some of her comfort outside the castle. That old crow was as right as rain. He turned back, not knowing what she thought. "Here in body, but where art thou mind, woman? And why the hell were you in the cage with O'Donnell?" he asked gruffly.

Emma heard his anger and it gave her a sense of satisfaction. "Well, the earl has beautiful eyes," she said to spite him.

Some of the wee ones of town seemed to enjoy the spectacle of their departure, running around the horses and yelping as they muddled their way through Dungannon. Oh, who was he kidding, the whole bloody town was watching. Ingrid had seen to that. "I told thee, that geezer was no good," Gowl mumbled. Then to his chagrin, he looked back and saw that Calvagh O'Donnell waved to Emma with a happy hand. He turned with a snap of his bushy head. The outrage. A blazing red flash of his scar revealed his displeasure. "It'll be different in Omagh!"

Emma waved back. "See," she said. "He's a kind a man as any."

Gowl scrunched his brow. *Not soon enough*, he thought, as Calvagh, who upon seeing the crowd disperse, began shouting his love and affection to Emma of Colley Town. It was his tone that made Gowl's innards a queasy soup as they trod away with their bundle bouncing behind them.

"I wish O'Donnell dead!"

The unkind words struck her heart. "There be no honor in that speak. He is more kind and dear than I have ever known. You were wrong to leave me amongst those women and should speak of the matter no further." Emma replied.

London England

Swan Inn sat within the bridge ward and served a most delicious tea. Here the influence of gentlemen was filtered like the dark fluid dripping from the strainer. The beverage came relatively cheap but it was always served in good porcelain. The tea was fine, that was true. It was fresher and a more aromatic blend than was available elsewhere but that was not why Thomas Smyth entered briskly on his way back from Southwark. Crowded, noisy and ideal for discussing his riskier business, Swan Inn was ideal for a secret meeting of friends. Today he awaited a privateer to England and a pirate to all others who knew him. Captain Roderick had not yet arrived.

"What have ya, sir? Black Indie, Thomas?" the serving girl asked.

Thomas looked up at the comely figure. She was slender and dressed in all the right fashion. The waitress had it all, except for the carriage which would prevent her from gliding through the set of narrow tables. Her buxom breasts pushed right up in two little perfect mounds, tight and cinched in a way that caused his eyes to dally. He felt a stirring as his gentle hand touched her hip and with his pleasure she smiled and slipped deftly to the side. "Oh... what finery have thee adorned yourself with in that bonny green felt?"

"Present from me father, Thomas," she replied.

There was a distraction that caught her shimmering eyes; she turned back, "Black it is then?"

"Aye, and lest not forget a cube of sugar," Thomas reminded her.

His chair settled with the bend of his knees and the wait began to annoy him. Southwark? What a pig hole and a day of it he had had. The streets were wider, cobbled from brick to wall and the tourism there was a bloody catastrophe. Her delicate feet came padding back. How he wished he could see them, "You move with the grace of an angel."

"Me hast too, Thomas. How else, would ya be getting your tea?" She poured. "Ya been crossed the bridge again. I can still smell it on your fine jacket." He gave a confirming nod. "How many did they hang today?" she asked.

"Only five," Thomas said.

"Hum..." the waitress set down her finery and removed the lid, raised a pinky, and then plucked a cube of sugar, handing him her cherished silver spoon. He stirred and handed it back before testing his brew. "That doesn't sound worth the time of travel. Was it anyone you knew?" she asked.

Thomas took a neat swallow, taking his time to remain close to her. "I am aggrieved to say it was, my dear. I don't like the hangings..." he paused. She let her fragrance wash over him which encouraged him even the more. "I was utterly astounded to find out Horacio Philpot has been covertly giving accounts of trade to the Spanish," Thomas said with a hush and brush of his hand.

"Really?" she asked, relishing the confidence.

He nodded sincerely, "Indeed and his name was found written in the book of confirmation that was discovered underground. He never truly converted, I am afraid," Thomas said.

"Them Catholic's are a tricky sort. I guess that's why we have Tyburn," her voice trailed off curiously but the curiosity ended and business was good. "He never struck me as an evangelist. Who would have known?"

"Well at least it was quick. He only kicked for a few short minutes. It was much easier for him than for the old bar maid, Talles. That poor woman's rope stretched so that the very tips of her toes scathed the ground. Of course a cheer arose from the gallows hall, so much so that I dared wonder if she would expire at all."

The woman poured another steaming cup, pinched a cube of sugar with the delicate tongs and set him straight. "I must be off now," she said softly.

Thomas held the spoon, "Two please," he said as a tall sea faring sort ambled over in high boots and a brownish leather long coat. Captain Roderick had arrived and he had the look of swashbuckling mischief. Thomas took another tea and then kept her attention with an introduction. "Ah, my dear. Let me introduce our good Benjamin."

"Pleased," she said curtly, "tea for ya, Captain?"

Captain Roderick removed his cocked hat. He took a deep breath of satisfaction and fondled her with his eyes. The smell was intoxicating, "Indian Black," he hummed. The entire Swan Inn smelled of it and he eagerly joined his friend.

"You could have made a fortune in that hour, Thomas. If the crowd were right," the waitress replied as Captain Roderick took his seat.

"I did. There was a large crowd and my man Dodd's wife sold out of scones and bitters, so all was not a loss," he said.

She smiled, "Aye, and it is still a good day. Look at this business now that you have lifted the quarantine. I swear such a move me thinks intentional," she said with approval.

Thomas smiled at Captain Roderick, tellingly. "I have taken liberty to purchase your tea, Captain. I hope you like sugar," he said.

"Aye, I do," he replied. The tea was served and to both men's regret, the lovely woman moved to her other customers. Captain Roderick took his entire cup with a single swallow.

"Have thee found a safe passage into Clew Bay?" Thomas asked.

Captain Roderick held up his cup and examined it and for a moment Thomas thought he might pocket the little treasure. "Indeed and the Castle Brehon has been sacked by Lord O'Brien. There will be no more piracy from Grace O'Malley for some time," he said.

"Better for us then," Thomas said taking his tea with leisure.

Captain Roderick pulled his short pistol out and set it on the table. More than a few of the other customers turned with the clank of metal. Of course they also stared at the costly gold rings that clicked on the steel. "No trouble at all. Do ye have what I asked for?"

Thomas smiled assuredly, "Yes. The Isle of Man awaits you as soon as you can make ready," he replied.

"What is the offer?" Roderick asked.

"One hundred and fifty pounds for as long as Sussex needs. I imagine it will only be a few months. You will also have the right to claim anything sailing between Kintyre and Antrim to keep as your own," Thomas said.

"Has the Admiral agreed to this?" Captain Roderick asked.

"Aye. I have been told by the lord mayor that Admiral Hackett and Lord Burghley have gained your favor with the queen. The sea lane into the channel has been most profitable, Benjamin. I believe you stand to make good."

Captain Roderick passed a small leather pouch to him under the table, "These came from a Spanish galley wrecked along the rocks near Donegal. I believe they will give you great pleasure."

Thomas felt the shifting of stones and inconspicuously pulled a small gem out, "Diamonds?" he asked with delight.

"Aye, and there will be more now that I am permitted into the Irish sea," Captain Roderick reported.

"Splendid, but do not risk too much," Thomas said.

"The Abigail is fast, Thomas. It was a good investment and I have also repaired the *Humbert Keel*. The Isle of Man will provide very good cover for both vessels. There is little to worry about."

Thomas replied: "Only the royal mail. Radcliffe will need you, Benjamin, and when he does, you must be ready."

"I look forward to it," Captain Roderick replied.

"The queen has also given the ship, *Good Jesus,* to Admiral Hawkins and Francis Drake. I am unsure of their destination so be careful not to cross them. I have an interest in their success as well as yours."

Captain Roderick dipped his head, "Noted. Has there been any trouble for you since returning from Ireland?" he asked.

"Nothing I could not handle," Thomas said smugly.

CHAPTER 39

Windsor

uilt on a steep and imposing hill, Windsor stood with a
view of the surrounding country that embodied the
immensity of the castle. It was a tower, a fortress, and
a palace all at once, and Elizabeth felt small as she walked on
the north terrace. Her gentleman usher had not left her side since
he had arrived and even as Lord Burghley's monotone voice
drummed her ear, Robert Dudley stood at the battlement and
watched her accusingly.

"My Queen, it is time for us to discuss more than the
reconstruction of the chapel and the terracing of the North
Warf," William said.

She turned to him bitterly, "Did thee believe I would be humbled by your gift to Lord Butler?" William did not respond. His look was all she needed. "Why?" she whispered.

William answered: "Your actions have far reaching consequences. You are not a woman or someone who can freely love or give herself away. If you were, the worst that might happen is that you have a child out of wedlock. No. You don't get off that easy. If you succumb to such weakness, the country will suffer. You will be banished and Spain will surely impose upon England the harshest of reforms. Have you thought of that?" he asked.

"I think of nothing else," Elizabeth countered.

"Even you, Elizabeth... cannot know what damage will be accrued at the hands of Lord Butler. How many of your guards or perhaps even your stewards might perish if thee give in to indulgences?"

"I am not with child," she touched the soft elegant stitching that covered her belly. She ran her finger across the ribbon of purple silk that tied her bun at the waist. "I will never be with child until I am wed," she said.

"No, you are a child yourself. You can sing, and write, and play the harp. How beautiful your play can be. So speak in eloquence, your beauty, not in French or Latin, and do dine not alone with earls or dignitaries. You may even appoint knights to the Order of the Garter, but ye have much to learn about England," William scolded.

"Yes, Lord Burghley, and I have yet to learn much about you," Elizabeth replied venomously.

He took off his bonnet in its blackness to reveal long weathered creases and drapes of graying hair. "Perhaps,

Majesty... but only when you relieve me of my burden will Lord Butler be more than an escort for Shane O'Neill to your court. That is why he still remains here in London. Your infatuation with this married Irish lord must end."

Elizabeth felt a flush of her anger give way to reason. She couldn't reply. Her father had taught her better than to challenge the good interest of state. He had made many mistakes such as this. She looked at Robert Dudley whom she trusted but found unchallenging. Robert would jump if she motioned to him and that element of certainty repelled her in the moment. She felt like crying. She could not.

William took a softer note seeing that she was vexed: "I have known you as a child," he said. She stood firm and quiet. He wondered what she was thinking or if she would do as he advised. "Majesty, your virtue must never be challenged," he concluded.

"I am a virgin," she replied, as if it were a curse.

❧ ❧ ❧

A mournful day past since her scolding, and a beautiful note resounded as the Mother Governess of the Queen's House brought good tidings. "You have sulked in your temper for too long, Elizabeth. It is welcoming to hear such pleasure," the eldest of the royal accompaniment said.

Elizabeth put down her lout and ran her hand across the fine white paint of her chair in the sitting room. "I have no desire to entertain, Kat. Have the ladies bring my supper here at five, and I shall read for the rest of the day," she said stubbornly.

"Look at this room," Kat said.

"Mother Governess, do not dare to chastise, for it is I who have been abused!"

Kat Ashley picked up the papers that littered the floor. Some of the notes she recognized and others had been rubbed out and written over to the point that they were incomprehensible. "Pity…" she said softly.

"It is the privy sitting room. It is my room," Elizabeth said smartly.

"I understand, Majesty, but it is the house also. Have not the maids visited? Or would they have been dismissed in wait to stand outside your door?"

Elizabeth looked at the desk and the grand ornamental gold lion that stood over her writing's with the fiercest gaze. He was the guardian who would protect her: unmoving, unblinking, ever watchful, and proud. "Is not this castle large enough for the maids to find their worth elsewhere?"

"No, it is not. And the guards stand outside along the halls with boredom. You must announce yourself. You must make your presence with the lords."

She had thought as much herself. The boredom was indeed a great invigorator of fantasy, and a day alone seemed a lifetime. "Who awaits me today?" Elizabeth asked.

Kat turned up her nose at the room and felt the need to adjust herself with discomfort. She didn't care for Robert Dudley. Perhaps he might penetrate the wall which Elizabeth put up. Her hands smoothed the buckle of her grey dress and a black shoe slipped out to reveal the puff of her swollen ankle. Subtly, so that Elizabeth would not protest, she pushed the queen's slippers toward the couch. "Lord Dudley of course. March is but a month away and he has grand plans for the people."

Elizabeth made her wait before answering. It was her way of maintaining a quality of uncertainty in the certainty that she had been contained. "Send him in... I am ready enough for one whom has seen me a prisoner," Elizabeth replied.

Twenty of the queen's guards lined the halls of Hampton in their ornate uniforms with beautifully sculpted swords. They stood at rigid attention as the Lord of Leinster breezed past them in haste to see his Beth. When he entered, she appeared the same pretty red haired girl dressed too high for comfort. He bowed deeply before stepping into the room, taking one step and then another.

"Oh, do come on, Robert," she told him, having no patience for his grand display. Of course he ignored her, and took two more steps and dropped to his knees to prostrate himself without dignity. Before she spoke he raised a glance from the floor.

"Stop..." she smiled. "Stop it, Robert," she pleaded.

Seeing the queen's pleasure, Kat announced her visitor: "The Lord of Leinster, your Majesty."

"I know who he is. You may leave us," Elizabeth said coldly.

"Yes, Majesty," Kat replied as she closed the rich polished doors dutifully behind her.

"I have something I must tell you," Robert said as he leapt to the couch with youthful disregard. It made her giggle. He kicked his boots onto the polished table and a hard knot of dirt fell off. She loved him for it all the more. "I came here to Windsor, my Queen, to give the good news of our Maundy Ceremony. If it pleases?" he asked with enthusiasm.

"Oh... good master of the horse, it would please me greatly to hear your grand design."

"How many feet do you wish to wash?" he asked smartly.

"Not too many, I hope," she said with a raised brow of delight. "Have thee inspected every maiden, vigorously, Lord Dudley?" Elizabeth asked feeling a vicarious excitement that she had put off in her fit over the past few days.

He averted her glance adeptly, and smiled. "Surely, I have. Of which I found several with feet worthy of royal attention. There are some comely maidens here in Mosely, you might know," Robert said coyly.

"Tell me," she begged.

Robert was utterly enthralled, "There will be guards to escort them. While you enter ceremonious on a royal fleet at the lead of your navy royal. It will be spectacular, Beth. I have commissioned the ships work out of paper so that they can be carried by fifty men. The sails will be of streamers that take you to your people in most noble fashion."

She cooed, and clasped her hands with the thought of it. He continued with a wave of his arm, "And then, I will present the comely maidens whom I've personally selected for their feet to be washed by your very beautiful and loving hands. Such a spectacle of humble adoration it will be. With that type of love neither Pope nor King would ever dare enter this city."

"It sounds mesmerizing, my friend," Elizabeth said with a subtle douse of enthusiasm.

"Are thee not well pleased?" he asked her.

She put her hand on his knee with assurance, "It is not with thee that I am displeased but myself, Robert," she paused and considered if...

"Dare not speak it," he replied.

"I have been foolish and it will surely deplete the coffers. Will you do something for me?" she asked.

"Anything, Beth," he replied.

"It concerns Ireland. We will establish a communication through the Isle of Man; however, elsewhere, it is as Lord Gresham foretold in Antwerp. We have gained no loans or kindness there, war cannot continue without end, and I know not whether to embrace the O'Neill or kill him." Robert could see she was deep in her concern as she continued. "I must receive a certain assurance through our newly established communication before O'Neill sets his feet within these walls."

"I have heard the same," he said.

"O'Neill has demanded to be made a high lord in peerage," she said flatly.

"He couldn't possibly?" Robert asked.

"He could and he has. If he knows that Spain is posturing to our north, it will only embolden him. Yet, if he arrives before I know that certain things have come to pass in Antrim with clan MacDonnell, I will be at disadvantage. It is imperative that I hear from Radcliffe. Do you understand what I am asking?"

"I fear you are unclear, Beth. Pray tell, what does this have to do with me?" Robert asked.

"I want you to meet O'Neill at Broken Warf and put your talents for show to his good pleasure. When he arrives, his people should believe he has been accepted and comes to claim a glory. It will not be hard for him to believe in this since he is a prideful son of a bitch."

"He is," Robert conceded.

"His actions do not come without merit though, and I must admit that many of his tactics have prevailed. There must be people in the streets to greet O'Neill and his journey to Windsor should last for an entire day. Longer if possible."

"That does not seem so daunting," Robert said questioningly.

Elizabeth exhaled with the burden of her discomfort. "It comes with risk, Robert. Perhaps so much so that all of my judgement be put in question."

"Never," Robert replied.

"England requires that you accompany O'Neill all the way to the gate of this very castle. Lord Walsingham has rather good information that O'Neill and the Earl of Kildare have already set sail from Belfast. If that is true, then my cousin will certainly make his move, and I must know the outcome before meeting with O'Neill in person."

"I understand, Beth. I can delay him a day or longer," Robert said.

She looked fearful, "He brings nearly two hundred armed soldiers as well. These are not just soldiers but true barbarians and I cannot have such beasts within this castle. When you arrive here, if the gate is marked of red, you must flee but not before you get them all in the range of our archers. When the first arrow flies, you must ride like you have never ridden before and do not look back!"

Robert suddenly felt awash with the heat of his own perspiration. It came to his brow and along the flat of his hand. "They will wait on me before the loose?" he asked uncertainly.

Elizabeth looked at him as if she was saying goodbye, "You are the Master of the Horse, Robert. O'Neill knows your position in this court and he will not suspect if you are with him. Ride openly by his side, at the front of O'Neill's men," she said sadly.

Robert suddenly forgot about the Maundy, "I would do it a thousand times over, if that is what you wished of me," he told her.

"Go and tell Lord Burghley, who is the only other that contrives such a purpose. Tell him so that all can hear, that I have dismissed you from this court," Elizabeth said.

CHAPTER 40

The First Disciple

enry Colley stood on main street to observe a fresh
arrival of men. Real sustenance from England. A new
foreman to oversee the harvest season and an
accountant named Quincy who was experienced in the lower
courts. The rest he could see were clearly men who could fight
or work in the field. It was fitting that John Goodrich was
present to greet the comers.

"Gentlemen will report to the headmaster," John told two
suited fellows who had arrived by coach. The men politely
nodded and then marched directly toward Henry.

"Over here, good men," Henry called, gaining the attention of
his new arrivals.

Quincy recognized Henry immediately, and was glad with his greeting. He had heard much about the Captain of the Kildare Brigade. His single spectacle hung loosely from a top pocket and he nearly split his knickers to reach the man.

Henry spoke first: "Quincy Able," he extended a hand, "Good to see you have come."

"It's good to be here, Captain Colley. Your benefactor has told me much about your exploits. Have you slain any heathens lately?"

Henry thought of those men who turned his brigade with such ferocity. His soldiers gave everything. Many men had died while fighting the Irish. He hated them and he feared them, but they were not heathens. "No." He considered what to say next as his helpmates looked on expectantly. "No. I believe the heathen slaying is best left to Lord Radcliffe," he replied rather than explain himself. "You must be Guthrie Johnson?"

"In the person," Guthrie said smartly.

"Well, that is just splendid. Splendid. Come…" he extended his arm toward the castle, "come, we welcome you both."

As the gentlemen departed, Vicar Judas appeared from his morning stroll in the fields near the bog. He approached John Goodrich enthusiastically and smelled of grass and the sweet ale of Saint James. "God be, John," Judas said as he ambled past.

John turned to those holding their black canvas sacks, "Say hello to the fine Vicar Judas, lads," he told the newly arrived.

Such appreciation given, Judas took the opportunity to speak, "There will be no hell here," he said strangely.

John smiled, "I meant no ill regard, Vicar."

"Oh yes, none taken," Judas replied.

The men who waited looked at each other curiously. They had been sent in drab gowns, loose fitting trousers, and a mottle of other scarps of cloth between them. As they mingled and took a delight in the ale along the roadside, John began the preparations for their tents.

Judas watched them occasionally, as he sat in the clearing near the church on main street. A glance here, a judgement there, and back to his preoccupation of reading the sole surviving *Book of Common Prayer* that Adam Loftus had given him. It was printed in English, from a press no less, and its pages still smelled of ash.

Tents perked up with tall center poles and the gravel of main street became muddy. The new comers were housed close to the church. *Maybe a bit too close*, Judas thought. He held the *Book of Common Prayer* behind his back and struck a pace toward John. "Have the men assemble for blessings?" Judas asked.

Those that heard, peeked their heads out of their newly erected tents, wondering who was being so loud. They had worked hard, and it was time for rest.

"Come out!" Judas shouted with a calculated hint of indignation. "There is a church to be built here," he saw their faces, "not of wood or stone but of flesh. I need muscle. Surely there are those among you who haven't wilted from your travel?"

John was beside himself. Judas had never seemed so intense. "We need a disciple and have lacked in our doings of faith for the need to rebuild! But no longer. Who among you shall be my rock!"

The tallest man of the group stepped forward. Dressed in grey spun wool and canvas pants, the imposing individual stood with bare feet and an inquisitive brow. "I will," he said.

"And what shall I call you?" Judas asked.

"Bordeaux, but most call me Bu-jo," the man said.

"A Frank?" Judas marveled in admiration of the man's heft and he immediately thought of Hagan the giant. "Of great worth you shall be. Oh... Bu-jo. Yes! You will be my rock. Henry has said I may have one disciple. Do you wish for a position at my side?" he asked.

"I will do whatever I must. If it be God's will," Bu-jo, replied. *God, Bu-jo thought, the whole of reason for his departure from Vassy.*

"It is God's will Bu-jo... it is. I can feel it in my bones and through the spirit. You will be the first," Judas proclaimed.

Judas took Bu-jo's hand and shook firmly, "I will work hard here," Bu-jo said.

"Good. We shall walk a bit, but first tell me who among these men do you trust? And someone who is good at finding things."

"That one there. His name is Tong," Bu-jo replied pointing to an Asian man who stood silently at the end of tent rows. A strange sight among the planters and a man the likes that Judas had never seen. Black hair, braided and hanging down his back, and loose fitting clothes that were belled like trousers.

"Tong?" Judas replied. The man looked like a little boy in stature. You may bring Tong with us while the others work with John. There are some rituals that I will teach you both so that the faithful can blossom here in Colley Town. You will be the keeper of the flame and Tong shall be as David was to Goliath."

Seeing that Judas had found what he wanted. John sent the others back to their tents. He had already found an apprentice, and that fellow was known as Earnest. The others would need rest. Their labor would require every ounce of strength that they could manage. John knew that and soon the planters would also.

❄ ❄ ❄

In the Bermingham Castle, Henry sat with his new helpers as a maid servant poured them all warm milk. "Tell me Quincy, how is it in London these days?" Henry asked.

"Not so much different than it was two years ago, I imagine," Quincy replied.

Henry took a sip, "Surely there is news worth discussion. Does Thomas enjoy his duties at the port?"

"He does, sir, very much so. There was a bit of trouble a few months past, but I am sure you have already heard of it. It concerned Her Majesty's ship the *Pinnacle*." Quincy replied.

"I haven't heard anything about the *Pinnacle*," Henry answered curiously.

"Well... you are isolated out here. Have you not had any news from Thomas Smyth?" Henry leaned forward indicating he had not. "The ship ran aground at Blackfriars. Many were missing and according to the ships log some were even buried at sea. Everyone that was on board were dead before the impact, and those poor souls had the marks of the pox. The whole event took its toll on Thomas, I am afraid. He had to quarantine the lower wards and make governance in the chaos for the greater part of London. I was afraid myself for a short while," Quincy told him.

Guthrie sat forward and looked Henry in the eye, "It was a terrible thing. They say the ship's captain was cursed. The only thing that survived that voyage was a cat as black as coal."

Henry pondered the news gravely. "That would explain the delay in his support of this venture. Has he recovered?"

Quincy gave a polite nod, "When we left he was doing better. He even asked me if I would be interested in helping him with the accounting of duty there in London. Something about having a person of good trust, he had said. I am sure those matters worked themselves out."

"You declined a position in the port authority over this?" Henry asked curiously.

"Aye, Headmaster. Thomas's business is much too complex. I am still young and wanting adventure. What better place to find it than here where the land is unspoiled and opportunity arises with unprecedented regularity?"

Henry knew straight away that he would like this Quincy. "Well your opportunity is coming. It may come faster than either of you imagined because tomorrow I will show you the land we have acquired in Geashill. After, I will be leaving you to make your assessments." Both men raised their glasses and took a soothing draw. "Guthrie, you will begin planning to open the fields come April. That will take a good thirty men, I suppose. You may want more. I will let you choose who will accompany you to stake out the plots for settling." He turned to Quincy, "You will remain here and have an inventory completed of our assets so that Thomas can see the growth in his venture. When I return, we shall divide the tools, labor, and store of provisions so that come spring time, both Colley Town and Geashill are ready to seed."

"That is awful ambitious," Quincy replied.

"It is what's needed. While you make the plans, Warrant Officer Blanch will train the men in military tactics. We also have another shipment of goods arriving next week. Rest assured, there will be enough food and coinage to make it so. If nothing else, I truly know the strength of Thomas Smyth's investors and those sort of men will make this happen."

"Where are you going, sir?" Guthrie asked.

"I am afraid I cannot tell you, except that it is of a military duty," Henry replied.

Guthrie asked: "Is it true what we have heard, sir?"

"What have you heard?" Henry replied.

Quincy listened unknowingly as Guthrie broached the unthinkable: "That some of the poorer Irish have resorted to eating human flesh."

Henry choked into his cup, spilling a portion onto his lap. Guthrie's question did more than strike a nerve. It made the man change from gracious host to a snapping vermin. "Who told you that! Has the gossip of London begun to defy all morality!"

"No, sir, we have been told you are a hero," Guthrie exclaimed.

❧ ❧ ❧

Later that evening, Mary watched Judas out in the field with his helpers. They lit a fire and began erecting yet another of the ghastly scarecrows. It was rather unnerving she thought. "Annie Beth, what do they do out there?"

Annie cleaned the table, bringing the wooden bowls they had used to eat bread and onion soup over to Mary, who stood by a window. The vicar and his companions could do anything as far as Annie cared. The yellow house was a happy house. Even the boys sat like brothers on the floor playing with a marble. "Who knows, Mary. They were out that way last night, with two giant lamps. It seems the vicar uses evenings to instruct that big fellow, and the little one has been darting off into the bog almost every day now. What is his name?"

"Tong," Mary answered.

Annie's husband called out to her, "Annie... Annie lass, do thee not think it time for the boy's to go to sleep?"

Mary turned to her, "Go. I already put some rocks near the fire. They'll keep you warm all night."

"Thanks be, Mary," Annie replied, turning away to her husband.

Mary watched as another lamp was lit and she saw Bu-Jo holding up his arms. What was the vicar doing? Was he taking off his cloths? It was too dark to tell. Behind the lamp the men in the field appeared like shadows in their work. Soon they had built a fire and the wind made that awful scarecrow look like it was dancing. She couldn't help but watch them when she should be fast asleep, and as she did, she thought she heard a scream. *No, it couldn't be*, she thought.

❧ ❧ ❧

A cock crowed in the morning as Henry entered the stable where the soldiers slept. "It is good to have thee back, Blanch," he said hoping his warranted officer would offer a tea.

Warrant Officer Blanch moved as if to shake Henry's hand and realized awkwardly that only a stump remained. He pulled back. He had no hand. He could feel it, but it was gone. The sensation frustrated his peace.

"You'll get used to it," Henry said as a comfort.

Warrant Officer Blanch donned his coat. A new tan jacket with the sleeve sewn shut at the elbow. "Will I?" he asked as he put it on.

Henry looked around. The other men had yet to rise and he was happy to see a hot kettle hissing over the fire. "I will need ya here and am thankful for the skill of that surgeon who saved your life. Thank God and Dublin's miracle of modern medicine." Blanch raised a brow of uncertainty as Henry kept on, "What do you think of all that has been accomplished?" he asked.

"I am not sure it was worth it," Blanch replied.

"It will be. I'd like you to train up the new chaps as soon as you're able. They will need to drill and do it often," Henry said.

"Why not have Dennis or Hubert do that?" Blanch asked as he stirred his muddy pot of tea.

"They will be going with me. We'll be gone for at least two weeks. That leaves only you whom I would trust. Can ya handle it?"

"For what?" Blanch asked.

"We had nearly made it to the Strule." Henry referred to their escapade in military debauchment. "I intend to take a small party north and scout above the Strule to see where the strongholds are. Ralph Lane has been so kind to see to my orders. He has urgent information to gain about the north and the unsettled clans, but that will remain our secret. Do you think you are able to carry on without me?" Henry asked.

Blanch looked up with suspicion, "You are going to look for her aren't you?"

Henry turned a frown, "It would do no good. I would be obliged to bring her back for trial."

"We both know she would never have done such a thing. Not Emma. I hope ya find her Captain, and I hope to God you both disappear. You would give everything up for her, wouldn't you?" Blanch asked.

Henry looked encouraged rather than sad. "Will you see to things when I am gone?"

"Aye," Blanch whispered as he poured them both a cup.

Henry reached out his hand. A clay pot much too hot, a sip, and then approval. He held his piping tea and walked to the stable door. The barn had a nice smell to it. It smelled like pure country. Henry inhaled the aroma of leather, mixed with the particles of straw, and steeping tea. He truly loved the cool air that hovered within that stable. Emma had loved it also. "I will not be looking for Emma but for something else. I go truly on the orders of Ralph Lane from Dublin. He sends us with utmost urgency. Do you think Dennis Hill will be capable of speeding my correspondence, if I find what we seek?"

"I don't like him, but I trust him, strangely enough," Blanch responded.

"Good. I'll take Dennis and Hubert, then leave in the morning," Henry said.

Blanch stood and felt a tad off balance, "Don't get caught unaware. Those things are still out there. You know it now, and so does I. It could be bad. I also want to tell ya that not all the planters that Smyth sent from London should be trusted. There's one missing already."

"Who?" Henry asked.

"Your vicar came earlier to tell me. It is the little china man, which run off."

CHAPTER 41

Second Chances

Southwark by the sea, Miguel held Agnes' hand and Mary walked beside. Through the corner they darted onto the busy road. Scones! The crumple of partially risen flour, spice, and wee bits of raisins that Agnes had come to love. She held three, Mary another dozen.

"Are you ready, little girl?" Miguel asked.

Agnes skipped between them as a gentlemen of apparent status smiled when he passed. They looked like a couple, acted like parents, and behind them walked Julianne and the widows of Saint Bartholomew's. "I feel a need for shopping the markets, dresses for all, I would say," Miguel said smartly.

The air was stale and the streets of Southwark were filled with litter. It seemed perfect. That is what Mary thought as they arrived to the sooq without question. It was the lesser side of the city; sprawling out in the marsh lands like a vine beginning to take root. The buildings seemed newer, the roads a little wider, and then there were the fair grounds. Exhibitions and tart little shops that spoiled a richer customer with the latest fashions from Paris. Mary felt like an artist arriving to her studio and noticed quite a difference in Southwark from the drudgery of Cheapside. It was more European, maybe even a little dangerous. The sub cultured gentry and pretentious chatter of passersby brought an excitement she had never known.

"How is this possible," Mary asked.

"You have earned your day, you both have," Miguel told them.

"Can we look at that one?" Mary asked, noticing a tailor shop with a marque that read for fitting and delivery in five days.

"You can," Miguel assured her.

Mary took Agnes by the hand and ran. The widows carried bags with clean linen for under robes and Julianne grew impatient. "Slow down up there if you please," she shouted as the distance between them and Mary grew larger. Miguel kept walking, and Julianne turned to Deborah who was already winded and falling behind. "It's as if they're in a race. Do you even know where we are going?" she asked.

"Couldn't say," Deborah replied with some effort.

Linda and Jeanne held hands and pulled up the rear. They didn't say much. Their expression told Julianne that their recent blessing seemed contrary. "Stop," Julianne told the widows.

"But they'll slip away," Deborah replied.

"Oh... bollocks!" Julianne put her hands on her hips, "I'm getting too old for this nonsense," she told them.

Linda and Jeanne said it first, "We don't want to go…"

They paused for a moment to observe a contraption in the middle of the road. It wasn't a wagon wheel. No, it was much too large for that. A man ran out and lifted the wheel then found its small wooden seat. Throwing a leg over, he straddled the odd thing and then his mate pushed him up and took the handle to run him away as the wheel whirled through a puddle and then out of sight. "This whole place is nonsense. What could something like that be used for?" Julianne asked.

"Well, we cannot go back to Saint Bartholomew's; I'm still trying to figure things out," Linda replied.

"It's a big city. Likes it or not, it's home," Jeanne said.

Deborah looked around and then turned to the chapel near the bridgehead. "And what of Mary?" she asked. Shop keepers were yelling, a horse cart clicked by and all the orphans that darted here and there faded away with the thought of Mary.

Jeanne bent down to adjust her shoe. All the women's feet hurt, and even though they had been given clean gowns, they had sweated right through them. It certainly wasn't a comfortable feeling to be parading through the streets of Southwark.

"Mary is not a nun, Julianne," Linda said.

"Perhaps not, but she is not a harlot either and shouldn't be left alone with that man. We know next to nothing about him." Julianne said.

"If he weren't a good man, he wouldn't have freed us," Deborah said.

"Hmmm," Julianne saw that Miguel stopped and looked for them, "I'm not so certain we shouldn't worry more about Mary.

You girls know what it's like to be young. You have seen her drool over him," she said.

Deborah brushed Julianne on the shoulder, "Aye, and if I were a bit younger... Julianne, it would be me to receive your scorning. Don't ya remember?"

"You are utterly wicked, Deborah!" Julianne exclaimed.

The widows all laughed together. It was good to think about the other things in life rather than the noose. Southwark seemed to be a different world. They had imagined it full of ropes and that terrible essence of death. It surely wasn't, and as they talked, Jeanne straightened herself out a bit, flattening her gown and turning as if to walk away.

"What are ya doing, Jeanne?" Julianne asked.

"Did ya see that fella? I think he fancied us. Didn't ya see him smile?" Jeanne said.

"What in bloody hell is going on with you women," Julianne stammered.

"We aren't going anywhere, Julie," Deborah cocked her head and raised a hand, "That is what we are telling you. We'll have a little fun here. We'll keep our faith and chastity, God willing." The old women laughed some more and Deborah continued: "And then, we nuns are going home. Mary will be fine. More than fine by the looks of it."

"Talk of chastity at your age? My goodness Deborah, must you really?" Julianne said, knowing the women were right.

❧ ❧ ❧

Miguel waited a good distance up the riverside street. He could see the widows talking, Mary leaned over and gave a hug and then she turned and walked quickly toward him. Agnes grinning from ear to ear. It was most likely the first smile she had worn since being taken from Kintyre, he thought. Birds chirped in cages all around them and the fairground was ablaze with colored fabrics and perfume. It made him feel a little itchy. A thing he was willing to tolerate in order to avoid the circumstance of suspicion. They were like any of the other tourists from abroad and that is exactly what he intended them to stay. A simple holiday before departing for Ireland. It seemed believable.

"Pick your head up, Agnes," Miguel said as he watched the nuns walk back toward Southwark Cathedral. He turned to Mary, "Are they not coming?"

"It appears not," Mary informed him.

"Will you buy me some candy?" Agnes asked.

He had seen her looking at the crystals with longing for over a half hour. The girl had patience but at nine years old her patience had waxed. "Will you cherish it?" he asked.

"I will. I'll save a bit for my sister and brother even if it takes me forever to find them," she said optimistically.

Miguel held up a finger, "Shush now, we're not away yet." Agnes nodded her head with the eyes of a child who held a secret. He touched her hair, "I believe you. Why not get three and you can save one for each of them." She squeezed his hand.

They walked for another hour. All the way up the river side until there were no more houses or shops. Here the birds circled overhead and shrieked before plummeting into the black mud that oozed over the bank. The sludge was littered with tokens and clamshells. Little bits or gems, sparkling to entice the mud slogs to wade out in the muck and chance their reward. It seemed a fairly poor way to make a living, Mary thought.

Miguel looked around to see they were not being watched. "Can you remember this spot, Mary?" he asked her, pointing to an aged timber sticking out of the bank.

She answered him without question. "Aye, I can remember."

Agnes, pulled at his hand, "We will get to Ireland?" she asked.

"Yes, child. That is the place. For now, you need to be an English girl, cv and Agnes is a very good name." He lifted her arm lightly and they were off without further explanation. He turned back toward the Inn near the bridge where he had paid for their better keep.

CHAPTER 42

Do Tell... Dear Emma

Omagh above the River Strule was a very fine place to build a cottage. Emma Colley wore pants. Gowl had given them to her to protect her legs as they cut trees down, shaved off the bark and notched the logs for building. He had been strong and she willing, so together the cottage was nearly complete. It was not a castle of many rooms, it did not even have a stone floor, but clay was their mortar, and sod the sheltering roof. She loved it, and the man who showed her how to do such things she loved even more.

Emma walked across the field toward the cattle. In one hand she held a rope and in the other she held a spear. The pasture hinted of winter as her ankle felt the cold of its murkiness strike her. It seeped over her boot and down to her toes. The icy invader of warmth with creeping fingers dampening her stockings. The mud sucked at her heels to antagonize her step with the uncertainty of its depth. She pushed herself forward trying not to fall. *Keep my eyes on her*, she thought.

The small angus heifer disappeared behind a brooding cow with its rounded ass and thick tail blending into the inner herd. Gowl would want that tail she thought. They moved unknowingly and Emma progressed to smell the heat of the animals and sweet aroma of manure.

The cattle shuffled forward with their grazing, bovine eyes, and bristled haunches; they were black with caked hides, moving like a carpet to dwarf her. Their grunting sparked a primordial surge of adrenaline that caused Emma's heart to pound with a shower of stars exiting her periphery. Gowl needed this. They had not taken beef for the fear of wasting, and squirrel meat had left him thin. An hour passed, or perhaps it was less. Such was the shaking of her legs that she feared a stampede. She was close; closer now than she had ever been before and they seemed uncommonly fast, alert, and wild.

Emma held out her arms as Gowl had instructed and singled out the intended prey. She walked forward praying that the dominant bull would not turn and charge. He sensed her and snorted, alerting the cows whose ears turned upward in twitching anticipation. They appeared singular in mass. Their sound of protesting bellows echoed through the valley. Never had Emma thought she would attempt such a thing alone but as she moved forward she knew she was committed. It would be one of their lives or hers. If they trampled her she would die. If they wounded her, she would starve, because Gowl was too sick to help her.

Sickness, she thought. For all he had done he now lay near a fire unable to stand without help. At first he had told her it was nothing but in the night his shivering warned that it was more. The fever came slowly and persistently. She touched her belly and felt something move deep inside her. *Gowl will die soon*, Emma thought.

The bull turned away, "Yah!" She yelled and brought her spear down like a whip on the rump of a passing cow. She saw the bull startle and dash away toward the mountain between her cottage and Omagh. A tingle hit her toes, painful and numb as the greater portion of cattle followed him with a thundering of hooves. Their escape erupted quickly and then ebbed to a walk after just a few bounds. They were confused and those that remained between her and the herd wanted to join the great mass that moved slowly away. Soon, just as Gowl had said, the separated cows began walking toward her cautiously, and when they moved, she moved also. Always keeping her eyes on the young angus she intended to kill. She let another two cows pass and then held up her arms. It was enough to stop them and Emma kept herself between the herd and the few. They would move and she would motion, a dance on the grandest of scales. One by one, Emma singled out the prize. Trembling and exhausted, finally just two spear lengths away; the black calf took its step forward, and she made a desperate lunge. The sound it made caused Emma to cry…

❧ ❧ ❧

Smoke rose from the chimney of her home. A high rapid ascent of heat, whose sparks caught in the air to mix with snowflakes. A fresh fire, kindled and hot. Emma looked to the cottage with the blood of her victory smattered from shoulder to ankle. Her boots were caked in it and also the black hair that told of her gruesome work. She sighed and pulled hard on the hide, feeling it's fatty moisture slicken her hand. The quarter from the haunches was all she could handle, so she had bundled the meat into the leathery skin. The cold would have to keep the rest till morning. She prayed that the wolves wouldn't find it. She had removed the stomachs; rinsed them and then added the tongue, heart and organs. Those bits she hid in the creek. The liver she had eaten already.

Emma opened the door.

"You look affright, wife," Henry Colley said as he stood in the plaid of an Irish noble. Tall and thin, and looking as cold as she had ever remembered, he terrified her. Colley Town terrified her and she dropped the meat on the floor. "What... what are you doing here?" she whispered, looking to Gowl who lay unmoving, aglow in the firelight and limp.

"Do thee not have something to say to your husband?" Henry asked as she backed into the corner aghast.

"Did you kill him?" she hissed, expecting to plunge her blade into Henry's chest and then perish in anguish.

Henry looked to his side and whacked Gowl's arm with a musket he was holding. It struck the skin and bone and moved his arm without response. "It does not look as though he needs much help," he said coldly.

"Did ye come here to kill us both?" Emma replied, squeezing the handle of her blade.

"You were not hard to find," Henry said, as he stepped toward her. He leveled his gaze and saw the flash of her metal.

"Why not put down that weapon and give me a kiss?" he asked her.

"Don't come any closer. I am warning you, Henry," Emma whispered.

His gaze pierced her. His voice did the same, "I want to know why!" he demanded.

Why? Her heart felt like bursting. "Why do you think? Do you think it is because of Agnes perhaps, or that you left me out of sorts?" Her words came from within and kept coming, "I... I despise you!" she seethed.

He didn't recognize her.

Emma looked to Gowl and then faced Henry with scorn and felt ready to die: "You did not love me!" she screamed.

He had not expected it to be this way. The certainty in her resolve that pushed back as she slipped past him to that barbarian who lay at deaths gate. He wanted her frail and needy.

"You did not love me, Henry," she said, letting her breath dissipate in the small cottage that held in the warmth.

"I did," he said nostalgically.

She touched Gowl's cheek with relief and Henry observed in silence while his wife tenderly stroked the scarred face of her lover. It dashed him with regret and as she threw off her sheep skins he saw the roundness of her full belly.

"You did not come back to defend me..." Emma whispered.

"And you... you took the vicar's life. There'll be no saving your soul for that," Henry replied bitterly.

"He was no vicar of mine. Would you have me on that stake rather than he?" she asked.

Henry raised his hand as if he intended to strike her and Emma squared to him. No man would ever touch her that way.

She expected it to come, but it didn't and Gowl began to stir. "He will eat now and you may take what you please and go."

"With this barbarian?" Henry asked.

Emma nodded and reached out to touch Gowl's arm. "I think about Colley Town at times. I spent two years of my life there, and I felt alone and deprived the entire time. I carried our daughter in my heart and lost myself with that grief. Can you not understand?" she asked.

"Is this what Agnes would have wanted?" he replied dryly.

"She would have wanted me to be happy, Henry. Do you not remember how she ran across the fields of Connaught even as we knew we were prisoners? She didn't care about the castle or riches. She was a child. A dear and carefree child."

"I remember," he said sadly.

Emma reached up and wiped away a tear, "You left me alone and you needed not to. You asked to go. Me alone... alone... always alone except for those who despised me. I will die before I go back there. So you might as well kill me, Henry."

He did not want to hear her, "Even if I said we could start anew in England?" he whispered.

"Nowhere but here. No one but Gowl," she said.

❧ ❧ ❧

Dennis of the hill clan near Tipperary waited on the road with Hubert and two others. Henry rode toward them, holding the crude map of Omagh and the River Strule. Together they had weaved a clandestine path of investigation. Such was their discovery, that the clans and septs of Maguire, McCarty, and even those of O'Neill had left their war camps for winter. It was almost too easy for them to travel along the common paths of trade. Ulster was virtually unprotected.

"We have found them, Captain," Dennis said.

"Were you seen?" Henry asked.

Dennis held out the traditional Irish surcoat. "I doubt it. You best put this on just the same," Dennis replied.

Henry covered himself and then placed the banner of McMahon over his bridal. "Do you know your way around Belfast?" he asked.

"I do," Dennis replied.

Henry took the leather map and unrolled it as his horse tapped the ground, "Make sure you mark the valley here as passable," he said, pointing to the exact location of Emma's cottage. "I will head south to Ballygawley, then on to Moy. Hubert, you will go to Fintona and immediately return to Colley Town. Warrant Officer Blanch is training our new arrivals and they will need to be ready for war. I want you to help and then lead them directly to the garrison near Armagh."

"Back to Armagh?" Hubert asked.

"Aye. Radcliffe has returned from the Isle of Man. We will join him for this campaign." Henry looked at Dennis, "I can't tell you how important it is that you make it to Belfast, Dennis." he said.

"I will, sir," Dennis replied.

Henry continued with a quick in his voice, "Let each commander of the outposts be informed that the army's beef resides in the pastures near the River Strule. There are enough cattle in those fields to sustain a winter campaign."

"Did ye find her?" Dennis asked.

"No," Henry's tone was calculating, "there is no wife of mine in Omagh."

Dennis obliged his captain and then tied the map and returned it to his saddle. "It is the ship named Abigail that I look for?" he asked.

"Aye, soldier. And with speed. The captain's name is Benjamin Roderick," Henry replied.

CHAPTER 43

The Truth
and
Beef Stew

L ewes Inn, Southwark, London had a spacious single room with a terrace, and Miguel sat with Mary as Agnes rested on a real bed of down. Below them the elite played cards and sipped on burgundy in a lush parlor. It was absolutely lavish, and Mary sat in awe of such comforts.

"I saw birds in cages today," Agnes said.

His gaze fell on her warmly and for a moment, he hoped the feeling would never leave. "Indeed," Miguel replied.

"Have you lived like this before?" Mary asked.

His eyes rested on hers and his words gave her goosebumps. "Art thou learned in the faith, Mary?"

"I am no scholar, but as far as scripture goes, I have a measure," she replied.

"You ask if I have lived like this before, and I would tell you, no. Not because of the comfort or coin that I have now."

"Then if not for the coin, then how have you lived?" she asked.

Miguel reflected on his former life as if suddenly he realized it was lacking. He had always felt fulfilled, and if not fulfilled, he was earnest in his suffering for God. He also had a brother who brought both comfort and pain. It seemed now that he had a capacity for more.

Miguel's words were exceedingly sincere as he answered Mary. "I have not been alone on this earth, but with God to comfort me. I have known heaven and have seen hell and of man or woman I never wanted until now." Then he wondered, would God strike him down? He knew that God was a jealous God and that his calling was undeniable, but would not his Lord make room for Mary as well. It was an overpowering emotion.

Mary blushed, daring to believe what she heard. "It must have been lonely. I at least found company with the sisters."

He looked out the window. "I want you to trust me and know that I have thought of more. Could you be happy with a spirit such as I?"

His openness shocked her as much as it fueled her hopes; it also frightened her. Mary's eyes began to water. "What does that mean?" her voice trailed off like a whisper, longing for nothing else. "Happy…"

"It means that we are not out of danger. It means that if you commit to me I will no longer be a priest but a man. There are some things which have already begun that I cannot change, and for that I am sorry." She grabbed his hand so that he faced her. Mary was enchanted and Agnes pretended to fall asleep while she dreamt of a little girl's fantasy. They would become her Ma and Da.

"Let's go now. It doesn't have to be to Ireland. It can be anywhere," Mary said.

"I must do one last thing, but when that thing is completed, we will."

"Could we not go together to Spain?" she asked.

"It would never be safe for us there; I can assure you. We will also never live like this again."

"When then? How much longer?" she asked.

"Tomorrow we shall enter Bear Garden. I must hear with my own ears what is expected of me."

"You must know what that will be? I don't want a life of secrets," Mary said.

"I believe that I must kill the queen," Miguel confessed, and Mary wished he hadn't.

Colley Town

Down the hillside, below the water catch made of stone, Warrant Officer Blanch paraded out of the stable and turned egregiously to the men who waited. "Attention!" he shouted as the rod in his right and only hand teased at his trouser leg. "Attention... is the first command that ye filthy lot of ball sniffers will learn today!" He marched straight at them and his boots glistened of high polish. The men stood with mouths agape and arms falling loosely at their side. Hubert had returned the evening before and stood for promotion. "Corporal Hubert!" Blanch sounded out.

"Aye, sir!" Hubert responded.

"Corporal Hubert, you shall take these shit stained whelps out into the field and line them up proper. The tall ones will reside in front, the fat ones to the middle and those gangly, short buggers that might reach up to wipe your ass will fall to the rear flank. Is that understood, Corporal Hubert!" Blanch ordered.

Hubert faced about in his tan and dark brown uniform and the red sagum of his splendid form swirled in a fan of military precision. "Ya heard the Warranted Officer of our Queen's most illustrious brigade… now do!" The newly arrived men had never felt such a pressure. All had been informed of their solemn responsibility, yet none was truly ready. They were now a part, albeit the lowest form, of Captain Henry Colley's Kildare Brigade. With a sense of urgency, they ran to the field to brandish wooden swords and lances.

Blanch turned to his protégé with approval. "Tis good ta have ye back, Hubert. How fares our captain and that louse, Dennis of the hill clan?" he asked as they made quick time to the field of men.

"Joined with Ralph Lane and the greater portion of the army," Hubert puffed.

Together, Warrant Officer Blanch and Corporal Hubert parted the fledgling soldiers and soon the drill began. All the planters of Colley Town were about their business. The soldiers, the women, and even the vicar and his disciple Bu-jo. It was that time of mending and preparation that kept their spirit warm. The season itself persisted in cold, and the gray sky hummed with the flapping of the crows.

Not far from the soldiers near the murky bog, Bu-jo skinned a log with a draw blade. Several other men erected similar logs along the perimeter so that the edge of the fields were marked with the enormous tripods of Judas's construction.

"Two more, I think, Bu-jo," Judas said.

Judas reached down and pulled at a heap of limbs to drag off to the brush piles. These too he positioned all along the outer rim of the fertile ground. A perfect place for the heaps to dry. "Bu-jo, will you come here," Judas called. The huge man looked up and immediately began plodding over. "Take this and affix it to the top of that pole there," Judas said, handing Bu-jo the bright red swath of silk that had belonged to Tong. Bu-jo reached up and pinched it between the logs without a second thought. "A little higher, I want it to be able to catch the wind," Judas instructed. When it was done Judas sat below their work and put his hands to the ground. "Sit Bu-jo. Let us rest and talk," he said. Bu-jo took the time to rest, grateful for his work and also the vicar. "Tomorrow we will break the ground and have the clods of clay hammered out," he said with satisfaction.

"It will be a good day," Bu-jo said as he ran his fingers through his hair, "I am famished. Will there be an evening sup tonight?"

"Aye, and a good one. We will have plenty and should be making our way back to the tent line soon. After the meal there is a stone which I will have you move to the center of this field. We shall call it our altar, and over time and with your great strength it shall be chiseled into a cross."

"The tending of fields should come first," Bu-jo replied.

Judas looked at him sternly, "Nay… the Lord's work shall always come first. And it will be important to mark this field of God to keep the heathens away."

Bu-jo thought about Tong and how Judas had sent him out into the woods to look for the mysterious wild men. Tong was eager to be on his own and he was fast and quiet. He was also eager to earn a year's worth of wages for hunting what he thought was superstition: Bu-jo could hardly blame him. "Do you truly believe in these wild spirits you described?" Bu-jo asked.

Judas looked at him seriously, "I don't believe. I know."

"If they exist, Tong will find them," Bu-jo answered.

"We will know for sure when his silk has been removed from this marker. When that happens, you will have your chance to slay a giant."

"I have seen many things in nature and in war but there are none that I despise more than those who defile the dead. If the beasts come here, I will be ready." Bu-jo replied.

Judas shook his head knowingly, leaning back with reflection. "Yes, we will all be ready."

Gowl's cottage near the River Strule

"Are you well?" Emma asked. Gowl sat in a tin basin and she scrubbed his back with lithe of ash. It was frothy and Emma had found mint leaves to scent the bar. Gowl slumped forward in his nakedness and allowed her to reach all of his body. Her hands were soft and soothing.

"I have never felt stronger," he said.

"Good. The baby will be coming soon and you will need your strength. When do you think we shall be married?" she asked.

"Married? Why would I pay for the cow when I get the milk for free?"

She slapped him playfully, knowing she had misled him. Henry was alive, but her husband Henry had left her long ago. Long before the Irish ever came to Colley Town. "Do you love me enough to make me happy?" she asked.

"Of course I do," he said.

"I will tell you again then. We had a visitor while you were ill and he left no doubt that I am free to marry."

Gowl turned to her and pulled her into the basin. Her belly was round, his arms were tender, and she knew that her life had truly started again.

"Tomorrow the clan will arrive for the cattle and I will tell our people then. From hence forth, you will be known as Emma O'Hagen of clan O'Hagen, the keepers of Brehon.

❧ ❧ ❧

The next day, Gowl was good to his word and as the open valley began to fill with his people, he made announcements of marriage and visited each and every elder. They would be wed before the snow covered their pasture in the field by their home. It would be done in the old way and Father Calvin of O'Neill had consented to bless the marriage. That had been the custom and that is what Gowl wanted.

Of the clans that arrived, none were more welcome than the McCarty's. They were a proud people and known for breeding the finest horses. Their chieftain, Michael, was also legendary for his knack at assembling wealth. He owned a greater portion of the herd and Gowl knew him from their raids into the midlands. The McCarty's rode into the pastureland with their women and children in tow. Soon a camp near the south end of the field was quickly established and the atmosphere was like a family arriving home.

Seeing the horsemanship of the new arrivals, Emma walked out into the clearing that she and Gowl had cut in preparation. All the O'Hagen septs would arrive from Omagh, and the O'Neill of Dungannon would bring grain and hops for the inter clan celebrations. Gowl was more important it seemed than she had ever imagined, and Emma watched as the chieftain McCarty and his wife rode toward their small cottage to pay respect. She greeted them with her full belly popping at the buttons and felt too large for her tightly fitted blouse.

The McCarty woman greeted her as if she had known Emma for years. "Give us a lumbar," she said graciously. Emma held out her arms as Mistress McCarty approached her. She gave Judith a welcoming hug that brought a warmth to their first meeting.

Emma beamed. "So pleased..." she could hardly contain her blushing. "We have not a visitor in nearly a month. And look at me, I must appear a mess!"

"Not at all, lass," Judith said, then she turned to her husband. "Michael has told me of your village in the midlands. It is known as Colley Town?"

"It is," Emma replied.

"Well you are with us now and we are glad for it," Judith told her.

Judith and Michael allowed Emma to show them into the cottage. Emma felt enthralled. The place was small but it was theirs! Quite the accomplishment for a gentle woman of her former self. Seeing who entered, Gowl shot up from his chair to greet the McCarty chieftain and his wife.

"Some news for ye, I have," McCarty said squarely.

Gowl smiled and pulled a cork from his favorite scotch bottle. "Well spill it then, and I'll spill us a dandy drink," he said. "It's beyond cold out there, so ye might know we have cut wood to get you through the first night."

Mistress McCarty took Emma's arm, "It looks as though the child will be coming soon," she said happily.

"Perhaps," Emma said holding her side. "I've been feeling it hard today. A right mule this one will be, I'm sure." She glanced over to Gowl. The men were loud and she wanted to stop and listen as he and Michael caught up.

"We can let the men do their talking, Emma," Judith said. Then she turned her attention to more womanly matters. "We'll be staying through to the wedding. Have thee made ye-self a birthing bed, girl?"

"Aye, I put an extra bit of blankets down over there. I don't want it to come and not be ready. I have had a child before, God rest her soul, but never alone," Emma said.

Judith gave her a comforting look, "Well... perhaps you will not be alone. I'm no stranger to labor either. It'll come in God's time."

Emma heard herself talking and wondered how she had lost her proper English so quickly. It was as if she had absorbed the very essence of Gowl's unmannered Gaelic tongue. Somehow the language was a part of the fabric of her new self. It made her feel… different. It made her feel… Irish. "I'll manage it."

Mistress McCarty patted Emma on the shoulder, "Good for you. Good… good… good. It'll be easier on you this time for sure. And for me as well I suspect, should that bagatelle come squirting out this very eve."

"It would be my blessing. Lord knows Gowl's hands are more suited for the stable," Emma replied. They laughed and Emma realized the men had stopped talking and were apparently eaves dropping.

"Don't be nosing in on a woman's business," Judith scolded.

Michael laughed and so did Gowl as he poured the women a whiskey. There were four chairs and a table in the cottage and they all found a place. Emma took a sip and the heat burned her throat as she rinsed it down.

"God's speed. Gowl, she is a fine woman. Who'd a thought the ends of the earth would join for you so. If it's a boy do you have a name?" Michael asked.

"Aye, McCarty," Gowl replied. "He will be Gowl." Emma's cheeks went red as Mistress McCarty turned up her nose in jest.

The good cheer kept coming and along with the talk came more whiskey. Michael told a tale that brought Emma a measure of comfort. "I'll tell thee as surely as I stand here now that O'Neill will be the next high lord of Ulster. Damned hell with Radcliffe and his bloody campaign. His reach will go well beyond Tyrone and well beyond his father Conn. O'Neill will put an end to it all. He got that greedy English bastard Radcliffe scorned by the queen herself, I hear. The news puts a wanting in my heart that's fit for Christmas."

Gowl perked up. "So O'Neill has awayed himself?"

McCarty replied happily: "The ships left yesterday and I wish I were on one. Even as O'Neill sails, the pigeons fly from Ballycastle to Dunluce to announce the right of it to all of Ulster. The English court even paid him thirteen thousand pounds for the trouble of getting over there. Nearly all the army has stood down. He will be an earl and that is known now both to us and to the Scotts of Antrim. There will be no more war."

"It is true then?" Emma asked.

"Aye…" Michael said with firm conviction. We also have heard that Clan Campbell of Argyll will not oppose a marriage between Katherine and Shane O'Neill."

Gowl frowned when Emma asked: "What of the Earl of Tryconnell?"

McCarty's expression soured. He was no fan of Tryconnell and made no bones about his dislike. "The traitor will be released, Emma. Upon Shane's safe return and when he has been accepted as a peer, O'Donnell will go free. Of course we have not told O'Donnell of the plan."

"That puts us at ease out here. I can assure you, Michael," Gowl replied.

"Good," Michael took a sip and stood to face the fire. "So it seems we have to take fifty head of cattle out of the common field and drive them to Tullyhogue before the wedding. That's what it'll take to ensure the priory is set for winter and also secure your blessing. Does that number sound correct?"

"Fifty head?" Gowl asked.

"Aye… it'll be fifty. It'll be a large wedding."

Emma saw Gowl pause in thought and she recognized his poor reception of the news. She had never seen him more serious. "Do the good fathers of Dungannon Friary not eat anything but beef?" Gowl asked knowing that fifty head was near the limit of his wealth.

Michael saw the concern in Gowl's eyes burst into laughter, "Alright laddie boy, don't shite ye-self, they'll take just five."

Gowl grabbed his chest to feign relief, "Bloody hell, ye had my dander up there for a bit, McCarty. You devil. I'd have to walk to every elder once again if such a thing were so."

The night was good, and when it was over, they walked out into the McCarty camp under the stars. The fire made Emma ever warm to Omagh.

CHAPTER 44

Bear Garden

Bear Garden, the amphitheater of wooden grandstands overlooked an exhibition. Bear baiting was quite the attraction in Southwark. Miguel had brought both Mary and Agnes, and they wore the colors of nobility. Agnes couldn't take her eyes off the animal. Her father had slain a bear once and its pelt adorned the stone wall of Dunaverty. She wondered if it was still there, seeing it in her mind's eye and remembering his story. *A fearsome beast*, he had said. The one down below she saw for herself. The crowd roared and she drifted back in her memory. *Are there bears in Kintyre that might come to eat me?* she had asked. He had answered: *No lass, there be no brown bears here.* She missed the scratch of his beard and the smell of wood smoke on his flannel. She heard the dogs barking and it made her take Mary's hand. "Will it die?" she asked.

Mary looked down at her, "Be still child."

Agnes raised her voice, "Will it die?"

"I have never seen such a thing," Mary replied.

Miguel sat to their right and dutifully held Mary's other hand and he could tell that she liked it. He gave it a little squeeze every now then, comforting, reassuring, and tender. It made Mary wish that the excitement would never end. There was something about him that quieted her, even in the dire circumstance of being hunted. He made Mary feel safe.

The Spaniard who sat on Miguel's right did not. He was another thing all together. Count De Feria was cold to her and sat in his jeweled vest and perfectly fitted jerkin as if he were the king. He feigned a smile but it did not seem genuine. Miguel passed her a bag of roasted beechnuts, and Count de Feria settled back as Miguel whispered in his ear. They appeared to talk as friends and even took out their purses for wager, but Mary knew that Miguel had never seen the count before. It made her feel odd and somewhat guilty.

"Where are the dogs?" Agnes asked.

"Shhh, just watch and listen," Mary said, as she eyed the Spaniard suspiciously.

From the grandstand of the arena the vendors buzzed with the chatter and zeal of uncivilized combat. Wagers were collected all around. There were trinkets for sale- little necklaces adorned with wooden claws and fine beads of glass. Pamphlets could be purchased for a half penny; Miguel had bought two. The dogs depicted in the drawings looked ferocious. And the bear in the picture had long claws and teeth as it charged out of the page toward the reader in vivid detail. Clearly it was not the same bear that was taunted down below.

Agnes lifted her finger to see the blotch of ink that blackened her index, causing a smear on her fine new dress. "There they are!" she squealed as the handlers lifted the gate and paraded the mastiff's out into view. The huge dogs wore collars of spikes and trounced in front of their handlers with leather breastplates. One had a scar across his back the other was missing an eye. So was the life of a warrior, Agnes thought as the dogs yipped with fervor and panted. Seeing the hounds, the crowd cheered and the entire ramshackle of wood began to shake beneath her. She looked to Mary with horror.

Miguel turned to the ambassador of Spain as the fervor rose. Count de Feria looked at him gravely. "Have ye delivered the message?" he asked quickly.

"Si, and both O'Neill and Fitzgerald will be received by the queen," Count de Feria replied.

The mob stood and cheered as the announcer entered the arena. The screaming and the sight of the terrorizing dogs frightened the poor little bear who bawled like a stuck pig. Agnes looked at Mary pitifully, feeling ever so endeared to the little bear that she nearly began to cry.

"Turn away child," Mary said as the dogs dashed out. Merciless huge bodied dogs that darted for the bear with great speed. Miguel pulled Mary's hand and she fell back into her seat to hear the dogs growl and the painful cries which came from the beast. Agnes covered her ears. Mary turned with contempt and the bitter taste of rage that she felt toward the men who delighted in such things.

Miguel pulled her to his shoulder, "Do not look," he said and she felt mercy that he was revolted.

"Get us out of here," she begged.

Agnes began crying, hoping beyond hope that this terrible thing would be over soon. She saw the count lick his lips and tighten his hands over the bejeweled coat he wore and knew that he was pleased. The prettiness of his attire and fanciful rough barely concealing his lust for the blood. He raised his hand as if he had the courage to slay the terrible bear: "Matar! Matar el oso!" he screamed.

When it was over the bear was dragged away and a single dog remained standing. The poor thing whimpered as the handler pulled it without remorse to the kennel. The count turned his back on them all and departed. He had wagered that neither dog would die and was displeased. Miguel sat there quietly as the stadium cleared and paper drifted across the dirt below. He would not be leaving London. The count had given him his father's blessing and with it the instruction to go forth with the plan and bring his poison to Windsor. His affection and longing for Agnes and Mary were of little matter now. *How would he tell them?*

Mary stood, "I will never come here again," she said.

"No... neither shall I," Miguel replied.

CHAPTER 45

A Toast
to
Glendalough

Thomas Smyth assessed the bulk of the Great Harry, which floated off the pilings of Broken Wharf. The center gangway was already fastened to disembark, and he cleared his throat with anticipation as the Lord of Leinster joined the mayor and headed his way. It wasn't often that an entourage of dignitaries would be met in the person. Today, and for Shane O'Neill, the exception had been made. Thomas considered exceptions as he did with all his dealings with John Lodge. He dreaded the encounter.

437

"My lord and Lord Mayor, the honor of your company is my utmost pleasure," Thomas said in greeting. They nodded to him rather than the imposition of uttering a sound. The insult went unchallenged and Thomas ducked in behind to follow the lords to the waterfront. He had done enough for the city to earn a simple respect, he thought. Someday, perhaps someday soon, Lodge might not think him so small.

Robert Dudley was dressed for parade, his horse team was ready and he set his intention upon viewing the ship itself. His eyes scoured the vessel like torches. Had he done exactly as Elizabeth instructed? The streets of London were lined with people expecting a grand parade, and a large complement of English soldiers stood at the ready. Even as he had done so, he doubted O'Neill would buy it. As for the lord mayor, he had been told nothing except to instruct all the watchmen to set out upon the streets to enjoy the company of O'Neill and Fitzgerald on their glorious march to Windsor Palace. Robert felt nervous.

Thomas Smyth took note of the ships condition and then turned to Lord Dudley for his own affirmation. "It appears in good order, Lord Dudley," he said optimistically.

The lord mayor tightened his lips without reply.

Robert answered: "It is a crock of horse shit, Thomas. Parading about a Catholic renegade and making his arrival a spectacle before our great city. But we must all play our part. That is why the entire ward is out to see the great chieftain of Ulster."

Lodge nodded in agreement. "It is an uncommon honor for such a scoundrel. I heard he killed his own father among other hideous things. A true barbarian; savage, absolutely savage."

Dudley scowled. "Well, he will be escorted none the same. Don't get thee nickers in a piss all. At least we will have the company of Lord Fitzgerald."

Lodge looked disturbed, "I see no need to dally with either once the offload is complete. Why have you insisted that we march with them along the north wall and out the upper gate? Wouldn't it be much quicker if we simply rode directly to Windsor?"

Thomas listened, standing like a pup at the foot of his master and he almost wished O'Neill would come with spear in hand. The chieftain had it right. Why would he change a thing only to find himself ten rungs down the ladder of life in his own kingdom? Was it fear that brought him? He hoped so.

Robert Dudley's tone was stoic, "It is what the Queen wishes. I am counting on your opening New Gate and the Bide Tower for spectators. I want a crowd to follow or even proceed the march of nobles. It would be goodly to last all day. You have made the necessary arrangements I presume?"

Lodge complained: "I have. Although, I don't like it. There are too many soldiers committed to the safety of this ward. It leaves the castle itself almost baron of men, let alone an adequate guard for the tower."

Robert answered: "O'Neill did not come to attack the tower but if there is any hint of disorder, I expect your guards and all the watchmen will be able to handle his small band of Irishmen. Is that understood?"

"It is and we would like nothing else."

Robert felt the same and secretly wished he might not endure the anguish of expendability. For that is what he now knew he was. Just a tool for his Beth. Or was he? It didn't matter now.

He had made his bed and wouldn't let his voice betray him. "He has safe passage, Lord Mayor. Come now... let us go meet this bedswerver in person. I see the colors of the Irish already leaving the ship."

❧ ❧ ❧

On board the *Great Harry*, Gerald Fitzgerald stood near Admiral Hackett on the gangway. The deck itself was sparsely occupied in its gargantuan form, and much like the companion vessel the *Mary Rose,* which had sunk, it lulled in the water like a great beast of burden. Gerald looked gratefully forward to having his feet upon solid ground.

"You will be greeted and taken to Windsor, shortly," Admiral Hackett said dutifully.

Gerald felt small, barely noticeable as he tipped his head to acknowledge the Admiral. The old seafarer stood with his golden epaulettes in true English fashion.

A trumpet sounded on the foredeck and the crew of the *Great Harry* lined the gunnels in salute. It was time, Gerald supposed, to introduce England to the 11th Earl of Kildare. Ashore he could already hear the spectacle and fanfare which was overly done in his opinion. Appearing regal, he descended and stamped his cane down hard with each step down the gangway. The wide planks rattled and a garrison of English soldiers formed to receive him. He took his time, making his royal descent as gulls screamed overhead and all the tiny boats lapped against their mooring boards.

Robert Dudley turned to Thomas Smyth with disbelief. "Where is the O'Neill?" he asked. The Earl of Kildare marched directly toward them with his own complement of men.

Thomas felt a bit of satisfaction with his next words. "I was about to tell my lords, as you breezed past me, that our dock master sent word upon the Great Harry's arrival that only Lord Fitzgerald was aboard."

"Fitzgerald only?" Dudley said with horror.

River Thames near Gravesend

Having boarded a ship of his own choosing and taking the seven days to sail the round of England, O'Neill sat alone above his men. His thoughts returned to Antrim. The Scotts had aligned with him before, but on this voyage, Sorely Boy had adverted his calling. Perhaps Katherine would gain some information on what was happening with the Scotts. For now, Sorely Boy and the Campbell's were fast behind and he had taken the gamble to accept the queen's offer. The priest had made good on his pledge and Turlough was in control of the defense of the clan. The men he brought where loyal. Most, he thought, were the very best. He also had the assurance of fifty Gallowglass and his general, Barre Conn. They wore saffron shirts and carried their shields as if they intended to conquer England rather than receive it.

The weather was fair as Barre Conn came to him. "We will sail past Canvey Island within an hour," Barre said.

The bow cut a clean wake. The air was crisp and for all the worry; it had been an easy sail. Surely it was meant to be. That terrible marriage of necessity. "Make the men ready," Shane replied.

Barre handed him a cup of hot broth. "She will be wondering by now why her ship has arrived empty to London."

Shane remarked casually: "It's not empty. The Earl Fitzgerald set sail from Dublin two days before we. He will take the escort the queen may have sent on our behalf. It is for the best. My word was that we would arrive in London. I never said how."

"Aye, your Grace," Barre laughed, "you never said how."

"We will land in a place of our choosing and go ashore as warriors. We will ride our own horses and have enough men to defend ourselves if things go badly. Hell, if we are so entertained and welcomed within the walls of Her Majesty's castle, we may even have enough to occupy."

"That's a fools thought, your Grace," Barre replied.

"Perhaps. Almost as foolish as taking my person to the very devil who wants my soul." Shane stretched his arms confidently and finished his thought, "Let us hope that Lord Butler and Fitzgerald have enough influence to ensure things go in our favor. That is our only advantage. If not, do not forget good friend, that our Jesuit has devoutly pledged to cause a stir within the Catholics of London. If that be the case and he is successful, the queen may find herself pressured to accept my offer."

"God be praised if it were only so," Barre said.

Shane looked at Barre Conn with compassion. "I have not forgotten about your brother Jodia. You will have your blood from the Jesuit, I assure you."

"And when our ships begin to row up the Thames, what then?"

"Let us hope that England falls out to greet us. From all I have heard, Radcliffe himself has been recalled to the court. I am sure he has devil tongued the queen's ear and her promise of our stately arrival has already faded from thought."

"If he is here, he is planning your demise," Barre said knowingly.

"You will keep a lookout for me on the shores and have the ships remain a good distance one from another to prevent our entrapment. Should we be attacked, we shall disengage on the opposite bank and lay waste to every man woman and child that we can before making our retreat home."

"We will not be attacked openly, my lord. Of that I am certain," Barre concluded.

Shane nodded, "With God's hand, Earl Fitzgerald will distract our good queen, while we move safely ashore."

"It doesn't sound as if you are sure," Barre replied cautiously.

"I am sure you will make camp. I am sure that I will go with a small party to Maidenhead and after that, the surety of all things are unknown."

Windsor Castle

Two Fitzgerald's and not an O'Neill to be found, but the ceremony went without question. She had it in the garden, under a blue sky and beautiful tents. Overlooking the festivities, Queen Elizabeth sat on a velvet chair resting her arms on pillows. The Irish lords sworn to her service relished the greenery, and harpists strummed their notes to fill the air with music. Among the peers who had entwined their fate with England was Gerald Fitzgerald the Earl of Desmond. Gerald felt himself relieved to be spared the hangman's noose although he brooded over the queen's declaration that England would stand apart from the Catholic faith. He relied on the faith of his people. He had business in Spain and it was not just faith that put him off. A protestant Ireland would diminish his power in Munster.

Gerald stood at the side of Alvaro de la Quadra, who had the look of satisfaction in his eye, despite having lost his stately apartment. They both watched the lady dancers of court prance along the stonework between the green bushes and the queen's entourage. The dancers would curtsey, then hop. They kicked their stockinged legs up high. Elizabeth clapped unenthusiastically, and behind her, Lord Burghley and Thomas Gresham raised their tankards. The court was abuzz again with festivities, Gerald thought, and he had nothing but poor reports of the condition of his men who languished near Armagh.

Ireland was as inflicted by its allegiance as badly as it was divided, and Gerald resented the acceptance of it all. Perhaps O'Neill was right. The chieftains of Glendalough clasped their hands together in forgetfulness of the battle that England had waged just ten years past. He grimaced when a toast was raised to Glendalough, by none other than Elizabeth herself:

"To Father Coghlan, may he rest in peace outside the conical tower of Clonmacnoise. God rest his soul."

Watching their folly and wondering just how long a peace would be sustained, he dared say nothing. But what of Athlone, later this very year? Would they of Athlone hear the queen's toast and find comfort? Gerald doubted it. These chieftains would never truly be earls in Elizabeth's court. She would most certainly include the people's harvest in future tributes to the crown. God be damned for which taketh all away. He did not want to live like that anymore. Whether he be a knight or not, deep down he felt the distance growing between him and the protestants.

Standing in his fanciful white ruff and bejeweled black doublet, Bishop Quadra touched his shoulder, "Do not appear so distracted." Gerald faced him, and together they looked apart. One with a pale white skin and heavy thick beard, the other of olive complexion and a wisp of a mustache over his cleanly shaven chin.

I am in hell, Gerald thought, *I even find this arrogant Spaniard beautiful.* Taking a moment to calm himself as the count waited for a reply, Gerald chose his words carefully. "I will do all that is required."

"You are free. You must act like it," Quadra replied smartly.

"Aye, my lord. I'll be leaving with my house at daybreak tomorrow. At least in Desmond I will be received the hero."

"The bitch has released your cousin and has sent for Shane O'Neill. I also believe she may be coming into heat for Butler. Either that or he has wetted her with some ungodly promise. You mustn't leave us, Gerald," Quadra said.

"Butler is now without an army and O'Neill was right to fight against him. At least he arrives to London as a victor and not a whimpering piss-tail. As for my cousin and I, our fathers sealed our fate long ago. We were born to this. No, my Spanish friend, his father tried to bend him to England and thusly died because of it. I must admit that begs to be worth admiration."

Bishop Quadra took a glass of bubbling wine from the court maid and gave another to Gerald. "Spain prefers the House of Desmond to that of O'Neill. Remember that in the coming days as you wait on your countrymen. In the meantime, enjoy some tennis, take sport in the fields, and make yourself appear noble and without gloom. That is what I need of you."

"You presume too much. I am indebted to Spain and my influence would be far better served with a commitment from your king. Do thee not think I know he has abandoned O'Neill?"

Bishop Quadra replied: "The whole of Ireland has heard the rumors that we Spanish promised but failed to deliver the ships to end the lunacy of war in Ulster. There is only one problem with that. We never promised any ships. No. Not once did the offer of ships and soldiers come from my king. It came from a wayward Jesuit stepping way beyond the calling."

The count raised his brow and took a sip of wine as Gerald finished his thoughts aloud. "We would not need Spain if the three great houses of Ireland would stand against this queen together. Would we?"

The count laughed and then passed a hand toward the dancers as if it were he that was sent to entertain them. "Perhaps not. Were it not for your desperate Irish tempers, I might believe it." Gerald turned to walk away and the count grabbed his shoulder, "I have presented her Bitchesty with a letter from O'Neill. It came from the same Jesuit who made the false promise. If she does not read it and take heed, that very man will come to take her life. What do you say to that?"

"A letter?" he asked.

"Yes, my friend. Spain has not abandoned the whole of Ireland." The count stopped for a moment and bowed with smile to the royal tent. "The bitch must reconcile with Ulster, so I tell you today to put your pride aside and accept your place in her Bitchesty's court."

"I have an army of my own," Gerald replied.

"It is not an army that is needed. Your friends out there under the tents are quite happy to be among the English. Look at Thomas Butler who sits by her side. Look at the Earl of Thomond, Connor O'Brien, and those from Glendalough. Do you think they will protest if you decline your duty and run off to form dissention?"

"Of course not, they have to much to gain. Unlike the Butlers, I would rather be a chieftain in Munster or live among the wildlings of Lough Derg than remain an earl in her court."

The count whispered, "You will do as you are told."

CHAPTER 46

Conflicted

Miguel placed a letter on the table for Mary and left her sleeping at Lewes Inn. He was unable to tell her everything and the one truth that pervaded between them was his admission that he would take life. It altered how she saw him and that stung. Would she be able to find a love for him? He knew now that if she could, he would never betray her, and yet the distance between them grew with silence. She no longer cared for shopping or playing the role of a dutiful wife on holiday. He had exposed her inner most thoughts and fears. Miguel knew her beauty distracted him and put his mission at risk. Perhaps it was God's way to break her free and set him on his path. She was alive and frail and he pined for her.

449

Leaving the Lewes Inn, Miguel walked up River Street toward the bridge. To the very place where Count de Feria had told him he would be received. The underground of a newly formed Catholic resistance had taken root in Southwark and Miguel was on his way to meet the prior. It wasn't far, not as far as he would have liked it to be and the huge stone of Southwark Cathedral rose up to guide his way, late in the evening. He stopped to ensure he was not being followed at the very head of the gate by the bridge. When he was sure it was safe, he entered the coolness of the cloisters and the air chilled his skin and smelt of incense. He envisioned the Franciscan order who had occupied the Cathedral prior to King Henry's dissolution and wondered how many souls had been saved inside the great construction. Hundreds no doubt and perhaps someday, when the Queen was no longer estranged, hundreds more would raise their voices to heaven. Now, according to the law, it was an Anglican diocese, and the candles remained lit. Every hour of every day they would burn as they had for two hundred years. It was a reminder that England, although drifting apart with dissention, had not lost itself completely. The common had faith and there were many, many candles in Southwark.

He walked toward the sanctum with its hard stone floor and waited near the choir which was made of beautifully laminated elm. Not a speck of dust was anywhere. His heels fell softly; Reverently, he sat, he knelt, he prayed. "Lord have mercy. Post Your angels in my place that will guide and heal the hearts of the helpless." Many prayers ushered from his lips and all were directed toward Mary. She would need them. She would need all of God's angels to survive. He waited under the watchful eyes of a caretaker and wondered if the prior had been arrested or worse. Had the consort of King Phillip led him astray? Within the holiest of holies, Miguel found no answer at all. Only hours of waiting and praying with no contact at all. *Through the prior of Southwark Cathedral you will gain access to both West Minster and the queen's court,* is what he was told.

"The Cathedral is closed for the common at night," the caretaker told him.

Miguel answered in Latin, "Adeuva me," and he stood to leave with a sense of failure. Why did this place affect him so? He felt the power of the Holy Spirit come rushing through him and it filled him with remorse. Why?

The caretaker looked kindly at him and stood with the empathy of one who had seen many sufferings. His old fingers were round. His calloused arms poked out of loose fitted sleeves like weathered shafts of driftwood. "I understand," he replied. "You are a Spaniard?" And with a singular motion, he both stood and tossed his grey hair out of his face to convey a scholarly countenance. "I will help you, my son."

Miguel felt himself shudder as he was led behind the choir, and down to the hall of clerics. "Adeuva me... adeuva me..." he repeated. His plea came from somewhere deep inside and without control. The words meaning more than *help me*: more than his heart could bear.

"I will. I will help you," the old one said without further question. Suddenly they stopped in the middle of the passageway and the elder peered over his shoulder. He was cautious and quick to touch a hinge that swung a door open. The wall moved with such craftsmanship that it was nearly indistinguishable from the remainder of the woodwork and as they entered an adjacent and hidden hall, the door closed quietly behind them. Inside, Miguel bent down to avoid hitting his head and the caretaker struck a candle for light.

"I have been told what you have asked for. The Holy Father, will write you of his intent just one more time. I warn you though, Miguel Avaje Fernandez, to leave the order will come at a price. Your solace awaits you in there," the elder said.

He said it as if it were a dream, whispering and soft, "I will pay any price." Miguel's mind was swirling with the power of the Lord. The caretaker pushed him forward and he wicked away the perspiration on his forehead, licked his lips, and crouched within the very small brick chamber he was being forced into. It was like a prison with its narrow confining walls and blackness. He cared not because his heart ached for what he knew he could never have. As he felt his knees strike the hard floor, a cattail of knotted rope was dropped at his side.

"When the spirit dwells in sinful thoughts, the body must suffer. Only then, will you be strong enough to fight your demons," the caretaker said.

Miguel did not want his father's message, he wanted Mary.

Hours later, the old man pressed his ear to the wood of the secret hall and heard a most horrific struggle. He whispered to himself in Latin and then bent to his knees. "Give this one peace, my Lord. Release his poor and tormented soul from his vices so that I may not have to do the thing which was asked."

Lewes Inn, Southwark

When Mary awoke she took a chance and looked out the glass window of their room. She poured a murky basin of water and dampened her face. *I have paid for two weeks only and after that you must go*, he had written her. The words tore her spirit to the core because she did not want to. She wanted to take the purse he had left and pay for as long as he needed. How would she know what ship to board and where to go? She had seen the tension on his face and dared not ask him anything further of his intentions. She never imagined he would abandon her, but then she had never thought he would openly confess to murder. His instructions were clear. *Find the English ship to Dublin.* Mary looked at the bag of coins he had left and then to Agnes, "I am not leaving without you," she had wanted to say but instead she remained silent. The expectation of his promise made him leave even more quickly, and now she wished she had not pushed him. She wanted her thoughts to miraculously span the expansive city to find him, wherever he had gone: "We will not go to Dublin!"

She waited and cried and thought of all the things he had said. Outside the streets were coming to life, but inside she was dying. It was Agnes who saw and stood as the door opened. Mary held her head in her hands.

Miguel entered, Mary looked up, "You bastard!" she screamed at him. "You bastard!"

As he stood there without apology, Mary saw his blood soaked shirt. He let out a sigh, and Agnes fetched the basin of water. His lips were dry; his voice was brittle. "Do not scorn me. It would hurt me much worse than you could ever know."

Her anger quickly turned to solace and relief. He was hurting. She loved him. What else was there to say? Dangerous. Danger was written all over him and she should have known better than to trust the man of murder. She secretly wished for the wounds to make him need her but instead they tore at her heart.

Miguel reached out to Agnes who immediately hugged him and buried her face in his robe. He tightened his jaw, he stroked Agnes's hair and Mary saw that he was sorry.

"What happened to you?" she asked.

"Everything," he replied.

St. Bartholomew's

Rodrigo sat in his study thinking about Julianne who he saw near West Minster the day before. He was sure she spied him before vanishing into the Anglican congregation. For that he was truly sorry. The hospital was nowhere near as healing without the sisters. None were allowed to enter now except those who could afford to pay. The streets outside stunk of decay. *It was time*, he thought, *to make my move toward permanence at Oxford.*

A knock came at his door: it was an attendee. "Rodrigo, a very important man has come to see you, and he waits in the observatory."

An important man? He could only fathom who would be nosing around to ask questions and immediately felt suspicious. "What does he want?"

"It's Thomas Smyth. He and the alderman from Cheap Ward have asked to come to the offices. They said it was urgent."

"I have no business with the alderman or Smyth. They are criminals," Rodrigo replied resentfully.

"What should I tell them?"

"Nothing! I will tell them myself." Rodrigo said without moving. He picked up a drawing that Agnes had made which he really quite fancied. It was a sparrow and a rose. The girl had talent, and so did Julianne and the widows. They were necessary and now that they were gone- he despised Smyth all the more.

His attendee lingered worrisomely, "When will you tell them? I don't like the look of those men and they seemed rather impatient."

"When I am ready. Now go."

❧ ❧ ❧

St. Bartholomew's observatory was a wretched place, Thomas thought. He never liked churches and he certainly had no inclination to visit hospitals. It was death in walls and men who found their goulash endeavors rewarding. He had no faith in physicians, only faith that Rodrigo Lopez knew about the Spaniard and the girl. For that, and that alone, he entered the sacred place of healing. He turned to the alderman who waited also, "Come, the good physician appears to be away."

Rodrigo spoke as he entered, "I am here. I've been here all along. What do you want Smyth!"

Thomas replied with equal distain, "It seems all of Spain has invaded England. If not by shipping, then by reproduction. How many children have you sired?" Thomas said rudely.

Rodrigo turned his nose, "Portuguese actually. Schooled in Barcelona, and sent here by the request of Mary Tudor. What are your credentials?"

"Cambridge, and I am here on business," Thomas replied.

"Business? Is that what they call it at the gallows?"

Thomas looked pleased that his reputation preceded him. Catholics, Spaniards, or debtors all had their part to play in his world. It was the way of things and today he would deal with a doctor. "It matters not what I call it. I'm pretty sure you know why I am here, and I can see your helpers were smart enough to leave. Pity they had to depart your service so quickly. I am sure you miss them."

Rodrigo glowered: "People come and go from employment at a hospital. It's a temporary setback, I assure you."

Thomas nodded regretfully and the alderman who was surely in his pocket sat like a statue trying his very best to remain inconspicuous. As Rodrigo looked on expectantly, Thomas continued: "I came to assure you, that I have no interest in pursuing the Catholics in Cheap Ward. Not I, nor the watchmen. Even the queen has sent word through the clergy that we should not incite against the papists and stir up any more unwanted trouble. I presume her Majesty feels it better to embrace all of the Londoners in a hope that they will see the true measure of her grace. So with that spirit in mind, I shall not be looking for the nuns, should they find their way back here."

Rodrigo felt like vomiting. It would be the end of him, if Thomas ever found out what he had done. Or it would be the end of Thomas. "I don't know what you refer to? This type of thing should have been avoided in the first place. Or does it suit you to strike terror in the hearts of the helpless?"

Thomas sat back, folded his hands across his chest, and leaned on the influence he had purchased. "My man here feels the same. Did you know he had an affinity for the older madam of your employ? It seems she was responsible for the care of his mother in her later days. A thing like that does not go forgotten."

"Aye, Thomas," Rodrigo replied.

"Since it is so with the alderman, and others who are important to me, I will extend you a credit. The nuns may return. The only thing I ask is that you perform a surgery for me in the very near future. After the surgery, you will have an opportunity to visit with the queen. Are you up to that?"

Although he expected the offer to come in another way, he dared not, for the sake of his mission, refuse. "I am always at the service of the crown. If the court wishes me to serve the house of Tudor."

"We shall see. In a very short while we shall surely see."

Southwark

They ate a kidney pie with bits of carrots that Miguel turned over with his finger. He knew more now than he dared to tell Mary. It was time. If he waited any longer she would learn too much about him. That part of him, that he told to no one was thing that would surely doom her. "You will both leave London very soon," he whispered.

Mary felt a flutter in her stomach, that dread of the thing she feared most. "Alone?"

"It will be like it was before, when you stayed at the Alms House, except this time there will be friends to guide you. After I leave in the morning, you will wait here until a message arrives with my name on it. Then you will return to the mud flats of Southwark where the timber rises from the water. Do you remember where it is?" he asked.

"I remember the day," Mary said.

He considered the dangers for both her and Agnes and knew they could not be avoided. Her eyes said that she knew who he was. A glimmer of light in a long tunnel of sacrifice. He was afraid to show her more, he got up slowly and lifted a board he had loosened many weeks before.

"What are you doing?" Agnes asked.

Miguel knelt down and pulled up the leather satchel. It was the same bag which caused Agnes to remember the night he told her of Cora. The night she saw him for who he was. "You know what this is, child. Would you love nothing more than to spin a coin across this floor?" he asked. Agnes let out a yelp of glee. Miguel lifted out another bag that Agnes had never seen and spoke to Mary. "Everything that can be and should be is in this one. Her past, her present, and her future. Will you see our dear Agnes to Dublin?"

"I can, and I will if it will bring you back to us," she said.

"No, Mary." Miguel placed the bag in her hands. "This is her family seal and father's ring. The birthright cannot be bargained with." He saw the disappointment and inevitable sense of rejection. "I will come when I can, you well know."

Agnes sent a coin across the floor. "Is Dublin in Connaught?" she asked, remembering the story.

Miguel shifted uncomfortably, realizing he had errored in revealing so much to the little girl. No one could know of Connaught. No one at all and he turned her mind to the notion. "Let us say that Dublin is what we say and Connaught is like Jade MacAlister, the chieftain's daughter. We will speak of neither but know that one day the world shall see both Jade and Connaught together."

"Like a game you mean?" Agnes asked.

"Like a secret, Agnes. A secret that we cannot share until it is time. Can you remember?"

Mary began to weep, "I am tired of secrets."

CHAPTER 47

Father

William Cecil entered the council chamber anxiously. Elizabeth sat with her ladies in waiting, with tea and crumpets already served. The queen put down her cup upon his arrival. "I cared not to see thee, Lord Burghley. Where is Robert?"

William approached, "He has yet returned, Majesty. Mayhap it is I who needs a private audience?"

Elizabeth twitched off the crumbs from her fingers and gave a telling look to her company. They appeared to know much more than William cared to have them know. They were not coy, but they were informed.

"You may leave us," Elizabeth said, and her company of loyal rose up and left without giving a due greeting.

William looked vexed. "Walter Devereux has arrived this morning with his complement, and I fear he has no inkling of your intentions for his marriage with lady Knollys. As for Robert, he has not been seen since the Earl of Kildare was delivered. I imagine he is sore for you. Most assuredly as you are sore for me, and have so cunningly instructed the castle to show my position nothing but indifference!"

"Perhaps, or perhaps your actions cause your own condition. Either way, we are bound by more than our deeds, Lord Burghley." She put Robert Dudley from her mind, feeling a slight betrayal. William's countenance however, pleased her, and she focused on the matter closer at hand. The Viscount Hereford was a potential replacement for Radcliffe and her pursuit of a pacified Ulster. Her tone was calculating, "As for Devereux, I will meet him to discuss the matter of Lady Knolls among other things. Have you sent word to her father Oxfordshire?"

"Her mother has brought her back to court, but she is not pleased. Has something sinister befallen the Vice Chamberlain?" William asked.

Elizabeth looked at him calmly and kept her face free of guilt. Certainly, something had happened. Her Lady of the Bedchamber was a nymph and William was too stoic to notice. She sat stoically and regally in her chair and turned her face toward the window, rather than face him. Perhaps he was wise enough to keep informed on other meddlers in her court. Her tone was anxious, "Has Francis Radcliffe returned herself to Dublin?"

William did not exactly answer the queen, rather he thought to disarm her and sway the conversation from her whimsical folly. "What is all of this about? First, you dismiss lady Knollys, and then you summon her back to be courted by a man that has no idea he is courting. And then... you all but chastise the dutiful wife of your own cousin, Sussex. Do you not realize that when you spite these women, you seed the animosity of rebellion?"

"I'll worry less about the lords if they keep their lasses shut behind their bedchambers. They are all a mess of harlots."

William scowled at the queen's indifference. "Lettice has always been a fine and upstanding member of the royal house and if she was wrongly engaged by the Irish, then I might find a need to investigate. Her honor would demand it, your Majesty."

Elizabeth stood defiantly, revealing there was more to her interest in Lettice than an arrangement of marriage. A jealousy. "No! You will do nothing of the sort! Devereux is older and faithful beyond reproach. So too is he in need of a wife and for that, and his ability as a general, a better match could not be made. I am sure he will take pleasure in bedding and also wedding our lustful little tramp."

William balked, "If you plan to marry off the lady, her husband should expect a virgin of purity. Do you have evidence that she is not? Because if you do, she will be no match for the Viscount of Hereford. If you put on this thing, you must be sure, it fits."

"Have the slut examined if you're concerned. I want Devereux well pleased and ready to take a more vigorous role in Ulster."

William wondered if that was all she wanted from Devereux? It was a base decision he was sure, for Thomas Butler had endorsed the Viscount as a potential ally against O'Neill. He had heard as much himself and his warning was fading from memory it seemed. Butler continued to fondle the queen's ear.

Elizabeth turned the conversation back to William. "What news is there of O'Neill? Is he bound for London or is he not?" she asked, as he considered all that she was up to.

"He has departed with a goodly number of men. We have received that word through our couriers and the ferry between the Isle of Man and Liverpool. Along with that correspondence, we have confirmed that the reconnoitering of Ulster has been successful.

"Good, I want Sussex to finish what he started. Then whatever he cannot achieve on his own, perhaps Devereux will. I will not have this announcement made until after the wedding. As for O'Neill, let him come freely on his own and send word to my cousin that he may expand the border of the Pale into Tyrone.

Southwark

Miguel entered Southwark Cathedral to find a large order of priests about their business. Some were lighting incense while others sang at the choir. Today at noon, the pews began to fill and outside more priests called the people to worship. He had considered bringing Mary, but she did not come. His contact, the elder who had heard his urgent plea, wished to meet Mary. He also had expressed an interest in ministering to Jade McAlister and that had given Miguel a measure of hope. He would move forward with his father's wishes, and when his terrible burden was completed, he would have a life free of guilt or shame. He would have an earthly life. It was the only way, and he planned to bring both Mary and Agnes to a confessional.

The elder did not wear his vestments and moved freely in open heeled sandals as soon as he saw Miguel. His voice was pleasant, "In the old days the boys would do this before their supper," he said, wishing the old days had returned.

"You polish candle stands and silver?" Miguel asked humbly.

The elder wiped off his hands on a clean white cloth. "You may call me, Prior, Miguel."

Miguel was speechless. He had been in the company of the prior the whole time and never knew it. A little strand of hair fell down over the prior's forehead as a chorus of voices began to sing. How many blessings had he given? Miguel could only imagine. The old man appeared timeless... the essence of knowledge vividly captured in his expression. He was a keeper of secrets and the glint in his blue eyes revealed a depth of wisdom and sadness, that Miguel had overlooked in his own self-indulgence.

"The way for you has been made ready, my son. You will go to Windsor Castle in two days. On the south side, closest to the river, you will enter the sewer gate and make your way to the first quadrant inside the castle walls. There you will find a ladder that will take you up to the latrine behind the kitchens. Someone will be waiting for you before the sun rises. Have you tested the poison?"

The pleasantness of his thoughts evaporated with the elder's question. He knew that priests did not give the right to kill. The Holy Father had, his own father. Even with the promise of Mary, he sounded dismal. "I have and it is potent," Miguel replied, thinking that the taking of life seemed so much more corrupt when it came through the channels of priesthood.

"Good, and how long until it takes affect?" the prior asked.

"One day, perhaps two, and nearly all who consume it will fall into a fever. Most will die."

The elder shook his head regretfully. "I never dreamed it would come to this. Never in a million years. But enough is enough, and it is not a sin to protect yourself. Remember that Miguel."

Miguel felt sorry for him. He had become so calloused that he no longer questioned the sanctity of life, only the purpose for which he took it. He had always told himself that he was not killing the essence of a man but simply the body. He imagined that is why the Pope had given him an open account of absolution. It was his purpose. Of course it was, and he had never questioned because he had also heard the voice of God. Why did he not hear that voice now? Maybe he should say it out loud?

He did: "Think of all those who have been slain and tortured. Would it be worse to allow the slaughter of a thousand more?" Miguel asked.

The prior fell silent and looked red and uncomfortable. Behind the doors of the clerics hall, even the priests and laymen at the choir stopped singing. Something was moving in them and he briefly wondered if they were also listening for God's response. This time, the Lord did not answer.

"I understand," the prior said. "When you return here successful, I will make a place for you to hide."

Miguel could not help but think of Mary as he considered the weight of his mission. For the first time in his life he became utterly afraid to die. He wanted more time. He wanted to know the details of his escape and looked to the prior, knowing there should be more. "Is that all?" his words left him empty.

Silence, and then a damning tone, "Not all. I have something for you," the prior said as Miguel began to sweat. The elder held out a letter, "It was delivered to me from Count de Feria, just this morning, and he has assured me of its authenticity. It is for you."

Miguel saw the papal seal. He did not wait to open it but took out his knife to tear at the wax. It was certainly for him and he sat down in front of the prior on a wooden bench to roll up his sleeve and read. It didn't take him long. When he was done the tears streamed down his gaunt face.

"What does it say?" the prior asked.

"It says the Holy Father loves me and he has granted me everything," Miguel replied.

"And Mary?" the prior asked.

"Everything," Miguel answered.

Then as if he felt the greatest pity for him, the prior put his hand on Miguel's shoulder. "You may enter now!" he yelled.

Men darted into the sanctum of his confidence, and Miguel realized the prayers had ended. It hurt him. He had dared to trust the elder and there was nowhere for him to go. The old man, whose arms hung like driftwood held him down in his seat. "God does not give a priest the right to kill," the elder whispered, and then with a louder voice he said, "He does command that we entice the guilty to confess their sins against Christendom. Do ye understand?"

As he thought of Mary, Adam Loftus marched through the sanctuary with the ambassador of Spain. "Do you know what your last disciple calls himself?" Adam asked.

Miguel said nothing.

Adam continued; thinking of Judas and their long and fruitful talks. "Do not look surprised. You knew him as Jodia and I have spent many hours with him discussing your other disciples. Such good things will come from him. Pity it was not you, Miguel."

"And you?" Miguel whispered to the ambassador of Spain.

"The Pope has given his wish that a return of unity may occur through marriage. England is greater than just one priest."

Miguel responded, "My father declared that the righteous man shall not fall to my sword or be scorned of angels. Therefore, O'Neill's message was delivered and righteous in the promise of Spain. Is this the honor of both my King and Rome, that they betray the foot to save the body?"

Adam grabbed Miguel by his hair, "Where is the girl from Kintyre?"

CHAPTER 48

Gravesend

The waters were unusually calm on the River Thames
when the watchmen of Gravesend began to thrash their
quadrangles. In the poor suburb, a primal racing of
hearts, the thought of women and children dying, burning
cottages, and fear went surging through the streets. These things
they had learned five hundred years before, when Vikings came
rowing up the ancient river. The sound of a ram's horn answered
the alarm, with lapping oars and the vision of raiders on long
boats. They did not know how many came or how bad it would
be. Enough to rape and pillage?

Shane stood on the bow with the morning dew beading on his
forehead. Behind him and readying themselves for the landing
were fifty gallowglass. Three boats carried his warriors and they

had clattered and clicked, stomped, and found their position with spears and axes. He felt the surge of the unknown and an excitement of conquest as if it were his first call to battle. A horse whinnied and betrayed their position and then another bucked in anticipation. He heard the alarms go out on shore. The excitement and preparatory movement threatened to send water spilling over the sidewalls.

As the oarsman increased their pace, the animals knew something was different. They quivered anxiously with eyes that strained to see past their blinders. A warrior attempted to calm them. Feet and legs, elbows and arms, met by a flick of a tails– and all the gallowglass gripped their leather with cinching tightness.

Shane held his sword and then turned to the squire who stood ready to don his chainmail. "Put it on," he ordered, as the ceremonial custom of his warrior nature overshadowed any need for stealth. He wondered if the gamble would be worth it. He thought of Katherine and his nephew Brian who had unwittingly cast a doubt to his own legitimacy. Would the queen see who held the power of Ulster now? It was certainly not the child Barron of Dungannon.

The oars picked up and sent a heavy wake at each bow as the stones of Gravesend scuffed at the ships hulls. Knowing that they might find themselves beached, the captains had cast anchors one hundred yards behind each longboat and now the chains were running out of slack.

On shore the signal fires began to burn. "To the watch!" those people of Gravesend yelled. "To the watch with spears!" came the voices from town on the fateful landing day.

O'Neill's men heard the uncertainty from shore just before the abruptness of a forceful landing. They recovered quickly and out came the ladders and ramps. Shane was one of the first to make solid ground as he ran to mount his stallion. The other long boats followed suit and the foam of the beach became frothy and thick. They yelled, they ran, they found their measure in the cold water churning with the murk of great disturbance. O'Neill had made good on his word to visit London and with him came the might of Gallowglass warriors.

As his force menaced forward, the people of Gravesend understood one thing for sure, England was being invaded.

The Bridge

It took hours to cross the bridge. They rode in a carriage and Thomas sat in the company of two lords who he only knew remotely. The most imposing was Gomez, Suarez de Figueroa of Cordoba, who was both a count and nobleman empowered to negotiate with the English crown. Most referred to him only as Count de Feria. Adam Loftus he knew through reputation, and he was uncomfortable listening to Adam's dissertation on the mysteries of loyalty, and the need to scrutinize even those who held position within the court. The whole ordeal made Thomas's stomach churn as he sat impatiently waiting to reach the greater city of London.

"Senior Cordoba, England will be in your debt for many, many years for your assistance with this conspiracy. I myself have trusted this man and without your help we never would have found him," Adam said.

Count de Feria gave a not so humble bow. "You will tell this to the Queen?" he asked.

"As far as I can, Senior Cordoba. We have much to gain from this man and if you say he is rogue to Pius, and also to Phillip, it would be our duty to see his interrogation through."

Thomas thought of Henry Colley, who Adam had recently left and his thoughts spilled into Adam's conversation. "Well, this traitor's plague will finally leave us free both here and in the midlands. You must feel that that is something, Adam?"

Adam's countenance exuded his utter fascination with the details of Miguel's capture. He nodded politely and then mulled over several options for Miguel's treatment. He needed to know how he had been so easily deceived and who was involved. Was Miguel both the sailor and the priest that Henry Colley had told him of? Thomas Smyth thought so. But how could one man be in two places at once? There was evidence to support a Spaniard of his description both in London and Dublin at the same time. He knew that was impossible and yet, by Miguel's own words, he claimed to commune directly with God. It was a claim that was blasphemous, especially to a Jesuit. He also thought of the information that Judas gave him. Miguel was the teacher of disciples and the forbearer of war. There was no doubt that he would be executed, but before that happened he needed to know. Where was the girl from Kintyre?

"How long will we be able to keep him?" Thomas asked.

"I have met with the Archbishop of Canterbury and he is in agreement that we must determine the extent of this conspiracy before reporting to the queen. How many Catholics are subversive and where are the sympathizers? Do you think the good physician will be of help?"

"I do," Thomas answered.

"And you trust this man?" Adam asked.

Count de Feria eyed Thomas seeming to have severe doubts as to his judgement. "The crime is plotting treason and murder. Why, pray tell do we seek the physician?" He was clearly upset that they would be interring their prisoner at St. Bartholomew's.

"I have leverage with the good physician and he was appointed by Mary Tudor as a loyal subject when it was not unlawful to worship and be sanctified by the pope. If the count wishes for an official torturer, such a man must be endorsed and provided by a constable of her Majesty's court."

"I would submit that he should be returned to Spain for trial. I will ensure justice is done."

"This is not Spain, and it will remain in the hands of our court. We shall be merciful and preserve life for as long as possible. You may send that comfort to both the King and Pope on our behalf," Adam said. The count would have to deal with the fact that clergy here had no authority to inflict physical pain or suffering without the courts blessing. A surgery however was a different matter. "He will be interred for his own welfare."

It was late in the evening when Rodrigo met them at the gate near the quadrangle of St. Bartholomew's the Greater. Opening the massive doors, he allowed the carriage and dead-cart to pass and quickly closed them to the street. He knew Thomas, he knew Cordoba, but he had never seen the Archbishop of Armagh before. It was Adam Loftus' greetings that gave Rodrigo the greatest pause.

"Good man, we are pleased to have our talent at hand," and then he laughed with Thomas Smyth. They laughed and watched as Miguel was lifted from the dead cart and dragged to the front of Lady's Chapel.

"Tie him down. I have already lit the way for you," Rodrigo said solemnly.

Adam made sure that Miguel saw his face before he was taken away. He had a sense of purpose now. "Do you hear the voice of God now?" Adam asked.

Southwark by the river

Mary saw the lantern of an oarsman long before he ever arrived near the muddy log on the Southwark side of the city. She held Agnes's hand as the nose of the skiff slid silently onto shore and wondered if this was who Miguel had sent. She had never seen this chap before, and was glad to see he had a son. Miguel had never told her who was coming to help them. Perhaps these two were just robbers or mud slogs coming to start their day and it made her nervous. The lad jumped out happily and ran up the bank wearing a loose fitting shirt tied with a dandy piece of rope.

The boy skipped right toward them and stopped to hold out his hand, "You may call me Jimmy," he told Agnes with a broad and cheerful smile.

"Will you come with us?" Agnes asked.

"Na… I gots ta feed me mum. She loves me ye know. Shall we get thee across the river?" he replied.

"Do you know him?" Mary asked, referring to Miguel.

Jimmy fidgeted and turned back toward Kenneth who waved his arm for them to hurry. "I do. I know them both," he took

Agnes's hand. "Come, ye must not be seen, and we have a long way to go."

Mary followed Jimmy to the water, knowing she had no other choice but to trust him. Her feet slipped on the mud and Agnes slid as well. "Over here," Kenneth said as he lifted Agnes and put her in the center. "I know exactly where to take you, and on the far shore there are other friends who will help you both."

Mary hiked up her new dress. It was the first that she wore it. Maybe she thought. Maybe by some far reaching miracle or blessing from God, Miguel might make his way to the ship to see her. To hold her. To never let her go.

St. Bartholomew's

Rodrigo Lopez lamented and prepared his surgical bags as the screams of pain, came flooding out of Lady Chapel. It was the vacant portion of the interior, and a place only the widows were allowed to go. He looked up at the archways and down the length of south isle and doubted anyone would hear them. Having never met the tall quiet man who came with Count de Feria and Thomas Smyth, he presumed the man to be a torturer. He was tall, wore a wide brimmed hat, and was foreboding. The knowledge that he had become a part of this terrible thing pressed into him with overwhelming sadness.

Count de Feria paced incessantly as Thomas Smyth endured the intermittent cries of torture by clicking his boot heel against an old chair. Rodrigo did not fare so well and considered the crime to harboring Catholics and prayed his work would be over soon. For all three men, the treatment seemed to last for hours.

Finally, Adam walked out of the inner chapel with blood stains on his cuffs. "He will tell me nothing. It will be up to you now," he said coldly looking to Rodrigo.

Thomas stood quickly, picking up Rodrigo's surgical bag as he did. "I've told thee what is expected."

Rodrigo clenched his fists, "There's no guarantee I can keep him alive! This is madness!" He turned to the only person he knew well, but dared not to reveal the extent of his liaisons. Count de Feria appeared indifferent. Would he really have to do this thing? It was the look that confirmed their previous conversation that the priest must be made a martyr- a thing he was told would prove his loyalty to the crown. Count de Feria took his surgical bag from Thomas and forced it into his hand. He hated him for it. He hated him and prayed that one day he would see his Pope in person. He wondered if Miguel felt the same when the letter from the Holy Father finally reached him. It made him sick. How could a man who called himself civilized do such thing?

"It must be done," Adam said.

Rodrigo took a breath to gain his composure. "I will need a few moments alone with your prisoner to assess his strength."

Thomas, who had yet to hear the whereabouts of the girl, protested. "It is not over until I say! The Lord Deputy of Ireland himself will hear of this! We need the girl!"

Adam cleared his throat. "It's alright Thomas. A softer touch may indeed be required with this one. I will handle the Lord Deputy. If the priest tells you anything about a girl or those who aided him, you may yet be spared this thing we ask."

For a moment, a very brief moment, a glimmer of hope fluttered through Rodrigo's mind and then he was allowed to walk the eighty paces to the chapel alone. It was there that he once again found Miguel Avaje Fernandez.

"Do you know what they want from you?" Rodrigo whispered.

Miguel was tied face up to the altar stand. "I do," he replied.

A lantern sat in a cradle above Miguel's body and Rodrigo examined Miguel's feet. His first thought was that his poor friend would never walk again. His second thought was pity. Two of his toes had been pressed beyond recognition and another appeared to have been cut off some time ago. He reached for a goblet of water and lifted Miguel's head to drink. "Did you tell him about me?" Rodrigo asked softly.

"Not you, nor the girl, nor Mary," Miguel said.

"I will see to Mary's safety, but the girl I cannot protect. They will find her. They will find them both and then neither you nor I will survive this. Will you not tell me where she is?" Rodrigo asked.

"You know I cannot," Miguel replied.

Miguel coughed with his drink and felt the heat of the lamp begin to dry the robe he had soiled and cause his eyes to burn. The smell of himself and the smoke was overpowering. Rodrigo removed his medicine. A strong potion that he had used often when taking off a leg that was gangrenous or beyond healing. It might be enough he thought to keep Miguel from singing out in pain. It was something.

"I will spit it out before you force that on me," Miguel said knowing what Rodrigo intended.

"Will you?" Rodrigo asked pleadingly. "Would you rather feel the cut of my blade than give yourself a chance to fade away? There is no disgrace in taking what is given."

Their eyes met as voices were heard in the south isle, and the voices were coming quickly. Rodrigo plunged the medicine into his pocket. Miguel tightened his lips and turned his face away when he saw Adam Loftus enter.

"He told me nothing," Rodrigo said as he laid out the tools of his profession.

CHAPTER 49

Black Tea
and
Barley

Emma had tea. It was a gift from Judith McCarty, and her kettle sat in the coals to delight her. Today was a day of leisure and tomorrow would be the wedding. She poured her delicacy even as she heard wood being cut outside. The peace of her morning having been interrupted when Gowl woke before sunrise. *There is much to do*, he had told her. Now after he had gone, it was his kiss that lingered: warm, kind, and memorable. She savored her fist sip and felt like humming. Her heart was light, her belly was not, and as that delicious flavor brought back a fondness of her youth, Emma knew she didn't miss England at all. Not one bit. These were Gowl's people. It was home.

Where the pasture met the trees, camp fires sprouted up all around the edge of the woods. The tea had warmed her, and as Emma opened the door a crisp wind struck her face. To think she had feared that Omagh would be lonely. It was anything but lonely. There was life inside her and everywhere else. She walked out of her cottage and crossed the pasture. She leapt confidently over a stream where young lads of the clan filled clay jugs with cold clean water. Then on she went toward a muddle of men rolling out wooden kegs with iron bands that toppled off wagons. Gowl would be with them, she figured.

Sacks of barley had been stacked up between the campsites of willow domes and sheepskin. Horses ran unbridled in the pasture and the huge herd of cattle she had once feared gathered tightly near the far side mountain. She could hear the dogs barking off in the distance as children gathered cow pies to throw into the fires. All of this had sprang from nothing in less than a week. Gowl had said it was work but Emma came to the conclusion that if work was labor and labor was pain, then she did not see work at all. She saw freedom.

Near the center of the field where the stream cut a swath through the ground to naturally divide the pasture, Emma arrived at the gathering place. It was here that the women of clan O'Hagen had built their fires, cooked their meals, and tended to the many things that women do. She had come for Darley.

Darley O'Hagen, the daughter of Da O'Hagen was unloading her cart alone. Emma immediately began to help, knowing that the O'Hagen clan was grieving the loss of Kevin O'Hagen, and she surely wanted to lessen their heavy burden. It was also clear, that Darley was pregnant.

Darley greeted her with a nod and wiped the sweat from her brow. "Tá aithne agam ort. Do an bhean an asal gabhar, Gowl," she said.

Emma couldn't reply with precise understanding but she smiled. Darley smiled back, which was encouraging. After a few moments, the cart was unloaded and Emma grabbed her apron, feeling her child give a thunderous kick. "By the grace of God's wounds, this child will come soon," she said.

"Aye," Darley replied.

Aye, Emma thought. It was becoming their mutual understanding. *Perhaps Darley might do well with some English.* Emma spoke slowly: "Does your baby come soon?" she asked, pointing to Darley's ample belly and giving it a little pat.

Darley's eyes opened like saucers and cheeks turned red. "I have no have baby!" she replied moving Emma's hand away.

"Oh my," Emma said and then she turned to quickly pick up a sack of barley. Anything to avoid further embarrassment. To make matters worse, Darley either did not or could not continue with English.

"Is féidir leat dul. Go fírinneach ní gá dom aon rud ó bhean chéile Gowl," Darley said gruffly.

Some of the O'Hagen women who were near, abandoned the work when they heard Darley respond, and darted off toward the men. The reaction struck Emma as odd. "So… ye say Gowl has always been a handsome man?" she asked.

Darley sluffed off and flipped over a wooden seat with a haughty puff. The response gave Emma all the understanding she needed. Darley was jealous. It prickled her curiosity and made her want to stay all the more. She watched as Darley prepared her work space by unfastening a heavy grinding wheel and securing the sprocket to her peddles. She then wound a wooden gear clockwise and indicated to Emma that the stone was readied to spin.

"What do you want me to do?" Emma asked.

"Pour," Darley told her pointing to the sacks on the ground. Darley was a large framed lass, more suited to Gowl than her, she thought. She also worked well. So well in fact that she began to sweat profusely. A moment later, as Darley peddled with the determination of a vixen, Emma poured the first few kernels which popped crisply and slipped through the chute. The sweet smell of grain permeated her senses and dusted her fingers as the crude machine ground their meal for market.

"Gowl, mo thóin a imirt," Darley said in a huff. The words gave Darley's work meaning and she felt emboldened and giddy, knowing that she had just told the soon to be bride, that Gowl could kiss her ass.

"Aye Darley. He is handsome in his own way."

Darley looked at Emma, feeling frustrated. With each sack of barley poured, she would repeat herself, hoping that Emma would catch her meaning.

"Aye Darley, is féidir le Gowl tarraing mo thóin."

Emma's poor attempt made Darley cry out with laughter. After the third sack and the third time Emma repeated the insulting phrase, Darley was weeping tears with the fun of it all.

Emma put her hands on her hips with pride. What better way to make a friend and also learn a few things about Gowl's jaded past. Darley was no prize, and Emma would ensure he it. Even with the stitch in her side she thought of how she would tease him. It was a bonus that she was able to ease Darley's burden. *Is féidir le Gowl tarraing mo thóin*, she thought. The words she would never forget. Words of healing and words of the heart.

"Do ye think we have enough?" Emma asked.

Darley pushed herself up with a grunt and stood with her sweat stained gown, shaking her head and slapping her hands together with satisfaction. It appeared they did have enough and she hopped off the cart with a most determined expression. "Is féidir le Gowl tarraing mo thóin."

Emma replied the same and they marched together over to find her betrothed. It was a good feeling. Some of the barley meal would be sold at market, the rest could make splendid beer. Mixed with the right amount of cool spring water and a few scoops of hops to boot, the barley would be the last ingredient to keep the men busy for hours. It was the men's job to boil the mixture, strain it, and then add last years mash. That was the process, and Emma was heading with this knowledge to her man by the river. For Emma it seemed a fairly reasonable trade of labor.

Gowl and the others were sipping off the old leavings which had been scraped out of the barrels like pottage from a kettle and placed in wooden bowls. He was drunker than monk on Sunday. In some strange way, it made her happy. It wasn't any problem at all. She would have him in their bed before sundown and that made her happy as well. And this night they may even have a child warming between them. As she put her mind to her task, she found herself dreaming of Gowl and the family that they would become. It would only be a day and they would be married!

Gowl spat out his drink and the little bits of mash stuck to his neatly trimmed beard as he heard Emma's attempt at his language. He was dumbfounded that both Darley and Emma had found each other in the pasture. "It's best ya not learn that particular phrase," he told her.

"Aye, but I will and ye have no idea," Emma replied. Her moment of satisfaction ended with a painful contraction. "It's time," she bent over and felt another tightening as the water broke.

❊ ❊ ❊

Sitting near her shelter, an old woman passed the cool morning with the elders near a fire. They stripped the bellies of salmon and hung them out to dry. She cleaned off her hands, wished that she was young again, and pulled a quilt over her knees. *The children,* she thought, leaping boundlessly through the grass with full bellies. Her mind drifted and she started to nod off in happy thoughts, when one of the young lads grabbed her shoulder. "You must come! It's the English woman! She's having her baby by the stream! She keeps..." he was breathless, "she keeps calling out and we don't know what to do!"

Mam felt uneasy, "For me?" she asked, thinking of Emma Colley.

"Aye, Mam. She knows ya— don't she? None of us can understand what she's saying!" the lad said urgently.

"She don't know I'm here! She couldn't know I'm here!" Mam replied. She had seen Emma at the cottage and intentionally avoided the mistress. Their connection was of another life and one to be well to forget. Still, she considered that it must be hard for such a woman to survive outside of everything she had ever known. She wasn't a headmistress here. She was just a woman after all. A woman, who like her, had suffered. Mam reached for a walking stick and pushed herself up. "Where she be?" she asked.

Across the pasture Emma bit her lip and rolled to her side. Gowl had ran back to their cottage to gather linen but was taking too long. Was he so drunk that he had passed out? This time, the thought of him made her angry. She was in pain and he was nowhere to be found. Her stomach felt like little needles where pricking her all at once and the contractions began to shoot into her ribs. She closed her eyes and knew the worst of it was yet to come.

"Tá tú ar tí lass a pop," Mam told her.

Emma heard but did not recognize. She had no idea what the old woman meant. "Speak English!" she shouted out in pain. She opened her eyes and held up her hand. An old woman gazed down with hair that was long and white. As white as it ever was. She also had her hand sewn quilt wrapped around her shoulders and the material tickled her cheek as Mam reached out.

"Is it you? Is it really you?" Emma asked.

"I said it looks like your about to pop," Mam replied in English.

For some reason, Emma didn't quite fathom why, she started to cry. It wasn't sadness, it wasn't the pain she felt but it was something else. She wouldn't have thought she would have missed Mam. "How?" she asked.

"This is where I belong until the end of days," Mam replied. The familiar face, the eyes that sparkled with wisdom, made Mam appear as though she hadn't spent the greater portion of her life in servitude. She seemed kind and composed as her cheeks glistened with rosiness of a cold wind. She looked clean. "I had no idea," Emma said.

"The brown house, I reckon, makes a woman seem small," Mam said tellingly. Despite what she had endured because of Emma, she didn't seem bitter. She seemed pleased. "It'll be coming now, I am sure." She touched Emma's tight blouse.

"Aye. Could do," Emma said. Hearing herself and knowing that Mam had heard her also, she wondered if her old servant would forgive her and take her arm. Had Mam noticed how much she had changed? She wanted to change even to the point of trying to learn Gowl's language. She wanted to belong but had so far to go.

Mam saw that Emma's gown was soaked. "I didn't think ya would last a month. Good on ya, lass," she said as she eased Emma up.

"I don't think I can move," Emma panted.

"Ya cannot have it here by the river. Ye'll ruin the fishing," Mam smiled.

Emma felt a wave of heat course through her midsection and then a tingling and tightening between her legs, "It is easier here than inside the cold walls of that tower house. I am free," Emma replied.

Mam understood completely and after Emma's contraction eased she guided her to a dryer place where a few spruce trees dotted the middle of the pasture. Darley was there also, and had never left Emma's side. Their presence made Emma feel safe. She had her baby under the spruce bows and Mam covered Emma with a quilt.

CHAPTER 50

Barron of Dungannon

enry Colley rode again at the head of sixteen English horsemen. Captain Henry Colley was armed with powder and shot. No longer the undertaker of other men's dreams, he reckoned himself the commander. Having ridden all night, and because the winter began to release a flurry of snow, Henry found himself exhilarated. The Irish guards between Ballycastle and the River Strule had been few.

The thought of Ralph Lane's promise urged him on. *It was not common to make war in winter*, Ralph had said. There was something much larger at stake than a single plantation in the midlands. He was part of a winter campaign, and Radcliffe was eager to regain the advantage in Ulster.

It was time, Henry thought as Dennis of the hill clan cantered toward him with a prisoner. The thought of his soldier taking a hostage put him off. They needed no more information and he certainly didn't wish to risk an escape. He drew his musket to drop the man as Dennis drew closer, crossing an open field where his horse bounded to obscure his aim.

Dennis raised his hand. "We found him near the cottage just as you described. He was too drunk to offer much of a fight."

Henry replied harshly: "Did anyone see you?"

"None who are still alive," Dennis confirmed.

Henry recognized Gowl as he rolled over. "Was he dragged through the bushes?" Henry asked, seeing Gowl's cuts and bruises.

"Aye, Captain. It is the same man I saw riding with the mistress. I didn't think you would object."

Gowl was bloodied but alive. "Was she there?"

"The fields were full of people. No way could I have searched. She was not in the cottage," Dennis replied.

Henry thought of Emma as he put his musket away. "I have a bargain for you, my good man. Are ye a fighter?"

🌺 🌺 🌺

On the hills near Dungannon, where the snow had just left a good dusting, Brian took his exercise in the fresh air and pulled a bony sleigh. "Will you not sit down this time, Calvagh?" he asked.

Such a bright boy, Calvagh thought. Someday together they may even forge a strong alliance but he was not ready to sit his ass in the snow. They crested the hill and gazed down at the tracks of Brian's previous adventure. He could spend hours enjoying the cold clean day, and so it seemed could the little Barron of Dungannon.

"I hear your uncle is gone," Calvagh said.

Brian skipped by his side in a fine burgundy jacket and English riding boots. He seemed almost euphoric for a lad who had been given such grave news. "They say he was hung at Traitors Gate in London and his head will be put on the bridge," Brian told him.

Calvagh looked suspicious: "Who says that?" He put his hand on Brian's shoulder to stay him. "Who says that O'Neill is hung? Who Brian?"

Brian became serious, "I am a lord of England. There has been a messenger coming to me as of late. At first, I did not know who it was who played tricks on me, but every day I since my uncle has left, I have gotten a note in one of my biscuits. Baked right into the bread."

Calvagh felt the cold on the bottom of his feet. Other children were now taking to the snow so he turned so that none would hear. "Who?" he asked urgently.

"Someone who knows a lot about Lord Radcliffe and his promise to make me the sole heir of Dungannon. In fact, I have been answering the notes with my own messages that I tie to rocks and throw out my window."

"You have been casting notes outside your window?" Calvagh said with alarm.

A CROWN FOR TWO ISLANDS   489

"Of course I have. How else will Lord Radcliffe know that I'm ready to accept my title."

Calvagh took Brian by the arm with great distress. "You must go back and collect up all of your notes, and pray that none fall into the hands of my wife. She is dangerous Brian. She could be tricking you!"

Brian appeared unconcerned. "Come, let us go once again down this hill together."

Calvagh sat, Brian pushed and then jumped onto his lap. They were off like a shooting star, racing down the steep hill without control. Brian squealed with delight and Calvagh could not help feeling that the young lord was in the gravest of danger.

When they toppled over, Calvagh held Brian to the ground. "Do not trust this word or answer the messages from here on out."

Brian stood, then dusted himself off and Calvagh did the same. "You have pretty blue eyes Calvagh. You have seen too much me thinks." An inquisitive expression came over Brian, and then Calvagh thought the little Barron might cry.

"What is wrong?"

"It is not my fault!" Brian declared, with a sudden outburst of anger. "I did not ask to be the lord of Dungannon!"

Calvagh took his hand and they began walking back up the hill as Calvagh thought of his own family. His wife had forsaken him, his father had abandoned him and his brothers wanted him dead. If he returned to Tryconnell without the army of England behind him, he would most certainly die. "Have you learned anything else?" he asked as the child returned to focusing on his fun.

Brian turned confidently, trying very hard to remain convincing. "I have people in Dungannon that will follow me. Even if your wife weeps for O'Neill, I will not let her do anything that will harm you. O'Neill is dead, Lord Radcliffe is coming and the entire township knows this to be true. I did not need the messages to know."

Calvagh raised a bushy eyebrow, "Are you certain?"

"Soon Radcliffe's army will set us both free. The war is over, Calvagh."

"Not at all believe that. There are the Scotts in Antrim. Has my wife left the castle to seek their aid?" Calvagh asked, knowing that Katherine would do anything to remain free of England. Even if Shane O'Neill was gone.

"She makes plans with Turlough and will not see me. All the men from Dungannon are packing up their belongings to go north. All except the old sage Farleigh and the priests. I believe Katherine and Turlough plan to go with them."

Calvagh hummed to himself, and then turned back toward the castle. "We have walked together before, so this day is not uncommon. You talk of these matters no further and if they ask you to go with them, you do that. You do it and pray they no longer believe you are the Barron of Dungannon. Now, go back and look for the notes you wrote and threw outside your window. If you find them, burn them and never write again. If they are gone, do not let yourself be found. You come directly back to me and make sure that no one sees you."

Brian looked at him curiously, he kicked at the newly fallen snow, and grabbed Calvagh's hand to squeeze it. It felt warm. Perhaps Calvagh had a fever. The memory of his father returned to him as he felt Calvagh's hand. His father was a strong man,

A CROWN FOR TWO ISLANDS ❧ 491

much stronger than either he or his friend. His father was named Matthew, the bringer of peace. It was the fever that killed him. "Do not be unwell, Calvagh. I am the Barron and will forever be."

CHAPTER 51

Cold White Valley

Emma closed her eyes and pressed her newborn to the breast. The baby was nursing, she felt her child like a heartbeat and Mam whispered in her ear. "Ya don't move from here now, child. You don't move at all," and then Mam fell silent and the old gentle hands tucked her in.

The snow that followed Emma's birth was more than a sprinkling. It came down in a flurry of puffy white snowflakes that stuck to the leaves and branches. The softness of a wintery grasp covering everything. She slept for hours until the cold finally reached her. She woke to push the quilt off her head and a trickle of snow hit her neck and chilled her down to the spine. Her baby fussed. "Shhh…," she soothed feeling an emptiness begin to overtake her. The sky was grey and quiet. Her baby took a breath and she peeked under the quilt to see that she had a boy. It made her heart swell as his little mouth circled her nipple. His legs kicked healthily and has tiny fists began to press her. He was alive and his head was shaped like Gowl's. A little head with a full matting of hair. "Where is your scar little man?" she asked, with his impression. Emma loved him immediately.

Eventually, after dreaming, Emma put her hand to the ground and found that Mam had left a large wineskin. She pulled it up gratefully and gulped down a mouthful. Then the quiet struck her with fear. Did they not love her? Did Gowl not return? She scanned the snow covered pastures and realized that she should be seeing movement and life. Then as she instinctively looked toward her cottage, she saw the horror of smoke!

Her infant let out a cry that echoed her loneliness across the valley and she stood. She wanted to run as fast as her legs would allow. She did not see or hear the others who began to dust off the snow and rise up around her. She saw only the flames.

One of the children bolted from a nearby hole like a frightened rabbit and dashed toward the meeting place where Emma had helped Darley. *Da.... Da.... Da... they killed me Da....* the child screamed. Another child cried out, and as Emma began to understand, the sound of Mam's voice reached her. That rattle of harshness that endured. The old mother threw back her skins and stood from the ditch that had concealed them all. It took Emma's breath away. She heard only the insufferable wailing of women and children.

Dungannon Castle, Dungannon

A coldness within the stone walls of Dungannon Castle came not from the snow but from the servants who ignored him. Brian had not eaten. They brought no food for him nor started a fire in his hearth. With a sense of neglect, he left his chambers, walked down the grand staircase and nosed around the empty hall. The castle was vacant. Feeling his stomach rumble, he wanted food. There was always something cooking in the outbuildings he thought. Perhaps the servants were cleaning a stag. The snow had come, it was the ideal time for hunting and so he thought perhaps that was the case. In past winters, he had watched the servants when game had been found. The thought drew him outside and toward the kitchen. Something would be hanging on a fire there, he thought. There were tracks on the brick path and that made his heart soar. He was not alone after all. He hoped the skinning part had already been done so that the wait would not be to lengthy. Just to be sure the meat was already inside, he peered through a glass window at the kitchens door. There was a fire roaring and he saw Katherine and Turlough with a bundle. Then suddenly Katherine appeared to shout and storm outside and Turlough threw something on the ground and chased after her. As the back door closed, Brian entered through the front and quickly gobbled up some pieces of ham. He was still swallowing when he heard them returning and for an instant he thought he would greet them, then with a fierce curiosity of what had caused them to disagree, he decided to hide in the pantry so he could hear for himself.

Turlough entered first and spoke very loudly. "You will leave? You will not go to Sorely Boy at Dunluce and seek an alliance?"

Katherine did not sound like she was playing. She sounded different. Brian listened. "He will not accept me you fool!" Katherine replied quickly. Brian heard something hit the table but dared not peek out. "Sorely Boy has already been promised the trade with Kintyre. My father will not contest that arrangement lest he risk the anger of England. Neither my father nor Sorely Boy will intervene for you or I."

Brian had never heard Katherine argue before and he certainly did not expect Turlough to sound so bitter. "He will be more inclined to accept your offer if I can succeed here. We cannot wait. We cannot falter in this time or Sorely Boy will see the loss of O'Neill as Tyrone's weakness. I can repel the advance of Radcliffe's army."

"You will never be able to take Shane's place. England will not allow it!" Katherine spat.

"I will defeat them, Katherine!" Turlough insisted.

Katherine sounded despondent. Her voice giving tell to something dark within her heart. Something which Brian recognized as pure and utter hatred. "You will kill the boy. He deserves to die for what he is. Do not leave the legacy of my love to a puppet of the crown."

"He is just a boy," Turlough said.

Brian wondered who they were talking about. Who was it that had done something so terrible that he must die?

"He is the Barron!" Katherine hissed. Brian's heart pounded in his chest. He heard her and tried not to breathe.

"No! We do not need to do that. Sorely Boy will listen to you. You have the ear of Scotland and you alone are dowager of the isles."

Brian was devastated by Katherine's words. She had said she loved him. She had played chess with him and let him sleep with her kitten. She had lied.

"Do you not remember what your eyes have seen in Belfast? Sorely Boy will never turn on Radcliffe or risk losing his claim."

"He might, Katherine. He might if he believes that he has been deceived. The Jesuit that I told you about has finally written back to us. He has found the true heir of Kintyre! I have the message in my hand for you to read. Take it to Sorely Boy, Radcliffe has been hiding her away in London! Let him see that he has dealt with a traitor and liar. There is an heir to the province of the MacRihanish. An heir that your father and the Earl of Argyll will never deny."

"It's impossible!" Katherine said.

"Even the hint of such a thing would put question to Sorely Boy's claim. This letter bears the Jesuit's seal. If it is as he has written, it can be proved that Radcliffe was behind the massacre of Kintyre all along. It will not just be Sorely Boy who aligns with us, the Earl of Argyll will surely join us against England." Turlough replied.

"What else has the Jesuit written?"

"He has written that at all cost, the north must resist a union with England and that Spain and the Holy Roman Empire have failed us."

"When you will kill the boy, I will go. I will do this for the father of the child in my womb. There can be no English Barron of Dungannon."

Hearing this, Brian began to sob. He covered his mouth fearfully until they finally left the kitchen. The Barron of

Dungannon no longer hungered, he went out in the cold winter daring not to return to his chambers at all. He went to cower in a cage.

❧ ❧ ❧

Calvagh reached out for the boy who begged to hide under his blankets. "They will kill me, Calvagh," Brian cried.

"Shhh…" he quickly pulled his furs over the child and held him close. "We must find you someplace safer. Do you think you can get to the horses?"

"I can try," Brian whispered.

"Bring two. If what you say is true, your uncle is surely dead. It is no longer just a rumor and they will want me dead as well. Together we shall ride off toward Tryconnell and shelter on an island not far from my home."

Brian was distraught, "An island?"

"Hurry!" Calvagh replied.

"But what of our queen?" Brian asked with his notion of honor.

Windsor Palace, England

On the upper terrace Elizabeth paced near a battlement of the eastern wing, "Where is O'Neill, Lord Burghley?" The anticipation and dread of her most inner fears began to come back to her: an undefeated enemy who came calling at her gate. Word had already reached the royal guards that his troop of horses were nearing Maidenhead. Long spears, swords and axes, and all the materials of war came with them. Such fearlessness gave her concern.

"He is out there, your Majesty," William replied dryly. The royal guard was at high alert to ensure O'Neill's accompaniment could not make an attempt on the castle. It was highly unlikely but as Lord Butler had warned the court, O'Neill was unpredictable. Standing beside her, William watched the warning fires burning and tasted the bitter pill that the chieftain had provided. Such arrogance crept into his inner self like a quill itching at his skin.

"Oh, I know he is out there, Lord Burghley. The question is, what are you doing about it?" Elizabeth demanded.

The people of Maidenhead had deserted their dwellings and were fleeing into the fields. What were they running from? Why did they not stand their ground? Even as William took note of the calamity that was unfolding before his eyes he thought of Radcliffe and the message he had sent. His vision was now dampened with the improved communication to the front. The speed of the Abigail II and its captain, Captain Roderick would undoubtedly already have arrived to Belfast. *What would he do?* She asked. Had not the two of them all but guaranteed that O'Neill the prideful was to be cut down at Windsor's gate with arrows.

Earlier in the day word had come to court that the Earl of Kildare had also arrived, and Robert Dudley was on parade with the wrong Irish chieftain. It was a gamble that had not gone well at all. What a fool he felt in front of the young woman he was attempting to mold into a queen. "I would suggest we parlay," William replied after much consideration.

"Does he intend battle?" Elizabeth asked gripping the stone wall.

"For show my Queen," William tried to appear in control. "He does not have enough reserve to offer a serious threat."

Elizabeth pursed her lips flippantly, "Does he not know we have his kinsmen within our grasp?"

"There is no way he could. Nor does he know of our recent agreement with the ambassadors of Spain. So it seems this wayward chieftain is rogue, just as his messenger the Jesuit. Dungannon rests squarely in the hands of your cousin, so if he is smart, all will not be lost in Ulster."

Elizabeth thought of Spain, regretting having to make such concessions. It would be far better in the end if O'Neill would just come around. He certainly had the backbone to provide some stability in the Ire'. "I still loathe Feria, but if an alliance between Spain and the Irish can be prevented, I will entertain the proposal of King Phillip. Only long enough to put this matter to rest mind you."

"You do not have to marry him, your Majesty. In your acknowledgement of considering a potential Catholic husband, you will hold off both Spain and the Pope."

"I will never marry," she said despondently.

"I agree." It was time to turn her attention to things he might control, he thought. "Have you given thought to Adam Loftus? He has proved to be more than the head of your clergy in Armagh. He is resourceful."

"Perhaps. Has the Archbishop's prisoner provided any useful information?"

"He will be useful. We believe that the Jesuit is the natural son of Pope Pius. The Pope all but confessed to having two children at his council in Trent. His sin, it is said, weight's heavily on his position, and Count de Feria has confirmed that your so called assassin is undoubtedly Pius's agent. He is detained at the hospital of Saint Bartholomew's and has been questioned," William replied.

"Tortured?" the queen asked.

William hesitated and thought of how he might lessen the information he had received from Adam. "The spy is a citizen of Spain and we brought Count de Feria to St. Bartholomew's to oversee the interrogation. The methods were condoned by the ambassador."

Elizabeth knew all too well of Spanish methods. It made her anxious and unsettled. "I asked if he had been tortured," she said vehemently.

William nodded regretfully. "Both of his arms were taken. It proved to be virtually useless in gaining a confession. The man's skin is marked with a secret code that we believe he uses to correspond directly with his father. Since the Jesuit was working almost exclusively in Ireland, as Adam Loftus has said, we believe the code may reveal who in Ireland has been conspiring with Rome. Several messages which we have been unable to break have been intercepted that we have yet to understand. As such, I have had the arms preserved for further study. Our people are working as we speak to understand their meaning."

"I did not approve the means of torture for this man," Elizabeth said distastefully. She gripped the wall harder and leaned into the stone. "No. You will not continue with this treatment. If O'Neill has conspired, he will surely beg a mercy for our prisoner. And O'Neill is the only real threat we need worry about."

"We could not know for sure if O'Neill wouldn't just sacrifice this man. I would not give him the chance. We have enough reason to imprison him for his conduct," William replied.

Thinking of all that she knew of Ireland and all she did not, Elizabeth disagreed. She sensed a foul vapor to the very core of her soul. "Allow Lord Butler and the Earl of Kildare to ride out and meet their countryman and accompany him to my court."

"And if he pleads for the Jesuit you will then have another problem," William said stubbornly.

"I have tried it your way, Lord Burghley. If you cannot prove without certainty that O'Neill has conspired, he may well be heard by me. It seems this chieftain is both clever and bold enough to outwit you and my cousin."

William balked, "I would not say outwitted, you Majesty."

Elizabeth faced William squarely, remembering how he had been so cruel. She needed him without question but she did not have to oblige him. Thinking beyond the day, and how she wanted O'Neill on the side of England, she asked: "Have you heard through this new communication route, anything that would change my mind?"

"Sussex has advanced to the township of Dungannon and also writes that the McAlister must never return to Scotland. An agreement has been achieved with Sorely Boy MacDonnell for trade rights of the peninsula."

Elizabeth raised a brow. It occurred to her that Sussex had expanded beyond her advisements, but that was no surprise. It was a disappointment, "Kintyre is of Scotland."

"The Earl of Argyll has accepted the arrangement in the absence of a McAlister heir. A negotiation was brokered through the Lord Mayor of Belfast. It seems that O'Neill is the only thing that stands in the way of stability."

"Of course this is so, for with Kintyre and Scotland open for trade, the northern cities will once again prosper. That we have denied that it was Sussex who decimated Kintyre in the first place probably would not sit well with the Campbell's at all. So the cities and the Earl of Argyll make amends to benefit their own, but what do they want from me?"

"Nothing, your Majesty. Argyll wants no further disturbance on the border and that is all. Sussex believes this will keep Scotland from entering Ulster on the side of O'Neill. He also awaits your pleasure in regards to liberating the Earl of Tryconnell."

Elizabeth considered the implications, "I shall hear from the chieftain who holds our earl a hostage before we risk setting him free." She felt sure that the Campbell's must hold some grudge against, her and they certainly would hold a grudge against Tryconnell. Why else would O'Donnell's wife be consorting with her enemy. "And you say the priest was not only trying to poison me, but also had custody of a McAlister heir?"

"Adam Loftus has said so. He came from Dublin to testify that the girl is the heir of Alexander McAlister of Loop. The same heir that Sussex secreted away to London in case things did not go as planned with Sorely Boy MacDonnell."

"And how was this information obtained?" Elizabeth asked.

"Loftus has access to a defector of the Catholic priesthood of Tyrone. A disciple who was to work against the Anglican mandate. The man has turned," William replied.

Elizabeth began to loath the idea of putting such a young and eager evangelist in control of her Irish assembly. "It seems my

Archbishop of Armagh has an appetite for torture. That is not how we will win the hearts and minds. What else has he done without my knowledge?"

"It took no torture to sway the defector. He has converted and works freely as a vicar on a plantation in the midlands and takes the name of Judas," William replied.

Elizabeth replied skeptically: "How fitting. It is much too convenient, Lord Burghley. My entire council must think me simple! I do not condone the torture or manipulation of facts. A death may end something with finality but torture only brings more of the same."

William replied: "It is not easy, but it is necessary. If nothing else, it deters future uprisings"

The wind picked up and the sky hinted of rain. "I am hungry, William." She turned and began to walk away, "Have the spy transported here. I will see this man with my own eyes before meeting with Shane O'Neill."

"And if we cannot find the girl?" William asked as she turned her back to him.

There would be a storm tonight, she thought. A storm that would bring back her demons. "You will not rest until she is found. Sussex has put us in a pickle of sourness. This girl must not return to Scotland."

Omagh, Ireland

Having slipped out from Dungannon Castle, Calvagh and Brian rode toward Lough Ere and the territory known as Fermanagh. Their track took them near the River Strule where the country was hilly with thick vegetation and conifer trees.

Calvagh thought of the risks of going home to Tryconnell. That would not be an option. His brothers who had not chosen to align with the English were now firmly in control.

Brian, who was full of uncertainty, thought deeply. His father Matthew had wanted him to be his successor, at least that is what he thought. Even his grandfather Conn O'Neill, had once told King Henry that Matthew was his son, and if that was so, he didn't understand why Katherine believed he was a puppet. He was Matthew's son, the rightful heir of Dungannon. He wasn't a puppet toy. Why would she hate a toy? He wished that his father and grandfather were alive. They would set Katherine straight, but without them no one would ever know he wasn't a puppet. None except for Radcliffe perhaps.

The first snow was beginning to melt as they made their way unknowingly to the fields near Emma and Gowl's burned out cottage. Calvagh knew immediately that something terrible had happened. The smell that rose from a large number of shallow graves left little doubt that a goodly number of people had recently died. The fresh mounds also indicated that some had survived whatever might have happened. At least enough to bury the dead, he thought. Together, Brian and Calvagh examined the area and looked at the grave markings. Most were O'Hagen. One of the graves gave Calvagh a terrible pause: *Emma Colley*, it read. Near to Emma's grave was another marker that read, Gowl.

"Are you crying?" Brian asked.

Calvagh let out a long deep sigh, "I knew her, and she was good," he said.

"I am so very cold," Brian replied not taking an interest.

Calvagh reached out his hand to the lad. "Here," he said handing Brian a flint and striker. "Do you know how to use it?"

Brian did and he started a small fire and warmed himself near the graves as Calvagh rode out to examine the area further. The valley and stream which cut its path through a huge meadow that had been used heavily. There was evidence of campfires and also some broken barrels but otherwise it was deserted. The only clue as to what might have happened was the trampled ground from a very large heard of cattle. Someone or a group of marauders, he thought, had left the pastures and were driving the cattle south. With this new fear, he returned to Brian quickly.

"We must leave this place," Calvagh said urgently as Brian hovered over a small flame.

"Do you think they will follow us?" Brian asked, referring to Turlough and his men.

Calvagh considered the prospect. It would be a great risk to tramp across the countryside. He also thought of his wife Katherine who would undoubtedly use this opportunity to gain her freedom from him. As much as he hated O'Neill, at least O'Neill had honored his pledge to not invade Tryconnell as long as he remained a prisoner. Katherine would have no such inclination. She was as cunning and dangerous as she was beautiful. He measured his response to not alarm Brian further. "We will be safe on the islands of Ere. At least until the English have control of Ulster."

"Who did this Calvagh?" Brian asked.

"It could be Radcliffe's army," Calvagh said believing more that it was thieves.

Brian's face lit up with hopefulness. "Then they are close?" he asked with excitement. "Could we not join them?"

"Aye, lad. They are close," Calvagh confirmed.

"Then we must find them," Brian said. He remembered his messages that seemed to indicate that someone wanted him alive and well. He remembered the promise. This tiny bit of hope suddenly warmed him and it all made such perfect sense. He had not been forgotten. The English were coming to ensure his rightful place in Tyrone. Of this he was sure!

"No Brian, we should continue to Lough Ere. We cannot go to Tryconnell for there is treachery against me. We can neither chance the intention of those who attacked the valley."

Calvagh was startled that Brian set his jaw with resistance. "I think it is you who would rather avoid the English. Is that why you will not join me so that we may ride to Dungannon together?" The words stung Calvagh for he loved this child as if he were a son. Brian continued with a quick and youthful disregard for his feelings. "Come with me to Dungannon first and then we will go to Tryconnell, Calvagh. Radcliffe will liberate you as well as I. We need not freeze on an island. We only need out of this cold white valley."

CHAPTER 52

Bakers House

A ll the villagers gathered on the high ground near the
castle of Dungannon. Turlough held a torch above his
head and Katherine loaded herself into a beautiful
carriage. Inside the walls, large barrels of tar stood ready at the
foundations.

"They have come, but they will not concur!" Turlough
proclaimed. In a frantic state, he shouted with rage at the loss of
his soldiers. "There will be no use of this for England!" A brief
but unhappy roar consumed the crowd, and when their noise was
over, a great flock of riders sped away with Turlough to fight
another day.

Those that remained in Dungannon pulled their hair and
wailed as children wandered without direction. Many of the

farmers had died and the few warriors remaining were licking their wounds. They had been beaten and many hoped for mercy in the wave of Radcliffe's advance.

❦ ❦ ❦

A plume of smoke arose from Dungannon.

"It is done, Henry," Ralph said, as they rode toward Radcliffe's army.

The Kildare Brigade followed in trace of Ralph Lane and Henry Colley and they rode directly toward Radcliffe's tent positioned at the head of his army. The great encampment stretched from Armagh to Belfast in newly erected outposts and fortifications. Behind them lay Dungannon Castle in waste, and ahead was their salvation. They had been the first of the lord deputies lead element into battle and Ralph's promise was complete.

Ralph entered the tent to see Radcliffe taking off his armor. "Dungannon is deserted and the castle burns as we speak, your Grace," he reported.

Henry remained silent, standing proudly at Ralph Lane's side. He had made his way back into good graces. He also still held Gowl his prisoner and had taken great pleasure in the knowledge that Gowl would make him a great deal of money. And then rather than letting his thoughts drift beyond his company, he listened.

Lord Radcliffe appeared satisfied with the report. His tone was light, "I received a communication through Captain Roderick that O'Neill will be slain by arrows. Do you know what that means?" he asked with great optimism.

Ralph bowed graciously, "The war is over."

Henry listened intently, waiting to hear more. Perhaps he thought, he would be assigned to clear the countryside of dissidents.

Radcliffe placed his sword on a table and poured a snifter of brandy. He set out three glasses which made Henry thankful. He was included. He was still an officer and the lord deputy now knew his name. "I would not say the war is over, but Ulster is done. We are to send Brian O'Neill to England. The young lad found his way into camp last night, along with the Earl of Tryconnell."

Ralph sounded surprised, "Calvagh O'Donnell survived? I thought for sure he would have been left for the crows. What will you do with him?"

"Not a damn thing, but the boy is something else altogether. He must be protected." The lord deputy handed the men their brandy. "I will have you, Captain Colley, take them both to a safe house in Newry. They will remain in your custody until a passage can be arranged at the nearest port in Carlingford."

The men took a drink and reflected on all they had accomplished. Their thoughts were all the same: O'Neill would be killed or was dead already. It gave Henry the greatest of satisfactions. Ralph grabbed him at the shoulder with a confirmation that he had been right.

Radcliffe continued, "There is one thing I might add. If something happens to Calvagh O'Donnell along the way, there will be no questions put to you. I have no intention of expending the resources of this army to march toward Tryconnell. Therefore, our Queen needs not to hear his plea."

"I understand, your Grace," Henry replied.

The lord deputy nodded approval and took his final sip, indicating that Henry should do the same and leave. Henry did and Radcliffe's tone changed to one of concern. "The council has sent an urgent message to me. They do not trust that you negotiated with Sorely Boy MacDonnell at Dunluce Castle. You better hope that Antrim and the Scotts come into the right side of things, Ralph."

"Should not we both hope, Lord Radcliffe? Ralph asked.

"No. In fact, I will be short in my duties here in Ireland, and Francis and I have been ordered back to court. The Queen wishes for my replacement it seems. She has not told the council why."

"Do you know who will be appointed in your stead?" Ralph asked.

"Devereux, Walter Devereux the Viscount of Herford. I hear the earl is soon to be married."

"If that is so, your Grace, our Queen must desire nothing but ashes of these wild Irish chieftains."

Colley Town

It was late in the evening, and although Mary knew she should not be alone with the vicar, she continued toward the newly built church of Colley Town. An oil lamp was lit and sat in a window near the back door, and she picked up her steps quickly. He was more handsome than she thought she deserved, but Judas had taken more than a liking to her. He had been tender, and tonight she hoped he would kiss her.

"You came," Judas said as she entered through the back door. His hair was down to his shoulders and clean. "I almost thought you had forgotten."

Mary smiled shyly and stepped forward so that he might see her face. "I thought of nothing else, Judas. It has been a long time since I held the company of a man. Am I to work for you tonight?" she asked.

"The work has been done. All we must do now is wait. Tong has seen sure to that. He returned a short while ago, Mary, and it will not be long before I must confront a very grave evil," Judas said solemnly.

"I don't understand. You sent him away? We were told that Tong had deserted the farm." Mary took a chair and felt both confused and curious as to why Judas would do such a thing. She waited with questioning eyes for his reply, hoping there would be some reason to forgive such a thing.

Judas walked with bare feet on the stone floor and came up behind her. There was a moment of silence before he put his hands on her shoulders and then he let out a sigh. It was a sound that told Mary the weight of the world pressed upon his conscious. She remained still and listened, feeling the quick of her heart at his touch.

"I sent him out to look for the beasts that eat of human flesh. I knew that Henry would never let me do so. It may seem wrong, but I sent someone I knew that Henry would not follow. Tong did exactly as he was told, and do not fear, he will be rewarded."

Mary's voice fell flat, "It doesn't make sense, Judas. I thought you wanted peace for us in the midlands?"

Judas tightened his grip on her shoulders and his voice became high. "He taunted these creatures and then left a trail for them to follow back here. I cannot let the thought of their evil go unpunished. You do not know what they have done," Judas told her.

The confession made Mary's knees tremble. She did not know as much about Judas as she thought. His voice was different tonight. It seemed colder and void of the feelings he had shown over the past few weeks. She wanted him to return to the man she was growing to love. For Mary, Judas was a promise, and he could provide.

Judas did not want to hurt her, "You must trust me, Mary. I will slay them. Bu-jo is ready, and so are the few soldiers that Henry has left us. We must put an end to their sinister ways forever." His hands softened as she thought and he began to rub her shoulders. It felt so good and warm. He pulled her up from the chair and smelled her hair, and she felt him breathing on her neck. She wanted him and did not resist as he gently caressed her body. "Wait..." Mary whispered, feeling both guilty and enticed.

"I need you Mary. I need you more than you will ever know."

Newry Township Bakers House

Brian was well pleased with the accommodations. He slept in a bed of goose down and sat up to place his feet on the warm wooden floor of a two story building. The smell of hot fresh bread from Bakers House Inn of Newry wafted up from below. Being curious and also excited to make a trip to London, Brian forgot about his troubles and ran to look out the glass window.

He had never been to Newry or outside of Dungannon for that matter. He wondered briefly what Turlough and Katherine might think of the fact that he had escaped them. Outside he saw a wonderful place with smiling faces and English soldiers with clean uniforms. He marveled at the line of picket fences and gardens that seemed to follow the stream that split the town in half. England had made it safe, he presumed. Everything south of Armagh was safe. Ak nock came at his door and he ran to open it.

"Are thee ready, your lordship?" Calvagh asked.

"Aye Calvagh. Can you smell how delicious our breakfast will be?" Brian said happily. Calvagh, his old friend with the long weathered beard and clear blue eyes looked as he always did. He still wore sheep fur rather than changing over to the English garb they had been provided. Brian was not surprised.

Calvagh answered spritely, "Of course. Why do ya think I'm here, ya twit?"

Brian found Calvagh's humor delightful. With a bound of energy that only the young possess, he bolted for the staircase. Calvagh reached out and grabbed him by the nape and threw him to his butt. "Age before barony, your Grace," Calvagh chided.

"The first bread is mine!" Brian squealed as they fought for position down the narrow stairwell of Bakers House.

Soon they were sitting at the table and drooling. There were muffins as well as smoked ham in the delicious upscale establishment that catered to the officers of the English fort. Two days at Bakers House was something of a holiday for all they had endured.

"You will need to wolf this down," Calvagh said as he soaked up some gravy.

"So soon?" he replied. Another plate was delivered and he ate it all.

Calvagh gulped down a pitcher of milk and wiped his beard with a crust. "Our escort has arrived and we leave in an hour. We head to Carlingford by the sea." Brian nodded as if he were giving permission. "You will be delivered to an English sail captain named Roderick and then it is off to London."

Brian held up a finger. "Then it is off to England for us both. I told you Radcliffe would not desert you, old friend."

Calvagh's whiskers parted with a smile, "Sometimes the sun even shines on a goat's ass. No offense, your Grace. Now, let us go; I am as full and ready as needs be."

Not having anything to pack except themselves, Calvagh and Brian walked outside and went straight to the livery in the center of town. It was there that Calvagh was told to be by his escort Henry Colley. He had come to the conclusion on his own that the man who protected him was the very same animal that Emma had told him about. Most assuredly, it was Henry who was responsible for her death. As soon as Brian was safely on the ship, he intended to kill Captain Henry Colley of Colley Town.

As they approached the livery, it was not horses that Calvagh heard but sport. Men were cheering and wages were being made. He grabbed young Brian by the shoulder, knowing how betting men could be rough. "Stay close, lad. This is not what I expected."

The soldiers were thick inside the livery and threw a few elbows to get them a good view. Brian squeezed Calvagh's hand. There was a fight going on and the soldier named Dennis of the Hill clan was hot to take the bets.

Captain Henry Colley was holding up a hand full of English paper. "It will be coin or crowns only! I'll not take any Irish marks!" Dennis said.

The bets were cast and then the burlap sack that covered the combatant's faces were removed so they could see and fight. It was a sad spectacle of what the English did to Irish warriors who would not surrender. The conduct of such barbarity had grown out of control. It was hand to hand, with no weapons or rules except for death. Calvagh had seen the combat before and hated it. Someone threw a bucket of piss into the ring and the large fighter screamed out with rage. It was the sound of the voice which caught Calvagh's attention. He nearly fell to the ground with disbelief.

In the center of the stable where the crowd of soldiers held a tight circle, Calvagh saw the braids of an Irish warrior. It was Gowl! Gowl's opponent was of clan McCarty and the men stood resisting the urges to fight.

Henry ordered the lances turned in. A circle of five of his soldiers who slowly closed the ring around the two opponents with razor sharp points. Gowl cried out in rage and lunged forward. It was a struggle. A terrible sound of grunting and pain that ended with Gowl on all fours as the victor.

Calvagh and Brian watched with dismay and revulsion as Henry collected the winnings and had his expended gladiator tied to a pole. For all the clean uniforms that Brian saw, he wished he saw civility.

Seeing Calvagh, Henry raised up his arms. "It is time men. Get the carriage and make the horses ready."

Calvagh put his hand on Brian's shoulder and answered for them both. "We do not fight to the death for sport." Brian grabbed Calvagh's hand. "It's alright Brian," Calvagh said reassuringly. Henry nodded and moved off to supervise his men.

"Must we travel by carriage?" Brian asked.

"It matters not how we arrive, only that we arrive," Calvagh replied, looking at Henry with disapproval. There were several soldiers who remained behind when the stable cleared. It was a suspicious situation but one in which he had no remedy for.

Calvagh moved toward Gowl and nudged him, while Henry was distracted with his men. "I know you Gowl O'Hagen and I know your woman well. Is she alive as you are?" he asked.

Gowl's eyes were bloodied but he recognized Calvagh immediately. "Will thee gloat on me?" he asked.

Calvagh's tone was compassionate, "Never, Gowl. There is a grave with your name on it near the River Strule."

Gowl looked up at him, "It is right to be there, for I am dead."

Calvagh glanced over his shoulder to ensure he was not being watched and Brian walked toward the gate to keep look out. "Is Emma alive?" he asked.

"That grave remains empty as long as I fight or die for Henry Colley," Gowl replied.

"That is not a bargain, my friend. That is not what Emma would want," Calvagh said with compassion.

Gowl turned up his face, "It is all I could do for her. They killed our men and drove off the clan into the forest. All except for Emma and my son. Henry kept my head covered in burlap so she wouldn't see me. If you want her, she will return to the valley once the English have gone. She believes me dead, Calvagh, and England believes her the same."

Calvagh returned to his thoughts of murder, "Nay Gowl. I have only wanted her company and never coveted your woman. You will be together soon and we shall make each other a promise. When one of us becomes free, the other will provide the means to become so. Do you agree?"

"With all of my honor," Gowl replied.

CHAPTER 53

Peace be with You

There was a trickle of water seeping down the wall and Miguel felt it cooling his back and wetting his trembling shoulders. He cracked his eyes and saw a torch burning and a long narrow passage. Somehow he had endured the pain and no longer cared if he lived or died. It was his earthly body that was weak, but his soul he still managed. Had his father forgotten who he was? His first thoughts went to Mary and then Agnes. Were they safe? If they were not, it would be of his doing.

You are not finished!

The voice was overpowering. It was his awakening. At the far end of the dungeon below the walls of Windsor, Miguel surrendered to the Lord.

Out in the open fresh air and above Miguel Avaje Fernandez, the queen made her way toward the dungeon. Lord Burghley was with her, "I must caution you not to go down into that place. He is in no condition to bear true witness or be of able mind."

His tone vexed her spirit and was quickly replaced with surety. "It is not beneath me to see what has been done in my name. You better pray that what I find does not offend," Elizabeth said vehemently.

William thought of the cruelty of men and knew the queen was not ready. How many would be saved because of his actions? Would she understand? "I would do far more to preserve your life and liberty, your Majesty. Far more," he said as she looked at him accusingly. He didn't say so out loud but thought: *too much relies upon your young and inexperienced judgement.* His thoughts settled, his voice was made calm, "That one might consider otherwise is surely a sign that the gravity of a Catholic uprising is not fully understood."

"I will see him!" Elizabeth demanded.

As they came to the entrance of the prison, a guard snapped to attention and opened that door which lead down to the dank below. It smelled of rot and foulness: she covered her nose with a perfumed kerchief and entered. "I will have him removed from here once we have spoken. We are not barbarians, Lord Burghley." Even as she took her first step she wondered if she would be strong enough to see a man in such condition. *Would he even know who I am,* she wondered?

Elizabeth felt both intrigued and revolted. William had already described the torture in great detail, so that she would not have to see. The surgeon had taken his arms without the mercy of laudanum and a knife was used instead of a saw to sheath the tendons away at the elbows. She had even seen the preserved remnants of his poor body in a glass jar. The fluid of embalming was tainted with his blood but the markings on the arms were undeniable. They were covered with a mysterious code. A code that William had said, held the answers to the pope's ciphers against her.

They descended further and then reached the straw littered floor chiseled out of the same bedrock which supported the massive walls above. The atmosphere was daunting and medieval. They walked under torches and William pointed down the long passageway that followed the foundations. "He is down there, and I strongly recommend you reconsider," he told her. This was no place for a queen and he cringed as she kept walking, allowing the gutters to soak the edges of her gown.

Miguel was restrained by a thick iron chain attached to the wall. "He does not look so imposing," Elizabeth said sadly.

William's tone was cold and calculating, "You must never underestimate the power of faith." Together they moved closer. "That man told us virtually nothing. It was as if the pain was his only pleasure," he told her. She frowned and he knew his words had little effect. He tried desperately to sound more daunting, "He is dangerous!"

William turned to the guard who accompanied them and the yeoman picked up a bucket and doused Miguel with cold water. They watched as he shuddered and raised his head defiantly.

"You would have killed me?" Elizabeth asked.

Miguel's voice was hauntingly calm and clear, "Not I, but He who controls the world," he replied.

She looked into his eyes and wondered how he could have known her true fear of religion. *He who controls the world? It was the essence of all that she could not escape. Not of man, not of God, but somewhere in between; the words left room for free will: dangerous, mysterious and cryptic.* She leaned forward wanting to know where her demons lay.

William saw her fascination and urged her away. "Your Majesty has seen him, now let us go."

She bit back, "You go, Lord Burghley!"

William did not know how to respond. Was it her demand or a question?"

Elizabeth bent down closer to Miguel. So close that if he had arms he could dash her. "Is it not God's will that you have failed and I find myself in control of your destiny?"

"Failed?" Miguel questioned. "You are betrayed. Was not the Lord himself betrayed so that all could see his power?" Miguel saw that she was nervous and he knew immediately that his words touched the Queen of England.

William reached out to pull her away. "Get out!" she shouted, turning to her head of state with scorn and lost affection.

"I will not leave you alone, my Queen," he countered. *She is scouring me with her eyes and getting too close to the secret. How will our country thrive with such youth and disregard?* His manner was one of question. He did not obey.

Elizabeth returned her attention to Miguel and her words were damning. "Does it not seem predestined that those you have sworn to serve have failed once again to quiet my voice?"

Miguel was weak, "You have taken my hands; what else would you have me say? Kill me and set my soul on its course to heaven."

She had thought of nothing else. It had been a burden to her and pressed her heart beyond what she thought capable. Her father would have no such reservations. It was that weakness of men that presumed of death and torture justified. *I shall make my voice sound of roses to his ear, both bright and showing the trueness of my light.* She did, "And make you a martyr? I think not. You are much too valuable to me alive. How you spend that life will be up to you. If you cooperate, you may find your remaining days made easy. There has been much misunderstanding between the Holy Father and England."

Miguel looked to the dirty stone wall above. His cry was unnaturally high and she could not douse it from her ears. His melody rose, but not of roses, to echo the scouring of his soul.

This time, her anger toward William Cecil would not be denied. "Leave us, Lord Burghley! Your methods have proven inept and useless for such a man!"

William protested. "I will not leave you in this place without a guard!"

"The guard stays and you will depart from me or take his place!" Elizabeth commanded.

William departed woefully, she turned to the guard. "Unlock him!" she demanded. Then, "Turn away!" she ordered. In that cold dark tunnel, what she said, none will ever know, but when the guard returned his gaze the prisoner was on his feet. He could say nothing. His queen's fierce gaze was all the warning, so he stood, he would follow, he would protect.

She gagged with his smell as she tried to hold him stead. "You will take one step," Elizabeth told him. Miguel shuffled forward under the pain and began to sink. "And another," she said softly.

"I cannot," Miguel whispered.

"When you were tortured, you claimed to be an angel. Do you believe you are?" Elizabeth asked.

"There can be an angel in all of us," Miguel cried and felt a power return his strength.

"Take another step," she told him. He did. "Why would an angel of the Lord not smite down the wicked?" she asked.

"I have," he answered.

"And another," she demanded. He moved again and she took his weight. "I must know where my demons are. Why have you done this?"

He felt her hand at his waist, "He has put me in your path. Your demons are all around you, and I am not one."

❦ ❦ ❦

There was a quietness in the courtyard when the Queen emerged from the dark below. The courtiers, the ladies, and her council stood in a line awaiting her safety. Even William Cecil saw the Queen of England comfort the conspirator as they struggled toward the warmth of her castle.

Maidenhead, England

Inside a tavern within Maidenhead, the bulk of the men from Ulster took their mead from nervous barmaids who endured their rough manners and boasting. Shane and his small army had not been attacked, and messengers were dispatched daily to ride across the river and deliver his request for an audience with the Queen. Shane spoke with Barr Con outside where they both could see the silhouette of Windsor Castle. The great monument of power overshadowed anything that O'Neill could achieve in Ulster alone. It had taken years to build, and it would take years to tear down should England ever fall. Shane felt restless.

"We will wait just one more day and then away ourselves from this place. She toys with us, Barr," Shane said.

Barr nodded with agreement, "A long voyage for naught should we do so. I fear there is more treachery in those walls than either you or I can fathom. Perhaps we should leave now?"

"No, another day." Shane said. His men were getting soft on drink and soon something terrible would surely befall him. Either one of his warriors would overstep or an Englishman would finally gain the balls to confront them. Either way if something did not occur soon, his chance a gaining a lordship would dwindle to nothing. Perhaps Radcliffe was in the castle lying to the queen. Perhaps she had heard of the burned vicar? Whatever the reason for delay, he would give England just one more day. As he pondered, his last and final messenger arrived on horseback. The man was winded.

"Tomorrow, your Grace!" the messenger said.

Barr looked at him apprehensively. "We could leave tonight. It would not be a cowardly thing to do."

"Tomorrow, Barr, and I shall go with as many as are allowed."

On the road to Carlingford

There was one road between Newry and Carlingford, and Henry Colley's Kildare Brigade had no choice but to take it. Dennis of the hill clan rode at the back and between the lead and rear were twelve other horsemen, a prisoner, and the carriage that held Brian and Calvagh O'Donnell and appeared well guarded. The column moved as quickly as possible over the low land road that was abridged and swampy on either side. Newry was two miles behind them when they were halted by a felled tree across the road.

Calvagh peered out the window and pushed Brian to the carriage floor. "Stay put lad, this is no storm down," he cautioned. Brian took a deep breath and did as he was told. "I'll be back," Calvagh said, as he exited and ran to warn Henry Colley. "Get off the horses! It's a trap! An old Irish trap I tell you!"

His warning came too late. Before his words had left the air, several shots were fired, and Henry fell to the ground. Many of the men fell, and their horses ran off wildly, splashing through the water.

During the initial attack, Dennis of the hill clan sped forward on his charger with sword in his hand. He was cut down before reaching the carriage, and in this turmoil, Gowl kicked his mule into motion and turned to make his escape. The other soldiers hit the ground either from their wounds or from utter terror.

Calvagh buried his face in the dirt and prayed they would kill him quickly. He could feel the tremors of horses coming up from behind and knew the English soldiers were doomed. He tried vainly to inch back toward the carriage and lifted his head. He saw white wool leggings and the red hand of O'Neill painted on the horses. Two more shots were fired into the carriage and he heard Brian cry out in pain. He found his courage in time to see Brian's body thrown out of the carriage and trampled, and then he was struck from behind.

When Calvagh awoke, he found himself once again a prisoner, and this time it was Turlough who would secure him in a cage. "Why not kill me!" he screamed as Turlough gloated.

"I have word, as does your wife, that O'Neill is not dead at all. You are his prisoner by honor, not mine, Calvagh O'Donnell."

"It is a lie!" Calvagh shouted as they picked him up and tied him to the mule that Gowl had endured. To his utter astonishment and odium, Calvagh heard the voice of his wife Katherine.

"I have gone myself to Sorely Boy of Antrim and returned to you my husband to give you this news directly. My father, and all of clan Campbell have disavowed thee and so I am divorced of your cowardly heart and will freely marry O'Neill. This condition has gone directly to your new queen, where my love is surely waiting."

CHAPTER 54

Broken Angel

Windsor was a short carriage ride away from the town of Maidenhead, and once there, Shane found the busy talk of courtiers and those who might spy on him disturbing. Lord Thomas Butler was one, and Gerald Fitzgerald the 11th Earl of Kildare was another of the lords who were sent to greet him. These men he knew well for his family had been tied to their lineage for generations. Their discontent was that it was only Ulster and Connaught who remained free realms in the law of Brehon. They understood him, probably more than the Queen could herself, but he did not trust them. He gazed up at the marvel of the battlements and was escorted by either Thomas or Gerald everywhere he went.

Later in the day, at his request, some of his other men were allowed the privilege of joining him but not his general, Barr Conn. It gave him the sense of being shut down and powerless in a court designed to contain. The futility of moving against the order, was reinforced with the mortar of the tower. As the days passed he thanked God for his wizard who was wise enough to understand the same. Farleigh had dazzled the court with his whimsical tales and had been promised a visit with the queen even before he.

❄ ❄ ❄

The days also passed with softened interrogation for Miguel Avaje Fernandez. He was kept in chambers not far from Elizabeth's private quarters. A place where doors became walls and hid everything in between. After one of their sessions, and at his request, the surgeon who had taken his arms paid a visit. Rodrigo was pale with regret and shamed. They did not speak of the torture but there was an understanding between them that went beyond any words. A solemn reasoning that the things that had been done could never be reversed.

Rodrigo had dressed his arms at the elbow and tried his best to prevent Miguel's blood from seeping through his gown. "If you loosen these you will die in seconds," he had said as he tied a twine which Miguel could clench in his teeth over the oozing stumps of his handy work.

"I cannot feel them anymore," Miguel said as if to offer some comfort.

Rodrigo had designed a chair for him. One fashioned with handles and wheels. As he remembered he slumped forward.

Although Rodrigo had left many hours before he spoke to the empty room as if someone were there. "The Queen has said she will see me just one more time. I will tell her that I am the son of Pius IV. I will tell her that it was me who contrived the poison and the plan."

He heard an answer: "I am your Father."

"I do not know anymore," Miguel responded. He let out a deep sigh of regret. "O'Neill has not held the north for Belfast and he will be of England. Will you release me now so that I might be with her?"

"I am your Father."

Miguel looked at the twine that held his mortal body to this world.

Castle Place, Belfast

The town charter was the topic of discussion at Castle Place, located in the heart of Belfast. The Lord Deputy, Thomas Radcliffe and the Irish chancellors, met with the lord mayor of that city. The vantage of the outer terrace, gave scope in panoramic vision to the expansion of the city. Among the gathering of powerful men was a sailor and privateer. Captain Roderick had met Ralph Lane and the two continued in their covert alliance. The communication of her Majesty Elizabeth's royal mail. The lord mayor, who had invited them together served burgundy and wafers expecting nothing but jubilant news from England.

Radcliffe sat near a stone wall contemplating his latest incursion as the sound of finches flirted in the air. O'Neill would not be killed, and the information sat poorly with the power of

Belfast. The lord mayor in particular was concerned of O'Neill's influences. It was clear now to all that some fashion of diplomacy continued to serve the wayward chieftain. He wondered how his slippery foe continued to elude and sway the agents of the crown.

Ralph Lane came to his side and spoke quietly, "Brian O'Neill of Dungannon has been slain."

Radcliffe looked out to the port city causeway. Certain things could be put in motion to limit O'Neill's credibility. Should he even bother? "Do not provide that tragic information to Captain Roderick."

"Aye, your Grace. I agree and will investigate further. Perhaps Captain Colley will be of recovery soon. If so, we will know if O'Neill was involved."

"I will not dally any longer with the circumstances of these wild Irish. Francis is receiving Lady Lettice Devereux even as we meet here. Viscount Herford has assembled the Irish Parliament in Dublin and I am to leave once our turnover has been complete."

"Shall I not investigate?" Ralph asked.

"Leave it up to Henry Colley to come forward with whatever he knows. Or, if he dies, let it die with him. The young lord would never have been able to rule Tyrone."

"It is a travesty none the same, your Grace. I have taken your lead, however, and will accept your appointment as Sherriff of County Cork. My letters are going back with Captain Roderick to make my resignation official."

Radcliffe nodded his agreement, "Very good. As for Captain Roderick and Thomas Smyth, once I get London, I will engage them to expand our private shipping. That is where the future of

England resides and I am thinking that Smyth might consider naming our venture, the East Indie Company.

"So that is it then, we will no longer war?" Ralph asked.

"Of course we will. We have not found the heir of MacAlister and the Scotts of Antrim will see to more unrest. Keep your sword sharpened and work on getting us more investors from Cork. It is time to begin profiting with more than my cousin's superfluous titles and really begin to earn."

The lord mayor of Belfast approached them on the terrace. "Will you occupy Dungannon to keep the scoundrel out of the city?" he asked, referring to Shane O'Neill.

Radcliffe replied happily, "The Queen has ordered a withdrawal of the preponderance of her forces. Dublin will continue to be the primary route of trade, but as for O'Neill, I could not say."

The West Wing of Windsor

Miguel sat in his chair, unable to move on his own, gazing at the fireplace and hearing the voice of God. To the bones he was cold: his life was drifting away.

The time is yours alone.

"I do not want to burn, Father."

You will not suffer of the flame, nor of the cold or depths of hell.

Miguel let out a heavy sigh and the doors to his secret room opened. He saw Queen Elizabeth and William Cecil.

Elizabeth spoke softly. "As you can see, he is alive. Now, I will speak to him privately, Lord Burghley," she insisted.

"He should have guards at his doors and restraints," William advised reluctantly.

"Do you think he will run away? Don't be foolish. I have fed him and been his nurse for weeks now."

"He is not a pet, your Majesty."

Miguel heard everything and nothing. He was a man, like any other man, and he had a heart. In the recess of his spirit, somewhere he had never felt before, he hoped for mercy. He had a love, a desire, and as Elizabeth walked over to him near the fire, and sat down in a lovely velvet chair, he began to weep.

"You will tell me now who loves you," she said.

Miguel answered, "I am the son of Pius IV. I was not allowed to love."

"Do you want something to drink?" she asked.

"I do not thirst."

She looked at his body, which was now shaved clean of every hair. She had watched as her maids had uncovered all of him. Washing, shaving, and wiping the hairs which might conceal further secrets. She had touched him; she had drugged him with laudanum, to dull his senses and he was hers. He was quite beautiful actually, his body was perfectly formed. "Do you love her?" Elizabeth asked.

Miguel's eyes rolled back and she saw him fade away. She put her hand on his chest and her words in his ear. "Do you love her?" the queen whispered.

He startled, and as his eyes opened she saw the depth of his soul. "Yes…."

CHAPTER 55

Resurrection by Fire

Mary led the women out into the field where the men had made an altar. The entire plantation would raise their hands in prayer. That is how Judas reacted when Dennis of the hill clan brought Captain Henry Colley home. Both men had been injured and it was Dennis who was strong to ensure they survived. Henry had been bathed in oil and stripped of his bloody garments and then covered in white linen. Judas had overseen the preparations, and Mary marveled at how sure he was that Henry would be revived.

"Light the fires and burn them high!" Judas shouted across the field.

His words caused Mary's footsteps to quicken. What if the fires that Judas had lit finally brought those wild beasts out of the woods? It made her fear and feel vulnerable. What if Judas was killed? That made her feel worse.

"We will put our faith in the Lord tonight!" Judas said as the planters began to congregate around Henry.

"Will they come?" Bu-jo asked, referring to the wildlings.

Judas replied like a crazed man, referring to the same. "They are already here. Now go and do as I say."

Mary felt he was out of control. She had allowed his love and it was strong. His passion was hard to quench. She wanted him; she needed him; she would not run away.

"Hurry," Judas shouted.

As the men prepared and the women gathered, Judas calmed himself and prayed over Henry Colley. It was as if Henry was an offering. He had been restrained and his breathing was shallow. After praying Judas looked at Mary and the women of Colley Town. "When we are all gathered and they believe that our numbers are few, they will come."

Mary crossed herself and kneeled at the altar where Henry had been placed. After a moment of silence, Judas summoned the men to come and gather with uplifted hands. "We shall pray together as I have taught you and then we will wait. All of us will wait together and bear witness to the miracle of faith." He calmed his words and the congregation calmed as well. They knew that a trap had been laid and most did not believe in the wildlings of the forest. "All of us will pray!"

Think, O God, of our master who is ill, whom we now commend to Your compassionate regard. Comfort him upon his sickbed, and ease his suffering. We beg for deliverance, and submit that no healing is too hard for the Lord, if it be His will. We therefore pray that You bless our master with Your loving care, renew his strength, and heal what ails him. In this we claim through the power and blood of Jesus.

And the people said: "Amen."

After the prayer, Judas called Tong to the altar where he was told to stand upon a pedestal so all could see and hear. "You shall bless the air with music, Tong. For I know that you have confessed to me your love of our Lord. So dwelt you in the wilderness and resisted temptation that your song will be most pleasing to Him."

None had heard Tong sing before. Not Susan or John, nor Guthrie or Henry's new accountant Quincy Able. Only Judas and Bu-Jo had heard Tong during their nights together in the field. It was as if Tong had been forgotten.

Tong stood with a resoluteness of heart that they had never noticed. At the same time, workers set fires surrounding the field so that the landscape would show brightly. These fires cast their radiance to Tong who wore his pajamas and red silk belt, and his face glowed like gold in the evening. When Tong opened his mouth, the people hushed and he sang most beautifully to heaven. His voice prickled the arms until the crickets and things of the bog melted away. They heard only his voice, pure and true.

Adoremus in Aeternum.

Mary wished that his song would never end and Annie Beth began to cry. When it was over, there came a wind upon the plantation that sent the embers of their fires into the sky. It was then that Judas sent Tong out into the night.

After Tong was out of sight, the echo of Judas's voice fell off to nothing as the planters of Colley Town saw Henry Colley move. Henry's eyes opened for them all to see, and Henry stared vacantly at Judas. The people were shocked and they saw Henry's hand move in resistance when Judas bent over and kissed him on the mouth.

Rising and releasing Henry from the altar of stone, Judas cried out: "Halleluiah, halleluiah!"

His praises echoed into the bog, where the wildlings gazed upon them with hunger. A bush bent down and a branch snapped, as Hagen stepped onto the field. The gathering turned to the wildlings who emerged beyond their fires. Men picked up their lances and forks. "We will fight this evil together!" Judas shouted.

A moment later, Tong ran into their midst and pointed to the south. There were shadows out beyond the fires and the shadows were of giants, just as Judas had warned. John Goodrich had the women lay down near the altar. Mary began to weep and clung to her son as the largest of the attackers let out a scream that sent utter terror into the crowd.

"Ju-dous!" Hagan yelled as his wildling clan emerged to attack the planters. They screamed with hideous voices and looked as though they were covered from head to toe in hair. None of the planters ran away. They stayed their ground and the heathens which charged them with clubs and spears increased their speed with the promise of easy pickings.

"Now!" Judas commanded.

At that instant a horse darted across the field and Bu-jo pulled on a length of rope that was laced with razors and glass. Hagan and his clan fell as pieces of their flesh were stripped away. As the beasts howled in pain, Tong pulled out a sling and stone to taunt Hagan as he stood to charge again. There was a whirl, a rock flew out, and Hagan ran his spear through Tong and fixed his body to the ground.

Guthrie and Quincy stood horrified and unable to move. They had heard of the terrible beasts but never truly believed. John and the workers began to battle for their lives as some of the wildlings made it into the circle people at the altar. Guthrie and Quincy felt they would all surely die but John clubbed the wildlings away. From the rear, the remaining soldiers began to fire into the beasts with muskets. The lead tore at hair and sent shards of bone flying through the air. It was a battle of bared teeth and blackness that came throughout the night. A battle that put an end to the legends of the wood.

In the morning, as Mary and Annie Beth and all the others of Colley Town dragged the beasts toward the fires, Henry Colley stood weakly with a new understanding of his vicar named Judas.

"Burn them! Burn each and every soul!" Henry shouted as the planters began to recover.

Mary ran to Judas and wiped his face clean of blood. "Is it over?" she pleaded.

"It is over, Mary! It is done!" Judas exclaimed with elation.

Mary threw her arms around him and kissed his neck and shoulders. He hugged her, he whispered in her ear, and she knew that she would be his wife.

Later that night, well after the guard had been placed, and Judas laid his head down to rest, he had a vision. He felt a light all around him and a hand reached out of that light with the markings he knew very well. "I forgive you, Judas," Miguel's voice told him. The words of the spirit washed over him and he wailed into the softness of his blanket.

CHAPTER 56

Everything

Elizabeth thought of her conversations with the priest who had come to kill her. She felt an honesty in the Jesuit that put teeth to her own inclinations that indeed a peace might be achieved with O'Neill. All this went through her mind as Shane O'Neill and his gallowglass warriors took a knee before her, in the throne room.

"The lords of England may rise," Elizabeth commanded.

Her words filled Shane's ears and left him with uncertainty. Should he rise and gaze upon her? The thought paralyzed him for he was not a lord of her court. To obey would be to presume and how could he dare? He remained bowed as Fitzgerald stood with Thomas Butler. The two rivals who were tied to the crown had accompanied him. He had heard them, and also took the warning that Radcliffe was not in London at all. What did that mean exactly? Thomas Butler did not give further detail but said only that all was not well between Radcliffe and the Queen. That at least gave him comfort.

Elizabeth gazed down at Shane who remained still. "Rise, you wild and untenable steed. Rise and face me so that I might find some value in your life as you have shown so little regard for me!"

Shane took his feet gracefully and she could see in his eyes that he may indeed challenge her. Such a pity she thought, for like Thomas Butler, he was tall and lean and fitting of his elegant ruff. "What have thee to say, pray tell?" she asked.

"My most gracious and forgiving Queen, I have much to tell thee. Of which I am certain no word has graced your ear or been a vision in your eye, lest not for my gravest efforts to reach thee."

Elizabeth sat forward with intent. *What lies might he convey?* "Efforts?" she asked plainly.

"Aye, my Queen. It is true that a war and armament of men against Radcliffe has troubled Ulster and also the great chartered cities of Lisburn and Belfast. There has been no other choice for us who have been plagued in Armagh, I might add. Although unprovoked, it appears that Lord Radcliffe will take no pardon from my people but seeks only the blood which runs through their own veins, and also in mine. So after the great destruction of property and the sacrilege which Radcliffe inflicted on the body of Christ in Ulster, I did repel his army and took similar recourse on one small plantation. For this I am guilty of defending your people who love and adore thee, against such a tyrant."

The room erupted with a commotion of nays and chaos. So much so that Lord Burghley stamped his staff into the tile repeatedly to quell the unsettled.

Upon regaining the silence of her court, Elizabeth replied: "Love and adore their queen you say?" she sat back, "does the barbarity of cannibalism and burning of vicars not testify to the greater evil upon the Pale?"

Shane ruffled uncomfortably, "Never has such a thing been done to the innocent, and although thee might believe us uncivil and wild, like beasts, I assure you that no evil as you describe has been committed. To eat of human flesh is of the devil and the devil does not have welcome in Ulster. It sickens me. It is true that there are wildlings and such beasts must be hunted and killed. Such things that may defile are not men."

"You do not appear uncivil but unlike the lords of Ormond and Kildare, you have not accepted your place in the common order. From your father Conn O'Neill such an heir to the earldom of Tyrone has been given. What do you say of that?"

Shane was unshaken and held his ground. "My most gracious and loving Queen, you have been deceived in this belief. The proclaimed peer is the son of my half-brother who was a bastard child, born out of my father's lust. This bastard was named Matthew and Brian is Matthew's son, not the son of Conn. Brian, whom you have claimed, is not the ruler of Dungannon or of Ulster. Even my father would agree if he were alive!"

"That is outlandish! You dare disgrace your own father in this court?"

Hearing the queen's tone, the gallowglass stood to defend Shane if needed. He waved them off. "I was born of noble union, through the marriage between the sister of Gerald

Fitzgerald who stands behind me and of my father Conn O'Neill. Mayhap in my father's past visit to this court, his lack of English understanding caused some confusion on this matter. I do not insult him, but praise him for caring for his offspring, but I assure your Majesty that my father's kindness to his bastard son, was not his endorsement. It is simply our custom under the old law."

Elizabeth felt troubled by the reasoning Shane gave her. It was not the same reasoning she expected. Nor was it unfathomable for her warlike cousin Radcliffe to give a false account. And yet here stood O'Neill, looking to be of civilized nature. He dared to war against that judgement? "And your complaints should have come to me in letter or messenger," she stated.

Shane had the look of utter frustration and the tone that confirmed it, "For all that is holy, I have sent so many letters. First to Radcliffe who ignored them and concealed my plea and then through any agent of credibility that I could trust. One person must have reached thee?"

"One perhaps," Elizabeth confirmed.

Shane and his gallowglass, who stood with with shields made ofwood and bone looked intimidating. How goodly it would be for him to align with her on this very day. He was bold. "If it is proven that Brian is not of noble birth, would you allow him his castle at Dungannon?"

"I love him, your Majesty. He will be honored but love does not a baron make."

The answer pleased her. "You may stay with us for a while so that we might work out this agreement. First however, there will be an accounting. Your messenger was found with poison."

Shane stood in waiting and soon the courtier which William Cecil had sent to retrieve Miguel, returned alone. There was a clicking of teeth as he immediately prostrated himself before the court.

"Lift your head and tell me. Where is the priest?" William asked with alarm.

The courtiers voice was troubled: "He is gone, your Grace. There is no chair or clothes or anything to hint he was ever locked away. Only this letter from Connaught."

Again the court erupted with astonishment, "Silence!" Elizabeth commanded. She looked at Shane accusingly, "If thee truly know this man or have anything to do with his escape, it will be your feet that feel the fire!"

"No, your Majesty! I have been in the presence of your lords since arriving. I have no knowledge of this thing. My messenger, I am sure, was misled. He was a messenger of peace."

"A messenger of peace, or a spy?" Elizabeth asked.

"A spy your Majesty. To tell thee otherwise would be a lie. He was however, a man of peace."

Elizabeth held the vision of Miguel in her mind. O'Niell did not know him as she did: not even the Holy Father would ever know what she had done. Her voice became calm and sure, "This lord of Tyrone will be well received with honor and sport. He will act as will his warriors in defense of the crown from henceforth."

Shane again took his knee and replied to William Cecil's great distain. "By honor and my pledge to God, your Majesty."

The queen dipped her crown with acceptance and said: "The Jesuit claimed to be an angel. It will be up to the council to prove that he was not."

Aboard the Great Brilliant

On the very last hour of the second week at sea, Mary looked to the man who was the image of Miguel. Agnes had told her, that she thought Miguel was playing his secret and would reveal himself very soon. Mary was unsure. If it was Miguel, he had not reached out to her, or made himself a comfort. His hair was different, a bit shorter and cropped tightly. His arms had different tattoos than the ones she remembered.

"It is safe now, for you to be known for who you are," the Spaniard said.

"Aye," Mary said softly, wanting to cry.

He smiled warmly and took her by the shoulder. She could see the mountains of Connaught and a bay with many islands.

"I am again to be Jade MacAlister?" Agnes asked.

"For now and always dear girl," he replied.

Mary reached out and touched his hand. It was warm and gripped her fingers, just like Miguel. He smiled, he was the pilot and he would guide them the rest of the way. "May we know your name, now?" she asked, with a longing for Miguel that still hoped for his love.

"I am Simon," he said. "He is my brother."

"What awaits us when we arrive?" Mary asked.

"Everything, Mary."

The End

FROM THE AUTHOR

I have always found history fascinating and *The Golden Age* is probably my favorite. The politics, people, and exploration into uncharted territories was incredible. My interest in the period from 1560 to 1600 began when I was completing an on-line course in world history. What I discovered, at least in regards to the Tudor Dynasty, is that fact is sometimes just as surprising as fiction. My hope is that I have captured your attention with compelling and complex characters who exhibit both the best and worst of the human condition. As for the story, one cannot know the inner motives of individual people, but the historical record does transcend the barrier of time.

Above all, please remember the series is a work of fiction. If I were asked if everything in my tale is perfectly true, I would answer: "If you believe so, you must also believe in monsters."

83852143R00314

Made in the USA
Middletown, DE
16 August 2018